Her fantasy lover is real...

"Why are you wearing a suit and tie this time?" She squinted against the sunlight. *Please, God, let this be a dream.* He moved his head and put her in shade.

"*This* time?" He lifted an eyebrow, perplexed. "You'll have to forgive me, lass, but I've no idea what the devil you're talking about." He maneuvered himself off her and sat upright at the end of the swing.

She tucked her feet against her, sat up, and blinked at him in utter disbelief.

"I came to knock on the door when I saw you on the swing. You tossed and turned, and with the way you grunted, I assumed you were in the middle of some sort of a seizure."

He turned his head and licked his lips, full and abused by her kisses. A mushroom cloud of mortification bloomed inside her, steadily bigger by the minute.

"Erm, you...begged me to kiss you, and then you yanked me down. One thing led to another and, well, that was pretty much the way of it. I *am* only human, though I know it's no excuse." He swallowed and stared at her, his Adam's apple moving in his throat. "I apologize. I shouldn't have gone down when you pulled me, but it was strange—like you *knew* me or something."

Lark leaned forward and rubbed her eyes. This couldn't be real. He had to be a hallucination. When she opened her eyes, she'd see a man in his fifties with a receding hairline, glasses, and a beer gut. She reopened her eyes, and there he was: The full package.

PRAISE FOR AUTHOR

Roxanne D. Howard

WHEN YOU CLOSE YOUR EYES

"Sexually erotic, emotionally compelling, and spiced with evolving passion, *When You Close Your Eyes* is recommended reading for anyone who likes their romance stories steamy and powerful."

~Five Stars, Midwest Book Review

When You Close Your Eyes

by

Roxanne D. Howard

When You Close Your Eyes

Contact Information: info@thewildrosepress.com

Cover Art by *Diana Carlile*

The Wild Rose Press, Inc.
PO Box 708
Adams Basin, NY 14410-0708

Visit us at www.thewilderroses.com

Publishing History
First Scarlet Rose Edition, 2019
Print ISBN 978-1-5092-2360-2
Digital ISBN 978-1-5092-2361-9

Published in the United States of America

Dedication

For Luke

Author Acknowledgments

A profound thanks to Malinda and Marilyn, Holly and Patrick, Carole and Rod for their unfailing love, support, and good times throughout the years.

A salute to Brandy Dixon, a dear lifelong friend, for copy editing the novel in its infancy, and a day spent together in Park City in 2007 that led to a spark of encouragement to believe in the book's potential.

A shout out to Drill Sergeant Dennis Davis, who once upon a time taught a young soldier what a Ducati was, and the value of never giving up hope. The world needs more people like you in it.

I'm so thankful to the original editor of this novel, Ann M. Curtis, for her meticulous and loving care of the book's editing when it was acquired with Loose Id Publishing. Ann is an incredible editor, gentle soul, and good friend, and she provided insightful feedback and tremendous inspiration throughout the initial editing process.

Thank you to the management, artists, and editorial staff at The Wild Rose Press. I rest well at night knowing this book is cradled safely in your arms.

To my husband and children, who are the joy of my life and the strength of my heart.

Prologue

The lucidness of the dream defied all logic. Despite how real it seemed, Lark knew it was still just a dream. On a rainy morning when she was twenty-five, she'd given her virginity to Charles. She recalled how the pale sunlight had streaked through the window of her London flat and washed over their bodies. Her American tan overshadowed Charles's pale English skin, and his chest felt warm beneath her fingertips.

This man entangled with her, with a firm grip on her hips as his long fingers dug into them and he thrust his hard cock into her, was *not* Charles.

He whispered her name like a mantra.

Lark couldn't see him clearly, but the outline of thick hair fell across a smooth forehead. He slowed as he caught her stare. He trailed a finger down the side of her face, past her neck, over her breasts, and spread his fingers along her hip. Her nipples tightened, and she arched her back for more. His touch tormented her, soft as a whisper. He'd barely grazed her skin, but she lit on fire from that mere stroke.

His hips swiveled into hers, slow and deliberate. He reversed the course of his hands and voyaged the length of her body, setting her sensitive skin alight as his palms skirted her flesh. She trembled with unabated desire.

"What are you doing?"

"What does it feel like?" he whispered with a hint of an Irish brogue.

****

An alarm clock sounded and ripped her from her dream. She sat up and pushed sweaty hair away from her face. Charles's heavy palm touched her lower back from where he lay beside her.

"All right, love?" he murmured, his voice sleep-ridden.

She reached to her right, pawed the snooze button, and turned the alarm off. She placed her hand over her heart and willed it to slow down. "Yeah. Yeah, I'm fine, babe. Go back to sleep. I'm going to go run."

Chapter One
Flight

Lark watched the fat pigeon's head bobble as he scavenged along the pavement. He cocked his head to the side as she and Maisie Robertson sprinted toward him, spread his wings and flew a few feet away, then continued to forage in peace.

The rising sun spread over Regent's Park, and Lark pumped her arms for warmth. The brisk wind off the Thames River became more prominent, snuffing out the last vestiges of summer with cooler autumn days. Lark coughed and slowed to a walk. Wisps of hair escaped her ponytail and fell into her eyes. "Hang on. We'll run again in a minute, Maisie," she huffed. Yes, it was complete bullshit. They'd totally walk the rest of the way. She had no more *umph* in her. But it was nice to pretend and give it the old college try.

"No, let's stop. I'm done in," Maisie said, panting, her London accent labored from their run. Taller than she, Maisie's freckled, fawn-colored skin glistened with perspiration. She stretched her arms high above her curly black hair as they slowed their pace.

A few coughs rattled Lark's chest. She ignored the concern on Maisie's face as she fished inside her black velour sweat-suit jacket for her cigarette and lighter. She flicked the lighter open and brought the cigarette tip to the flame. She puffed and took a long drag. The butt dangled from her cold fingers with an ashy glow. She did try e-cigs a while back, but the plastic against her lips held no appeal. She paused to admire the neat green hedgerows and rows of blue-marbled crocuses nearby.

A bright blanket of sun lit the dewy grass. Lark blew the smoke out the side of her mouth and grinned as she joined Maisie and walked along the concrete path. "I should have run while you were on holiday, but I wasn't motivated enough on my own. Watch the sparks fly off my thighs."

"And mine. I ate way too much over there." Maisie laughed. "How did the temp do?"

The daft, nineteen-year-old London girl spent more time making updates to her Twitter account and flirting with the FedEx delivery guy than producing any actual work. "Christina wasn't you," she said lightly. "I'm glad you're back, though I'm sure you'd rather be in Goa."

Maisie scrunched her nose. "Why on earth would I want to lie on a warm, sunny beach and watch hot men walk by when I can stand here and freeze my ass off?"

Lark laughed. "No clue. Were there a lot of cute guys?"

"I didn't notice, mate. My job on this holiday was to keep the kids in line and yell at Thomas not to wreck his sister's sand castles."

"Did it work?"

"No. He's in a terrorize-his-sister phase. He wrecked them anyway. And time out at the hotel room isn't much of a punishment." Maisie chuckled. "Bless his naughty little heart. But enough about my demonic children. What's new here?"

Lark licked her lips against the cool air. "I had another dream last night."

"Same guy?"

"Yeah." A shiver which had nothing to do with the autumn wind spread through her.

"Was it any good?"

Lark gave her a pointed look. "Maisie."

Maisie laughed and held up her hands. "Hey, girl, I'm just asking! It's a sign you're overworked or something. Freud would say it's a manifestation you're not happy in the sack or because Charles has yet to make a decent woman out of you."

"And he'd be right." Lark nodded, then cringed as they walked toward the front gate. "We've been sort of...well, not fighting, but sort of distant with each other. We went to the Registrar's office three weeks ago."

Maisie froze, wide-eyed. She seized Lark's arm and stopped them in their tracks. "Get out."

Lark shrugged.

"You're serious?"

"I know. I was as shocked as you are," Lark confessed with a lopsided grin.

Maisie frowned. "He actually *took* you there? What happened?"

"I had no idea where we were going. He said he wanted to get our names in the books for when we do set a date." Maisie's face brimmed with doubt.

"Let me get this straight. You've registered legally, but you still have no idea when you want to get married? Kind of odd he'd take you there but not tell you, isn't it?"

"Well, that's why it's been weird lately," Lark said

as they continued walking. "But I suppose it's no odder than staying engaged to him for the last five years." Lark shrugged. "Hey, it's a step *somewhere*. Better than limbo, which is all we've been in for the duration of our relationship. There you have it." Her friend's unspoken desire to say more lingered in the air like exhaust fumes. Lark crushed her cigarette under the heel of her sneaker and drew a shaky breath. She clapped her hands and mustered what enthusiasm she could without a caffeine fix. "Well now, big day ahead of us, hmm?"

"It is," Maisie affirmed.

They turned out of the park and walked toward Lark's silver Lexus parked a few yards away. The London traffic was light for six-thirty as they crossed the street. Lark turned on the lights and pulled into traffic.

A few blocks later, she pulled to the curb in front of Maisie's modern Tudor-style, semidetached house. "Here we are. The kids awake?"

"I hope not," Maisie muttered darkly. "Mummy needs a long shower. Anyway, it's Graham's turn to get the darlings ready this morning."

Lark laughed. "Have a nice break. I'll see you at work."

****

When she returned home, the flat echoed with a male tenor voice singing an indistinct West End tune in the shower. It rang out through their fair-size flat—deep, pleasant, and English. Lark laid her keys on the travertine kitchen counter. A small smile tugged at her lips. They had niggling problems, and he wasn't her favorite person these days, but the man could certainly sing. She unlaced her shoes and padded across the clean hardwood floor, past the sectional suede sofa and German floor lamps, to the bedroom. The low Japanese bed was unmade, the dark blue-and-silver duvet peeled back to reveal an indent in the Egyptian-cotton sheet from where Charles sat at the edge upon waking. Lark undressed and threw her sweaty clothes into the nearby hamper. She reached for her terrycloth robe and tied it around her waist as she headed for the bathroom.

Steam emitted from the bathroom door as she pushed it open, and the hot air blew toward her like she'd stepped into a sauna. Through the gummed glass of the shower door, the tall, muscular outline of Charles worked his hands through his short and spiky, light-brown hair as he sang.

Lark grabbed a towel off the rack and stepped forward with it draped over her arm. She applauded on the last quavering note.

He opened the door, grinned, and wiped water from his eye as the shower poured on him. "Thank you." He bowed, and wet droplets slid the length of his chest. "I do weddings." He paused before he stepped out, and his dark eyes scanned her frame. "And I take special kinds of gratuities." He tugged at the knot on her robe, pulled her to the shower mat, and slid his fingers into the knot. "Come in with me."

She covered his fingers with hers, peeled them away, and shook her head.

"Oh, come on, don't be prudish. We've got a bit of extra time." His eyes gleamed.

Charles, ever the opportunist, solicited any off moment to break their dry spell. As much as she loved him, it rubbed her the wrong way. She wasn't in the mood. It had been over three weeks since they'd last been intimate, and she believed their problems were, on some level, related to the dreams she had of the other man. Charles's reluctance to commit had never truly bothered her, but since his promotion in the last year, he spent less time at home. She'd come to understand through trial and error that life wasn't all about shooting straight to the top of the corporate ladder. Lark wished she'd procured stability with him earlier and had known for *certain* he didn't want anyone else when she'd given herself to him.

Lark held the towel out and smirked. "I can't say I'm not tempted. But I need these next few minutes to rehearse the presentation."

"No, you don't." He took the towel from her and left the water on.

She slipped past him, eager to step beneath the warm spray. "I mean it, Charles. Don't distract me. We don't all have the gift of magically owning the room without working on our topics."

He shrugged and wrapped the towel around his hips. "Fine. But don't blame me if you're stiff, babe. Enjoy the shower."

She slid the glass door closed.

****

Perched on the kitchen stool a while later, Lark speared her fork into a bowl of chopped melon and wished it were a chocolate croissant. She watched the news on the TV and half worked on a crossword puzzle, not really into either as she replayed the dream from the night before in her mind.

She was dressed for power today in a sharply cut black-and-white Armani suit, her long hair curled at the ends and layered around her face. As she'd put her makeup on, it hit her when she'd woken from the dream, she'd been aroused, her panties damp. It troubled her. The man in her dreams had paid her nightly visits off and on for the past six months, but though the touches and feelings seemed real, they'd never manifested themselves in her real life.

Until now.

Charles walked out of the bedroom in a three-piece navy-blue suit. His tie laid around his white collar, ready for assembly. An arresting man in his thirties, he watched her with his dark, penetrating eyes as he continued to fasten his left cuff link. He was handsome and crisp, ready for action.

"Did you have a nice time running?" he asked civilly, as though she hadn't snubbed him.

She ate another forkful of melon. "Mmm, I did. I'm glad Maisie's back. I've missed her while she's been away."

Charles strode over and bent to kiss her. He finagled the remote from her hand and turned off the TV. "I'm glad you have a workout buddy again, though why you chose your PA is beyond me." He opened the fridge and extracted an apple croissant in a clear plastic box.

"Hey you," Lark brandished her fruit at him. "Whenever I run with you, you go ahead of me and holler to keep up. Maisie helps keep the pace, and she likes to talk. Give her a break, would you? She's married with three kids, and *still* finds time to work and finish dental school. She's a superwoman. You're just jealous because she worked for you for a year and moved on. I can't help it if I'm a cooler boss." She took a bite.

He lifted a little white china pitcher full of fresh milk over his coffee mug and eyed her as he poured, then stirred it with a small silver spoon. "Touché. Well, in a few years, she can give you Hollywood teeth. What I mean, Lark, is you can find many other women in our company much higher up who would be better to fellowship in a lucrative sense. You never know what you might get to talking about." He gave her a pointed glare above the brim of his cup and ignored her annoyed expression. She hated it when he did that. "Before I forget, there was a number on the Caller ID this morning. It said Unknown Name, and they didn't leave a message, but it came from the States."

Lark rose, rinsed her empty bowl in the sink, and stacked it in the dishwasher. She frowned. "The States? I didn't know my mom had our number. I haven't talked to anyone there in years, and as far as I'm aware, I closed my bank account. Are you sure they didn't leave a message?"

"Yeah, I'm positive. I checked. I'm sure they'll call back if it's important. Don't stress it." An old-fashioned ringtone dinged, and they both looked around. Charles tightened his tie as he headed for the coat rack. "Mine," he hollered, as he retrieved his Blackberry from a coat pocket.

Lark watched him go into the next room to speak to a client. She collected her briefcase and keys.

It seemed far-fetched the missed caller would be someone from her family. She hadn't spoken to her mother or brother, or anyone in Oregon almost as long as she'd been engaged to Charles. *But what if...* Something didn't feel right. She tried to shake it off as she fixed her fall coat and put on a soft red scarf. Pre-

presentation nerves tended to get the best of her. She needed to push it to the back of her mind, at least for now.

Charles met her at the front door. "Are those the earrings I gave you last Christmas?"

Lark touched the white diamond studs on her ears. "Yeah. Why? Are they okay?" She waited as he scrutinized her. He was brutally honest, and it worked for her.

"They're all right. You'd be better off with the long silver ones, though. Less sheepish. Are you all set?"

"As I'll ever be." She gave him a shaky smile. "I'm going to head over in a sec to review everything."

Charles checked his cell and sifted through his messages, preoccupied. "Sounds good, babe. I'll be along in a bit."

On a normal day she would have given him a standard peck and left, but she nodded and tried to smile. She shut the door behind her, drew a breath, and headed off to work. In the car, she engrossed her mind in bullet points and statistics for her presentation to circumvent the reality that she and Charles were in trouble.

****

Ultimately You was housed in a nice high-rise in the central urban London sprawl close to the Thames riverbank.

When Lark entered the first floor, Maisie waited for her near the elevator, prepped and ready, in her element as she described the morning's agenda. The mini spirals of Maisie's high black hair were tapered with a dark barrette. She wore a tasteful, chic white dress, pinned with a red paper posy. Despite the banter with Charles earlier, Lark counted her lucky stars to have someone like Maisie as a best friend. She also happened to be the best executive assistant in the world.

For a Saturday, the elevator sure took its sweet time on the way to the fourteenth floor. Lark shifted from foot to foot and eyed the floor numbers above the elevator doors.

"Did you catch *Idol Mania* last night?" Maisie asked. "We watched it after we got in, after the kids fell asleep. I love Donovan."

Lark smirked. "Nah, I can't get into it. I have a hard time fantasizing about a random, middle-aged Justin Bieber wannabe. Hell, I have a hard time fantasizing about Justin Bieber."

"So does everyone else on the planet, mate." Maisie laughed.

Lark's cell phone rang, and Maisie tamed her giggles as Lark answered the call. "Lark Braithwaite."

"Lark? It's Doug," a quick voice boomed. "I've a dilemma, and I hope you can help me."

"I'm a manager, Doug. I don't fix or create problems." She smiled and winked at Maisie as Doug chuckled on the other end. "What can I do for you?"

On the way to her office, she gave him the correct code for a database entry he'd erred on, closed the phone after the call, and handed it to Maisie.

"Here. Don't let me even *look* at this until after the meeting."

"You've got it, boss."

Alone in her office, Lark went through her PowerPoint presentation and ensured the information was where it ought to be. Finished, she gathered everything into her laptop case and zipped it up. Satisfied she'd done all she could to prepare, she walked, arms folded, to the series of large windows in her office. She stared at the vast London spread below.

Her mind reeled like a salmon caught in the upstream, rushing toward a tumbling, raging current as she perceived the ancient rooftops, cathedral domes, and modernized office buildings outside her window. The oblong-shaped Gherkin skyscraper towered in the distance near the Thames River, and the bright sun reflected on its impressive, blue-black tinged windows.

She spearheaded today's merger-acquisition meeting, and though she was gifted when it came to public speaking, her nerves flared every time. Behind not-so-closed doors, a handful of her professional associates considered her abrasive. In a role where women had to be twice as good as men simply to survive, she had to surpass them threefold to succeed. She had indeed stepped up to the mark, and she had the cushy office and pregnant paycheck to prove it. But beneath it all, an indiscernible element, a wide hole left a gap in her life.

Charles acted quiet and bland when they had gone to the registrar to put their names in the books, and it didn't sit right with her. It seemed more like he did it out of a sense of obligation. There was no "I want to spend the rest of my life with you," no "I love you," no joie de vivre. It bordered more along the lines of, *Right, love; let's go get Chinese takeout, then go to the registrar's while we're at it.*

The sex with him had been great. In the beginning, he doted. He'd acted ardent and the epitome of what she pictured her first lover would be. He engaged her often, but during the course of the years, he'd fallen into a routine of sorts and did the same things over and over again out of habit, and it got old quick. Perhaps he became too comfortable with their relationship. But it seemed off, a strangeness to his behavior she couldn't place. Like he didn't care anymore. She had qualms about an existence in a loveless marriage. And nothing helped her make heads or tails of the dreams; the crazy, erotic, lust-filled dreams of the other man, a *total* stranger.

"Tell me you're not thinking of jumping," Charles remarked drolly from the doorway. "We just had your suit cleaned."

She turned around. He slouched against the door frame with his ankles and arms crossed and watched her.

"Not quite yet."

He entered and walked toward her. "I like your view," his eyes darted to the window. "But it's much nicer a few floors up. You can see Big Ben and the stars on clear nights. Makes it worthwhile when you have to stay late."

Lark smiled. The telltale rustle of nutshells filled the quiet office as he lifted the lid to the large, clear jar on her desk in which she kept pistachio nuts for visitors. He joined her at the window.

After years of being with this man, his effortless poise still impressed her. His immaculate suit spoke of money, and the polish on his shoes sparkled like diamonds.

"Well, maybe I'll join you someday."

"Sooner than you think," he popped a nut into his mouth and tossed the shells into a nearby bin.

"What's that supposed to mean, exactly?" She turned to him.

Charles narrowed his eyes. "Well, we'll see how today goes. I'm not making any promises." He gave her a quick once-over. "But I've heard a few rumors, and I wouldn't get too comfortable here if I were you." He inclined his head. "See you in there. Good luck." He stroked the small of her back with his knuckles and left.

****

The boardroom was a modern, state-of-the-art, rectangular glass fish tank of a room. As Lark walked in alongside her colleagues, memories surfaced of when she'd come here for the first time with a pile of collated handouts as a new employee. Nigel Pritchett worked as the regional sales manager at the time, and she'd assisted him with a presentation he gave to the Board of Trustees.

A sociable old fellow, Nigel was what Charles referred to when they were alone as a *luvvie*—someone who liked to speak as though he'd swallowed a thesaurus and acted posh when, as Charles said, he came from middle-class Yorkshire.

When Lark later took his position, Nigel had wished her the best of luck, but there was no mistaking his condescending undertone. Not like she blamed him; a man of fifty-seven respected years did not smile when someone younger waltzed in on a position he'd occupied for most of his career. But times were changing, and the company wanted new blood.

The chatter grew louder and more animated as she neared the front of the room. The room itself was decked out more than usual for the company merger with Osaka-Nayaweni, LLP. Colorful orchid arrangements and bamboo plants were dotted on the tables, and a large projector screen showed her PowerPoint's title page. The company logo displayed on a nice dark background.

She watched Maisie adjust the knobs on the bottom of the projector until the screen was where it ought to be, and her fingers grazed the USB drive she'd pocketed in her suit jacket, should she need a backup.

Lark approached the conference table as Maisie dimmed the lights a notch. A nearby table was covered with an assortment of breakfast croissants and pastries, ice-water pitchers, fruit, and coffee. The conference table itself was long and sleek. Leather swivel chairs and pitchers of ice water with crystalline glasses were placed around the table. Twenty or so people sat, ready. The heads of departments had been called in for the merger.

Nigel Pritchett sat near the opposite end in a dark suit, with his trademark bowtie. His glasses were perched precariously on the end of his nose, and he read the meeting's agenda with his pinky finger elevated. The overhead light caught the more reflective parts of his short, salt-and-pepper hair.

Nigel seemed to sense her and beheld her atop his Homer Simpson glasses. The steam from his pretentiousness funneled into her from ten feet away like a hydraulic hose to an inferno. She had forgotten how cunning his blue eyes were. They nodded at each other. Dear God, he took himself way too seriously.

Charles sat confident and relaxed at the head of the table. He chatted in Japanese with Mr. Osaka from Osaka-Nayaweni to his left. She sat beside Charles. His natural bravado came into play at the perfect times in meetings.

To her right, a young man with foppish red hair, an old classmate from grad school, dropped into the seat beside her, chipper and enthusiastic.

He appraised her like a dear cousin. "Hey, Lark. Thanks for your help this morning."

She shook his hand and smiled. "Doug. Anytime. Wonderful to see you. Do you plan to offer a few statistics from Finance for us, then?"

"Certainly. Though it's nothing compared to what's on your plate."

"Lark!" Lark's grin faded as Maisie dashed in with her cell phone in hand.

"There's a call for you. Important. Can't wait," Maisie breathed. She extended the phone to Lark, a frown etched on her cheerful face. "It's from Oregon."

Lark held up her palms and shook her head. "I can't take anything right now. Tell them to call back."

"You *need* to take this call," Maisie said in a low voice. She leaned in. "It's about your family."

Charles watched. He put his hand over Lark's wrist before she made a move and shook his head. "Lark, I don't care if it's the Prime Minister himself—*now* is not the time," he urged in a harsh whisper, a strained smile on his lips. "We're about to draft a several-hundred-million-pound merger here. We need you. Half of this merger is on *you*. Whatever it is will have to wait."

Lark nodded. "Have them e-mail me," she told Maisie. "I'll check it on my phone." She turned back to Charles.

He stood and dinged his fat silver pen on the edge of a water glass. "Ladies and gentlemen, can I have your attention, please." The room silenced.

A gold bracelet slid down Maisie's slim brown wrist as she set the cell phone in front of Lark. "When you read the message, you'll want this," she whispered. Maisie glared, then clipped out of the boardroom at a snappy pace. Something was definitely up.

Lark laid the cream-colored agenda over her cell phone and gave Charles her full attention.

"Ladies and gentlemen, I'm Charles Chase. For those of you who don't know me, I'm the senior advertising executive in the marketing division of Ultimately You. It is my privilege to welcome you all here today, to join in and witness the hopeful merger between our company and Osaka-Nayaweni, LLP." He paused as the room applauded. Lark smiled but eyed the agenda under which her iPhone lay waiting.

"We believe today will mark a significant course of change in the histories of our two companies, and bring about a beneficial outcome not only to the products and merchandise we sell to our millions of customers but to the way we do business as a whole." He continued with his introduction for the next several minutes and acknowledged the corporate directors from Osaka-Nayaweni and the Board of Trustees who were there. He asked them to stand and say a few words.

The phone vibrated under the agenda when Mr. Osaka stood to speak in immaculate English, and she ached to check it.

She took advantage of a momentary applause, grabbed the phone, and hid it in her lap.

Once Charles stood to circle the table as he continued his rehearsed monologue on service branding, she read the message.

It was from Aaron, her brother. The subject line read: URGENT: Open ASAP! Lark opened the e-mail and glanced at the message.

Hi Lark,

It's Aaron. I know it's been a long time since we even talked, but I have to get in touch with you. I feel awful to have to tell you this in an e-mail, but this morning, Dad passed away.

She froze, and reread the last sentence. An ice-cold sensation shot through her body, and her stomach churned. She could hardly breathe, the room overclustered with too many people, *far* too many people.

Doug leaned over. "Lark, are you all right?"

Her hands shook, and her throat was parched. "I—I need a drink of water." She gulped drily.

Doug handed her his ice water, which she took and managed not to spill as she sipped.

Charles walked around the opposite end of the table, handsome and at home in the boardroom. He continued speaking, oblivious to her dilemma.

Lark set the glass down. "Thank you," she whispered to Doug. He watched her as she continued to read Aaron's message.

Dad's had terminal cancer the last three months, but he didn't want us to tell you. Mom needs you here, and so do I. We need to fly you home TODAY. We're planning to bury him in the next few days, and I booked you a flight with American Airlines—but you need to be at Heathrow Airport for check-in by 11:34 a.m. today. Your time. It leaves at 1:07 p.m.

Lark checked her watch as Charles commented on the possibilities the merger would bring.

I hope you get this in time. Please call me ASAP. We love you and really want to see you.

Love, Aaron

He'd left his phone number next to his name.

"Lark?" Doug whispered. "Are you all right? You're pale."

"I-I…" The entire room turned its attention to her.

Charles was right across the table now, beaming. "And so, ladies and gentlemen, without further ado, I'll turn the time over to our regional sales manager, the number one reason this is happening today, and might I add the pride of Ultimately You, Miss Lark Braithwaite." The room broke into polite applause as Lark stood and flipped on the switch to the wireless microphone attached to her suit.

"Good morning." Her voice wobbled but came in crystal clear over the speakers.

"Good morning," everyone replied, and for a horrifying moment, she went blank.

"Mr. Osaka, ladies and gentlemen of the Board, distinguished colleagues, thank you all for gathering here today on our behalf." She slid the cell phone, still in her hand, to Charles.

He took it from her as he sat, baffled. She nodded to the iPhone and watched him check the message. She lifted her PowerPoint remote and clicked to the first slide, her nerves on fire.

"In October of 2001, our company had a major downsizing, as you all know. Due to the events of 9/11, productivity came to a standstill as most of our global commute came in and out of the World Trade Center." She paused and cleared her dry throat.

Charles followed her with wide eyes.

She clicked to the next slide. Her hands shook, but her voice held steady. "Operating out of London, we had to restructure, rethink our strategy, and engineer cost-effective solutions. Luckily, we had fast thinkers with brilliant ideas on our team, one of whom introduced this meeting," she nodded to Charles.

Charles dipped his head to applause. He focused on her once everyone had directed their attention back to the screen.

Lark clicked to the next slide. "I bet you're all wondering what the squiggly lines in this graph represent. No, it's not a television at two a.m. in the nineteen-seventies," she delivered. The joke scored a few chuckles from a couple older colleagues in the room. Worth a shot. "Our revenue is begi—" Charles stood, and she paused. "Yes, Charles?"

He normally interjected remarks whenever she gave a presentation—he loved to show everyone how smart he was—but never so soon.

"Forgive me, Lark," he said, considering the cream-colored paper in his hand. "But the agenda's incorrect." He kept face. "I believe Mr. Stephens was meant to speak first if I'm not mistaken."

"I was?" a confused, gray-haired Mr. Stephens piped up from the other side of the table.

"Yes," Charles pressed. "Mr. Stephens, if you'd like to present, please? A slight change in plans, ladies and gentlemen." A small murmur carried through the room as Lark motioned to an executive assistant to turn off her presentation, and a bewildered Mr. Stephens took the floor with a sheaf of unorganized papers.

Charles approached Lark and put a hand on her back as Mr. Stephens joked with the audience about being glad he prepared.

"Let's go into the hall, hmm?" Charles said near her ear. Forty pairs of eyes grazed over them as they left, but she remained calm and collected.

He shut the door behind them, leaned down, and put his arms around her. Lark clutched him back and buried her head in his shoulder.

"I'm sorry," he said in a low voice.

A torrent of sorrow passed through her, and she held on to him. "It's all right. It's fine. I mean, my dad and I weren't close. We haven't spoken since I left the States. But what a time for it, huh?"

Charles pulled back and searched her eyes. "Lark, even if you could leave right now, do you think you would make the flight?"

She disentangled from his arms, flustered and confused. "I don't know, um, possibly?"

"Then go."

Her eyes widened. "Charles, are you out of your mind? Not right now. You said it yourself; we're in the middle—"

"Forget what I said." He put a hand to her cheek. "This is your family. You should go. I can stay and do your presentation. I've heard you practice it enough bloody times."

Lark leaned into the warmth of his large palm as tears stung her eyes. She cleared her throat. "I'm sorry for the last few weeks."

He pulled her close to him again. "It's all right."

She closed her eyes.

"Lark!" They turned, and Maisie hurried toward them through the hall with a small carry-on in tow. A black leather folder was tucked beneath her arm, a set of keys hooked through her long fingers.

"Thank God for my time abroad," she gasped. "I don't think I've ever packed so fast in my life." Maisie rolled the small suitcase in front of Lark and set it upright. "I used the keys in the safe you said to use in case of emergency and ran to your flat since it's close by. Hope you don't mind. There's not much here, but you have a few changes of clothes and some hygiene and makeup gunk. I also grabbed a few black dresses. I wasn't sure which dresses you'd want, Lark. Sorry." Maisie handed the portfolio to Charles. "I had your secretary print out an emergency leave of absence so you could sign it before she goes."

Lark looked incredulously at Maisie and stepped forward to give her a grateful hug. Maisie glowed and nodded at her once they broke apart.

"Lark, I'm sorry about your dad. There's a taxi parked out front if you want to hurry and get whatever you need from your office. Heathrow's about forty-five minutes away, so you should make your flight if you leave right now."

"How long is the flight?" Lark perused the flight itinerary Maisie had printed and put in the folder.

"Thirteen hours total; the information is in there. The taxi driver will wait for you, and if you leave me your keys, I'll sort out your car, but I'd suggest you get a move on it. I'll get your leave approved after you've signed it."

"I'm the one who has to approve it anyway," muttered Charles. He handed Lark her phone back, took the folio from Maisie, and added his signature with his fountain pen. He glanced back at the conference room as he tucked his pen away. "Leave granted. I'm going to head back inside and take care of things." He looked back at her. "Lark, I'll call you when you land. I'll see if I can book holiday time and come out there tomorrow."

Lark touched his chest. "Are you sure? I don't have to bail on you like this. I can still stay."

Charles squeezed her hand and gave her a quick kiss. "Let me deal with the merger. It'll be fine, all right? Don't stress it. I'll get this settled and find a flight out there when I can. I have to go back inside before poor Stephens makes a complete ass of himself. I'll see you soon," he said, his hand on the doorknob. "It'll be fine." He winked, strode back inside, and called for everyone's attention as the door shut.

She and Maisie eyed each other, and the next twenty minutes were a complete and utter blur. If someone had asked her later, she would never have been able to repeat what had occurred in the last half hour.

Lark hardly remembered Maisie steering her everywhere—they gathered her coat and handbag from her office, she had a brief and weird conversation with her brother Aaron on the phone to tell him she was indeed headed home, and then Maisie shuffled her into the taxi outside.

The ride to the airport was quiet and uneventful, which she appreciated as she needed to pull herself together. She smoked out the window and made a few phone calls to tie up loose ends before flying out. As London passed by, a sharp breeze assailed her flesh through the open window as questions nagged her. What would Oregon be like after all this time? Would the merger be okay? And why did this have to happen *today*?

At Heathrow, she bought water and comfort snacks as well as a chicken Caesar sandwich wrap at Boots. She drifted through the hectic security checkpoints in a dreamlike state. She didn't hate airports, but they brought on anxiety these days, never as relaxed as they used to be.

The wait for the flight was short. Once aboard the plane and in her seat, Lark unwound as the plane lifted off. Her backbone dissolved, and the first daggers of grief pierced her heart. She drew the shade over the window to block out the bright sunlight and put in her earbuds to drown the pain with music.

Much later into the flight, when the flight attendant came around, she ordered a glass of wine, then sipped it while she flipped through a *SkyMiles* magazine. A sweet calm washed through her and dulled the pain. She leaned her head back and closed her eyes as the plane chased the night. She hadn't slept well these last few weeks. The abyss of sleep overtook her, and she welcomed the escape…

****

"Relax," he said, as his lips skimmed the shell of her ear.

Needing this, she closed her eyes and tried to do as he bade. She had no idea where they were; it was different each time. This time, they were in a bright and airy white bedroom somewhere. She wore a sexy light sundress and sat at the edge of a soft bed. He slid his large, strong hands over her tense shoulders from behind and massaged them. The stress lifted away as she melted into his touch.

She couldn't recall the last time anyone had given

her a massage. His hands were exquisite. He lifted her hair and twisted it over her shoulder, then worked his thumbs and fingers to draw out the tense knots of her upper back.

"That feels wonderful." She leaned her head back as he pressed his lips against the side of her neck.

"*You're* wonderful," he murmured against her skin. "I need you, Lark."

She sighed as he kissed a sensitive spot below her ear. His lips were full and warm as they explored her collarbone. He stopped massaging her altogether. He trailed his fingers along her shoulders and smoothed them over her skin as he stroked the taut muscles above her breasts.

A dream again. This wasn't real, but it was heaven to be touched and attended to after so long.

"I wish I could stay here, with you. You make me feel so good." She gasped as his hands slid lower to cup and knead her sensitive breasts. She turned her head to the side and met the sweet warmth of his mouth. His tongue demanded entrance, and she met him eagerly, moving in tandem with the rhythm of his hands, caught in the slow, steady rush inside. Wakefulness approached the more they kissed, and she pulled back. "Wait. This is… We shouldn't be doing this." The last thing she wanted was for him to stop.

"Don't think about it."

His Irish brogue trickled the consonants like a gentle stream. He closed his mouth over her earlobe and sucked, hard. A surge of hot energy shot through her straight to her core, which pulsed with demand.

"Relax. You deserve this. You deserve to be loved."

She yielded, and let the guilt wash away with the flow of his words. He used his lips like a weapon, assaulting her neck until his long, strong fingers turned her chin toward him. He captured her mouth again and pulled her back on the bed with him. Her heart pounded as he shifted position. His arm encircled her midriff, and he lay her beside him. He wore black silk pants, his body well-built and coltish, and the coarse hair on his broad chest grazed her nipples as he loomed over her.

She slid her hands beneath the waistband of his pants and grasped his hard cock. He growled and paused to yank them off. His cock fully free now, he pressed into her, his stiff heat against her thigh. She opened her legs and cradled him with her hips.

His warm mouth enticed hers to yield to him, and they exchanged long, drawn-out kisses. Lark closed her eyes as his kisses drugged her. He slid his hand beneath her back and rubbed her ass, while his other hand combed through her hair. Lark squirmed beneath him, bucking up, hoping he'd take the hint. She wanted to open her eyes, to see this man who had invaded her dreams, but his kisses became more ardent, more persuasive, and she drowned in them. His tongue stroked hers, and she moaned at the taste of chocolate and oranges. While a part of her comprehended this was a dream, and she had another man, a *real* man in her everyday life, this dream-lover's kisses sent her over the edge into a delicious inferno.

He reached between them, holding his cock as he drug the tip slowly across her wet pussy. He pressed the tip inside, and she welcomed the weight of him. She rubbed against him and arched her back, unable to get him to come into her. She gasped as he continued to drug her lips with ardent kisses.

She wrapped her legs around his hips and pulled him into her aching need with a fever she'd never shown any man. He groaned and sank inside her.

"Lark."

She opened her eyes. His face hovered close to hers, and for the first time, she could make out how strikingly handsome he was as if he were a real flesh-and-blood person. He had a full head of thick, dark curls, hawklike green eyes framed by thick brows and dark olive skin which lent an exotic air, a straight nose, and full lips, and a look on his face that told her he was about to devour her.

He thrust deep and groaned with delight as they became one. Lark held on to him as he moved, then tightened as he pounded into her. He drove so hard into her, her breasts bounced.

Trembling, she reached lifted a shaky hand and touched his strong, smooth jawline.

"Y-you're real!"

****

Lark opened her weary eyes as a small dinging noise signaled all passengers could remove their seat belts. She'd flown coach. The other passengers stood, and passive-aggressively milled around each other to get their luggage out of the overhead compartments.

Lark tucked her empty plastic wineglass in the seat back pocket and put her crumpled-up napkin inside. She lifted the window shade. All she could see of Oregon outside were a few planes in the queue for takeoff and a weak, late afternoon sun in the sky.

Deep in the pit of her stomach, a long-lost familiarity surfaced. She was home.

Chapter Two
Forest Grove

As she walked through the jetway at Portland International Airport, Lark spotted her younger brother, Aaron, who stood off to the side. He was dressed college-boy casual in black trousers and a burgundy polo shirt, and he held a sign with her name. He resembled their father so much, she swore she must be having a flashback. Aaron had the same sturdy oval Braithwaite jawline, short and thick sandy-blond hair, and their father's light-blue eyes. Unlike her father, he sported a trimmed, light goatee.

The last time she'd seen him, he'd been fifteen; a lanky, goofy teenager with a squeaky voice and an endless amount of energy. He stood there, twenty-one and a complete stranger. Taller than she'd expected, he had at least five inches above her five-foot-six frame. She could tell he was less like her statuesque father, though, from the way he slouched to the side.

Would he still have the same comical spirit he'd had as a kid? She recalled the good-natured, free-spirited ham of a boy who loved to tell jokes and participate in the musicals and plays in elementary school.

She rolled her suitcase behind her and stopped a few feet in front of him. She'd pulled her hair into a low side braid over her shoulder before she left the plane, and she still wore the black-and-white suit from the meeting.

"Hello," she managed. "Long time no see."

He smiled but didn't say anything. Then, as if he realized who she was, he did a double take. His jaw dropped, and his face lit up in a huge grin.

"Holy *crap*, Lark, you look like a model! You have lost so much weight. Mom's going to freak out. It's awesome to see you."

His blue eyes sparkled with sincerity as he stepped forward to embrace her. A fragile kind of ache spread through her when he put his arms around her. She closed her eyes and hugged him back.

"It's good to see you too, Aaron," she choked. She couldn't believe how deep his voice was now. "Look at you. You're all grown-up."

He stood back and scratched behind his ear. "Yeah, I shot up one summer. For a while, I worried I'd inherited Mom's short gene, but the Big Guy let me off easy. Mom wanted to come and meet you, but she's got her hands full with Dad's funeral. She has a lot of stuff going on. She wanted me to tell you she was sorry she couldn't make it, but she'll be there when we get home. Thanks for coming on such short notice."

Lark smiled at his down-home Oregonian accent. "Thank *you* for the e-mail. Otherwise, I wouldn't have known."

Aaron grinned and grabbed the handle of her suitcase before she could object. "You look pretty tired, sis. Let's get you home. Come on. I've got my pickup parked. It might smell like dirty laundry from college, though, just to give you fair warning."

Lark adjusted her purse on her shoulder and

walked next to him out of the terminal. "I'll consider myself warned. It couldn't be worse than what I must smell like at the moment, so I'd say we're good to go."

The pickup in question was a white Ford truck with an extended cab. It had computerized wraps of a cowboy on a horse on both doors, along with the logo and tagline: BRAITHWAITE BOXING COMPANY— MOVING YOU RIGHT ALONG.

"I sent a quick text to Mom to let her know we're on our way," Aaron commented after they got settled in the cab. "It's been getting darker earlier," he said as he backed the truck out of the stall. "I hope it'll still be light when we get home, so you can see the old place. We're real glad you're here." He smiled at her.

"So am I, Aaron."

They had brief small talk about what Aaron's school life was like and her own journey home; then the cabin of the truck fell silent save for the light country music on Aaron's plugged-in iPod. Lark turned her head toward the window and watched as the evergreen forests, rolling hills, and vineyards passed by as they drove through the countryside toward her father's ranch.

Lark leaned against the window. She recognized many of the white houses they drove past as well as the private, iron-gated entrances of the various ranches in the area. In a few months, the branches of the pine trees would be weighted under newly fallen snow. London didn't get much snow in the winter.

The neat, manicured hedgerows she'd become accustomed to gazing at while on trains in England were replaced with fences, their pastures filled with overpriced, well-bred mares and colts, cattle, and sheep.

Patches of short brown grass dotted the hills, a sure sign of autumn.

As the late afternoon idled by with each passing mile, Lark averted her gaze from the window. *How bizarre to be back here.*

Aaron sang along to a Keith Urban song, and Lark watched the road, relieved it wasn't more awkward between them. He'd been easy-going as a child, and the good nature stayed with him. At least she had an instant friend in her brother. How weird to see him behind the wheel of a truck, driving through Tualatin Valley with her in the passenger seat, when she still remembered him in her mind's eye as being fifteen. He and Pam visited her at her master's degree graduation ceremony before she left for London.

It counted as even stranger when a mere eighteen hours ago, she'd been about to give the presentation of her life in a merger-acquisition deal. The two worlds were so far apart, surreal.

She'd tried her best to forget all about the town of Forest Grove and the past while diverted in London, where being busy as a catalyst in charge of major, successful deals had taken all her time and attention. But the Ford turned, climbed the winding hill, and crested the top. She gasped as memories of the ranch and home flooded forth in a great deluge at the panoramic spread before her.

Evergreen trees lined both sides of the paved driveway—save for one angled to the side, which she'd crashed into when she was sixteen—and a cast-iron, rustic welcome sign read BRAITHWAITE RANCH in a soldered arch overhead.

Aaron cleared his throat and lowered the music

volume. "'Bout four years ago, in wood shop, I carved a sign that said THE OTHER SIDE OF THE MOON and hung it below the insignia. Took Mom and Dad a few good weeks before they realized it was there. Dad made me take it down. He said it looked unprofessional. I have it in my dorm room."

Lark touched her hand to the window, warm inside. "They should have let you keep it up. It sounds cute." She let out a small sigh as they drove and neared the ranch house. The red, gold, and sun-kissed fall leaves added a colorful array to the magnificent charm of the large structure—a brown and dark-red composite of huge cabin logs, aluminum siding, stone, large windows, and glass skylights. It stood two stories high at the end of the lane, four windows on the top floor, four on the bottom, with wooden trim and roof etching. The long, gabled porch had a wooden banister, and the portico area was decorated with warm-colored, modern patio furniture. Rustic, like her dad. A large, ornamental autumn wreath adorned the wooden front door, and what flowers were still in season scattered among her mother's front garden, plants and herbs surrounded by fir trees.

To the right of the house stood the horse stables and a barn, as well as a dusty arena area with worn grass. Three charcoal-colored Appaloosa horses grazed in the late afternoon light. With a slight pang, Lark recalled the passion her father had for Appaloosa horses in particular. He loved to have their small family trail-ride through the mountains on outings late in the summer. She smiled. He would go on at length about the good quality and uniqueness of the horses. Their lineage, racing quality, and mere existence fascinated him.

"Good stock, Lark. There can't be any finer."

As the Ford turned into the paved semicircle driveway in front of the ranch house, Lark managed to catch a glimpse of the covered swimming pool out back as the truck pulled in front of the porch.

A stone water fountain stood adjacent to the pool. Hmm. A new addition since she'd last been home. A sheet of water trickled over the side of the large, flat stone and collected in a man-made pond beneath it.

Her mother stood on the front steps, shielding her eyes with a hand against the sunset, which cast a warm glow on the front of the house. Despite the slight fog from the drink she'd had on the plane and the inertia of long-distance travel, Lark's heart beat against her rib cage at the sight of her mom.

A slender woman like Lark, Pam Braithwaite had short, blonde hair, cut at the neck and layered with light and dark highlights, and warm, brown, doelike eyes Lark had inherited. She smiled tenderly as she waved at them. She wore dark blue jeans and a V-necked brown shirt and held a crumpled tissue clenched in her hand. She stepped down from the porch and put her free hand to her chest. The Ford slowed to a stop a few feet in front of her.

The truck hadn't stopped before her mother was there, trying to pry the door open. Lark unlocked it.

"Lark," Pam sighed and leaned in to hug her. She stopped, shocked. "Oh my goodness, you're so skinny!"

"Surprise?" Lark laughed and put her arms around Pam. She held her as best she could from her awkward position. The smell of sandalwood and rose oil filled her senses, a smell she had long forgotten. "Hi, Mom."

Pam pulled Lark out of the truck and embraced her. "Oh honey," she whispered. She put a hand to Lark's cheek and gave her a maternal head-to-toe assessment. "You're amazing."

Tears threatened to surface as Pam hugged her full-on. Lark struggled to stay in control as her mother sobbed on her shoulder. She breathed deep, and the gravity of her father's death sank in. She put a hand on Pam's hair. Coming home had been the right choice, no matter what.

"It's okay," Lark whispered as her mother sobbed. "I'm here. Everything will be all right now." They held each other, two lost souls. The truck doors closed behind her, and Aaron stood beside them with her luggage. Lark took her mother's hand.

Pam shook her head. "I can't believe it. I know you'll think I'm a hormonal old bat, but I'm so proud of you, honey. You've always been beautiful, but to have worked that hard..."

Tears overfilled Lark's tired eyes and spilled out. Other than escaping to her dream lover for a brief respite, she had not slept well on the flight, and her body craved a shower, a supportive mattress, and soft, warm sheets. Maybe being home, where the pace of life was so much slower, would enable her to catch up on much needed rest. She wiped her eyes and did her best to smile.

"Well, I figured if I got a master's degree and landed a great job in London, I at least ought to physically fit the bill, so I worked out in addition to dieting." Lark sniffed. "I have Weight Watchers to thank for the rest." She draped an arm around her mother as they moved toward the porch steps.

"You sound so cultured, Lark. I can't explain it; it's like your accent sounds the same, but you talk with the rhythm of an English person."

Lark shrugged. "Must have been all the time I've spent with them. Good to know I still have my Oregonian accent. You can take the girl away from the country, but not the country out of the girl, I guess."

Pam shook her head. "I can't believe you're home again. It's like a dream."

Lark tightened her arm around her mom's waist. "I know. It's amazing to come back here after all this time. I'm sorry it had to be in this particular way."

Pam leaned her head on Lark's shoulder as they neared the front porch steps. The porch veered off to their right a bit. A white swing occupied a great portion of it under the living-room window. "That wasn't there before."

"No."

"What happened to the one attached to the ceiling? The old, rusty, creaky number?"

Pam wiped her nose with the wrinkled tissue in her hand. "Your dad got rid of it years ago. It was old, and I wanted something soft to sit on. It wasn't butt-conducive for visitors."

Lark eyed the plush cushions and the white throw pillows on the overstuffed swing. She walked over and sat. The soft cushions molded to her form and enveloped her thighs like a soft cotton cloud. The countryside in the distance stretched for miles in a stunning spread. She couldn't remember the last time she'd felt so peaceful.

Pam watched her. "I'd give a million dollars to know what's on your mind right now."

A strong wave of fatigue hit Lark, and she sighed. "I thought about how the old swing used to creak all the time when I would sit on it. It's been so long, I can't believe I remember."

Pam leaned against a thick log gable. "I'd wager you'll have a lot of deja-vu in the next few days. Let's go inside, hmm? I have a crockpot of chicken pasta all warmed and ready to go for you guys. We'll get you a bite to eat, and then you can get some rest." Lark nodded, took her mother's offered hand, stood, and followed her inside.

Her mother redecorated, though the layout of the place hadn't changed. All the furniture in the visiting room had been replaced in brown, tan, and burgundy colors. The framed portraits and paintings on the walls were still the same, as was a watercolor of the Seine in Paris her mother and father had chosen on their many excursions. Even the photograph her father had taken of the ancient ruins in Greece, blown up on a canvas print, still hung on the wall.

Pam led her through the long hallway, past the living room, and into the kitchen. Lark glanced to her right and glimpsed the library her father had treasured. Rows of books and encyclopedias lined the walls. She caught a peek of the unlit stone fireplace, in front of which sat a large mauve couch, and the corner edge of her mother's black baby grand piano.

A calico cat slinked past her. If that was who she thought it was… He'd been a kitten when she was last home. He ignored her and headed straight for his food bowl.

"Ignore Bandit. He's an old miser and a total drama queen. I'm sure he'll warm to you in no time.

Sit," Pam ordered.

"Laminated or real wood?" Lark eyed the new floor.

"Laminate. We wanted real wood but not for the price."

Her mother remodeled the kitchen. All the countertops and the kitchen island were a mixture of black oak wood, and monochrome, dark marble. Pam had a good eye because Lark had to admit all the different textures and colors complemented the house. A small, round table with four cushy chairs stood by the back door.

"This is new," said Lark as she slid into a chair at the table. She was sad to see the old set was gone.

Pam dished up a plate for Lark at the counter. "Brand-new. Well, two years old, if I'm being picky." She set a plate of warm chicken pasta in front of her. Lark put her hand on her mom's before she could leave.

Lark softened her voice, something she hadn't done in a long time. "Mom, you shouldn't do this. Come sit with me."

Pam lifted her chin. "Nonsense. I need to move around, remind myself I'm still here and functioning. Would you like a drink?" She moved away and took out a glass from a nearby cupboard.

Lark's mind whirled, and she longed to go lie down. Good old jet lag. "Can I have a glass of water, please?"

"You've got it."

She ate small bites of the delicious pasta. She looked around and noticed new things mixed in with the old around the room.

Aaron entered the kitchen and took a seat. "Smells

good," he murmured.

"It is," Lark said between bites. She savored the tasty flavor. "Do you not use the dining room anymore?"

Aaron leaned back in his chair and rubbed the back of his neck. "Not unless we have guests over. It's less hassle for Mom since it's just the two of them...*was* the two of them."

Lark offered him an empathetic look. "How's school going? You're about finished, aren't you?"

"Yeah, I graduate next June," he sipped the water their mom handed him.

Lark picked at her food while they visited. She learned Aaron had driven home from Berkeley, where he studied political science. He dated another student, Giselle, off and on.

After she finished eating, Lark went upstairs with her mom. The shag carpet she recalled had been replaced by a nice and plush light champagne-colored Berber. Everything seemed bigger than London, more spread out. Her flat was half the size of the downstairs alone.

Lark eyed her luggage against the wall. Aaron must have brought it up. Her heart softened as she surveyed her childhood room with its cherrywood furniture and dark orchid, silver, and blue theme. A fresh flower arrangement stood on a small round table next to the plush lavender armchair in the corner. She used the bathroom, frowned at her tousled and disheveled appearance in the mirror. Screw it, she needed a shower. She pulled the shower curtain aside and stepped in.

Out of the bathroom and in pj's, Lark half smiled

as she remembered the astonishment on her mother's and Aaron's faces when they'd first seen her. A lot had happened since she'd moved to London, but it was nice to know all her hard work in losing weight wasn't for nothing. She was an emotional eater, but she'd learned over the last six years to work off any extra food she ate. Exercise had also become a good way to drive away the demons of the past.

She turned around, and the smile left her face as she spied an old framed photograph on the nightstand. She picked it up and sat on the bed.

A heavier, younger version of herself in a black high-school graduation gown and tassel hat stood in an auditorium with her mother's and father's arms around her. A blue-and-gold banner overhead read, THE GRADUATING CLASS OF— Her father stood in front of the rest of the banner. She touched her hand to her face in the photo. Such a broad and happy smile, even a dimple in her left cheek. So young and unweighted down by the cares of the world. Her gaze traveled to her mother and then her father. He beamed with pride at the camera. About a week after this picture was taken, she'd found out his secret.

Everything had changed from then on out.

She reached over and replaced the frame on the nightstand, then brushed her damp hair and fell back on the bed. She stared at the vaulted ceiling fan. Memories swarmed her mind, but in her weariness, none were decipherable.

She kneaded her scalp, and her neck became more relaxed. Her father stood at the window of his office in her mind's eye as he'd been in his younger years, his hand lifted in greeting. She recalled a picnic spread on a soft, checkered yellow-and-white blanket out on the lawn, the scent of freshly mown grass in the back garden, a red kite against a blue wash of sky. Her eyelids grew heavy, and she drifted...

****

The patchwork quilt laid over the green grass beneath the shade of the oak tree cradled her back like a soft mattress. They were in an open area, and the gentle kiss of a cherry-blossom-scented breeze cooled her skin. The gurgle of water crept over stones and alerted her to the clear brook a few feet away from where she lay naked in his arms.

They faced each other on their sides, legs entwined, his half-erect cock against her thigh. His spent seed warmed her insides, and he kissed her tenderly, slowly, with more affection than she could have ever hoped for.

"Lark," he growled against her lips. Soft waves of his dark hair tickled her forehead. He tilted her chin back, moved his lips down her throat, and burned a line of fire over her skin. His large, warm palm trailed along her back, then slid from her hip to her bare thigh.

She stuttered a breath. "Touch me."

He gripped her leg and draped it over his. He kissed her shoulder, and she whimpered at the touch of his hardened cock as it rubbed against her sensitive slit. He closed his hand around his cock and brought the head to her clit. He teased her, coating it with her essence. She moved her hips closer to relieve the tension, but his determined look broke no argument — he controlled the pace.

He dipped the head of his cock into her pink folds, teasing her entrance with the barest of pressure. He pulled back again to brush it along her slit. A soft moan escaped her lips. God, she wanted him. She clamped her thighs about him, closing her folds over his length as she slid against it, driven by wild need. Each touch he gave her further ignited her body.

It was wonderful to lie outside and in the sun; for the first time, she saw him plain as day. His face had a noble quality to it and was sexy as hell. He had high cheekbones, and the aura he exuded made her think he belonged to a different era.

He smoothed his fingers over her hip and along the curve of her ass. He tilted his hips back to free his cock from her hold and hauled her in closer. His mouth plundered hers, and she was lost to him. His fingers dipped in the cleft of her ass as he kissed her, and she let out a small mewl. She writhed against him like a cat in heat. He stroked her rounded flesh, and she hitched her leg higher over his hip, desperate for friction. It wasn't enough; she needed him inside her. As if she'd spoken aloud, he curved his palm beneath her ass to her front and cupped her dainty mound. His lips parted as he drank her in with his eyes.

"What have you done to me? What is it that makes me want you so much?" The lilt to his Irish tone was husky and somewhat raspy. His gaze roamed over her.

"I've been wondering the same thing," she whispered, her heart pounding.

"I want to fill you up, Lark," he growled. "I want to bury my cock inside you."

He kept his eyes locked with hers as the hand on her mound sought its way through her folds, and his thumb caressed her tender nub. Lark trembled and grasped his shoulders as he slid a finger inside. She clenched her inner walls, closed her eyes, and shivered as he located delicate, receptive nerves and worked her into a frenzied state. He kissed her and nibbled her lower lip, then slid a second finger inside to join the first. *Sweet God.* Her eyes rolled back as he formed a steady rhythm. She gasped.

"I have to have you," he growled. "And I'm not talking about your body. I need all of you. Every inch. Every breath."

He moved over her. She stared at him as he stroked the hair from her forehead and kissed her there. The tenderness with which he did so surprised her. She met his eyes, moved by the love in them. The raw passion in this man was unparalleled. He separated her legs, thrust his hard cock into her entrance, and stretched her until he was sheathed to the hilt inside.

"It's you for me, Lark," he growled as she raised her legs and crossed her ankles over his lower back. He slid out, and thrust forward, hard. She cried out at the bliss and held on to his shoulders as he spoke into her ear.

"It will always be you."

****

Lark sighed and rolled over, awake. She'd fallen asleep next to her open suitcase, drooled on the quilt, and good God, with damp panties to boot. These dreams were getting way too lifelike. She sat up, her back stiff. She brushed wayward hair out of her face, wiped a smidgen of sleep from her eyes, blinked, and looked around.

It seemed so impossible to be here, back home. The gentle trill of the birds outside twittered away. It was like she'd stepped through a portal in time. The stillness of the room drove home why she was here, and her dream faded. She'd conked out with the lamp still on. The sun streamed in through the window and warmed her back and legs.

Lark slid from the bed, rotated her neck to relieve the stiffness, and clicked the lamp off. She went over to the window and looked out of the partly opened curtains. The beautiful Oregon countryside spanned everywhere she could see. She glanced at the alarm clock on the nightstand. It was almost noon.

"I can't believe I slept in so late," she muttered. She selected a pair of black slacks and a cranberry-colored, long-sleeved shirt from her things, laid them on the bed, and hopped in the shower.

Later, she emerged from the en-suite bathroom with her hair back in a tight, slick ponytail and her makeup done. She froze in the doorjamb as she took in the clean room. No, she wasn't in a *Twilight Zone* trip – her bed was made and the color-coordinated pillows splayed against the headboard. Her suitcase had been moved and sat against the wall by the overstuffed armchair. A quick peek in the nearby dresser revealed her clothes were folded and put away. She shook her head with a wry grin and grabbed her pack of cigarettes and lighter from the dresser top as she left the room. "Some things never change, Mom. Either that or you have an OCD poltergeist."

Chatter wafted up from the kitchen below. She met her mother on the stairs.

Pam held a tissue as she talked into the phone. Her eyes were reddened, stark against her black shirt and black pants.

Hi, Pam mouthed, her jaw quivering. Lark returned

the silent greeting and stood on the bottom step with folded arms.

"All right. Thank you, Niall. You've made this so much easier. I don't know what we'd do without you. Okay. I will. See you tomorrow. Bye."

Pam clicked a button on the phone and smiled sadly at Lark with tears in her eyes. Lark gave her a gentle hug. Death was never easy on the living, and it hurt to see her mother in any kind of pain.

"I can't believe Rick's gone." Pam sniffed. "It's like I roll over in the morning and expect it to be a crazy dream, but it's real. Sorry, sweetheart. I'm a complete wreck."

"Mom, of course, you are. You have every right to be." Lark hugged her again. It was all she could do to try to convey how much she loved her. "Is there *anything* I can do to help with all this, with the funeral?" she asked near her ear. "It's tomorrow, right?"

Pam nodded and wiped her nose. "Eleven. The viewing is tonight at six at the funeral home. Our attorney's taken care of all the arrangements. He went out of his way to get the flowers ordered and the programs for the funeral done up. All that's left to do is cook and get things ready for the after-party tomorrow."

Lark lifted her eyebrows, impressed. "Wow."

"I know. He's been amazing." Pam put a hand on her cheek, and her eyes traveled to Lark's long ponytail. "Do you wear ponytails a lot?"

"Not all the time, but sometimes. It's professional and practical; I can throw it back and go."

Pam lifted a fair eyebrow. "Well, it sure has grown

out. It's so healthy. Could you do me a favor and wear it down for the funeral?"

"Of course."

"Thank you. Let's get you some food." Pam steered her in the direction of the kitchen. She'd set the table for a light lunch.

Lark sat with a glass of apple juice, picked at a few pomegranate seeds, and spooned bacon bits from a white china dish onto her salad. She set her cigarettes and lighter on the table and poured dressing over the salad. She waited for Pam's inevitable antismoking lecture, but it never came. Her mother was distracted by other things.

Pam smiled. "It must seem so different to you, all of this after London."

Boy, what an understatement. "Oh, it is. Everything's bigger. I don't think I had a concrete idea what portion control meant until I moved to England. This tastes fantastic."

They ate in silence, then Pam snapped her fingers. "I'm sorry, I've been so preoccupied, I forgot to tell you a man named Charles called earlier while you were asleep."

Lark pinched the bridge of her nose. "Damn it. I forgot he said he'd call after I landed. What did he say?"

Pam smiled as she set more dishes on the table. "Well, he charmed my socks off with his nice British accent; more so when he said he's your fiancé."

Lark swallowed and dabbed the corner of her mouth with a napkin. "Mmm. He is. We've been engaged a long time, though." She lifted her hand in a blasé way and showed her mother her diamond engagement ring.

Pam brought her hand closer and examined it. "Nice. So, what's he like? Where did he grow up? Do you call him Charlie?"

Lark scraped her food around her bowl with her fork, not sure how to answer what Charles was like anymore. *Brilliant, evasive, trite, insensitive?* "He's…handsome, successful, very English, I guess. He's an only child, and his parents are divorced, but he grew up in a nice house and went to a private school in Cambridge. He hates the nickname Charlie with a passion, so please call him Charles."

"Well, he sounded respectful on the phone. I seem to remember your taste for a different sort of man. He seems on the ball, though."

Lark nodded and picked at her salad. They did need to talk, but this wasn't the time or place to divulge personal hardships to her mom, so she kept it pleasant.

"Did he leave a message?"

Pam poured apple juice into her glass. The ice crackled and shifted beneath the liquid. "He said to tell you he's booking a flight out here, and he'll try to call you later. How long have you two been engaged?"

Lark glanced at the beautiful ring she'd known for half a decade. How many times had she asked the exact same thing, but in a much more sarcastic and colorful language?

"Five years. We don't want to rush anything."

"It's safe to say you're in the clear for rushing into it, dear." Her mother laughed.

It was good, in a way, to come back home so she could have time to think about things with Charles. She gazed at Pam's beautiful, careworn face. Still youthful, though graced by a few wrinkles around the eyes and mouth. "You look great, Mom. You haven't aged a bit."

Pam thanked her and paused between sips. "Grape seed oil, like I've told you. Does the trick."

"Are any family members coming to the viewing?"

Pam nodded. "Niall's taken care of it. Your distant cousins and aunts will be there. Great-aunt Bernice couldn't make it; she's too old, bless her heart. How's your salad?"

"Good."

Aaron opened the door and walked into the kitchen in boots, jeans, and a red plaid shirt. He set his keys and a large, brown paper bag on the kitchen counter. Lark tilted her head, endeared by his humble attire. He seemed more like someone's ranch hand than a college student at Berkeley. "Hi there, cowboy." She smiled.

"Hey." He cocked his head to the side. "How you feelin'? You were pretty wiped yesterday."

"Aaron," Pam chided.

He laughed, a glad release in the quiet kitchen. "What? It's true, Mom. No point beating around the bush. So, uh, sis," he pulled up a chair beside her. "I've got something to ask you, and it feels like the right time. Here's the deal. Before Dad passed away yesterday morning, he was sick for a long time. While he was still well enough to talk, he made me promise him something."

Pam drew upright in her chair. "I never heard of this. Go on, Aaron."

Aaron eyed Lark's nice trousers and blouse and scratched behind his ear. "Well, uh, the thing is, he made me promise before he was buried, if you ever came back and we had the opportunity, you and I'd take

48

the Appaloosas for a ride as one last salute to him."

Beside her, Pam clasped her hands together. "Typical Rick." She turned to Lark. "You don't have to, Lark, of course. Though I know Rick would like you to."

Though her mother and brother were wide-eyed and eager, it was all a bit invasive. Still, she didn't want to seem rude. "I...my assistant packed workout clothes and black stuff for the funeral, but I don't have any suitable clothes to wear for riding. What—you didn't want to go now, did you?" She glanced at Aaron's cowboy garb.

Oh hell. She shouldn't horseback ride today of all days—namely the likelihood she'd fall off the horse and land flat on her ass. But she could name a few reasons why she might like to.

"Nah," Aaron said. "We can eat first."

Chapter Three
Dustings

Two shaky cigarettes and half an hour later, Lark, filled with trepidation, leaned on the corral fence a few feet away from a calm mare, who lowered her head and drank from the high-perched trough. Large thigh muscles shifted beneath the mare's smooth, gray-spotted coat, sheer power and sinewy grace enveloped into one magnificent creature. A beauty with a charcoal-gray-colored mane and tail, she continued to chomp on her feed.

Pam ransacked an old box and gave Lark an old, loose denim shirt, blue jeans, socks, and thick hiking boots she managed to fit into.

"Something wrong?" Aaron asked beside her with a rein draped over his shoulder. He had donned her dad's black cowboy hat, and with the exception of his light, trimmed goatee, he could have been a younger version of their father.

"Hmm? Oh, nothing. Unless you consider I haven't been on a horse in about a hundred years…" Her voice trailed off as her mother approached with reins in hand. She led another Appaloosa from a nearby pasture.

Aaron placed a high wooden stool on the ground for Lark to use to mount the mare.

"Well, try to look at it this way. You're like, what? A hundred pounds lighter, so you've got that going for you. Vertically challenged people, this way." He took her hand as he helped her up. "What's the old saying about riding a bike?"

"Yeah, yeah, laugh it up," said Lark. "You gave me the nice horse, right?"

Aaron steadied the mare while she swung her right leg over the horse's back.

"You know, Aaron," Pam called as she guided his horse into the corral. "When Lark was a little girl before you could talk, she used to call these guys 'Appley-loothas.'" She grinned. Rosy color lit her cheeks, and aside from the black she wore, her face lightened.

Aaron grinned up at Lark. "Did you?"

Lark glanced away. "I had a lisp until I was ten. There's no way you'd remember. You weren't even born. Dad was horrible and made me try to say 'Appaloosas,' and it became the brunt of every dinner joke for nine straight years of my life."

Aaron chuckled. "Well, I do remember how I called you Lard."

Pam snorted from a few feet away as she slipped the reins over the head of his horse. "Lark got so mad at you when her friends were over, and you would follow her around and torture her." Pam lifted her face to the sky, closed her eyes, and breathed in deep through her nose. "Mmm, smell that."

"What?" Aaron crinkled his nose. "The manure?"

Lark laughed, and Pam chided Aaron. "No, wiseass. I mean the grass, and the fresh air, and the soft breeze. Rick's here right now, as sure as I'm alive. I can feel him. Thank you so much for doing this, Lark. I know he appreciates it. I can't tell you how much I do."

"Well, I'm glad my discomfort and sure-to-be-sore ass are appreciated by someone," Lark quipped.

"Now, you'll be fine," Aaron reassured her. He stroked the horse's neck as it adjusted to her weight. "This here's Penny. We got her a few years back, and she'll take real good care of you." He tapped the horse's rear flank, and they were off at a toddling, rhythmic walk.

As she passed Aaron, he mounted his horse and fell in line with her.

They went at a snail's pace through the pasture at first. When Lark was confident Penny liked her enough not to throw her off, she turned to Aaron, who rode beside her. "Look at you. You're like a young John Wayne or something," she teased.

He tipped the brim of his hat. "Well, if John Wayne was into politics and had ideas about economic reform, I guess I am."

"I don't think he was involved in politics, but you *do* both have the whole androgynous name thing in common. His real name was Marion, yours is Aaron—"

"Hey now—"

"Hey, what," she bantered. "It's payback. How long have you had your goatee?" It would be interesting to see how much of a resemblance he bore to her father beneath it.

He smoothed his fingers over it. "A couple of months. I placed a bet with Niall on who could grow theirs faster, and I won." He grinned.

"Oh. Can I ask you something?" She glanced at him.

"Sure."

"It's about all this. Was there any particular reason

Dad wanted us to ride together?"

Aaron leaned forward in his saddle. "I'm not sure, but I think he regretted things and wanted us to have a kind of adventure before he was buried. He never said what it was. He said to me a few weeks ago, 'Before they bury me, go for a ride with your sister.' And he made me promise. I don't know why, but thanks for doing it."

Lark stroked Penny's long neck, close to the saddle. "I'm glad to. Charles isn't into this kind of thing, so it's a nice change, if not weird to be—" She paused when she caught Aaron's amused expression. "What?"

He shrugged. "Nothing. You seem at home in the saddle, is all."

"I do?" She smiled.

He nodded and glanced ahead of him. "Hey, want to trot? We'll keep it slow."

Lark clicked her heels twice into Penny's flanks, and the horse bobbed her neck as she set off on a trot. Lark leaned forward and enjoyed the way the wind played upon her face. A while later, Aaron talked her into a full-on gallop.

As the strong mare eased into a run, the wind whooshed against Lark's flesh. The horse kicked clumps of dirt and grass, and she flew with the breeze, free.

****

A while later, when they returned to the open corral, Pam stood beside the fences. Aaron helped her dismount Penny.

"Well, how was it?" Pam asked.

Lark approached her, thighs jittery as though she

were still on the horse. "Windy." She turned with Pam toward the house, while Aaron and a ranch hand fed the horses after they removed their saddles and tack.

"Lark," Pam said as they walked. "I've thought about you and Charles. If you want to talk to me about anything, I want you to know, I'm here, honey. I'm not breakable because your dad died; quite the opposite. Also, I'd like to get to know you again."

Touched by the glint in her mother's large, brown eyes, Lark stopped and embraced her.

Pam put her chin on Lark's shoulder. "I want you to know how much I love you, okay? I know it's been a long time, but you're still my little girl, and you always will be. Even when you're an old, wrinkly lady in a nursing home."

Lark's eyes stung, and she shut them. "I know, Mom," she whispered back. She pulled back sooner than she wanted to, opened her eyes, and patted her mother's shoulder. "Before all this is over and I have to go away to the UK, I promise we'll have a good, long talk, okay?"

"All right, honey." Pam wiped the corner of her eyes with her hand.

When she returned to the house, Lark meandered in the library outside her father's office. She shuttered her fingers across the plump spines of the weathered works she found on the bookshelf and named them off in her mind: Shaw, Ibsen, Hemingway, Shakespeare, Thoreau.

How many times as a child had she been in this room, lying on the large merlot Persian rug in front of the fireplace, surrounded by piles of books and listening to her father on the phone in the next room, comforted by the sound of his deep voice? She longed for those days as a child when she could remain content from the sound of her father's voice. She envied the ease with which children were satisfied. If only it were so simple as an adult. Lark walked into the office. He'd modernized it; the only remnant from the earlier years was the small, rectangular wooden table. A nice, new, and large cherrywood desk upstaged the bright room. It sat close to the window, with two black leather chairs in front of it. A treadmill and couch bordered the rest of the room, and a flat-screen TV was mounted on one wall.

Lark sat in the chair behind the desk. The soft leather soothed her sore thighs. From the corner of her eye, she spotted an old photograph on the desk. She scooted forward in the chair to retrieve it.

She swore under her breath as she picked it up. Her big hair and straight bangs stared back at her. Aaron had been eight at the time, and his cute, soup-commercial-kid-with-the-basin-bowl-haircut face beamed out at her. Pam's arm wrapped around his shoulder, and he stood between a teenaged Lark and their father.

"I'd forgotten this," she whispered, staring at how young and happy they had been. She was surprised at the clear quality of the photograph, taken so long ago. They had all been close. Happy. Her dad appeared to worship the ground her mother walked on.

Yet it was all an act.

A flood of emotions—mainly rage—took her over. After all her hard, diligent work in high school, she'd graduated as valedictorian, then won a scholarship into Berkeley with an informed English composition she'd written about the fruitlessness of supremacist organizations. Her academic scholarships had seen her through four years of college.

Before Berkeley, she'd taken the summer off and, along with her high-school friends, had gone on a parent-chaperoned European excursion she'd saved for. Upon returning a day earlier than planned, she'd driven home from the airport to surprise everyone, but the house stood empty and quiet. She'd gone upstairs to her parents' bedroom to borrow her mother's quick-drying nail polish.

The smells, the sounds, the grotesqueness of finding her father with a woman who was not her mother, in the bed he and Pam shared, were imprinted on her mind's eye forever. She'd flown out of the house, threw up in the yard, and escaped to her car. Her father threw on clothes and came after her, but she had shifted gear into drive by the time he got outside.

Revolted and distraught, she'd called her mom and told her what happened. Her mother further broke her heart by rushing to Rick's defense.

"It's okay, Lark," Pam had said when Lark called her on her cell phone. "I've known for some time now. Please come home so we can talk about this."

Lark had hung up, paid a cash deposit, and checked into a cheap Motel Six for a week before her first semester as an on-campus student at Berkeley. She used a local laundromat to clean her travel clothes, ate instant noodles from boiling water she made in the coffee pot in the small hotel room, and lived on cheap fast food the entire time.

She refused to go back home and was too mortified to tell her friends. This all took place after they'd made a big public-service announcement for Rick's Man of the Year award. His deceit and infidelity imploded her world. Her family was her one true stronghold, and it had been the last time she'd ever seen him.

A bitter laugh escaped. "I haven't thought of you for *years* now. I've kind of shoved it all on the back burner and gotten on with my life. Isn't that sad?" She took her cell phone out of her back pocket and flipped it over in her palm. She frowned and set it on the desk. Emotions had a shelf life, and this late in the game she ought to let bygones be bygones. But certain scars festered and didn't heal the same.

Her dad made every effort to reach out to her, but she wouldn't forgive him. He'd sent her a letter of apology and a fat check. She never read what he wrote, but she did cross her name out on the check, put Pam's on it instead, and sent it back to her mother's attention without a note. She'd made her own way, right until the end, summa cum laude, and Pam and Aaron had come to visit her a few times throughout college and at graduation.

When she was twenty-five, Ultimately You headhunted her for the position in London before her graduate ceremony. She'd kept in touch with her mother and Aaron, but it was awkward. She'd never been able to understand how Pam could have forgiven him. It seemed as though she didn't think twice about it. Twenty years of marriage shot to shit, and she lay down and took it. Like it never happened.

Lark stood, folded her arms, and walked over to the window. She couldn't be near her father's photo anymore. "I was so devastated, Dad, and she went about her life as usual, not a care in the world. You didn't deserve her, and I resent the hell out of you for what you did. I *love* Mom. With all my heart, I do. But I can never respect her for forgiving you so fast."

A strange, cold sensation flitted through her, as though someone was in the room with her. Lark glanced around, grabbed her cell phone off the desk, and headed upstairs. She dialed Charles's number on the way. It hit his voice mail on the first ring, so she hung up and called his office number instead. He said he'd put in late hours due to the merger. The line answered on the third ring.

"Ultimately You, Gemma speaking. Oh wait, it's the States. Charles?"

Lark glowered at the sound of Charles's young, pretty assistant, who was also London's biggest tart.

"Is that you, darlin'?"

A coldness shot through Lark's body at the way Gemma intoned *darlin'*. She kept quiet and held on to the door frame.

"Hello? Baby, are you there? There must be a delay. I'm glad you landed, though. Call me back when you can, yeah? Okay, bye now."

The line went dead, and the phone slipped from her hand to the floor. She shut her bedroom door and leaned against it, covering her mouth so she wouldn't make a sound as she sobbed. She slid to the floor, tucked her knees into her chest, and rested her forehead on her arms. This couldn't be happening.

"I don't know why I dream of you," she whispered aloud to her dream lover. "But I need you tonight. I *need* you."

****

Everyone was quiet on the way to the funeral home later that evening. Aaron drove them, and they arrived thirty minutes before the viewing.

The funeral home was nice. Classical music played in the background as they milled around the foyer. It was a closed-casket viewing. A poster-size canvas print of Rick in his twenties sat on a nice easel. In it, he dressed to the cowboy nines in simple jeans and a red plaid shirt as he guided a beautiful, smoke-colored Appaloosa by the reins.

She trudged through the meet-and-greet line. She managed to interact, but every word came out automatic, each gracious, quiet smile fabricated as reality sunk further and further in. After the call to Charles's office earlier and hearing Gemma's sultry, insinuating tone which all but screamed *affair*, she wanted to go back home, close her eyes, and disappear into her dreams.

"Well, the funeral's tomorrow." Aaron yawned as he took a seat beside her on the sofa in the foyer.

"Seems weird, doesn't it?"

He nodded. "Yeah. I mean, Dad never slowed down for anything. When he was alive, he was *alive*." He waved a hand. "He *lived* his life, you know? Well, no matter what, sis, I'm glad you're here."

She squeezed his hand, and put aside her own problems. "Me too, Aaron. I'm glad I came back."

****

Lark drew in a sharp gasp of air through her nose and bolted upright. It was the middle of the night, and she had the distinct feeling of being watched. She reached to switch on her nightstand lamp, but a low Irish voice stopped her.

"Don't. Keep it dark."

He stood in front of the window, his gaze riveted

on her. The contour of his powerful frame and halo of thick, dark hair etched against the moonlight. She was pretty sure he didn't have any clothes on, and a thrill of excitement shot through her.

She touched her face and blinked. "This can't be a dream. I'm awake."

"Well, good. I *want* you awake for what I'm about to do to you." He moved toward the bed. She sat up. This wasn't a dream at all. He sat next to her and leaned in to kiss her with those thick Cupid's bow lips. Thrown off-kilter, she put her fingers up to stop him.

"W-wait. This feels way too real. I mean, we're in my old *room*."

"I don't choose the location, Lark."

His fingertips caressed her cheek, and in the shadow of night, his eyes were like dark gems. His lips tickled her ear when he leaned forward.

"I'm here to please you, and right now, that's all I'm interested in doin'."

He pressed his lips to hers, and at first, it was soft and sensual and everything she missed about what it was like to be touched, to be loved. She'd forgotten what raw love felt like, when someone wanted you so much it was like powerful medicine to a dying man. Then he moved forward, pushed her onto the bed, and braced himself over her. He groaned and sucked her lower lip into his mouth. A current traveled through her. She opened her mouth to him and returned his passion. He thrust his tongue deep into the cavern of her mouth, mimicking what his cock might do, and she nearly lost it. She mewled. He made a low noise of approval in the back of his throat and continued to plunder her mouth, ruthless in his utter and total possession. Lark laced her arms around his neck.

He was on her then, touching and exploring her with a careful but roving hand. As he continued his blissful assault, his fingers hooked into the band of the pajama bottoms she slept in. She let out a sigh as he slid them down her legs, marking a path with his hand along her skin. She groaned with encouragement when he took them off.

"I want to see you. All of you," he muttered as he slid her T-shirt up. Deep in the fog of lust, Lark helped him tear off the garment, and the shirt soon sailed across the room into the darkness.

"Yes." He stared at her bare breasts with tender reverence. Lark bit her lip and followed his glance as heat colored her cheeks. She was sensitive when it came to her breasts. Some body issues would never go away, no matter how much weight she lost.

He lifted her chin with his index finger. "Your breasts are sexy as hell, Lark," he said, his voice rough. "I want to put my mouth on them and suck your sweet nipples." Hot wetness flooded her pussy. She nodded as he enclosed a nipple in his warm mouth, tugging it with his teeth and suckling it as if he'd never have enough. Cool air kissed her nipple when he moved to do the same to the other, and she gasped as her pussy clenched. As if he sensed her predicament, his other hand smoothed the flat plane of her stomach. She blushed as his hand explored her mound. His mouth released her nipple, and the soft curls of his thick head of hair brushed against her flesh as he lowered himself.

"Yes. I love the way you touch me," she breathed as he marked a trail of tormenting kisses down her stomach, past her navel, until the first long, flat stroke of his skilled tongue had her whole body bowing toward him. She let out a whimper and entangled her fingers in his thick curls, frantic to have him closer. "Feels so good. Please…"

He growled his approval below, sending delicious frissons of pleasure through her oversensitive body. "I'm going to make you come on my tongue, Lark."

Lark cried out and clenched her fists in his hair as he fucked her pussy with his mouth. She wished she could call out a name or tell him she loved him; anything. But all she could manage to say was *please*.

Chapter Four
Niall

The metrical, high-pitched alarm on Lark's phone pierced the silence. She let the beep carry on and savored the emptiness of her sleepy mind before the cogs turned and her brain awoke.

Once she realized where she was and why, she stretched her arm out and pawed around, then picked up the cell phone. She opened her eyes and checked the time.

6:17 a.m.

She slapped a hand on her forehead. "Great," she croaked. "I dreamed of my dream lover, and I was lame enough to do it in my old bedroom. I need to seriously get laid." She kicked a foot in the air, swung her leg over the side of the bed, and sat upright. She turned on the lamp and rubbed her tired eyes, then forced herself to stand and go to the bathroom. She almost tripped over the leg of a chair against the wall, but she made it. Ten minutes later, she emerged with her hair in a messy ponytail and a clean but sleepy face. She also had on the sweats Maisie packed for her along with sock liners and her running shoes.

She turned her face away from the framed graduation photo and drank the last of the water she'd left on the nightstand. She grabbed her pack of smokes from the top of the dresser, opened the door, and tread silently downstairs. She set the items on the porch railing and stretched her body out.

Her father's body would be laid to rest in the earth today. In a horrible, numbing way, it was like attending the funeral of a distant cousin. She should feel *something*, but she couldn't. The apathy pinned her chest like an anvil.

Solar lights in the garden lit her way as she left the house, and the trees in the woods were barer, the leaves stripped away from their branches.

She took a deep breath and ran.

She timed her breath to match her pace, and air escaped her lips each time her left foot hit the ground, like a military cadence. *Left…* She pictured dirt being shoveled onto her father's coffin. *Left…* Her mother grieving by his grave while she watched from the sidelines without emotion. *Left, right, left… "Is that you, darlin'?"* Lark scowled and cast her eyes upward. The weather was cooler here than in London in the mornings. Her visible breath testified as much if not her chilled skin.

The breeze stung her watery eyes and crept down the sides of her neck. She continued running, each footfall a mantra as she breathed in and out. It was here, in the quiet hours, when she became at peace with the world. Mornings were sacred, no matter where in the world she was. No pretenses or people to worry about.

The sky lightened. Lark checked her watch as she looped around the trail and retraced her steps. 7:08. She returned to the house, her mood lifted, as though in tandem with the rising sun. She made it a few feet from the front porch steps when a wave of dizziness fell over her.

She staggered forward and caught herself with her hands on the top step. She turned, sat on the step, and leaned her head against the rail post as her heart pounded and her mind spun.

Must be the jet lag. She tried to steady herself, praying the vertigo would subside.

After a few minutes, she stood and walked up the steps but found the house locked. And she didn't have a key. She turned around. Aaron's truck was no longer in front of the house. Lark frowned. He must have gone into town for chicken or horse feed and didn't know she'd gone out. She peered in the window, but there no light streamed in from the kitchen through the hallway or from the stairs. Her mother must still be asleep.

Lark made her way over to the plush porch swing and settled on the cushions to wait.

She hadn't brought a bottle of water with her. As she rocked, her eyes closed as fatigue swept over her. Aaron would be back soon from wherever he'd gone, and it wasn't too cold out. She lay on her back, rested her head on a plump pillow, and crossed her arms over her chest as she dozed.

****

The blindfold was tied on and made of soft, black material that caressed her skin. Though it was light out, the mask bathed her in darkness. His constant, heated, pulling kisses moved away from her lips and trailed down her jaw to her throat, over her collarbone, toward her breasts.

A little tug pulled her hoodie. He unzipped it and yanked the front of her T-shirt down, her bra right along with it. She couldn't see anything but knew it was him. Her dream lover.

She expected him to latch on to her nipple, but he didn't. He caressed the tip instead, flicking his fingernail along the sensitive bud as he marked a trail of pebbling, tantalizing kisses around the entire circumference of her right breast. He laved the sensitive underside with his warm tongue, while his hand fondled her left breast.

He seized her nipple with his teeth.

She groaned. He chuckled, and vibrations coursed through her. She clutched him tighter. Lark wanted to pull off the blindfold, but he had her pinned. He continued his ministrations, and kissed his way over her bared, flat stomach, across her hip bone, and closer to his ultimate goal. She covered his hand at her hip with hers and grasped it. She was a sweaty mess, but he didn't care. He took his time and appeared to enjoy every second of it.

"Wait," she said. "I-I can't see you. I want to. Take this off."

"I'm here," he assured her, crawling back over her body.

Knuckles brushed her cheek, and the weight of his gaze fell on her. "You're so beautiful," he murmured.

Lark gave up her blind fight and self-lamentations as his lips pressed against hers. "Mmm, yes," she moaned between kisses. "Kiss me, God, *yes*. I don't want to feel anything anymore but you." The freedom of the darkness emboldened her. She touched his chest and encountered the lapels of a jacket. She yanked him down, moaned, and sucked his lower lip between her teeth.

His body yielded to her, but his kisses changed. Where they had demanded and enticed before, they became timid and reluctant.

Yet the more she gave to him—putting her arm around his neck and releasing the fury of her frustrations out on him—the more he relaxed and responded. Tentative at first, with a hint of hesitancy he'd never shown before. What was this? A cool breeze blew past her face, and a sense of déjà vu of the night before overtook her.

****

If the kiss had stayed careful and guarded, she might have continued to question it. But the blindfold disappeared. She'd fallen asleep. Her eyes flew open, and *he* was there. Oh, my God. He was there! Heated eyes watched her. Rakish dark hair fell over his forehead as he breathed hard, and the morning sun lit up the world behind him. She shuddered and took a deep breath to speak, but his hands moved to cup her face. He held still and closed his eyes as his lips took her mouth. Right then and there, she knew with crystal clarity *this* was real. This was the weight of a real man on top of her, clothed. He smelled citrusy and freshly laundered. *What in the* hell *is this*?

How did *he* get here? He was only her dream lover. Or was he?

Confused beyond all comprehension, Lark didn't have any time to contemplate a single thing. His lips delivered a breath-stealing, soul-shattering kiss, and then they were all over each other. This, ah, *this* she knew. Lark hooked her ankle over his, put a hand on his shoulder, and tried to rid him of his jacket as she drew him closer. She fisted his hair as he devoured her mouth. He tasted the same as her dream lover, and she put her tongue in his mouth to savor more of his tangy sweetness.

They both made noises they never had in her dreams, breathy gasps and blasts of air as their mouths met and separated as they sought new angles and depths to their passion.

He made a disgruntled sound as he tried to get more comfortable in the cradle of her hips over the hindrance of clothes. This *wasn't* a dream. He nibbled on her lower lip as she opened her mouth to tell him to stop, but then he carried her away in the undercurrent of his large, warm hands, which caressed the skin of her stomach beneath her hoodie and T-shirt. She continued to accept his kisses but pawed her zipped-up sweat jacket. Okay, so she was still clothed. He was rock hard against her, and he ground his hips into her. A disbelieving grunt escaped his lips. Lark shivered at the jolt that went through her.

"Wh— Mmm. *Whoa.* Stop," She managed against his mouth. She furrowed her eyebrows and scrutinized him as he breathed in and out. He braced himself on the weight of his hands above her, his bright green eyes bearing into hers. His face was the face of her dreams— the sensual bowed lips and cleft chin, the built body, and the thick hair. His hair... She blinked. His hair was cut at the nape and styled for a day at work. She glanced at his clothes.

"Um, why are you wearing a suit and tie this time?" She squinted against the sunlight. *Please, God, let this be a dream*. He moved his head and put her in shade.

"*This* time?" He lifted an eyebrow, perplexed. "You'll have to forgive me, lass, but I've no idea what the devil you're talking about." He maneuvered himself off her and sat upright at the end of the swing.

She tucked her feet against her, sat up, and blinked at him in utter disbelief.

"I came to knock on the door when I saw you on the swing. You tossed and turned, and with the way you grunted, I assumed you were in the middle of some sort of a seizure."

He turned his head and licked his lips, full and abused by her kisses. A mushroom cloud of mortification bloomed inside her, steadily bigger by the minute.

"Erm, you…begged me to kiss you, and then you yanked me down. One thing led to another and, well, that was pretty much the way of it. I *am* only human, though I know it's no excuse." He swallowed and stared at her, his Adam's apple moving in his throat. "I apologize. I shouldn't have gone down when you pulled me, but it was strange—like you *knew* me or something."

Lark leaned forward and rubbed her eyes. This couldn't be real. He had to be a hallucination. When she opened her eyes, she'd see a man in his fifties with a receding hairline, glasses, and a beer gut. She reopened her eyes, and there he was: The full package. In the flesh. He was impossibly sexy, and an air of intelligence graced his eyes as he scrutinized her. She planted her feet on the porch, then put a hand to her head. The vertigo from earlier returned. "No, *I'm* sorry. I was dreaming…"

"Excuse me for saying so, but it must've been one hell of a dream."

Lark nodded and tried not to black out as a wave of dizziness came over her.

"You look like you're dehydrated. Hold on."

The lilt of his familiar Irish accent soothed her like warm milk. He stood and walked over to a black laptop case propped near the front door that had several thick manila folders sticking out of its open center. One read BRAITHWAITE in large, capital letters on an index label. He crouched, unzipped the front pocket, and extracted an unopened plastic water bottle.

He unscrewed the cap and held the bottle out to her. "Here."

"Thanks." She accepted the bottle and took a long sip. The cold water instantly revived her. She wiped a drop off the corner of her mouth with the top of her knuckle as he watched. She offered the bottle back to him, but he shook his head and reclaimed his seat next to her.

"Keep it. Drink."

"Thank you." She closed her eyes and took several large gulps, the cool liquid a balm to her throat.

"My name's Niall O'Hagan."

His deep and pleasant voice sounded different, lighter than the sultry bedroom voice she was used to from her dreams.

"I'm the Braithwaites' attorney."

Lark paused in midsip and lowered the bottle in her hands. "You—*no*." She glanced at him.

His mouth lifted at the corners as if it dawned on him he was the butt of a joke he wasn't aware of. "I…what?"

Oh, the irony of dreaming about her father's lawyer this whole time. Oh, God. She giggled like a madwoman. This was it; she'd officially lost it. She rose and walked to the top step of the porch, put a hand

70

over her face, and plunked down. "I am so messed up."

An unwanted flash of Gemma's flirtatious *"darlin'"* to Charles yesterday surfaced, and tears stung her eyes. She went silent and willed them not to fall. Nice try, but no use.

Niall sat on the step beside her. "I'd offer you a drink, but I quit ten years ago."

Lark laughed, despite the tears. "An Irish attorney who doesn't like Guinness is like an Englishman who doesn't like fish and chips."

"I know; shameful," he said with mock contrition. "Don't hold it against me. I'm doing the world a favor. Trust me. I was a horrible drunk. Are you okay, miss?"

Lark scoffed and gesticulated with her hands to the sky. "It's Lark. And what a loaded question." She couldn't look at him, not after what happened. She clenched the edge of the step on either side of her and stared out at the trees.

"Well, since we've already nailed second base, we might as well be open with each other. Forgive me if I'm candid, but it seems you were in the throes of an alleged, eh, *intense* dream, and you awoke and believed I was him. Is that right?"

Horror dawned on her at what she'd done, and her jaw dropped. "No!" *Yes.* She glanced at him, and his knowing expression begged to differ.

"I see," he said, his tone careful but persistent. "Then why did you kiss me like that?"

"I-I don't have to answer." She lifted her chin with defiance.

He scooted closer to her. "No, you don't. But I wish you would."

She scratched her head in frustration and jumped

up. Screw this, she needed to get inside before she made even more of an idiot of herself.

"I'm sorry to embarrass you," he said, and she paused with her hand halfway to the doorbell. "I'm decent. I would never— I never meant to take advantage of you at all, please know that. When you kissed me like you did, so familiar, I…"

Niall acted like more of a gentleman about the whole situation than most men would. And she, meanwhile, was being a total bitch. And the poor guy had no clue as to why.

He met her in two nimble strides. His proximity alarmed her because they'd never both stood in any of her dreams. He was a big guy, at least six-foot-three, well built with wide shoulders and a lithe, muscular frame to complement the height.

He stepped even closer and assessed her in return, appearing to like what he saw. His mouth opened, and his eyes widened with realization. "Wait. Lark? *Lark*, Lark? Rick's *daughter*? But… You're so little," he said, surprised. "From the pictures, I assumed you'd be, erm—"

"Fatter?" she asked, glad at least to be back on sure ground. She could always toss self-effacing jokes around about her heavy days. "It's okay. You can go ahead and say it. I've lost a lot of weight."

Niall put a hand to the back of his neck. His eyebrows rose. "I think 'a lot' is an understatement. Good on you. My mam struggled with her weight too; I know how hard it was for her to lose it. My hat's off to anyone who has to do it. Well, you look amazing. Wow."

He rolled his eyes at himself and glanced away.

She was so used to his prowess as a smooth sex panther in her dreams. This was bizarre as hell.

"I'm sorry. God, I sound like an idiot. Look, I hope you don't think I'm a leering wanker or anything. This is…awkward."

"You can say that again," she murmured. What would he say if she told him she'd had erotic dreams of him every night for the last six months? It was bad enough she'd just made out with the guy. He probably had her pegged as a crazy nymphomaniac.

She held out her hand but didn't make eye contact. "Listen, how about we forget that ever happened, okay? I'm Lark Braithwaite. I flew in a couple of days ago from London."

He took her hand and closed his long fingers over hers. "Niall O'Hagan. Pleasure." He stepped closer. "And I'm all for a clean slate, but forgetting's not on my agenda, lass. I'm taking it to the grave. Hands down the *best* snog I've ever had in my life. Client's daughter or no, you can't take it back."

Her face heated. "Fair enough… And thank you. I guess."

"Thank *you*."

His index finger stroked the top of her cold hand, and she shivered at the pleasant warmth. They stood there, staring at each other. Her lips parted, and he glanced at them. This was insane, but would he think her strange if she kissed him one more time? She shouldn't, but she wanted to. The hungry look in his eyes told her he did, too. He narrowed his eyes and leaned in. Before she could muster the courage to meet his lips, the front door opened and her mom stepped out onto the porch, holding a cup of coffee. Lark pulled her hand from Niall's.

"Niall. Lark. What are you doing out here? I thought you were still sleeping." Pam studied Lark's face and glanced at her hands. "How long have you been out here? Are you cold?"

Lark shrugged. "I was, but I warmed up." From the corner of her eye, Niall's lips pursed into a smirk, and she wanted to smack herself. Genius. "What I *mean* is, I got up and went for a run," she babbled. "It's the time difference. My body's still adjusting. I set my alarm before I went to bed to get a regular schedule going." Oh hell, she needed a cigarette. Now. She put a hand into her sweat pockets only to find them empty. Shit, she'd left them on the porch steps. She bent to retrieve them.

Pam's eyes fell on the unlit cigarette in her hand when she turned around. "And now you're having your celebratory cigarette. Well, that's one way to do it, I suppose. You're your father's daughter through and through. Niall, this is my daughter, Lark, who came in from England."

He regarded Lark with humorous, glittering eyes. "We met."

Lark caught a waft of his citrusy aftershave. Jeez, and she must smell like a sweaty garbage can. She put the unlit cigarette back in the pack. "Never mind. I'll smoke later. I need a shower."

Niall beat Pam to the front door and held it open for them both.

"Better make it a cold one," he whispered as she passed. She scowled at him, and he grinned wider.

Pam patted his arm. "Thank you for coming, Niall. Lark, why don't you come join us after your shower? I made blueberry pancakes. Rick's favorite. He'd call it a catastrophe if we didn't have them today."

"I will. Excuse me."

"I'll be along shortly," she heard Niall say.

Lark glanced behind her. He still held the door open, his eyes trained on her. He winked. She turned back around and pressed her lips together as she followed her mother through the hallway. A pleasant feeling traveled through her.

Lark vigorously scrubbed her hair and body in the shower and tried to focus on what she was doing when she blow-dried her hair and applied her makeup, but her passion-clogged mind reeled from his kiss. When he took her face in his hands, he'd stepped out of her dreams and into her messed-up life. He'd made the kiss his own, and the evidence of it was stamped on her face. She looked at her hooded brown eyes and full, dewy lips in the bathroom mirror. Then she spied her engagement ring on the sink countertop. She frowned with mixed emotions before she slipped the ring back on.

Chapter Five
Willingly

Lark took a deep breath before she turned into the kitchen. *Get a grip. This was a freak coincidence. Stress manifesting itself through dreams. That's it. I'm cool, confident, and collected. I'm a woman who knows what she wants—*

"Coffee?"

"Yes, please." A large hand appeared in front of her, and though she couldn't meet the eyes of its owner, she supported the bottom edge of the hot mug and took the proffered handle. She nodded her thanks to Niall.

Lark took a seat across from him at the kitchen table, selected a stevia packet, and poured the powder into her coffee. If Niall spotted her engagement ring, he seemed impervious. She watched as Pam portioned pancakes from a spatula onto three plates and scattered fresh blueberries around them.

He scooted his chair back and retrieved a glass, pausing at the fridge to consider the ice maker. "Has the ice valve worked since I fixed it last month? Hasn't been wonky, has it?"

"So far, so good," Pam replied. "I'll give you a call if it acts up. I know I've said this before, but with all you can do, it's a wonder you aren't married, young man. Now, go have a seat. Breakfast is up."

Niall did as he was told and sat to pour apple juice

in his glass. "Why don't *you* sit down? You need to let someone else serve you on a day like today," he chided.

"I need to keep busy," Pam said. "It…makes this easier."

She gave Lark a soft pat on the shoulder as she set a plate before her. Three stacks of golden-brown, fluffy, saucer-shaped cakes topped with fresh blueberries and syrup stared back at her. They let off a mouth-watering aroma. *Ah.* She'd missed her mother's pancakes. Of all the changes in the last several years, the one comfort she could take was in Pam's unyielding domestic fortitude.

"I'm sorry about your dad," Niall said in a quiet voice. "I meant to tell you when we met. He spoke of you often."

"Thank you." She took a sip of the warm coffee and peeked over the top of her mug. He draped his suit jacket over the back of his chair before digging into his food. She liked the pleasant contrast between his bright white shirt and dark, handsome features.

Pam leaned against the kitchen counter, where she'd set her plate, and randomly picked at it. "Your hair's pretty, Lark. Did you have a nice run?"

Lark sliced her pancakes. "Thanks, Mom. Yeah, I did. Good for clearing cobwebs out of the old brain. Plus, it's good to feel in control of your body."

"Oh, aye," Niall agreed. His face grew wistful. Then he recited: "*It is not in the stars to hold our destiny but in ourselves.*"

"William Shakespeare." Lark took a bite.

He lifted his eyebrows. "*Nice.*"

"Lark has always been a bibliophile," said Pam.

Niall nodded in deference to Lark, and she hid a

smile in her coffee mug.

The back door opened, and Aaron came in. He wore a deerskin coat and dirty work gloves. He removed his black cowboy hat and wiped his feet before entering.

"It's getting cold out there. Hope it doesn't rain for the funeral. It's clouding over. Morning, Mom." He kissed Pam on the cheek.

"Morning, hon," Pam greeted. "Have a seat. I'll get you a plate."

"Okay. Hey, Niall." He sat in an empty seat, took off his gloves, and laid them over his right thigh. A hearty sigh left his lips.

"Hey, mate," Niall returned. "Old and cold, eh?"

Aaron snorted. "Not too old yet. Give me a few years, though. I'll get there."

"Yeah, sooner than later." Niall smirked. Pam and Lark laughed.

"Shut it," Aaron quipped.

"These pancakes are moreish, Pam."

Pam brought Aaron's plate to the table and inclined her head to Niall.

"Mom's an awesome cook." Aaron dived into the pancakes before Pam could even set them down. Lark stifled a grin when he added with his mouth full, "Why do you think I'm home all the time whenever we get a break from school?"

Her mother bopped him on the head with the oven glove she'd used to hold the warmed plates. "To have me do your laundry."

"Hey," Aaron hollered, ducking.

"The correct answer would be because you miss your dear old mother and want to come home for the holidays. Niall, what time should we head over to the funeral home?"

Niall checked his watch. "The service is at eleven, and then we'll proceed outside for the burial."

His voice dropped, and he spoke in a softer tone, his Irish brogue playing upon his consonants like a gentle flute. He charmed the hell out of her. His accent was strong and urban. By the sound of it, she'd bet he was from somewhere north of Dublin. She'd worked with several Irish people who'd been transferred to her London office from there. He had an intelligent, playful manner to him which never manifested in her dreams, and she liked it.

"Everything's good to go. You don't need to worry," he said as she zeroed in again on their conversation. "Let me know if you'd like to say anything at the ceremony, other than the song if you feel well enough to. As to when to leave… Well, it's up to you. I'd suggest you leave here before ten, so you can get there before the prayer, and it will be private and not overintrusive. You can talk to everyone afterward."

Aaron nodded beside him. "Yeah, sounds about right. We pretty much said all we needed to with everyone last night at the viewing. It should be immediate family right now."

Pam turned around and sipped some apple juice. "Well, there's the party afterward, and there will be plenty of time to reminisce then. That seems best," she said. "I need to clean these dishes before I take a shower."

Lark had finished and stood to relieve her mother. "You're not planning to cook for everyone this afternoon, are you, Mom?"

Niall answered before Pam. "No. I've arranged for your neighbors and Rick's colleagues to handle the food and give your mam a break."

Lark lifted her eyebrows, glad he was on top of things with the stress Pam had to deal with. She took her plate over to the sink.

Niall shifted in his chair and turned to Pam. "Which brings me to another point. Have you decided what time you'd like to have a sit-down and go over your copy of the will? You mentioned you had questions."

"I do. About a billion of them. I know the kids will have questions too. Can we do a reading of the will or something to make it easier, where we're all present and can talk about it?"

Lark looked from her mother to Niall. "Do they even *do* readings of wills? I thought it only happened in books and movies."

Niall nodded. "You'd be correct. There's no legal obligation to read Rick's will or *any* will. Normally, within thirty days after the date of the death, I'd pull each of you aside or arrange a time to meet with you and give you—as beneficiaries—the opportunity to ask questions about your inheritance. I have a copy for each of you, and Rick made a video he wanted you to watch. However, given the time you're here, Lark, and the assets listed in the will, it may be to your benefit to talk it out, if everyone's so agreed."

"I'm cool with that," Aaron piped up. "As long as there's food involved."

"Could we do this at your office, like you mentioned a few days ago?" her mother asked Niall.

He shrugged. "Sure. As long as you know it's not necessary. But if you wanted to go there instead of the living room, I'd be happy to grab a pizza and drinks for everyone and just have an informal gathering. My assistant can come into the office from six to eight tonight if you decide you still want to, after the funeral, or we can hold off if you'd prefer. Your call."

Pam covered her lower lip with her hand and leaned back against the counter. "Well I, for one, need to get away from the house after being cooped up for so long. Lark? Aaron? What do you think?"

Lark met her brother's eyes. He seemed tired but in good spirits from his hard work outside, and his upper cheeks and the outer edges of his nostrils flushed red with cold. He scratched behind his ear, and a strand of his dark-blond hair fell into his eyes.

She hadn't even considered the will until now. "Well, should we ask anyone else to come? I mean, wouldn't he have divided it?"

"No," Niall said. "Everyone on the will is in this room."

Her mother sighed and tugged her bathrobe tighter around her. "All right. Well, we might as well have done with it today and go over the will tonight after the funeral. It would be good to discuss it as a family and ask Niall questions while we can, collectively."

"I agree," chimed in Lark.

"I'd prefer today, anyway. Then we can spend some time together, hmm?" she said, eyeing her daughter.

Lark nodded, heartened. Of all the unbelievable and, okay, weird things that had happened in the last couple of days, the chance to see her mom again counted as the best.

Pam eyed Lark's tasteful black dress and then looked down at her robe. "I need to go get ready if we're going to make it." She picked up a nearby washcloth.

"Oh no, you don't."

Lark blinked, and there Niall was, plate in hand, right next to both of them. He took the washcloth from Pam, then scooted her aside as he set his plate in the sink. He donned a plain black apron from a nearby cupboard hook and placed opening at the neck over his shirt and tie.

"Excuse *me*, Mr. O'Hagan," Pam reprimanded him with her best mom voice. "You're a guest here, dealing with our estate. You're not here to fix things and wash dishes."

Aaron snorted. "Whatever, Mom. It's not like he doesn't do DIY all the time or anything. He's as much a member of the family as anyone. Put 'im to work."

"Now Pam," Niall chided as he tied the apron behind him. "Me mam'd go mental on me if I didn't help out. My mam put my brothers and me on kitchen duty. It was the law in our home. Being the estate attorney doesn't mean it should be any different." Pam opened her mouth to object, but Niall whipped the dishcloth out at her jokingly. He turned on the faucet. "I won't hear any more of it. Off you go. Off with you, now. *Off*. Take free advice here, and never argue with an attorney—'tis a losin' battle."

Lark glanced at him with budding curiosity. So, he had a playful side. He winked at her, then schooled his features. "Now, then, young Miss Braithwaite. You rinse, I'll wash?"

"Fine," she replied, getting to work. The edge of his shirt sleeve rubbed against her with his movements, but she didn't pull away. Instead, she shifted closer so she could smell his delicious aftershave. Shit, he pulled her in like a magnet.

The doorbell rang with a loud chime.

"Were you expecting anyone?" Aaron asked Pam.

"No. Could be Evelyn or someone from the church. I'll get it," she said, heading for the hallway.

"I'll just sit here and finish this while you two do everything," Aaron said with his mouth full of food. "Scrub harder, Lark. Put your back into it."

"Wanker," Niall bantered.

Lark laughed, and he joined her.

They worked in silence, then she mustered up the courage to find out more about him. "So, uh, how long have you, you know, been my dad's attorn—"

"Guess who I found at the door?" Pam asked as she burst back in, rosy-cheeked. She held off whoever it was in the hallway behind her with barely contained enthusiasm.

Lark blinked. "No clue."

"You got me," Aaron said drily.

Pam moved aside and nudged forward all six feet four of Charles wearing black slacks and an expensive blue sweater. "Surprise," she sang.

Lark dropped the plate in her hands. The dish hit the floor and shattered. She couldn't breathe; then she realized what she'd done. "Oh, shit. I'm sorry, Mom."

"It's fine, Lark. Everyone, this is Charles Chase, Lark's fiancé."

"I've got it, don't worry," Niall assured her. He crouched and delicately lifted the larger pieces of the cracked porcelain.

"Thank you," she whispered.

"Well, it's good to see you too, darling," Charles said, amused. "I must admit, I've missed your clumsiness. It's been my constant companion for half a decade." He strode forward and swept her up in an over-the-top kiss.

"Wh-what on earth are you doing here?" she asked once she could breathe.

"He flew out so he could be here for the funeral," Pam said, overjoyed. "Isn't it romantic? He got dropped off by a cab."

Aaron studied them with a blank expression, and Niall had his back to them as he swept small shards into a dustpan.

"Yeah. That's great." She sounded dumbstruck, but she couldn't help it. She studied Charles's handsome face, with Gemma's voice on the phone from yesterday still burned fresh in her mind. Her face hardened. There was no way she'd feel guilty. He tilted his head to the side, assessing her with a question in his dark eyes.

"Would you two like to be alone?" Pam asked. "We can get a room ready for you, Charles, but Rick's old office is open if you two want to talk while I get the guest room ready."

Charles thanked her with impeccable charm.

He held the office door open for her until they were in the room and then made himself right at home, propped on the edge of her dad's desk. "Well," he said after a moment. "I believe that was the coldest greeting you've ever given me. What gives?"

"What's going on with you and Gemma?"

His face took on a spectrum of emotions, from

shocked to amused to affronted, then mad. "Please. Spare me, Lark. You're not the jealous type. Don't be coy. What the hell has happened to you in the last couple of days?"

"Don't," she warned.

He balked like he didn't know her. "Don't *what*? I save the merger and make sure you're able to get back in time, and then you treat me like a distant relative when I come here to surprise you and support you at your father's funeral. Aren't you happy to see me? What's going on?"

"I asked you first," she said coolly. There was no way in hell she would let him worm his way out of this. He lied like a Persian rug. "I called your office yesterday, and the way Gemma answered your phone led me to believe you, and she are on pretty intimate terms. I believe she called you…what was it? Oh yes, *darlin'* and *baby*!"

He waved a flippant hand in the air. "Please. The girl's an absolute tart. She's like that with everyone. The whole world knows it. I wanted to keep Maisie, but she went to you, and I got the airhead."

The way he spoke too fast didn't sit right with her. "No. I don't believe you. There's unprofessional, and then there's intimate. When she got the notion it was you calling, I'm sure you can guess which one her voice was."

He laced his fingers together in his lap and scrutinized her as if she were a difficult crossword. "Are you certain you want to have this kind of conversation on the day of your father's funeral? I came here for *you*, Lark, nothing else. I'm here to support you."

"If that's true, then why won't you answer my question?"

Charles folded his arms. "Because I don't need to," he growled. "What are we here for today? Let's skip this insipid, foolish talk and focus on your father. My God, you complain about how I need to be more romantic and spontaneous after we watch those Godforsaken Channing Tatum movies, and when I do something you whine I never do, all *you* do is throw it back in my face!"

Lark pinched the bridge of her nose. She didn't want a fight. "Look, I'm—"

"You don't have to apologize." He rose from the desk, put his hands on her arms, and kissed her forehead. "It's been a rough week. But I'm here now. Let's get through today."

He drew her to him, and though his condescending attitude and the way he avoided her question pissed her off, she fell into the hug because she needed it.

****

The next several hours waxed on like a strange dream. Pam came into Lark's bedroom while she got ready and showed her a long column printed in the local paper. The wording was inside a border, and a black-and-white picture of her father in his later years occupied the top of the page. His obituary.

Her eyes skimmed over the words "beloved father and husband," "great outdoorsman," and a list of his various accomplishments in both business and community. The final paragraph caught her attention.

We have a wonderful opportunity through our actions and words to make a difference in the lives of our family, friends, and strangers. This man did. Rick, we will miss you.

"Who wrote this?" She read over the words again.

"Niall," Pam replied, brushing Lark's hair.

"You asked him to write it?"

"He teaches English Lit at the community college once a week, Lark. He and your dad hit it off and grew close in the last few years."

Lark turned back to the article and pressed her lips together. So, he was a real nice Irish guy who happened to be a lawyer and an English Lit professor, who also starred nightly in her erotic dreams? Paging Dr. Phil. "Do you think he's in the will?"

Pam sighed. "No. He made your father promise not to include him. It's his way of showing respect. He valued their camaraderie too much to get money out of it. He used to help your dad fix everything around here. I don't know much about him except he grew up poor, so he's been through more than most people have. He's a fantastic handyman."

Doing her best not to fantasize about Niall wearing a tool belt, Lark slipped on a bracelet. "Does he have a wife or kids?" The question was ludicrous; she had no right to get jealous, especially since she was with Charles, but the idea of Niall kissing another woman bothered the hell out of her.

Pam finished brushing Lark's hair. "No, he's single. No kids. Nice-looking man, isn't he? But then, Charles is too. He could be a movie star. He reminds me of a young Pierce Brosnan."

Lark shrugged and feigned indifference.

****

The skies were cold and gray as they rode to the funeral home. Parking took a while with overcrowded cars and SUVs, and some parked down the road in overflow for lack of space. The service itself was beautiful. Lark eased through the funeral by focusing on helping her mother, who broke down a few times. She handled it with grace until Pam stood in front of everyone before the lowering of the coffin and sang "Dream a Little Dream of Me"—her and Rick's song.

Tears formed in Lark's eyes as she listened to her mother's beautiful, clear voice, which broke at first but then grew strong. Tears coursed down her face. She did not bother wiping them away. Her mother could really sing, and it got her right in the gut. Charles stood at her side, hands clasped in front of him as she cried. She seldom wept, but she wished he could cotton onto emotional cues for once. Aaron took one look at her and walked around Charles. He wrapped her in a warm, tight hug.

Relief washed over her when the service ended. The heaviness of having to say good-bye drained her, though closure was good to have. At the funeral party, she chatted over finger sandwiches and was amused to find there was such a thing as funeral potatoes. She nattered with women and men whose names she'd forgotten five minutes into the conversation, listening to stories about her crazy, "one heck of a guy" dad.

Charles separated from her as they were prone to doing at long social gatherings, and near the end she spotted him in an adjacent room, talking with two colleagues of her father's.

She needed to slip away. She extricated herself from a small chat in its infancy before having to hear about what a great guy her father had been from a man who'd worked for him at the office in Portland over many years.

Lark retrieved her cigarettes and lighter from the main pocket of her black leather purse she'd hid behind the desk in her father's closed office. She slid a cigarette from the pack and headed past several clusters of people as she made her way to the front porch.

Once she'd stepped outside, she cupped her hands over the cigarette, lit it, and drew in a long drag. Peace settled over her as the nicotine did its job. She walked along the porch.

The strong breeze proved a pain in getting the cigarette to light, and it dawned on her in an abstract way how much actual time and effort smoking took. She regarded her cigarette, then shrugged and took a drag. "Fetishes take effort," she murmured under her breath.

A scraping noise came from the porch, and Lark looked over her shoulder. Niall came out the front door, briefcase in hand. He eyed her and stopped, studying her. The attraction in his eyes was palpable. But then he glanced away, appearing to consider the appropriateness of his actions.

"I'll see you in a bit at my office, Lark." He nodded in passing.

"Thank you for coming," she got out. Their eyes raked each other. He should go. She should let him. But damn it, she hoped he'd stay.

He descended the steps and then turned back, lifting his head. His eyes were reddened, and she wanted to hug him. "Whatever mistakes your father made in his life, he did right by you." He adjusted the handle of his laptop case in his palm. "Well, I'll be on my way. See you later."

"Bye, Niall," she said softly. She watched him go, then crushed out her cigarette. She needed to lie down somewhere quiet. She found her mom and told her she'd be in the office. Once there, she shut the door and lay down on the black leather sofa.

It hurt too much to think of her father. She turned her train of thought to Niall. The dreams were becoming more and more frequent, and she couldn't hazard a guess as to what they meant, nor did she put much stock in the idea of fate being planned for anyone. Yet, from the moment he'd kissed her, Lark was connected to him, not merely physically, emotionally, or spiritually, but a marriage of the three that let her know he was in her life for a reason. Blurred images formed of their time together, twisted and shadowed collages of their brief discussions, the vivid dreams she'd been having, and even the wayward glances between them melded into an indiscernible film in her mind.

She sighed and combed her fingers through her hair as she got comfortable. She dozed off, replaying meeting Niall in her mind. As brief as the encounter had been, she wanted him to hold her again, to listen to his heartbeat beneath her cheek, and feel his warm skin touching hers. She fell asleep, and right away, the dream was different...

****

Warm lips skimmed along her neck. Niall's curls tickled her shoulder as he kissed her. From what attention she could pay beneath the heat of his lips, they were in a large, grand ballroom. The word Opulence came to mind, a word her father liked to use during her childhood when telling her bedtime stories of the galaxies and their beauty. She didn't have much capacity, though, to do anything but melt into Niall's arms as he embraced her from behind. He caressed her bare shoulders. She wore an elegant ball gown and exotic jewelry.

"Lark," he said warmly, using two fingers to turn her chin toward him. His eyes glittered like brilliant green gems, and Lark couldn't think when he looked at her like that.

"I love the way you say my name," she whispered. His face became a blur as he leaned down to claim her mouth with his.

Niall enveloped her like a huge, warm blanket. He kissed her, peppering soft kisses on her upper and lower lips as his hand spanned her waist. She was aware of a sort of webbed, silver piece on her head, like a veil, coming to the middle of her forehead. She released one hand from the rock-hard muscles of his arms to touch the hairpiece.

"What is this?" she managed between kisses. The metallic nubs were cool beneath her fingers. She curved her finger over the small, smooth surfaces of gems at the interlinked points. As the kiss verged on becoming more passionate and Niall's palms slid along her shoulders, his fingers traced her collarbone. She summoned her strength and came up for air. She pulled her lips away from his. "Niall, where are we?"

His breath was ragged when he pressed his forehead against hers. "Together, Lark. We're together. Look." His large hand cupped her chin and lifted it slightly. She let out an audible gasp. A few feet away stood a floor-to-ceiling mirror. They were reflected in it, him wearing Roman-era soldier regalia and a scarlet-red cape, she in a silver-colored, exotic gown that complemented his shining armor. She looked resplendent, as if she belonged there. But the gown wasn't what alarmed her. It was the insignia the headpiece formed on her forehead; a crown. Was this a costume party they were meant to attend?

He leaned toward her ear, his lips brushing the bejeweled lobes as he growled in his husky, melodic voice, "I want you. I'll never stop wanting you."

Lark drew in a sharp breath as an image flashed in the mirror's reflection of them both stark nude and in this same position. His palms massaged her full breasts, and her head was thrown back as he plunged his hard, thick cock into her pussy from behind. In the mirror, her face reflected sheer ecstasy. Her gaze traveled down to where they were joined together, passion suffusing both their faces as he drove in and out of her hard, his long cock coated with her juices as he slammed back into her. Niall's hands tightened around her. "This is a mere glimpse of what we could have, Lark," he whispered in her ear. "And so much more."

****

She bolted upright on the sofa, her nipples tingling from where he'd touched them, her breath heavy, and her pussy sopping wet.

Charles squatted down next to her, frowning, his eyes narrowed. "Welcome back," he taunted. "It looks like you took quite the trip."

****

At a few minutes before six, Lark got out of her brother's truck, admiring the nice skyscrapers in downtown Portland. Charles couldn't exactly deride her because of a dream, but he'd acted moodier than usual after she wouldn't tell him about it. She smoothed the back of her hair and reddened at the memory of how exquisite Niall's heat had been, his arms enfolding her.

Once inside the building, a young Asian security officer located their names on a list and showed them to the elevators. Lark spotted a physics textbook while they passed his desk, and she remembered those days of swing shifts and hardcore studying.

Niall's law firm was on the tenth floor. The foyer was furnished with dark colors, colorful art, and nice leather sofas. The secretary—a thin, late middle-aged, pleasant red-headed woman—welcomed them in a librarian-quiet sort of way and asked them to have a seat. She told them Mr. O'Hagan would soon be with them.

They sat in comfortable chairs along the green-painted wall. The paintings were a theme of crests and Celtic emblems.

After a few minutes, the office door beside the secretary's desk opened. Niall came out wearing a pair of reading glasses, a set of keys in his hand, and a firm but compassionate expression on his face.

"Thank you, Sherrie," he said to his assistant. "Are we all ready?" Everyone stood. "Follow me, please."

Niall led them down a hallway to a conference room. Lark expected something bigger and more luxurious, but it was a small, modest room with a nice table and a built-in overhead projector. Eight leather swivel chairs stood around it. A projection screen covered a light-brown wall.

They sat. Niall fiddled with his open laptop at the head of the table and plugged a blue adapter cord from his laptop into the projection system. His long fingers tinkered with the cord, and Lark tried not to stare at them and relive her dreams.

Sherrie came in with paper plates and two savory-smelling pizza boxes and set them down in the center of the table with a maternal smile. "Here you go."

Aaron grunted in delight and attacked the lid of the top box, lifting out a slice of pepperoni. "Ah, now you're talkin'. Come for the drama, stay for the grub."

Niall chuckled. "Not too much drama. This should be fairly straightforward and relaxed. I'll try not to bore you. Sherrie, could you please bring in the soda?" He passed around stapled copies of her father's will, and Lark perused the first few pages. He'd emailed them to her earlier, but she hadn't gotten a chance to look at them. Aaron slid a paper plate with a slice over to her.

"Thanks," she said, taking a bite.

"No probs." He drummed his fingers on the tabletop. "Aren't we supposed to like, yell at each other and go nuts over who gets what?" He ate a full mouthful of pizza. "Someone should have a bottle of booze, too. We need a drunk uncle."

Lark rubbed her temples. "I'm more likely to ask for an aspirin at this point."

"We have some at the ready," Niall assured her.

Sherrie returned with a two-liter of soda and plastic cups, and soon everyone was fed and watered. The older woman took a seat to Niall's right, ready to take dictation. She turned on a digital handheld recorder.

Niall stood, pausing as he took his reading glasses off and looked at them in his hands. "Well, now. In this situation, you'd normally receive a registered letter, telling you about your inheritance. But for a multitude of reasons, I wanted to give your copies to you myself.

I know you're going to have questions for me. I've asked Sherrie to sit in and record this for documentation. I hope you don't mind. Rick was a special client, and he wanted to say good-bye in his own way. I respected him, and I'm going to honor that."

Niall glanced at Lark as he addressed them. "Once in a while, people come into your life and hearten the atmosphere, make it a more pleasant place to live. Rick was such a man.

"Now, we all make mistakes and learn and grow, and Rick was no exception. For whatever he did wrong in his life, he did other things to balance the negativity out and make up for it. He was a good man, deep down, where it counted. I came to know him many years ago when I became his attorney, but he became more than a mere client. He was a close friend." Niall's voice softened.

"I was younger, but he never took it into account and sought legal counsel the same way you would with anyone else. Not only did he teach me how to fly fish and use tackle, but Rick was also a skilled carpenter, and I learned a great deal from him and Aaron on the ranch in our off time. I can't say enough about what a caring guy he was. He'll be missed. He made a video for you to say good-bye and let you know what he's leaving you. He wanted to, so I'll play it, and then answer any questions you might have about your assets. As a personal note, I'd like to mention if you need anything from me, legal advice, something fixed at the ranch, or a listening ear"—his gaze roamed to Lark's, and her insides heated— "I'll be there in a heartbeat. All you have to do is ask." She dropped her gaze to the will to avoid the blaze in his eyes and fidgeted with her hands.

Niall played the video, and Lark watched with mixed emotions. Her dad came into focus in the barn, grooming an Appaloosa with a paddle brush. He spoke straight into the camera as though he were shooting a company promo.

"Right. Here it is, gang. I'm dying. My will is short and simple. Most of my close friends have wealth and family, and beyond charity, I can't think of anyone else whom I'd like to leave things to other than you three. I've chosen to divide the estate in three different directions; my property and ranch, my business, and a significant portion of my money. Everything else I want divided among the different charitable organizations to which I donate.

"On with who's getting what. We'll go with ladies first. Pamela, my bear."

Lark glanced at her mother, who dotted the corners of her eyes with a tissue.

"I'm leaving you my money, minus fifty thousand each to our children. Sweetheart, you've hung in there during the good, the bad, and the...well, in between. You should have left me hundreds of times, but you didn't, and I love you for that. You are an incredible woman."

"I love you, Rick," Pam whispered.

"After I'm gone, I want you to live your life the way you want to live it. Go play the piano again, get remarried. You're too young and beautiful to be an old fart's widow, and a lot of good, eligible men are out there who could try to deserve you if you wanted. You made my life worth living, and I am—well, was the

luckiest man alive to have you when I did. I'm sorry for hurting you. Thank you for loving me. If I make it to heaven, I'll see you when you get there."

"You bet you will," Pam said.

Rick paused. *"Aaron, m'boy, I'm leaving you the business and profit shares. You are now the proud owner of the Braithwaite Boxing Company."*

"The *hell*?" Aaron shot up, sitting upright in his chair. A bit of his drink spilled on the table, and Niall mopped up the mess with a napkin while Aaron kept his eyes glued to the screen.

Her father carried on, saying his good-byes. Aaron had expected the property and ranch, then. But if Aaron had the shares, that meant…

Lark's eyes widened as their father bid a loving farewell to Aaron, who paled beside her, his mouth open, shaking his head. She turned back to the screen, not saying a word. Her dad wouldn't. Would he?

"Lark. Now, I know you're upset with me and don't want to have anything to do with me. I don't blame you. I would feel the same way. I admire everything you've done in sticking to your guns and getting through school at the top of your class. From what I hear these days, you're doing well at your company in London.

To touch on my affair, what I did… Well, all I can say is, I regret it. I regret what happened and what I put us through did to us as a family. Not a day goes by when I don't think about you and wish I could go back and undo the hurt I caused. You were my princess, and I let you down." He stopped a moment, chuckling.

"I have this memory of when you were two or three. You used to watch me shave every single morning, and I'll never forget your little hands on the

edge of the bathroom counter, this tiny nose, lots of hair, and big brown eyes peeking over it, watching me in the mirror. I want you and Aaron to know I love your mother with my whole heart. I am one lucky man that she forgave my mistakes. But Lark, if you've come home for my funeral, it means you're willing to turn over a new leaf as well. I'd like you to. You're too young to live with bitterness. It's my department as an old man." He winked. Lark smiled.

"So here we go. I'm leaving you the entire property and the house, as well as my timeshares."

Aaron swore, and she could tell he'd set his heart on getting the ranch. A veteran of countless meetings, she remained quiet, despite her shock. This would complicate matters in a major way. Today was Monday, and they were due to fly back to England next Monday.

"When you were born," Rick went on in the video, *"your mom and I used to say you were the life of the house, the spirit which made this place tick."* He laughed. *"You'd climb trees and read books, and come back with your knees bruised and scraped, all proud of yourself. You embodied everything about the ranch—free living, comfort, happiness.*

Lark, I hope the light you had inside you didn't go out on account of me. It would be a waste of your time to let go of something so precious because a dumb man made a mistake. I wish I could rewind the clock and change the foolish decisions I've made in my life, but like the doc said the clock's ticking. I want you to have the ranch, to do what you'd like with it, keep it up, have kids if you want, work in the garden, ride horses, and be happy.

There's just one catch," he added when she

expected him to wrap it up. "*I don't want you to smoke. Any of you. I kept joking throughout my life, but it's what's killing me. If you are smoking, it's my last request that you stop. Breathe in fresh air. Be young and healthy. Take care of yourselves, and make smart decisions. And know I love you. I always will,*" he added, and she had a gut feeling he directed that last comment to her.

In the video, Rick got off the stool and, as he unlatched a stable door for a saddled Appaloosa, he said, "*Well, since I've said what I need to say, I think I'll go for a ride. Niall, want to follow me out?*" The camera bobbed as it trailed him outside to the corral.

He took a hefty breath and swung a leg over the horse. He turned the horse toward the camera, flicked his hat back, and leaned forward in the saddle. "*I want you to know, gang, I'll be watching from a distance as you get older and live your lives. If you're ever alone or somewhere where you feel a little breeze, that'll be me, saying hello or giving you a nudge.*" He sat back, and the horse fidgeted, ready to go. "*Well, there's my will. Guess there's only one thing left to do now.*" He turned the horse, the Western sun descending as he galloped off, his horse hopping a low hedge. The video faded to black, and Niall brought up the lights in the conference room.

"Typical Rick," Pam said, shaking her head as though speaking of an old dog.

Lark resisted the urge to sigh.

"So much for no drama," Aaron said, helping himself to another slice of pizza.

****

In her heavier days, Lark had had trouble sleeping

and would wake around three or four in the morning. But since losing the weight and being so busy with work, she pretty much crashed and slept all night long. Not tonight, though. She blinked at the ceiling. Still dark. She eyed the clock on the nightstand. 3:30 a.m. She switched on the lamp and rolled over to sip from her bottle of water, then sat up. A bath might help soothe her sore muscles and troubled heart. She got up and went into the bathroom.

She set the plug in the drain and turned on the faucet, then sat on the side of the deep tub, watching the water oscillate against the rim as it leveled out and filled up. She sighed and rubbed the rising goose bumps on her arms, then lifted her nightshirt off and stood to slide her panties and pajama bottoms down her legs.

She stepped into the warm water, leaned her head back against the rim of the tub, and sighed as the soothing heat covered her like a blanket. The last few days had wiped her out. "Mmm, yes," she whispered. "Heaven." She closed her eyes and lay there for what seemed an eternity, letting her body and mind relax as she soaked.

The funeral and will threatened to overload her. She didn't want to think about any of it. She focused instead on Niall and their clumsy but passionate first meeting. The unconscious habit she'd learned he had of sometimes lowering his dark eyebrows. The sensual dreams and exotic locations.

****

Lark tried to relieve the tension in her shoulders and rubbed the back of her neck. The massage helped. She moved her hands to her breasts, where she smoothed her fingers over the nipples. She closed her eyes and cupped her breasts, kneading them. Her hands were too small to completely cover them, but she let her overactive imagination take over and pretended they were Niall's. She loved the way he'd kissed her on the porch, a potent mixture of wild passion and tenderness. He looked at her with intense devotion, and he seemed not only emotionally available but considerate of her. In a way, his emotional availability was more erotic than a touch could ever be.

A fresh draft of cold air from the furnace kicking in hit her nipples, hardening them, and she sank farther below the water. Ah, warm again.

Letting go of her right breast, Lark slid her open palm down her rib cage and to her sex. She rubbed her fingers against her soft folds, picturing Niall there, where, damnit, he belonged. She spread her legs farther apart and brushed the bundle of nerves at the top, stroking back and forth along the edges of her clit. She tossed her head back and inhaled sharply through her nose. This wasn't something she did on a normal basis, but then again, meeting, literally, the man of her dreams wasn't either.

"Put your mouth on me, Niall," she whispered. She pictured him licking her pussy with a slow drag of his tongue, enticing her into responsiveness. She licked her lips and spread her folds, easing a finger inside her tight, slick walls. She released a small whimper and bucked her hips against her hand as she pumped her finger and imagined him inside her, plunging into her.

She squeezed her left breast tighter and tugged it as she sped her finger up, but it wasn't enough. She needed more. Needed him. She withdrew her finger and reinserted two, trembling at the difference. "Oh," she breathed, her hips rising with the new sensation as she gave over to her fantasy. "Niall—"

"I'm here." She jumped in alarm, and water splashed over the sides. He crouched down next to the tub, calm as could be, wearing nothing but black pajama bottoms.

She crossed her arms over her breasts, sinking low. "What in the *hell* are you doing here? Get out."

A sly smirk grew on his face. "But you wanted me here."

Lark gawked at him like he'd grown a new head. "Are you perverted? I'm taking a bath. You need to leave. What are you even *doing* here at night?"

"Being at your disposal, as ever."

The smoothness of his accent and the capricious way he tilted his head to the side set off alarms in her head. She couldn't be…was she?

"Wait. Is this a dream?"

He put his hand in the water, prying her fingers off her breast one by one, sliding his own against them. "You tell me." His voice dropped to a velvety tone, and she drew in a breath as his thumb grazed her nipple, his mouth open and hovering over hers. The predatory gaze in his eyes scared her.

"W-we should talk about this," she stammered as his face came closer.

"Lark? I'm not here to talk," he said roughly, and his mouth crashed down on hers. He pushed his tongue into her mouth and splashed water as he yanked her hand away from her sex. He steadied her abdomen with a large, heavy palm, and traveled lower to her pussy. Kissing her fervently, he plunged a long, thick finger into her, and she cried out, twining her tongue with his and moving her hips toward him.

He drugged her with his kiss and fucked her with his hand, thrusting his finger deeper than she'd ever be able to do on her own, and she bucked against his hand. He supported the back of her neck with his other hand as she lost herself, savoring the sweet, languid taste as his tongue dueled with hers.

"More," she gasped. "I need *more*."

"You'll get it." He withdrew his finger and drove two more back in, hard. "You're going to get everything you want."

"Niall."

"Never forget it," he hissed against her cheek as he thrust in and out of her sensitive walls, making her tense up. "It's *me* doing this to you. No one else. I'm the one fucking your pretty pussy with my fingers." He thumbed her clit, and she convulsed against him, sending a fresh splash of water over the tub.

"Yes! Oh, please…" She'd never begged Charles for anything, never had a reason to, but she'd bow down in damn supplication to this man if it meant he'd give her the release she desperately desired. Her body sang, on the edge, and her eyes watered. "Niall, I-I need this, need *you*," she sobbed, biting her lower lip. His fingers stuffed her pussy, and he sped his thrusts to an almost punishing pace, stroking her back wall with each impact. His touch gave her everything she needed, and if she never had so much as a glance from the man in her waking moments again, she wanted this to last forever. "I want you so much. Oh, God, *yes*." Her body trembled, and she threw her head back against the support of his palm as the climax washed over her. She shuddered and cried out her release.

He kissed her tenderly, and then his fingers left her body. Lark opened her eyes wide, blushing.

****

After a few shaky breaths, she realized several things at once: her breath emitted little fog clouds as though it were winter, and the bath had gone cold, ice-cold. She stood, shivering. She held her arm across her rock-hard nipples for warmth and reached for a towel.

An hour had passed, and she was alone.

Chapter Six
Close Quarters

Later in the afternoon, everyone gathered in the main living room. Lark sat on the sectional next to Charles, who texted on his BlackBerry, oblivious. Niall, dressed casually in dark-gray shirt and slacks, pen in hand and holding several documents, stood in front of the fireplace.

"The will cannot be changed. It is final and legally binding."

She looked everywhere but at Niall. After last night, she could hardly look at him without the dream replaying in her mind. Her mind needed to focus on what they were talking about, but the intimate bath scene kept intruding. His luscious body in front of her didn't help either.

What would actual sex with him be like? He'd proven a walking legal encyclopedia during the past hour. Not as if she could even entertain the notion of being intimate with him, but would he be anything like his dream counterpart? Or would he be a stuffy career man? Lark frowned. He didn't act like one in her dreams.

Charles shifted on the cushion beside her. He stood to stretch and then rummaged through the minibar. A few bottles clinked as he extracted one. He handed her a glass filled with amber-colored liquid. By standard an occasional social drinker, Lark took a generous swill, draining it in one go. *Yes, please, inebriate me. God knows I need it right now.*

"Uh, sis, we have plenty more. You don't need to worry about running out any time soon," Aaron joked.

The ice cubes knocked against her teeth, but the effect was instantaneous. She swallowed the sour liquid with a slight grimace, handed the glass back to Charles, and nestled against the couch. Charles poured a drink. He'd been sleeping in the guest room, and they were distant but civil with each other. She still didn't trust him when he said nothing had happened. He'd been trying to get on her good side by acting the perfect gentleman: opening doors for her when she didn't need it, getting her things. The act didn't sit well with her.

Aaron stood by the window with his arms folded. Pam sat in an armchair with a glass of wine in her hand.

Charles joined the conversation when appropriate, but during the past hour, his cell phone kept going off. It rang again.

"Excuse me. I need to take this," Charles said as he retreated to the office.

"Here's what I don't understand," Lark snapped, annoyed with the entire mundane legal monologue. She wanted this resolved so she could go back to her life. Niall stopped and listened. "Why can't I just hand the house over to my mother? Why is it such a big deal?"

"Because the estate was bequeathed to you, not to her, and the estate ownership was Fee Simple Absolute, which means it was in your father's name when he bought the ranch. We can do this without too much hassle, but there *is* a time period for releasing the deeds to you—several weeks postmortem—until everything's been certified and documented, and we're going to have red tape."

"Then it should be simple," she growled, standing and walking around. "If he left it to me, I should be able to sign the deed over to my mother or something, if we're all in agreement. I'm sure you've had this kind of problem pop up with previous clients, Niall," she said, taking on a seasoned managerial tone.

Niall took a step toward her, steadfast. "Over inexpensive things you can sell on eBay and Craig's List, aye… Not ranch estates worth almost two million, Lark. One way we can resolve this is the estate could remain a life estate in your name, which means Pam could continue to live here, and you could sell the property when you decide to later on in your life if that works."

Her mother shook her head and looked out the window. She had suggested the same thing to Lark after watching her father's video when they'd both taken a bathroom break. She could still hear her mother's voice in her head.

"I know you have a lot to think about, but I'd love to have the house be in your name, if that's what you want, honey. I could stay here until you felt like you wanted to move in, and it'd be yours, no matter what. I know it's a big decision, so whatever you want to do is up to you. If you don't want the house, you don't have to take the house. What's important to me is you're back with us, Lark. I only want you to be happy. I love you."

At the time, she'd been too pissed off and shocked to even know *what* she wanted and had simply walked off, shaking her head. Her mother must have taken it personally.

"My damned father," Lark scoffed, her blood boiling from having been hashing everything out for far too long. She was pissed. "No, we already told you. I don't want ties to this place, and it's not fair to my mother either. I have a life in London. Let me claim I don't want the house and wish to sign it over to her on a clause or an addendum or something."

Niall scratched his eyebrow with the earpiece of his glasses, sighing. He seemed frustrated too. "Lark, it's not that simple. I wish it were. The process itself isn't complicated, but it takes time. We have to put it through the probate process, and I've never seen it take less than sixty days. Some can take years.

Rick was adamant about not having a no-contest clause when we drew this up, and he had three successful psychological evaluations after he got diagnosed. You wouldn't be able to petition the authenticity of the will and expect to win. If you sell your mother or Aaron the house, you have to pay for a home inspection, an appraisal, and whoever buys the house has to make a certain offer which isn't a ridiculous offset to what it's worth.

But first, it has to be probated. We have many forms we have to fill out. I'll be more than glad to help, but it's not something I can magic up overnight, and you need to understand that. Anything worthwhile takes time and effort. I'm a thorough man, and I never do a half-assed job on anything." *Anything.* She gulped when his eyes bore into her. She glanced away under the heat of his stare. He clearly meant it in a different context, but the words drained straight to the gutter of her mind. Niall frowned, oblivious to her inner struggle.

"I will pull whatever strings I can, but the soonest—and I mean the absolute soonest—I might be able to do it is in two to three weeks' time, but I still can't guarantee you—"

"Great," Lark retorted. To hell if she would let him have the reins. "I'm sure my father paid you enough. You've got to be good for something. Get on it, and get it done. God, my *assistant* can work faster." She grabbed a cigarette from her pack on the desk and the lighter next to it and stormed out of the room.

"Lark," Pam called after her.

She knew what she said and the way she'd said it, but she didn't give a hooting hell. Added to the almost certainty Charles shagged Gemma, and was talking to her on his cell right now, it was the last straw.

Once outside, she drew a frustrated drag and leaned against the front porch pillar, blowing smoke out of her mouth and wanting her office, her organized, scheduled, pragmatic, business-oriented life, to have her outstanding executive assistant back, and iced caramel macchiatos from Café Nero for her midmorning pick-me-up. Anywhere but here, with this monumental load her father dumped on her, on everyone.

The door opened behind her. "Niall, if you're expecting me to apologize, I—" She turned, but Aaron strode out onto the front porch, not Niall. He walked past her, rotating a cigarette between his fingers as he took in the view, his cowboy hat dangling from his other hand.

"I don't expect you to do nothin'. Got a light?" he drawled.

Stunned, she lit his cigarette. He seemed far too

preppy to be a smoker. "I didn't know you smoked."

He paused before putting it to his lips. "Don't tell Mom," he replied. "There's a lot you don't know about me."

He took a drag like James Dean. Who was this guy, and what the hell had he done with her kid brother? He let out the smoke and then broke out into a series of spasmic coughs.

Lark patted him on the back and laughed her head off. "You big faker! First cigarette?"

Aaron's face contorted as he drew breaths, and the coughs subsided.

"Yeah." He pitched the cigarette over the balcony and stuck out his tongue. He searched through his pockets before taking out a miniature can of breath spray. "Ugh. How can you *stand* those things?"

Lark considered her cigarette and snorted. "They grow on you, I guess. Like an irritating facial hair that keeps coming back." She threw Aaron a guilty glance. "I'm sorry for my behavior back there. This is hard to deal with."

"Well, we're all having a hard time with this." Aaron squirted the breath spray twice into his mouth. "There's nothing wrong with that. At least we have each other."

"Why do you think he did this? Messing with things when he didn't need to?"

Aaron sighed. "My take on it is he wanted you back."

"Well, it's a helluva way to reunite. Honestly, I'm happy to give the ranch or whatever I have to you or Mom or anyone," Lark said, defeated. "I'm fine enough as is, and I don't need anything to remind me of Dad.

I'm sorry if that's cold, but it's how I feel. He hasn't been a part of my life for years now, and it doesn't matter to me." She took a drag, pissed off. "I don't understand why he gave the ranch to me and not to you in the first place. I think it's weirder he didn't make Mom a co-owner. I mean, what was he *thinking*?"

Aaron leaned against the pillar and sighed. "Not a clue. He seemed all there before he died, but what the hell do I know? Dad liked to stir the situational pot."

"Yeah, he did. My guess is as good as anyone's, but I would assume he'd leave the ranch to you or Mom, and a few shares to us."

Aaron chuckled. "What am I supposed to do with a damned boxing company? I planned to go into the Peace Corps."

Lark gasped. "You were?"

"Yeah. Don't tell Mom. Dad told me how you wanted to join, but you never did."

"Well, your secret is safe with me, but I may have to tell her about your smoking."

"Go on. She won't believe you anyway."

They looked at each other and laughed.

"Well, I'm sure Niall thinks I'm a nightmare," Lark said, glancing at her nails. They needed filing.

"Nah, he'll let it roll off. He's cool that way. He gets what we're going through. I, uh…" Aaron swung around the pillar. "I know you've heard this before, but you need to step back and chill."

Lark arched an eyebrow, surprised to get advice from her baby brother.

He softened his tone. "Things suck right now, okay? I'm not going to lie. I have no idea what to do with a corporation at this point. It's about as far out of my element as I can get; I know a darn sight more about breaking in Appaloosa mares than I do about being a corporate tycoon. And I'm not even done with college yet. I'm not leaving school with a year left to go. But I believe things are the way they are for a reason. We'll get it straightened out. All right?"

A week ago, *she'd* given a pep talk to a troubled employee. Oh, how the tables turned. She let out her breath and nodded. "All right." She crushed out her cigarette and turned to the front door. "Come on then, Coach. Let's go back inside. You can watch me apologize to everyone and admit what a snot I was."

Aaron stepped down the top step instead. "Not right now. Hold off. Mom wanted a break. She went upstairs to take a nap, and I'm going to go for a ride." He motioned to the stables. "Want to join me?"

She shook her head. The drink had affected her, and riding a horse wouldn't be the smartest thing to do right now. "I'll go back inside, I think, and try to deal with this without being witchy." She smirked at his skeptical expression. "Okay, that's a lie. Did you see Charles in the office when you came out?"

"Well, I didn't see him come out before I left, so yeah, he must still be in there."

Lark turned the door handle.

"Hey, Lark?"

She paused and looked at him. "What?"

He glanced down, and she envisioned a timid boy about to ask something important. "Does he treat you well?"

Lark didn't know how to answer. Before she could, though, it hit her that Aaron didn't seem interested in her answer. He considered her, then said, "Humph," as though it were better to keep his comments to himself. He turned and descended the steps. He put his black cowboy hat on before he rounded the corner of the house and disappeared from view.

She went inside. The house was quieter than when she'd left, save for someone rattling around in the kitchen.

Lark strode back into the living room. A ray of sunlight captured the waxed shine of the baby grand piano, centered upon a carpeted dais near the larger windows. A lone sheet of piano music graced the stand above the keys on the otherwise bare piano.

Tiny dust particles in the air caught the light and glittered like miniature, sunlit stars, and she mentally traveled back in time, sitting as an eight-year-old girl on the piano bench while her mother played a beautiful rendition of *Für Elise* beside her.

Lark approached the piano. Music used to fill the house, fluid and invigorating and alive.

She slid to the center of the piano bench, where she got comfortable and lifted the dusty lid from the keys. She took in the ivory whites and the beautiful black notes spread out before her in perfect symmetry.

She'd forgotten how to play. Her fingers found the usual middle notes, though: *C*, *E*, *G*, and she pressed her fingers down. The sweet harmony of a *C* chord played. She sat upright at the keyboard. Her mother's small but skillful hands used to glide along the scales when she played them, the sound echoing through the house.

It had been such a long time ago; the memories of how full the house used to be with music faded away, the warmth replaced with iPods and apps, meaningless emoticons, and busy meetings she *had* to get to in time.

The hushed living-room air carried the sound of the gentle autumn wind rustling the leaves of the trees outside.

"Oh, she plays *and* reads. The plot thickens."

Lark turned her head toward the doorway, and Niall stood there with a glass of milk in hand, his eyes kind and gentle in the soft, afternoon glow of the setting sun. His glasses were off, and he appeared relaxed. He kept his eyes on her while taking a drink, and her core clenched by habit. Damn it, those were the same looks he gave her in her dreams.

Recalling her actions earlier, she reddened and half turned back to the piano.

"No, she doesn't. She *used* to, though," she added as he came toward her. *Please, please don't sit next to me.* Since meeting him, she'd avoided staring too directly. Her insides were a flaming pile of nerves which could blow at any moment, and if he did that smoldering thing where his eyes raked hers with naked clarity one more time, she would lose it and jump him.

Niall set his glass down on a coaster on a nearby lamp stand.

He sat close to her. "Scoot over." His arm touched her shoulder as she moved to the right, warm and solid, and stayed pressed against her when he got comfortable.

Feeling it an appropriate time to apologize, Lark tucked her hair behind her ear. "Niall, listen, I'm sorry for how I acted earlier. I know you're doing everything you can, and I appreciate that. I—" She cut off when his hand took hers from her lap. Pleasant tingles shot up her fingers.

When their ankles brushed beneath the bench, a charge ran through her. Her body seemed to gravitate to his. Against her better judgement, she constantly sought him out, despite knowing she shouldn't.

Ignoring her babbling, he placed her hand on the piano keys. They were smooth, foreign, and cold beneath her fingertips, but she was more distracted by his hand covering hers.

He turned his face to her, and in the shaft of diffused sunlight pouring through the skylight and falling over them, his eyes gleamed.

"Play."

He narrowed his eyes with a toss of his head toward the keys as if to dare her. He glanced at her lips. *Please, kiss me. No, don't kiss me. Yes, do.* He eyed her hair, then looked back at her lips.

"I don't remember how to play. It's been forever."

Niall took his hand off hers, but she kept hers on the keys.

He slid down the bench and put his hands above the other end of the scales. "D'you know any melodies?"

"You play?" Jeez, was there anything he *couldn't* do? His continual competence impressed the hell out of her.

He nodded, playing a few measures of a haunting Irish tune with both hands. "Yep, I also tap dance. I'm pretty good at it too. My mam put bottle caps on the underside of our shoes. Later on, we took actual classes. So, eh, did I do that in your dreams too, or was it straight-up shagging?"

Lark's jaw dropped, and she grew horrified. "I— I—"

He held up a hand. "You don't have to answer. Except you kind of already did. Kidding. I'm *kidding*, Lark. Relax." He chuckled and turned back to the keys. "We had piano lessons every day growing up. Five o'clock sharp. If my brothers and I weren't at the piano, ready to go, it meant our hides."

He didn't seem bothered by the revelation he'd managed to get from her, even though a small smile lingered on his lips, so she pretended it didn't bother her either. "Sounds like your mom meant business when she raised you guys."

"Aye." He winked at her. "Poor woman had to deal with five hoodlum boys. Who could ever blame the poor thing? Anything coming back to you?"

Lark asked herself the same question, tapping her right forefinger on the key.

She fiddled with different notes until she flowed out a single-fingered tune she learned from her mother, an old ballad. Halfway into it, he picked up a simple harmony on the lower end of the scales, humming beneath his breath and patchily singing the words in a low timbre.

Not for the first time, he'd brought her to a hard spot between elation and awkwardness. And damn he smelled good. It exhilarated her to play after so long, though it sounded sketchy at best.

"Not bad," he concluded, smiling at her when they finished. "Don't know if we're ready to take this one on the road, though."

"It's a work in progress," she offered. She gulped and stared at his throat, still guilty over how she'd acted earlier. He was, plainly put, a good guy, trying to do his job. "Niall, I—" Something about the way he tilted his head, and the spark in his sharp eyes, gave her the distinct impression he read her like a book.

"You don't need to do that with me."

His hand slid closer over the piano keys, until his fingers moved over hers, taking her hand in his. A warm energy emitted from within, and before she could stop it, she locked stares with him. She had no idea how long they gazed at each other, but she didn't want it to end.

"Lark?"

They both turned at the sound of Charles's voice from across the room, and Lark slipped her hand out of Niall's. A light noise sounded as her fingers depressed the keys, and they both stood.

"You're all done?" she asked Charles.

He analyzed them both, his expression heated.

Niall nodded at her and moved away to retrieve his glass of milk. He took a sip. He seemed to sort of ignore Charles, regarding him only in a professional manner when required. Given how affable Niall was toward people, she got the impression he didn't think too much of her fiancé.

"James left. He stayed late so we could talk to Mr. Osaka," Charles said, coming toward her.

"Excuse me. I'll leave you two alone. I'll be in the kitchen if needed." Niall retreated.

"Is everything okay?" Lark sat beside Charles on the sofa in front of the fireplace, trying to relax while her heartbeat tripled.

"Yeah." Charles rubbed the bridge of his nose and shut his eyes. "Well, it will be, provided we get back there on Tuesday." He rolled his neck. "I could use a Scotch. Mr. Osaka extended his stay until Tuesday, so we can get things taken care of and work through the contract."

"He's still there? Are we putting him up?"

He nodded. "Don't ask about the cost. He insisted on staying when he heard we'd be back within the week. We couldn't say no, of course. He's enjoying all the comforts of the Savoy and the sights London has to offer, courtesy of UY."

Lark winced. "That's— I'm sorry, Charles."

He shrugged. "Don't be. We can afford it, as long as it's kept in close quarters. No one needs to know beyond a few of us higher-ups. Still, we're going to take a financial beating." He brooded and then glanced over the couch at the piano across the room. "What were you and O'Hagan doing over there, playing 'Hot Cross Buns'? What were you two up to?"

Her nerves caught on fire, but she managed to meet his eyes. "Nothing."

Chapter Seven
Callings

They made no further progress concerning the estate that night. She spoke to Niall a few more times as they worked out what could be done. After conversing with her mother and brother, they decided she would have to stay until things were settled so she could sign off on certain documents which required an in-person signature. The rest could be scanned and e-signed from London.

Their discussions had hashed out that Pam would buy the house from her with Aaron as a co-owner, and he would give Lark a significant portion of his inherited shares, delegating the leadership of Braithwaite Boxing Company to the current CEO while still retaining ownership. Then, when Aaron graduated next year, he would oversee the business.

Lark spent the rest of the night in her father's office, arranging a different flight back home. She'd spoken to Charles, who'd drunk after his calls, and they decided she needed to stay to have more time to get things situated. However, he would go back as planned.

She booked a nonstop flight out of Portland for the following Friday. Niall had said before leaving it might be possible to get everything settled by then, and she had to be there for the closing to sign the papers.

With so much weighing on her mind, when

bedtime came, she took a dose of generic sleep syrup and fell into bed, exhausted.

****

She walked toward a rose-covered stone cottage in the middle of a rolling green countryside on a beautiful day. The building looked old—at least a few centuries old—and it sure wasn't in America. Her hair hung loose, and she wore a floaty, light-blue dress which stopped at her knees. The cottage appeared clean-kept, tidy, with trimmed shrubs adorning either side of it beneath the narrow windowpanes. The lush dark green of the nearby hills leant a colorful charm to the dusky-pink roses and the light gray of the cottage. The perfume of the roses wafted over to her, sweet and heady. The wooden door creaked open, and Niall stood there, waiting in an unbuttoned white shirt and black trousers, his dark curls mussed, the open tails of his shirt lifting with the gentle breeze. She held her hair down as the wind played with it and made her way toward him.

"I've been waiting for you." Though his tone bordered on agitation, he slid his hands around her waist, his fingers grazing the curve of her spine. His eyes softened as he leaned down to kiss her.

"Sorry to keep you waiting." Lark moved her fingers through his thick hair, breathing quicker when he clenched her sides, then searched her with his hands as though he were mapping out terrain he intended to conquer. He deepened the kiss, and she marveled at how he could cause her heart to thunder with the simple stroke of a hand. She wanted to lose herself to him.

He held her close and rubbed his nose against hers. "C'mon." He turned and walked her inside, kicking the door shut with his foot. A cheerful fire crackled in the hearth on the far side of the small room. In the center of the room stood a bed, fitted with a white sheet and nothing more.

Niall moved behind her, inching up the hem of her dress to the top of her thighs. She lolled her head back onto his shoulder, kissing the underside of his jaw as he moved his hands beneath her dress over the flesh of her stomach, spanning his fingers over the gentle curve of her waist before moving his hands to palm her breast. He pinched a sensitive nipple, and she moaned, pressing the cleft of her ass against his hard cock. His hips jerked in retaliation, and slowly, his hardness rolled against her.

"Keep that up," he growled into her ear, "and I'll take you right here."

"I wouldn't mind," she whispered. Why did he make her feel so naughty? He let out a restrained "mph." His fingers dug into her hip, grinding the defined shape of his cock into her ass through their clothes, hauling her closer. She mewled in delight when he grabbed hold of her chin, turning her face to the side while holding her against him. His eyes were vibrant and alive, reflecting the firelight as he regarded her.

"You're glorious, Lark. And you're mine."

He kissed her, his tongue demanding entrance to her mouth, which she eagerly granted. She slid her tongue against his in a sensual dance. He smelled of warm, fresh bread, and his breath had a minty taste.

His hand squeezed her breast, then slid down to dive beneath the edge of her panties. His fingers moved over her slit and between her pussy lips. She couldn't hide how damn wet she was. He let out a guttural sound at the discovery, and she smiled into his mouth, tangling her tongue with his. The kind of power she held over him from her response alone made her feel all the more special, valued. She gasped when he yanked her hips back and pushed her forward.

"Bend over," he crooned in her ear. He slid the dress up over her ass, his hands exploring every inch they came into contact with. "I'm going to fuck you now. Hard."

Lark shook as his fingers bunched the dress above her breasts, pausing to stroke his thumbs over her nipples and pull on them. She moaned. "You're so damned beautiful, Lark." His touch caressed and soothed. She straightened to help him take off the dress.

"Put your hands back on the bed."

She did, her nipples tingling from where he'd tugged them.

"Stay there, my love," he murmured into her ear. His hand lingered on her throat.

She didn't give up control often, if ever, but she trusted him without reservation. She hazarded a glance under her arm as he knelt behind her, slowly sliding off her panties. Tremors filled her body as he clutched her hips and dragged his soft, warm tongue from her clit to the base of her folds, kissing her pussy with the same passion as he had her mouth. Lark reared against him, shivering as he tongued her clit.

"That feels good. Fuck me, please, Niall. I want you to."

He stood, and his belt buckle clinked. The zip of his trousers whizzed, and oh my, he dragged his long, hot cock against her ass, teasing her with it. She looked over her shoulder, and the naked craving in his eyes nearly undid her. He'd watched every breathless tilt of her head, every arch of her back, and the various muscle spasms her body had had, and now she wanted him to fuck her hard with a ferocity that frightened her.

"I think about you more than I ought to," she admitted as he teased her sopping wet entrance with the tip of his cock, bathing it in her wetness. "You're always on my mind."

"Oh, yeah? What do you think about?" He slid the head of his cock along her backside as he smoothed a palm down her spine.

"What we're doing now." Her cheeks burned, and she trembled beneath his touch. Her nipples pebbled as they rubbed against the cool cotton sheet beneath her. "What I'd *like* to do when I'm awake, but never find the courage for." He stilled his movements, and his hardness pressed against her.

"Lark?"

"Mmm?"

He leaned down and spoke against her ear. "You'll find the courage." He slammed his cock into her wet pussy, and she cried out. He stood, took hold of her hips, and pounded into her. He set an erratic pace, frantic with need, and all that mattered was them, flowing into each other in a delectable rhythm. Niall moved his hand between them and rubbed her clit mercilessly as he slid his cock in and out of her. She came undone as he rode her, abandoning everything but how he made her feel. He pulled her hair back and turned her head to the side. His tongue took hers, and he said something against her mouth she couldn't make out. But then it didn't matter because she came.

****

The sun filtering through the curtains roused her from a deep slumber Wednesday morning, later than usual. She blinked at the alarm clock on the nightstand as she pushed hair out of her face. It was after nine.

For a reason she couldn't explain, an intense need surfaced to run hard today. She dressed, went outside, and gave it all she had. She came up short of breath but didn't stop as she neared the house at the end of her run. She locked her arms above her head and sucked in fresh air as she winded down.

A clear, plastic liter of spring water stood in the middle of the bottom step on the porch.

Pam must have left it before she'd gone out to get groceries. Lark twisted off the cap and drank. Much better. A familiar, nagging mental pang took over as she headed inside. She hadn't smoked all morning.

Her cigarette pack wasn't where she'd left it on a corner stand in the hallway. She bent to see if it had fallen behind the stand. A strange sensation overtook her of being watched.

She turned, and Niall paused in midstep from one room to the next, fresh and smart in a light-gray suit, the jacket discarded and his shirt sleeves rolled to the elbows. His dark hair was a mess of curls, and he had on his reading glasses and a pencil perched between his full lips. An open law book lay balanced in his palm. He considered her and took the pencil out of his mouth.

"They're on top o' the cabinet."

Lark nodded and stood on tiptoe until she spotted her pack and lighter, then retrieved them. Her body bumped against his on her way down, but he didn't pull away or step aside, and his closeness drove her mad. His chest rose and fell in time with hers, and his eyes focused on her lips. Shit, she stared back.

"I see Rick's last wishes haven't persuaded you to stop smoking yet," he teased with a mischievous grin, his gaze flicking to her eyes and back to her lips.

She bit her lower lip, trying to get on solid ground, but from the hunger on his face, she shouldn't have done that. Last night's dream left a fresh imprint on her mind, and she went for a bitchier approach, hoping to deter him. "Please, Niall. My dad was more of a do-as-I-say-not-as-I-do type of parent. So right now, I need these more than I need a lecture, thank you."

He shrugged a shoulder, and a wayward dark curl fell over his left eyebrow. "Fair enough. Could I make an observation, though?"

Lark put the cigarette between two fingers and played with the lighter in her other hand, prepared to take it outside. "Could I stop you?"

The corners of Niall's mouth twitched. He glanced down, and she moved in for the kill.

"What? Oh, I'm sorry, are you intimidated by strong women?"

His gaze fixed on hers. "On the contrary, I find it alluring. I find *you*, in particular, extremely alluring, though it's unethical."

Panic shot through her. What in tarnation was she doing? She should tell him she and Charles were engaged, discourage him. But the way his eyes caught the hallway light, turning them a deep viridian, reminded her of their tryst in the cottage. She said nothing, but her nipples peaked and pressed against her shirt like hard pebbles. He glanced down at them and moved toward her until her back pushed against the wall, trapped. She wasn't an expert at reading people or anything, but *I want you* might as well have been written on his forehead in permanent marker. He dropped his law books on the floor without preamble and cupped her face in his hands, leaning forward to kiss her, with no uncertainty this time.

Stunned, she dropped her smoking items as his mouth claimed hers. She let out an involuntary whimper as he touched his tongue to hers, and it appeared to be all the encouragement he needed. With a groan, he fisted the lower back of her shirt and tugged her toward him as his other hand sought the side of her neck.

She sucked on his tongue, twining her leg around his as she devoured his mouth. He nudged his cock against her and then pressed harder, rubbing it into her pussy through their barrier of clothes.

She should push him away—she *should*, this was insane—but he tasted like her dreams, warmth and earth and mint, and she craved him again, needed him. She brought her arms to his shoulders, unsure. He covered her hands with his own and placed them around his neck as he dived into her mouth again, groaning. She kissed him back, the tentativeness fading away with each pull of his lips, each stroke of his tongue.

Liquid warmth rushed to her pussy as his hands slid beneath the back of her shirt, exploring her skin. The amount of passion she got from this single kiss trumped anything she'd ever experienced. She shivered as he rocked against her, hard and hot in the cradle of her hips. He grabbed her bum, tugging her closer as he rubbed against her, his staggered breath against her mouth. Oh yes, he wanted her.

126

A distant lock turned, and the front door creaked open.

They drew apart, but Niall's fiery expression burned into her. He bent to pick up his law books and pencil, and with a heated look, he darted into the library. Grocery bags rustled nearby, and she stood there like a zombie with her mouth open. She crouched down to gather her things and tried to breathe.

"Lark?" Pam rounded the corner. "Honey, are you okay?"

Lark remained crouched. Looking winded was the easy part. No trouble there. "I'm fine, Mom. A little out of breath."

"Well, jeez, you must be. You sound like you got a real workout."

Lark shut her eyes and wanted to disappear. Her heart tried to make a break for freedom against her rib cage. "Yeah, I did. I'm fine. Give me a sec." She watched as her mother's flats walked past her into the kitchen. She looked around and located her smoke supplies.

"Well, if you're up to it, want to help me bring in a few bags from the car? Your fiancé seems busy in the office, and Aaron's out. I know Niall's working on our case."

"Sure," Lark said, regaining her footing. "I'll be happy to." She passed the library on her way out. Niall sat on the couch, his law books covering his lap. She walked out to her mother's car, wanting to believe what happened was a daydream. After she'd brought a few grocery bags in, she noticed her mother standing in the library doorway, nattering with Niall.

"How did it go at the title company?" Pam asked.

Niall's voice carried toward the kitchen. "Ah, had me nose pressed against the glass when they opened. I've got my mobile on me in case they call. I'm waiting to hear back from Karl Cheney on how fast we can get this done and seeing if there's a faster route to use in the meantime. Karl's checking with his contacts, and I've phoned the home inspectors. We're shooting for Monday or Tuesday. I'm working on it. You'll be sorted."

"I have complete faith we will," Pam returned.

Niall caught Lark's glare as she went out again to get the last of the groceries. He raised his eyebrows as if to say, *Hey, I can't help it if she thinks I'm great.*

What in the hell was she doing? Lark brought in the rest of the groceries from the car, chastising herself six ways from Sunday when a tall, curly-haired shadow towered over her. "We shouldn't have done that," she said without turning around. "What happened in the hallway w—"

"I didn't come out to talk about that."

She turned around. "I'm with Charles." She held up her left hand, frowning as she showed him her ring. She'd been stupid to act upon her fantasies, to even entertain it could be real. By doing so, she'd opened a giant can of worms.

Niall smirked and shook his head. "I could care less about Charles. He's a git. What I wanted to say earlier was, aside from the incredible mind you've been blessed with, it'd be a shame to waste such natural beauty God gave you by smoking when so many people have a lack of it. You're stunning. Don't ruin it."

She ducked her head, pleased. No one had ever bothered to say something like that to her before. He fixed his eyes on her as he fiddled with his car keys.

"Anyway, that's all I wanted to tell you. See you later," he said, striding toward his SUV.

Lark set the groceries down. She had a smoke after depositing them in the kitchen but gave it up halfway through.

****

Closer to noon, she showered and dressed. Charles opened her bedroom door after a quick knock. She'd finished drying her hair and had closed the two top buttons on her blouse.

"Hi, haven't seen you in a while." She turned toward her vanity mirror, intent on finishing her hair. He'd set up shop in her father's office.

"I need you to come down to the office."

His breath smelled sour. Oh, my God. She could smell him even from here. Had he been drinking already? It was still morning, not even noon.

She frowned. "What is it?"

"Most of the execs are in the conference room back in London. They want to speak with us and are having an impromptu conference. I'm dialed in. They gave me a toll-free conference bridge. Mr. Osaka is with them."

The pit of her stomach tensed. They needed to tie up the merger quick. She nodded and followed him down.

"I don't like your hair loose and hanging. It's too dowdy," he commented over his shoulder as she tailed him down the stairs and through the visiting room, not giving her a chance to respond. "It's better up. I'll be right there. I need to use the loo," he said as they entered the living room. "I've got them on mute. Wait for me, and I'll be there."

"Okay." All right, so his remark stung. Charles usually focused on one thing, and like most one-track men, when he devoted his attention to a single task, it consumed him. Her emotional skin had thickened the more she'd come to know him, so she didn't let it bother her. In her line of work, those who were able to progress had the strength to multitask as well as having an ironclad shield. Both were a useful commodity which gave her vantage points. She clenched her fist. Still, it didn't hurt any less.

As she walked through the library into the office, Niall sat on the couch, typing away with his ankle resting over the opposite knee, balancing his laptop. Stacks of documents lay in neat piles around him on the couch and floor.

He glanced at her while scratching something down on a yellow legal pad with a pencil, his glasses halfway down the bridge of his nose. "Funny that," his melodious Irish brogue floated over to her like a cheerful little cloud. "I think having your hair down becomes you."

Lark threw a reluctant smile his way before she turned and went into her father's office. As she closed the door, he met her eyes.

Charles must have received faxes in the last few days. Several contract agreements littered the small wooden work table to the side of her father's desk area. A business phone sat in the middle of the desk. A sharp, blue light indicated he had them on mute. The London end stayed silent. They had her and Charles muted as well. She pulled back a chair and slid into it, glad to be doing business again.

She picked up a sheet of paper with Charles's

chicken scratch in black ink. Lark scrunched her nose, trying to decipher the words.

85 account records (before?)

94 affair—Toledo

When Charles returned a few minutes later, however, she did not have a chance to ask him about it as he strode right in, commandeered a chair, and leaned over the table. He depressed the Mute button on the speakerphone.

"Hello, this is Charles. I have Lark Braithwaite on the line with me." He nodded to her.

"Hello, everyone. Mr. Osaka," she acknowledged.

"Miss Braithwaite," Mr. Osaka countered over the speaker.

Charles cleared his throat. "Now we're all here. First of all, I want to dispel any rumors that might've been flying around about us withdrawing from this merger."

The call dragged on due to the need to iron out everything left undiscussed with the merger. Charles kept shaking his head, and at one point, he pressed the Mute button and swore, calling Mr. Osaka every name in the book, the gentlest of his verbiage being "bugger." The ice-cold way he said it made Lark numb inside. Knowing the meeting got him riled up, she tried to relax. He would be back to normal afterward. But she was agitated. Had he always been like this when they'd worked on big deals? She didn't recall him ever using such colorful language before. She glanced at the door, which remained ajar, and rose to shut it before returning to her seat across from Charles's.

When they'd sorted everything out, Charles received a message on his BlackBerry. He turned it so

Lark could read the message while he spoke with Mr. Osaka in Japanese.

Charles, I'll call you afterward. Have something important to discuss. Have Lark hang around as well. James

Lark nodded to Charles, and once the call ended, the phone over on her father's desk rang.

"It's him," he said after checking the Caller ID.

Lark pressed the Speakerphone button. "Hi, James," she said. "We're here."

"Brilliant. We have an important client of ours, the chief executives from Jagger—a cologne firm based out of New York, still in its infancy. We've collaborated with them to create a venue for a London base, as we believe their product lines along with Ultimately You could be fruitful. As fate would have it, I've learned they're staying on a layover in Portland tonight. It would be a great opportunity for you to take them out to dinner somewhere nice, on the company. I've had Cynthia arrange for the car company to send a rental car to your house. All you have to do is fax a copy of your driver's license to them when they arrive. They'll pick it up again tomorrow morning, everything free of charge."

Lark exchanged glances with Charles, who beamed. "It sounds fair," she said.

"This is a *perfect* opportunity for us to get away," Charles raved. "It'd do us both good to get out for a night. We've been penned in here for three damned days." He directed his attention to the phone. "James, we'll do it."

"Outstanding," James barked.

Charles stored the number for the salesperson's

contact and ended the call. He seemed in better spirits. "Go sling on that sexy cocktail dress you brought," he said, dialing the number on his BlackBerry as they left the office. "Get all done up. Oh, and put your hair up, please. No country-music-awards hair."

Lark scowled. "Knock it off with the hair insults, would you? Jeez. Maisie put it in by mistake." She lowered her voice as they walked in front of Niall, who seemed ensconced with whatever he typed on his laptop. "I'll wear the one I wore to the funeral. It's more tasteful."

"Lark." Charles smirked. "The cocktail dress." He frowned, and she could see the cogs turning in his brain. "Now we need to know where to take them."

"Take who?" Pam asked. Lark hadn't seen her mother beside the piano, watering a plant. Pam's brown eyes shone with interest.

"We're taking two clients into town for dinner tonight." Lark flashed a glance at Niall. She explained about the rental car.

"Courtesy of UY," added Charles. "Are there any good restaurants in Portland with an air of prestige?"

Pam continued watering the plant. "There's Genoa. Your dad did lots of business dinners there, Lark. They may have an open table. I'd call in advance, though. The phone book's in the kitchen drawer."

Roxanne D. Howard

Chapter Eight
Dinner

Lark hadn't worn the cocktail dress in a while, but it still fit. She borrowed a sheer, silvery shawl from her mother which flattered the dress and covered its more revealing parts.

Colin Fields and Matthew Harte were waiting in the lobby of the Benson Hotel when Lark pulled the black Camry rental out front. Both men appeared closer to Charles's age, in their mid to late thirties, and they had the same seasoned office-veteran aura about them. The taller of the two had a leathery orange tan, out of kilter in the cold autumn weather.

When they arrived at Genoa restaurant, live piano music played as they entered the establishment. Covered glass candles adorned the middle of each white-linen topped table. Classy. Lark raised her eyebrows, impressed. She'd never been here before.

Charles kept his hand on her back as the concierge at the podium in the entranceway welcomed them in a strong French accent, asking what name their party was reserved under. Charles formed the word, "Chase," but stopped, staring at the cloakroom ahead of them.

Lark stared as well.

"What in the ruddy *hell* is O'Hagan doing here?" he whispered to her.

Their guests behind them took an interest in Niall

134

as well, who ducked his head as he took off his scarf, handing it to the cloakroom attendant. The Irishman turned on his heel and caught them watching him. He'd changed into a nice dark dinner suit and bowtie, his striking features more defined than usual in the soft light.

Conscious of the hot blood burning her cheeks, Lark tried to focus on something else. Much to her chagrin, he walked over to them, holding out his hand to Charles, who shook it guardedly.

"O'Hagan," Charles said with tapered enthusiasm. "Well, this is the last place we expected to bump into you."

"There's no avoiding me, I'm afraid," Niall joked, glancing at Lark. "I'm here with a couple friends who're visiting. I come here often."

"Ah," Charles sneered, "What are the chances?"

"Well, 'tis a small world, after all," Niall countered. "Hello, Lark." His voice dropped a notch as he locked gazes with her.

She nodded, speechless. What was he *doing* here?

Charles introduced Matthew and Colin to Niall, and a weird silence ensued as the men shook hands.

Niall seemed comfortable though, quirky. No way in hell did he simply "happen" to be at the same nice restaurant they'd chosen to take their clients to, this exact night, at this precise time.

"We're ready to seat your party, sir," the maître d' called to Charles from the dining-room entrance, holding four leather-bound menus with a red tassel hanging from each folder. "Right this way, please."

"Excuse us." Charles pushed past Niall, who turned to avoid bumping into him. Niall grinned at Lark as she passed him.

"Have a nice dinner." He winked at her.

"Thank you." As Charles guided her into the dining room, his hand on her lower back, her insides hopped with excitement and curiosity. Niall had come for a reason. Did it have to do with her?

Their small circular table sat near the center of the elaborate room, two tables over from the vacant dance floor, where the pianist occupied the corner and played soft jazz.

At the table closest to them sat an attractive dark-skinned couple, a man and woman, both tall. Charles pulled a chair out for her. She paused on the verge of sitting down. Niall approached, then walked past her and took a seat behind her, sitting with the couple.

"You ordered yet?" he asked, adjusting his silverware.

Lark stood there, staring down at him. He turned in his seat, saw her, and stood back up. "Excuse my bad manners. I was a local lad. I don't believe you've met my friends. My dinner companions, Anthony and Deidre Ajayi."

The Ajayis nodded to Lark's party and said hello in accented English. Lark took Anthony to be a quiet, studious man, based on his demeanor, and Deidre was a beautiful woman with dark, wide-set eyes, high and riveting cheekbones. Overall, she had gorgeous features.

Lark sat, and Charles took a seat next to her, his back to Niall. "Excuse us," he said over his shoulder once Matthew and Colin sat. "Have you decided what you want?" he asked Lark, pointing to her menu. She perused it.

"I'll have the veal." She'd volunteered as the designated driver and could not drink, but Charles insisted on ordering French wine for her as well. She sat it out and stuck with the club soda.

The waiter came around, a sliver of a man in his late twenties with short, thick red hair. He asked in French what they would like. Lark couldn't speak French to save her life and watched with slight annoyance as Charles ordered for the table in a flashy French patois.

"Madame, may I take your shawl?" the waiter asked, indicating the coatroom entrance at the opposite end of the room.

Niall turned around in his seat when she stood. The waiter helped her remove Pam's shawl from her shoulders.

A number of male eyes zoomed in on her like paper clips to a magnet as the waiter stepped away with her shawl, which was undoubtedly the effect Charles had been after from the moment he'd told her to wear the dress. The soft sheen of the Versace silk clung to her body, showing every plane and curve. Six years ago, she would never have attempted to wear anything like this. Doing it now still made her self-conscious.

She tried to avoid Niall's gaze, but couldn't. He'd angled his chair in a half-turn, making him more visible to her, and the heat of his stare drew her in. He gave a sharp intake of breath at the sight of her. From the rise and fall of his chest and the expression on his face, he was clearly in the grip of strong emotion. He did not seem aware he'd stood.

Though she could feel herself blushing from his rapture, Lark remained calm and collected as she sat back down. Niall took his seat as well.

"Breathtaking," Charles commented. He made a show of Lark, toying with her fingers in front of the men, appearing half-interested in what Matthew and Colin were saying as he traced his finger down the side of her arm, eyeballing her. She did not return his sentiments. She could feel the slight movements from Niall's chair mere inches from her own, and heard the cadence of him talking with his friends. Prickles of annoyance needled her as Matthew and Colin ogled her from across the table.

Before the waiter left, Charles took a pen from his breast suit pocket and circled an item on the menu. "You've misspelled *mignon* here. You'll want to show it to your manager and get it corrected."

Behind her came a bark that sounded like a laugh. Niall cleared his throat. She turned her head, and he fell silent. A second later, the warmth of his hand settled on her shoulder.

"Yes?" she asked.

"Deidre would like a word." She turned around in her chair, and the beautiful woman appraised her.

"You have pretty hair," Deidre complimented in her thick African accent.

"Thank you. I love your necklace," Lark said, admiring the intricate chain she wore around her neck with its wooden shapes, unusual stones, and multicolored beads.

"Thank you. The children in our village gave this to me for my birthday several years ago."

"Deidre teaches English in the school she and Anthony manage," Niall offered, his gaze roaming over her dress. His eyes lingered on her breasts, and he bit his lower lip and glanced away, his cheeks reddening. She hid her blush into her glass of water at his struggle, flattered.

"You're both teachers," she said, setting her glass down. "How wonderful. What ages do you teach?"

"As young as four, as old as sixteen," Anthony replied from the other side of Deidre. His voice was deep and resonant.

"Lark."

She looked at Charles, then back to the Ajayis and smiled. "Have a wonderful meal."

Lark turned around. The wine flowed freely at the table, and it looked as if the guys were on at least their second glass. Charles seemed to be getting intoxicated—Charles never got drunk off two drinks, which meant he must have imbibed more back home. She sighed. When he became intoxicated, he became an unmitigated ass.

While waiting for the food, Charles insisted on dancing. She looked around. "But the dance floor is empty."

"Come on, be a sport. One dance."

His voice took on the belligerent, whiny tone he got when he drank. If dancing with him staved off a temper tantrum, then fine.

"Just one."

She gave their clients a polite nod as Charles led her to the dance floor. Charles put his arm around her waist and took her hand, and she understood how a pedigree poodle at a dog show felt.

The pianist struck up a slow contemporary song, singing a little. Charles held her close as they danced. Though he'd always been light on his feet, there was no lightness in her heart when he said in her ear, "I do declare, Miss Braithwaite, you are the most stunning woman in the room tonight. You look ravishing. Well done."

"I'm glad you're enjoying yourself," she muttered as he turned her about.

Lark danced with him, aware and knowing everyone watched them, as Charles wanted. Meanwhile, her gaze betrayed her and traveled over to Niall, who followed her with his eyes.

Charles dipped her at the end of the song, but she'd never felt more alone, despite their closeness. People applauded. He led her back to the table without another word, mission accomplished. He dived into full-blown business conversation with the guys from Jagger, having their full attention now. He was The Man.

Lark half listened to Charles's conversation with the Jagger representatives while she kept her other ear on the conversation at Niall's table behind her. Deidre and Anthony shared experiences they'd had in the last year with their work and plans for the upcoming year.

Lark nibbled at her salad, wishing it were Ben & Jerry's. After talking to the two Jagger execs about her department, it was clear this would be a "dating dinner," where the most amount of business which transpired would be what team won what Super Bowl or World Cup.

She injected questions where Charles gave her an opportunity to squeeze a word in on their sales ratios compared with other international firms, but between times she grew more interested in eavesdropping on what Deidre and Anthony had to say. She scooted her chair back a few inches to hear them better.

The men beside her got louder the more they drank. They'd be wasted by the end of the night. Colin and Matthew were like the kind of men Charles hung out with when he needed male-bonding time—brash and egocentric. He was on his playing field. The wine loosened their tongues, and the masculine power play ensued.

She listened with a hard ear while picking at her entrée as Anthony went on to describe the starving and ill children in the villages of Tanzania, compared to the village they lived in now, how light their frames were or how distorted their bellies from malnutrition.

"Well, it's good the G8 Summit did something," Niall said close behind her. "But action has to happen, or nothing's ever going to change the way it needs to. There's been so much bloodshed in Kenya, enough for the whole world."

Deidre spoke up. "It will happen over time, I believe."

"Well, the peace talks are progressing," Lark said, and she turned in her seat to face them. Niall backed his chair up, and she had everyone's attention. She went on. "The problem is, how many people, how many children, are going to fall by the wayside in the meantime before action is taken?"

Niall raised his eyebrows. "I didn't know you were passionate about the situation there."

Deidre nodded in Niall's direction. "Mr. O'Hagan comes with us down to Africa every June to do an assessment of the needs of the smaller villages. He also helps coordinate the petition for supplies and takes care of the legalities, the nonprofit status of the school. He has been most supportive to our cause."

"I only wish I could do more." Niall bowed his head toward Deidre.

Lark took a good look at Niall, fascinated. "I'm impressed you go over there. I may not have a lot of time to devote to it because of work, but of course, I'm passionate about it. I mean, we can't see the molecules in the air, but it doesn't mean they don't exist. It's a beautiful fantasy to imagine a mythical, hidden African country armed with magical technology and kick ass heroes who save the world, but the reality is it's a third world country and in dire poverty. While we're fighting a political battle and dealing with greed and corruption here in the states, our ignorant comfort doesn't excuse that Rwandan children are sitting on mud floors as we speak, with only a spoonful of rice in their bellies."

"Well said." Anthony lifted his glass to her. Lark caught Charles's eye from her side, aware he listened in.

Niall leaned his elbow on top of his chair, giving her his full attention. "Please, go on," he said, and the others seemed glued to her words as well.

Lark glanced down and came out with it. Her own table grew quiet. "Well, when I think of the fact children in Rwanda are working at age four, I'm sickened. They're barely getting out of toddlerhood, learning how to string sentences together. And my one major issue is the wrong sort of people in positions of power. It's the whole joke about embracing a political leader who emboldens chaos and violence among his people. But my biggest concern is the utter disregard that's had and the attitude toward women. Raping is like a sport to the men in the militias, who tear through small villages, cutting off women's brea—"

"Lark, could we please keep the subject to something more suitable for dinner conversation?" Charles interrupted with a forced, polite air. He picked at the salad left on his plate, and his fork lingered in midair as he glanced at her with an odd, harassed look.

Matthew and Colin acted polite, but their awkwardness might as well have been a cloud above the table. She remembered why she was there in the first place.

She dotted the sides of her mouth with the edge of the napkin in her lap, reached for her glass of water, and turned back to the table. "Yes, of course. Excuse me."

"You'll have to forgive Lark," Charles said to the men, taking over the reins. "She's hard to stop once you've got her going. But she's a tiger in the boardroom," he added with a wink.

"And other places too, I'm guessing." Colin snorted, nudging Charles's shoulder with his own. Matthew chortled beside him but offered Lark a fake apologetic grimace. Charles did not say anything, yet from the smarmy look he gave them, he might as well have.

Her insides burned hot and uncomfortable, and she set her napkin on the table. "Excuse me," she said, scooting her chair back to go to the ladies' room. She put the strap of her evening purse over her shoulder. The legs of the chair bumped into Niall's. His hot gaze stayed on her. He grazed his finger against her dangling left hand near the leg of her chair.

She met his eyes, and the fire in them consumed her.

"I'm fine with Lark continuing," Niall challenged.

The two parties stopped talking and looked from Charles to Lark and then from Niall to Charles. She'd seen men make asses of themselves and break into brawls before, but she didn't like being the reason.

"By all means," soothed Deidre. "Finish what you were saying, Lark. We've seen things you wouldn't believe. We were there through most of them. We won't be offended. Please."

Lark gulped, aware of the giant scowl dying to surface on Charles's composed face and the awkwardness at both their tables. She continued down a safer road. "Well, nothing infuriates me more than to deprive someone else of their humanity. I read an article not too long ago about how most of the children in Rwanda speak three languages or more, and they don't have video games and inner-city conveniences. They're smart, but they lack the resources and wherewithal to learn to read and write." Deidre and Anthony nodded their agreement and soon immersed her in conversation about their village.

She chanced a glance at Niall. His eyes lit up as he lifted his glass to his lips.

Halfway through the chocolate mousse, Lark left the table and made it to the restroom. Decorated in white, pink, and gold tones, it was vast and luxurious and even had an adjacent sitting room. She finished with the posh toilet and left her bathroom stall to wash her hands at a gold-faucet sink.

A toilet flushed, and Deidre emerged as Lark dried her hands. They nodded at each other in the mirror.

Reaching for an excuse to linger longer, Lark removed her engagement ring as she depressed the lotion dispenser and moisturized her hands and wrists.

It had a sweet, floral scent.

Lark peeked at Deidre in the mirror. "May I be blunt?" Deidre asked.

"Of course," said Lark, rubbing the lotion into her hands before replacing the ring.

Deidre washed her hands. "You strike me as a passionate young woman. I can tell you are driven. I am like that as well. I also see you do things to please the man you are with. This is good, but you shouldn't do them if you don't want to. If you put him first in everything, child, you will always be treated as second class." Deidre wiped her hands.

Lark wasn't sure what to make of it. The woman was a complete stranger, yet her words drove straight into her. Odd, considering not many people could affect her in such a way. Lark blinked. "Um, thank you. I'll bear that in mind."

Deidre motioned to join her at the door. "Come."

They walked back out to the table together, chatting along the way about the ornate ceilings of the restaurant and how old the place must be.

When they arrived at their tables, Niall and Anthony stood. Deidre sat, but Lark remained standing. Where were Charles and the two other men?

"They went downstairs to smoke," Niall said, watching her with a knowing expression.

The way he stared at her, *into* her, unnerved her, and it seemed like the right time to go out for a cigarette. It was too warm inside anyway, and fresh air might do her good. The door to the balcony stood ajar along the south wall, with fairy lights glowing like fireflies through the white curtain, hung outside the open door. The perfect escape.

"I'm going to go get some fresh air. It's stuffy in here," she said, shouldering the small silver evening purse her mother lent her. Niall inclined his head to her, and the weight of his stare stayed with her as she headed toward the veranda.

The lights of Portland twinkled in the distance, and a sweet, fragranced breeze blew past her. There must be an autumnal fuchsia plant hung close by for any late migrating hummingbirds nearby.

More than displeased with Charles, Lark listened to the rustling leaves from a potted tree. Her arms broke out in goose bumps, and she rubbed her hands over them, chilled at her neck and where the low-cut dress stopped at her cleavage. The balcony door creaked open behind her. A few minutes later, a large jacket slid over her shoulders, enveloping her in warmth. She turned around.

"Thank you, Char—"

Niall put his hands on her shoulders. Behind him, farther in the restaurant past a couple of tables, Charles sat at their table with the men from Jagger, loud and boisterous in their conversation, oblivious to her absence and more than a little intoxicated. Way more.

"My pleasure," Niall whispered.

She shivered again, this time having nothing to do with the chill. The jacket covered her, warm and comfortable upon her shoulders.

"Lark, I need to speak with you. I'm sure by now you've gathered the real reason I'm here tonight?"

Lark shrugged. "It doesn't take a genius to put two and two together, yes."

He took a step closer, his face but inches from hers. "I have a confession to make. I overheard your plans for dinner back at the ranch."

"So, it's no coincidence you're here." Her eyes searched his.

"No, it's not," he admitted, pausing to gaze at her.

"And the table?"

"I came early and tipped the maître d' a Hamilton to seat you next to us."

She gave him a commiserating look, shaking her head. "W-why would you go to all that trouble? I told you, I'm engaged."

Niall stepped forward. "I had to see you."

"You see me every day."

He eyed her, moving his hand toward her cheek as though he were approaching a wild animal. "I'm drawn to you," he murmured, caressing her cheek and jawline with his warm fingers. "You *keep* drawing me. I never had this with M— Never mind."

Lark gasped and moved away from his hand. "You're with someone?" Sadness passed across his features, and her stomach plummeted.

"Yes. No. I mean, I was. Twelve years ago. She died in a car crash."

Lark swallowed and turned away from him toward the city view. "I'm sorry. I don't mean to seem insensitive here, but please don't tell me I resemble her or something. Is that why you—"

He chuckled, and the pressure of his chest warmed her back. "You *look* nothing like her," he said into her ear. His large hands encircled her waist from behind. "You *act* nothing like her." His full lips pressed against the side of her neck, and despite knowing she should put an end to this dangerous game, she leaned back against him and closed her eyes. "Taste nothing like

147

her. I'm drawn to you. I know it's crazy—I can't explain it—but I…I want you, Lark."

She inhaled as his right hand slid up her stomach to tentatively cup her breast. He grazed his thumb over the nipple as he kissed her neck, and her breath became labored. When she didn't object, he slid his hand into the open V of her dress and slid his fingers beneath her bra. The dinner jacket provided a safe cover for his actions from any potential onlookers, and she clutched his trouser leg as he chafed the pad of his thumb over her nipple.

His hands were warm and smooth, strong, like in her dreams. This was wrong. She needed to stop him, but she couldn't. She yielded to his touch, and he turned her face toward him with his other hand and kissed her full on the mouth. His tongue sought entrance, and she met it with her own, her pussy drenched and throbbing with demand.

"Lark." He kneaded her breast as he made love to her mouth.

They kissed as he cosseted her, and if this carried on much longer, she wouldn't be able to stop. He could fuck her right there on the balcony, and she'd let him without reservation. His hand left her breast and descended at a tortuous pace down the flesh of her ribs and past her abdomen. She held a hand to the dress clasp at the back of her neck to avoid the front of the dress dragging down as he slid his hand beneath the rim of her panties. She whimpered as he neared her pussy and shook herself as she came to her senses. She drew his hand away with great effort. "Niall, we can't," she gasped. "I'm sorry." She looked away as she straightened her clothes.

He breathed hard behind her. "You want to, though. I know you do. I feel it. Though not like this. I'm sorry I lost control in a public place."

She turned back to him. His gaze lingered on her lips. She'd never be able to hide her attraction to him; it was as transparent as air.

"It's okay," he reassured her as he rubbed her arms through the jacket. He pressed his lips to her forehead, then walked off without another word, back into the restaurant and toward the bathrooms.

She turned away from the door, grateful for the privacy they'd had. She sniffed the jacket, infused with his scent, pine and nice cologne, woodsy. She waited for her heart to return to normal and stayed out there until the wind increased and she no longer throbbed with want. She pulled the jacket tighter around her, the maître d' opened the balcony door for her, and she went back inside. Their waiter placed a black leather folio on their table as she approached.

"Wait, Charles." The nitwit was about to leave the receipts on the card plate at their table. "We need these for expense reimbursement."

Charles draped an arm over her shoulder. "Don't worry," he slurred. "Maisie'll take care of it. She takes care of everything."

"Maisie works for me now, remember?" She collected the receipts and folded them into her purse.

"Perhaps I should've stuck with the low-alcohol-content American wine instead of going with the French version."

"That would've been best." She retrieved her mother's shawl from the cloakroom and came across Niall in the foyer.

"Will you be okay getting back?" he asked with a slight frown.

She nodded. "I'm fine. I didn't drink tonight. I'm wide-awake." She slipped Niall's jacket off her shoulders and handed it back to him. "Thanks."

He took the jacket and put it right back around her shoulders, fixing it over her bare arms. "Keep it," he said in a low voice. "It's cold out there." He leaned forward, and in a husky voice, whispered in her ear, "At least something of mine will touch you tonight."

Lark quivered as he pulled away, and she tried to stay composed. Deidre and Anthony had their coats on and were waiting for him by the door. Deidre nodded at her.

Niall leaned close. "You'll have instant friends if you ever visit Rwanda. Deidre likes you."

"Yes, I like her as well." She enjoyed Deidre's tactful, naked honesty. She'd love to talk to her again.

Charles appeared beside her and shoved Niall hard. Niall bounced back, his expression fierce.

She grabbed Charles's arm. "Stop it, Charles," she hissed, wide-eyed as they gained a few onlookers. Did he know about the balcony? They'd been pretty secluded. Had he seen?

"I'll take it from here, thanks, O'Hagan," Charles snarled as he yanked Niall's coat off her.

"I'm sorry. He's drunk," she apologized as Charles tossed the coat on the floor.

"Are you sure you're okay getting back?" asked Niall, concern evident in his voice.

"She's fine, you twat," Charles sneered.

Lark moved to step between them, but Niall held up a hand to tell her to forget about it. He wished them good night and left with his friends.

Charles took off his dinner jacket and put it around Lark, serious and solemn. The jacket fell like a parachute over her shoulders and stunk heavily of wine and cigar smoke. The stench vexed her, heady and nauseating, like too much cologne.

"Let's go." He turned her toward the elevators, where Matthew and Colin stood waiting. He was courteous and pleasant as she drove them back to their hotel, but in the brooding silence on the way back to the ranch, she sensed his defensive shield, despite the wine he'd consumed. It hit her then how domineering he was.

Chapter Nine
Dessert

At home and in her bedroom, Lark stepped out of the black dress. Off came the stilettos, stockings, and bra. She put on comfortable sweatpants and a T-shirt. She could breathe, except each one became a sigh as she thought about Niall's touch, his kiss… How every time he came near, her body all but screamed at her to go to him. But she didn't have that liberty right now.

It was close to midnight. She took an earring out as she sat at the vanity in her bedroom. She caught Charles's reflection in the mirror. He wrapped his knuckles against her door and leaned against the door frame, studying her.

"Hi," Lark said, crisper than she intended to.

"Did you have a nice time at dinner?" Charles asked in a low voice.

She took her other earring out and placed them both in the brown leather travel satchel in front of her. "It went well. They seemed interested when they gave you their contact details. Of course, they may be too drunk to recollect the conference call we arranged for December 4. You may want to send them an e-mail."

"You know what I'm on about, Lark." Charles glared at her with a frown.

"Niall gave me his coat when I went outside. It was cold, Charles. He was courteous."

He traipsed into the room as she took off her engagement ring and bracelet.

"You've got to be kidding me. The man's a complete bellend," Charles said loftily. He loosened his tie.

"Oh? I thought our waiter was rather nice." Lark wiped behind her ear and down her neck with a moist makeup-remover cloth. Of course he meant Niall, but she hated it when he mouthed off about people when he was three sheets to the wind.

"O'Hagan's three seconds shy of getting his ass whooped. And I'm ready to do it if he steps out of line again," he slurred.

Lark rolled her eyes. He was hammered. "Oh, go to bed. You're drunk and don't know what you're saying."

He considered her. "Enjoy this, because I'll never say it sober, damn it. You're right." He stopped right behind her, leaned down, and ran his finger down the side of her cheek. "You're so hot."

In the mirror, his eyes flashed with adoration, flattering and disconcerting at the same time.

"Well, thank you. Go to bed, Charles," she whispered, grateful when he kissed the top of her head and then left. Deep down, she loved him—or she loved what they'd had. But he could be so extreme. And the whole Gemma situation didn't sit well with her either.

Her mother had attacked her bed again after she'd left for dinner. Lark's folded and laundered clothes sat in a neat pile on the edge of the bed. Damn, it looked immaculate. Did Pam take out a ruler for those hospital corners? She shook her head and drank water.

She climbed into bed and shut off the lights, then lay there wide-awake. Niall's touch, the way his voice sent shivers through her, sent her heart into overdrive. Charles *never* touched her like that. His touches were calculated, either sexy or mechanical, always with an end purpose behind it, something he wanted from her.

Wired and nowhere ready to close her eyes, she left the bed and went to the window, opened the curtains, and sat on the window seat. She shouldn't compare, she shouldn't even entertain the notion of Niall... But it was impossible not to. It had been nice to escape for the evening, to not have to deal with her father's passing and the issues at hand. Her eyes grew heavy, and her head fell back against the wall.

****

She sat in a tree and watched Niall below. It was twilight. The full moon gave off good light, enough for her to see him. He wore an old blue shirt and worn jeans. He tethered the reins on a gray horse to a thick, gnarled tree branch. She stayed hidden while he made a low campfire. He cleaned a large, flat rock and set fresh green leaves on it, then used a hunting knife to debone two fish and set them on the rock-plate against the campfire to broil. His chin sported a light beard, and he had a tribal sort of talisman around his neck.

He shouldered the rucksack from his shoulders and took out a container filled with something. He faced her from where he sat, and the muscle in his jaw moved as he chewed and set what looked like nuts to roast in a pan. He sprinkled a thimbleful of something on the trout and set water to boil in a kettle perched over the fire.

He appeared at peace, as though he liked the silence and stillness. She followed his gaze to where the moon reflected on the lake like a mirror. He stood, unbuttoned his shirt, and let it fall to the ground. She watched as he shed the rest of his clothes, then waded into the lake a few feet away. She admired the outline of his frame. Niall lowered into the water, disappearing from her sight. When he resurfaced, he closed his eyes as he slicked his hair back from his face. Droplets cascaded down his muscular chest, etched in the moonlight, radiant from the fire. He leaned his head back and floated, staring at the stars. Lark climbed down from the tree and walked past the campfire. She intruded on a private moment, but she wanted to share it with him, to know more about him. He saw her and stopped floating, instead treading water.

"Lark, what are you doing here?"

She shrugged. "I have no idea. I hoped you'd have an answer for me." She took in the rough terrain, the thick plants, and the surrounding bamboo trees, the heaviness of the air. "We're nowhere I've ever been. Do you know where we are?"

"I do." He glided backward a few feet.

"Good." She lifted her T-shirt over her head and stripped. "Then you can tell me when we're done."

"Lark, wait."

She paused in the middle of taking off her panties. "What?"

He shook his head, but he was troubled. "Nothing, I just… This place."

"Isn't it great?" She waded into the coolness, a few feet away from him and treading water as she kept afloat. "It's primal, but there's something sexy about it. I like it when we go somewhere new."

"But that's just it, this isn't new for me. I *know* this place."

She swam forward and reached out to place her hand on the tattoo over his heart. "And I know *this* place. Want to take me there?" The staccato of his heartbeat beat beneath her fingers. The warmth of his close body heated hers, despite the chillness of the water.

They barely made it back to land. Niall tasted every inch of her skin he could reach, filling her mind and body with a heated flood of desire. She wanted control this time, to bring him to the breaking point of rapture, as he had for her.

"I want to touch you," she whispered when they were next to the fire. Niall nodded and stood still as Lark skimmed her cool fingers up his abdomen. Her touch lingered on his rib cage as she kissed his chest. She moved her hand back down and closed it over the length of his hard cock. He shut his eyes and inhaled her hair.

"You smell good," he murmured as she enclosed her hand over his cock, spreading the bead of moisture at the tip with her thumb, massaging his length with long, tugging pulls. He shivered beneath her touch and bent to lick the shell of her ear.

"Like roses and woods."

"Stay still." Lark fell to her knees before him and stroked him at the base, working her way to the slick head of his cock, which glistened with pre-cum. He groaned and put his hand on her cheek. She locked her gaze with his as she enveloped the tip in her mouth, circling her tongue around it. She curled the flat of her tongue over the edge, and he thrust against her, his head thrown back and hips tilted forward, caging her head between his palms.

Smiling, she took him in her mouth.

He groaned, fisting her hair. "Oh *yes*, sweetheart. Fuck me with your gorgeous mouth." She continued to suck, spurred on by his reaction.

****

Lark jerked and woke up, disorientated. She'd fallen asleep in the window seat. She looked across the room to the alarm clock beside her bed. The neon-blue display told her it was after three in the morning. She didn't feel like crawling into bed. She used the bathroom and then padded downstairs to the kitchen.

As she rounded the corner at the bottom of the stairs, she collided with Pam. They both jumped.

"Heavens to Betsy, you scared me," her mother exclaimed, putting a hand to her heart.

They both laughed once they recovered. "Sorry, Mom. What are you doing up?" They turned and walked to the kitchen together.

Pam put an arm around her. "I've had trouble sleeping alone. Thirty plus years sharing a bed with a man every night. Well, I decided to sin and have some ice cream. Clear my head and clog my arteries. Care to join me?"

Ice cream sounded like heaven. Lark opened the freezer as Pam turned on the light over the stove.

Her mother stood a few feet away, her highlighted hair loose and soft around her face. She wore a deep, dark-blue satin pajama set unbuttoned at the throat.

Lark blinked and stood back, studying her mother. "What is it?"

Wisdom emanated from Pam's limpid, dark brown eyes, much like her own. "Nothing. I realized we have the same lips. Our mouths are the same. And your hair

157

sort of has a glow to it, Mom. I don't know if I ever told you before, but it's real pretty against your eyes. You're a beautiful woman."

Pam beamed and joined Lark at the freezer door. "Hon, I don't know if it's the ice cream talking, but keep it coming. Now, I knew you had to have a weakness somewhere. Moose Tracks or Mint Chocolate Chip? Hmm. Decisions, decisions."

Lark glanced at her mother. "I don't do this all the time."

"Neither do I," Pam shot back. "Okay, that's a lie. I do this on a regular basis. Who doesn't? If ice cream can't cure it, it can't be cured." Pam extracted a half gallon of Moose Tracks and went over to a nearby cupboard, where she drew out a few decorated bowls. "Pick your poison, hon, or come join me in sin with this one."

Lark joined her mother at the kitchen island, getting out two spoons from the silverware drawer.

Pam took them, then shooed her over to the table. "Have a seat. I'll scoop it out for you."

Knowing better than to argue with a kitchen commando, Lark complied and did what she was told.

"How do you like being back home?" Pam asked as she set the bowl in front of Lark before she sat.

"It's a mixed bag. I mean, it was hard going at first because of Dad. But it's nice now, sort of like stepping into someone else's life and revisiting the past. There's a different pace here than what I'm used to. Aaron's grown, but he's still the same."

Pam nodded. "Tell me about it. He still plays practical jokes on me whenever he gets the chance. Rick was a cowboy. Aaron takes after him. Otherwise, he's like me." Pam tasted a spoonful of her ice cream. "You remind me of your father. You both have a head for business, and you're both so stubborn. You can deny it till you're blue in the face; you know it's true."

Lark nodded. "Hey, I'm not about to argue with the woman feeding me ice cream."

"Good girl." They ate in silence, and then Pam asked, "How's it going with Charles? He seems pretty busy these days in the office. Did dinner go okay?"

Lark dug out a scoop of ice cream and took her time.

"Honey, you *can* tell me things. I want you to."

Lark sighed and put a palm to her forehead, leaning on the table. "It's—it's complicated. We were fine the first few years, but before we came out here, well, we haven't been gelling like we used to."

"I'm sorry to hear that. It was nice of him to come over," Pam offered.

Lark took a bite. "I agree. There's a lot going on, and it's messed things up."

"For everyone."

"Mmm."

"Poor Niall's been working himself to the bone to get this mess sorted. He puts his best foot forward with everything."

Lark sighed, anger and lust warring within her over the man. "Yeah, well, sometimes he should put his foot in his mouth instead."

Pam pointed her spoon. "Be careful of bitter things said over ice cream at so young an age, Lark. Once you say them, there's no going back, and they'll haunt you for years to come."

Lark released her rage between spoonfuls of ice

cream. "I feel like things wouldn't be as screwed up if he wasn't here. I mean, why does he think it's any of his business to walk into my life and say what I should or shouldn't do? Who does he think he is?"

"I suspect," said Pam as she stood and took her bowl to the sink, "he's trying to be your friend. True friends tell you what's good for you, though you don't want to hear it."

Lark scraped more ice cream from her bowl. Images from the restaurant last night flitted through her brain. It bordered on ridiculousness, how she'd read something into each fleeting glance, each brush of his arm against hers which set her nerves on fire. "I disagree. Good friends know when to shut the hell up."

Pam smiled. "What I'm getting at, hon, is Niall's heart has always been in the right place, and he's good. Real good. Not a lot of people like that these days."

Lark toyed with her spoon, thinking of his comment to her the previous morning after her run. "Oh Mom, I meant to tell you earlier. Thanks for the bottle of water yesterday. I needed it."

"I'm sorry?"

"That wasn't you?"

"What wasn't me?"

"Someone left me a bottle of water yesterday morning. I thought you did."

Pam fished around in her bowl. Her mother scraped out the last of the dregs with her spoon, then glanced up. "No, hon. I was out shopping. Must have been your brother—or Niall. I wouldn't put it past him."

Aaron had been working in the barn, and Charles didn't leave her things; he presented them to her on a diamond-encrusted platter. He was showy. It had to have been Niall.

"I have an idea," Pam said. "Why don't you do a little year-end gardening after Charles goes back to London? Niall's not going to need us while he gets everything settled, and it'd be perfect to get you relaxed before you go back to work. You know, plant a few bulbs. I have more clothes to rummage through. I'm sure they'd fit you. Let's find something and see how you feel after work in the garden."

Lark smiled. "All right." Ice cream made everything okay.

****

The sun had not yet risen when she rolled out of bed and used the bathroom, emerging ten minutes later ready to go. She hadn't slept much after her early-morning ice-cream binge, but a small amount of sleep could go a long way and refresh anyone. She took a deep breath as she put her hands into her sweat-suit jacket pockets and found her smoking paraphernalia. She'd smoked before going out last night but oddly didn't feel the need to now.

She walked out the door, heading downstairs. After depositing her smoking stuff on the kitchen table, she went outside. Before she could take more than a few steps, she spotted Niall stretching his long muscular legs out on the deck. Her cheeks burned as she remembered spending time between those legs in her dream. He looked bright and awake, wearing black tracksuit bottoms and a hooded top.

"Mornin', Shakespeare," he sang, fog emitting from his breath.

"Niall?" Lark checked her watch. "It's *way* early. What the hell are you doing here?" She eyed his attire

161

as she came close to him with her hands in her jacket pockets to keep them from the cold morning air. What was his hidden agenda? *Oh, come on. This is—*

"Well, good morning to you too. I forgot to mention last night... Since I've been going back and forth, burning up gas, your mam invited me to stay in the guest room downstairs until all this is resolved. It'll be easier to work from here for the next couple of days instead of having to commute ninety minutes each way to my condo. I've been living out of my office the last week to get everything done."

Lark relived her conversation with her mother earlier. Had he been privy to it? "Did you sleep here last night?" Redness etched his nose from the cold. How long had he been out here? Had he been waiting for her? "I didn't see your SUV in the driveway."

"Nah, I got in about an hour ago. Aaron let me in on his way out to the stables," he said. "I was with Dee and Anthony late last night before taking them to the airport. They caught the red-eye. Didn't get here until about five. I tried to go to sleep, but I'm something of an insomniac. Unless I'm deadbeat tired, sleep never happens. So I figured I'd come out here. I thought you could use a running buddy."

She smirked. "A *running* buddy, huh? I do fine on my own." She eyed the property, then looked back at him. "Besides, I'd hate to have you lagging behind, eating my dust."

Niall grinned, his green eyes spirited and bright in the murky morning light. "Is that what you think I'll be doing, now?" he ruminated. "Hmm. Guess I'll have to try to keep up with you, then."

"I guess so. No time like the present." Without

another word, she took off, past the patio steps and through the garden path and onto the trail in the woods. She played with fire, but this was the first time in a long time she'd felt desired or important to someone. She glanced back, and he watched her from the patio, his hands clasped together as he leaned over the railing.

"I'll be along soon, Shakespeare. I'm admirin' the view," he called. "I'll see you in a bit."

"Don't count on it," Lark murmured beneath her breath, and she ran for it, as she and Maisie did when they were training for a 5K where they always ended up walking. It was sadly more motivating to know someone was watching, and she hoped to God her ass didn't look fat.

The wind swooshed against her in pleated gusts, but she didn't care. The temperature had dropped, and she welcomed the icy sting of the breeze to the back of her throat and neck. The constant pumping motion of her legs and arms soon warmed her, and she breathed deep. Her footfalls fell light and fast, and it was easier to breathe than a few days before.

As she neared the crest of a hill, a swarm of gnats congregated in the middle of the path. She dogged it and kept her mouth shut, trying not to breathe while swatting to clear the air. Her pace slowed after she cleared the gnat kingdom.

A few moments later, Niall's sneakers crunched on the pebbled path as he caught up with her. She jogged in place when he fell in step with her, swatting in front of his face.

"Got to love that extra protein in the morning, eh?" he sputtered, wiping his cheek.

She laughed. "Let's go, then."

He let her set the pace, which she appreciated. After being overweight for most of her life, the movement liberated her soul. She'd never run around the property as a teen, and the physical freedom was damn good. But she was no marathoner by any stretch.

The shadowy pines loomed in the distance, and the sky washed into a pale blue. The morning light played over their heads, zigzagging as they tread, with various shades of orange and red from the rising sun. Once or twice Lark caught her shadow along the path before her, a dark silhouette against the brightness of the morning.

Lark glanced at Niall out of the corner of her eye. The man had a complete runner's build, like a damn greyhound. He was born to run, sturdy and broad-shouldered, but tall and robust. He breathed easy and seemed to enjoy the pace. She bet he could run much faster, given how comfortable and fit he seemed, but he kept the pace beside her as he looked around. A stream gurgled beside them, and multicolored foliage covered the trees as they went into their winter hibernation. Golden leaves littered the path.

Near the end of the trail, Lark glanced at Niall, then focused straight ahead. "Hey, thanks for the water yesterday."

"Anytime." His voice lightened. "I saw you out here. Figured you might need it."

They sprinted the last twenty-five meters. It went faster than normal, and though an unspoken discomfort lingered between them after last night, she was happy to have someone to talk to again. As they walked it off on their way back to the house, he remarked on the peacefulness of the property.

"Your dad did a fine job with the landscaping." He nodded toward the stables beside the house.

Lark agreed. "They both did. My mom did most of the earlier stuff—the gardening, what went where. Of course, I was too busy with school to notice. I was never home much."

He normally seemed careful with how personal he went, but he surprised her. "Let me get this straight. Aside from what I already know about you from your dad…"

Lark reached the porch steps and commenced to do her stretches. She glanced at him.

"You were a serious student, have a love of poetry, are a top-field competitor in your profession, and…you're active in your local Toastmasters, am I right?"

"Great talent. You should do that at parties. You pretty much nailed it, but I'm not active in Toastmasters. I was a few years ago. Two out of three isn't bad, though. Care to keep going?"

Niall stepped closer, his eyes bright. "Okay. You don't like it when people belittle themselves. It irks you. Your favorite color is yellow—"

"How did you know that?" she asked, stunned. All right, so it was a weird color to like, but it always reminded her of fresh spring daffodils. How on earth did he know?

Niall went on. "Your heart is always in the right place, whether you have it closed to certain people or not. You've a more sensual and romantic soul than you let on."

Lark blinked, afraid. Afraid of her dreams of him, afraid of what they meant, afraid of what would happen

165

Roxanne D. Howard

if she continued to let him remove those well-built bricks from the walls of her heart. She cleared her throat and fought with herself to take back control. "Impressive, Niall. You should join a psychic call-in show."

He shrugged. "What can I say? It's a talent. But I wouldn't join a psychic show. The pay is crap. I know, I can be a newer version of the Magic Bullet guy. I'll be the Irish version with the messed-up accent. Don't tell anyone, but it's been my secret dream to leave law and go into show business." They laughed as they finished stretching. He put a hand on her arm as they went up the porch steps. "Lark, wait. About last night—"

"We need to stop this. We shouldn't have done that," she whispered, guilty.

"No, we *should* have. But not there, not in a public place. I should have been more of a gentleman, and it's not how I'd like you to think of me. Hear me out. We're both here for the next few days. Would you like to run together again in two days' time?"

Tell him no. "Of course." *Good job, Lark.* "I mean, it's nice to have a *friend* to run with," she said harsher than she meant to, the same way she said good-bye to rude clients after long meetings.

He returned her smile as if he understood, despite her demeanor. He followed her into the house.

They entered an empty kitchen, and Lark picked up her cigarette pack from the table, considering them. She lowered her voice so she wouldn't wake anyone. "It's strange, I haven't had a cigarette since yesterday afternoon."

"Good." He put his hands on the back of a chair on the opposite side of the table. "There's no reason to

166

break a good streak. Throw 'em away. There's no time like the present."

Lark sighed. "You sound like a friend of mine. Still, it was easier to breathe when I ran today than it's been in a long time. I thought it might be the altitude difference at first, but I think it's not smoking."

Niall's voice echoed in the kitchen, deep and down-to-earth. "Well, it *is* easier to breathe when you're not smoking. Smoking constricts the blood vessels in your lungs, so without it, you're getting more air now. I noticed you didn't drink last night either, and it increases your desire to smoke."

"It does?"

"Aye. Most times when people go to parties, it's not the alcohol that gives them the hangover. It's the cigarettes *and* the booze. I'm not anyone to tell you what to do or not to do, but it's never too late."

"I am going to need one before the day is out." *Maybe.*

He shrugged and walked around the table toward the cupboard, where he withdrew two glasses. The long finger crooked around the rim of her glass as he handed it to her sending her imagination into overdrive. *Show me what you want, Lark.* She followed him to the water dispenser on the fridge. They drank their water in silence. His Adam's apple bobbed against his throat as he drank, and she did her best not to stare. *Tell me what you want. Say it.* The water nourished her dry, thirsty throat. *Yes, Lark.*

Niall stepped closer to her. Their breathing slowed in the quietude. His gaze bore into hers, and she panicked. Could he read her thoughts? Was she too transparent?

She turned to avoid his gaze and drank more water, finishing her glass. She'd tried to keep a decent distance between them and had even sidestepped to keep from brushing against him. This craving, nervous charge wouldn't go away. It increased, painfully so, with each innocent graze of an elbow or swipe of hip to hip when the path had narrowed. She was selfish, but she wanted him to take her as he had in her dreams, to make her forget. It got harder and harder to trust herself around him. Every time he stepped into her comfort zone, she yearned to wrap her arms around him and throw caution to the wind.

Then there was the fact Niall was actually a great guy. She turned and studied him covertly. He had this simple, lighthearted air in the way he carried himself. That, coupled with knowing the facial expressions he made while in the throes of passion, were messing her up big-time. The sultry way he looked at her over the rim of his glass didn't help either.

She cleared her throat. "I, uh, I should go upstairs and get ready." *And take a cold, cold shower.*

He nodded. "I've got things to do today too. Once your mother is up, I'll need you both to sign your life away on a few forms I brought with me, and then I'll be in and out, getting the probate papers ready. I'll see you later."

"See you later," she said, turning to leave.

"Lark?"

"Yeah?"

"Good run."

He winked. She went weak in the knees. His arresting eyes lit, accenting his strong Irish features. The rugged morning stubble framed his jaw and sensual lips, and his windswept dark curls fell into his face.

"It was." Though she said it with a light tone, her body had other ideas. She put her empty glass on the counter and left before she said or did something she shouldn't. Once she reached the stairwell, she paused to lean her head back against the wall and closed her eyes. If only her rapid pulse would stop racing. It didn't even occur to her she'd left her cigarette pack on the table until she was upstairs.

She was so in trouble.

Chapter Ten
Character

An hour later, Lark flew with a purpose into the kitchen. Everything seemed in full swing—the lights were on, the window above the sink cracked to let in a small breeze, and the small TV on the counter blared out the enthusiastic news correspondent's morning reports. She glanced around.

Pam leaned back against the kitchen counter, talking to Charles, who sat at the table, sipping coffee and reading the newspaper.

"Morning, sunshine," Pam said with subdued cheer. "Thought you were still in bed. You can go back to sleep if you want."

Charles motioned for a good-morning kiss. She obliged, giving him a quick peck on the lips.

"Morning, Charles. No, I've been awake since six," she said to Pam.

"Wow, you're a step ahead of the rest of us. Take a seat, hon. I'll get you something to drink."

Lark's hands shook. She picked up a discarded bit of newspaper to keep them busy as she sat next to Charles. "How are you feeling after last night?"

It was a coin toss every time he had too much to drink; he could come back fine or moody. Charles proved his usual impeccable self, though he looked exhausted. He wore black slacks and a white polo top with the UY logo stitched above the left breast pocket.

"I'll get back to you once I've woken up," he brooded, nursing his coffee.

Moody it was.

Lark skimmed over the articles in the newspaper. "You know," she commented over her shoulder to her mother. "I forgot how small the newspapers here are in contrast to the *Evening Standard* and the *Telegraph*. They're kind of cute. Everything else here seems wider-spaced, bigger portioned. This newspaper is one thing that's smaller in size."

"Not the *only* thing, I imagine," Charles threw in, turning a page.

Lark cleared her throat. He looked smug and sipped his coffee.

"Lark, I hope you don't mind. I, uh, found your cigarettes on the table this morning," Pam said, setting a tall glass of grapefruit juice in front of Lark on the table. "I threw the pack out, thinking they were your dad's old ones. They took the garbage about an hour ago."

Crap. "I was craving one, Mom."

"I'm sorry, hon."

"Well, I mean, I did resolve to quit smoking this morning. I haven't had one since yesterday afternoon," she reminded herself, trying to keep her hands from fidgeting.

"Have some of the grapefruit juice," her mother advised.

Eyeing the glass with disdain, Lark recalled when she'd refused certain vegetables as a child. "Thanks, but I'm not a big grapefruit juice fan."

"You don't have to be," countered Pam, tapping

her nose. It had been so long, Lark forgot how she used to do that. "The taste will get rid of your craving, and if you have it right after each meal, it'll lessen your desire to smoke. Your dad drank it after his doctor diagnosed him with cancer. It ended up being more effective than the nicotine patches." Pam's voice softened when she mentioned Rick, and she turned to wipe the counters with a damp washcloth.

Charles glared at Lark.

"What?" she shot at him, not liking the scowl on his face.

He set his coffee cup on the table and leaned forward. "Lark, be honest—how many times have you done this? Let's face it. You're not going to quit."

She frowned at him.

"A fine attitude," Aaron's cheery voice joined them as he came into the kitchen with a plastic-wrapped bouquet of autumn flowers. He held a fishing pole, and a small metal tackle box in his other hand. He leaned the pole and tackle against a corner wall.

Niall followed behind him. They both donned heavy fall jackets, though Niall wore a nice work shirt and tie where his jacket opened. He inclined his head to her. She nodded back, feeling the charge in the air that had become the norm whenever they were in the same room.

"Never give up, I say. What are we talking about, again?" Aaron hung his hat on the back of a chair.

Pam brightened upon seeing the flowers. "Are those for me?"

"Uh-huh," he replied. "We were at the gas station a few miles away, paying an ungodly amount for fuel, and I grabbed 'em for you. I know we've still got the arrangements from the funeral home, but I figured you could use something special."

"Thanks, honey." Pam removed the plastic wrap and buried her nose in them. "Mmm. Better put them in some water," she said after giving Aaron a kiss on the cheek. She opened a kitchen drawer and withdrew a pair of scissors. "Your sister's decided to quit smoking."

Aaron turned to her. Now she remembered why she steered clear of small towns. News traveled faster than lightning.

"You have? That's awesome, Lark. Going cold turkey?"

"Something like that." Lark cringed and pursed her lips after taking another sip of the sour grapefruit juice. Why couldn't it taste like peaches?

"Well, hey, Dad wanted you to. If nothing else, it's awesome you're going for it."

Niall sat at the table and nodded at Charles.

Charles checked his watch and frowned. "Why are you here, O'Hagan?"

From his cagey expression, last night hadn't quite erased everything from his memory.

Pam turned her back as she worked on the flowers, but Lark noticed her perked ears as she listened a little too intensely to their conversation. Before Niall could open his mouth to answer, Pam piped up.

"That's right. I forgot to mention. Since Niall's home is so far, and he'll be traveling from our house to Portland every day for the next week, I've invited him to stay here until everything is settled." The tone of her voice added, *Let that be an end to it*.

Charles scowled, and Aaron checked the

entertainment section of the paper with a diplomatic air. He was staying here, then.

Lark took another sip and shuddered from the strong, bitter taste of the juice. It tasted like citric death, and she couldn't pretend it was chocolate or anything good. She'd never taken to grapefruit juice, but her mother was right about its power to relinquish any oral desires. She'd be lucky to want to put anything in her mouth ever again.

Lark watched Pam take a bottle of aspirin out of a drawer and shake out a tablet. Pam deposited it in a stone-accented mortar by the kitchen windowsill and ground it with a matching pestle.

"Well, guess what infamous Hollywood star's in rehab again for like the tenth time. No surprise there." Aaron chuckled, shaking his head. "This guy gets paid millions to play superheroes, but what does he do with his life? Acts like he's back on the block. Man, if I had that kind of chance, I wouldn't waste it getting stoned. I'd spend my free time supporting causes I care about. It's surprising the studios don't fire him. It takes a lifetime to build character, and a second to destroy it."

"Well, character's a tricky thing," Pam muttered, sprinkling the crushed aspirin from her fingertips into a large glass vase. "It has to be anchored at a certain point." She switched on tap water from the sink and set the vase beneath it.

"Mom, what are you doing?" Lark asked. "You're supposed to mix the packet of flower food in the bouquet."

Pam took each of the flowers from the cut-open plastic bag, trimmed the bottoms of the stems, and arranged them in the vase. The powdered aspirin inside swirled like tiny molecules.

"Home remedy," Aaron muttered, buried in the article. "She does it all the time." Aaron shook his head. "This guy's an effing joke."

"Sometimes," said Pam as she arranged the flowers, "the things we nourish ourselves with don't have to come from the most *obvious* source. There. Lovely." She placed the vase in the middle of the table.

Lark touched the edge of a musky, rose-colored carnation petal, inhaling the sweet, enticing perfume. When she opened her eyes, Niall studied her from across the table. When their eyes met, his darted to his drink, and she picked up her grapefruit juice. His ankle grazed hers beneath the table, and he slowly rubbed his foot around hers. Her eyes widened, and he raised his glass in front of his face to cover his smirk.

"I assume you'll be using the office?" Charles asked Niall.

He shrugged. "Here and there."

God, how could he be so calm while he played footsie with her and tantalized her with that sparkle in his eyes? She cleared her throat and moved her ankle out of reach.

"Oh, Charles," Aaron cut in after taking a sip of coffee. "By the way, I meant to ask you. I'm heading up to Hagg Lake in about an hour or so. I'm going fishing today before I have to drive back to Berkeley Monday morning. You want to come?"

"Hagg Lake? Sounds charming," mused Charles.

"Don't let the name fool you. She's gorgeous," Lark told him. "Hey, feel free. I'd go with you myself, but I've got to stay here for the signing. It might be better than being bored out of your mind while we do paperwork."

Charles inclined his head to Aaron. "All right, then. I've never fished, though."

"Hey, that's okay, man," Aaron encouraged. "We'll kick back and let the fish do the work. I reckon it might be a good chance to get to know the guy who's going to marry my big sister."

"Well, all right, then. As long as you don't mind me lighting a Cuban while we're out there."

"Dude, it wouldn't be a Braithwaite male-bonding experience if someone wasn't smoking."

****

The two men set off an hour later. While everyone ate at the table, Niall had Lark and Pam sign probate paperwork. He then excused himself and took off to his office in Portland, saying he would be in touch.

Pam wanted to send old pictures to Rick's extended family. Lark agreed to help her. They would need to go down to the basement to sort through photo boxes. Descending the long, wooden stairs, it hit Lark how much they'd renovated it in the last decade. Finished with carpet, painted walls, and a spacious gym, the basement was like a separate house. Lark peeked into the small room her mom told her Niall stayed in as they passed it on their way to the den. It had built-in shelves and wood-paneled walls. It was a nice guest room with furniture, nice bedding, and a small bathroom that she caught a glimpse of in passing. A small, black suitcase lay open on the bed, the clothes Niall had worn earlier bunched in a ball.

"Here we are." Pam came into the den from another room with one medium-size brown box and sat on the old couch beside her.

They lifted the lid, and Lark was locked in the past.

After looking through hundreds of photos, Lark pulled out an old photo of herself at fifteen with some friends from high school. "Wow. There's the old gang. Hello, bangs." She laughed. "We fell out of contact after high school. I wonder what happened to Janae." Her finger traced over the blue eyes and light-blonde hair of a beautiful young girl making a funny face, with her arms around Lark and another of their friends.

Pam sighed. "Last I heard, she's living with her mother, Patty, with her four kids."

Lark's eyes widened. "Four?"

Pam nodded. "Patty's so wonderful to take her in. But what mom wouldn't. She got pregnant with the Bryson boy's child. When she told him she was carrying, he joined the Army and never returned after boot camp. That was the last anyone heard of him. He took off."

"For good?"

"Yeah."

"Oh, no." Janae had been a close friend, vivacious, caring, a complete free spirit.

"I know. The poor girl. She went through two bad marriages after that and moved back here from Iowa last spring. I hope she's doing okay. She seemed worn-down when she first came back. I see her in town once in a while. She shops at the deli counter in Leibowitz's from time to time."

Lark's heart went out to her old friend. "How sad. I don't know if I'll get a chance to see her before I fly back to London, but I hope she's okay. Mom, do you think her problems with men changed who she was? She wanted to dance with Ballet Central West. She could dance too. She danced the dream sequence in *Oklahoma* our senior year. But what I mean to say is, do you think by choosing the wrong men, it altered who she was, and she lost herself? Or do you think it was who she would become anyway?"

Pam pondered the question with the same expression Aaron wore a few days ago out on the front porch when he'd pretended to smoke.

"I think we're all products of our decisions and goals. For better or for worse, Janae chose those men. I don't know the whole story behind it or what went on behind closed doors, but in the end, what it boils down to is the choices we make for ourselves, what we're each willing to accept and tolerate. There's a fine line of compromise in relationships."

She avoided her mother's eyes. "I believe if someone loves you, the last thing in the world they would do is hurt you." There was no need to sugarcoat it. Lark never shied away from her disgust about Rick's indiscretions. And she wasn't judgmental; he'd slaughtered the moral persona he'd displayed to the world, and the emotional dent he'd put upon their family. When her mother stayed silent, Lark chanced a glance at her through the tousled curtain of her hanging hair.

Her mother tilted her head. "Lark, I love you, but that's a load of bull. There's a fairy-tale myth girls are spoon fed which tells them those who love you will never hurt you, but it's ridiculous. They *have* to hurt you. It's part of loving and growing. What you have to decide is if you love them enough to forgive them. With your father, I didn't have to think about it. I was hurt beyond comprehension. I mean, we were happy and tightly knit before the mess—it shook me to the bone. But I had to put it behind me, honey. For all our sakes."

Lark set a picture frame beside her and glared at her mother. "Why *did* you?"

"Lark—"

"No, please. I want to know." Every time she cornered her mother about it, she evaded, but something told her to keep pressing. "He's gone, Mom. He's buried. Just tell me."

Pam rubbed her forehead. "Sweetheart, you have to understand how things were. Your dad had a lot of family support growing up, but the truth is, I didn't."

Lark blinked at the solemnity on her mother's normally cheerful face.

"I know I never talked about it much, but there's a reason why. My parents weren't the most loving. Part of the reason I love cooking so much is that I didn't have it growing up. I had to fight for every scrap of food and love I ever got. Rick came into my life, and he was a game changer. Rick..." Pam's eyes darted down. "Well, he was my prince. I never imagined as a child I'd have anything that even came close to this place, or you, or Aaron. Being loved and cared for by Rick, and raising you, gave me the greatest joy of my life." She twisted the wedding band on her finger, a wistful tug at the corners of her mouth. "Beyond playing the piano, I didn't have any kind of skill other than a patchy high-school education, and with raising the two of you, I had no way of making ends meet in any capable way if I left him. I *did* think about it, though. It hurt to the core because we loved each other fiercely. But I didn't hate Rick. I could never hate him."

Lark nodded and put a hand to her heart. *This* was

Roxanne D. Howard

why Pam turned conversations around if they ever wandered to her side of the family and her childhood. "I didn't know you grew up like that, Mom. Oh, my God. When you said your parents were dead, it never crossed my mind it might be something else. What made you stay, though, after what happened with Dad?"

Pam crossed her arms. "You, your brother, the potential downfall of the company. It wasn't doing too well at the time his affair came out in the open, and if I pressed for a divorce and alimony, your dad would have given it to me in a heartbeat but gone into bankruptcy in the process. I couldn't cripple him, not after how hard he'd worked to build everything. And I couldn't do it to us as a family, no matter what it cost me or my pride. I've never been made of as strong a moral fiber as you, honey."

Lark leaned in and gave her a hug, aching for her. "*So* not true. You have more moral fiber than all of us put together. It's one of the many things I admire about you. What's the old Winnie the Pooh saying, about being stronger than you think you are?" she whispered. Pam laughed through her tears and held on tight.

It was nice, learning about this coveted piece of her mother's past and taking time to reminisce. Every second of her professional life tight-roped between a hectic schedule and impossible deadlines. Beyond company-related discussions, there was no time to talk or connect with anyone in this warm way. Lark frowned, and she pulled away from Pam. That wasn't a good thing.

She prided herself on not being the kind of person to phone in sick or take time off work due to menial colds or flu, but she wished she'd taken one sick day,

180

one day to herself, to do what *she* wanted to do, and not have to worry about being everywhere at precise times and places. It was a good thought to have, like a relaxing balm to her spirit.

Several hours later, Lark heard the front door upstairs open, and heavy footsteps trod through the house.

"Must be the boys back from the lake." Pam set the open photo album in her lap. Lark sat on the floor with her legs tucked under her to the side, leaning her elbow on the couch. "I want a cigarette bad," Lark confessed. Her fingers wobbled.

Pam considered her. "Well, the option's open if you want to quit so soon. The gas station's not too far. If you feel like you're dying, you can go get some. But why don't you try sucking on a piece of hard candy instead?"

"Now, there's an oxymoron if I ever heard one. I'll exchange something that stains my teeth for something that rots my teeth." Lark stood and stretched.

"Well, try it. What have you got to lose? I put a bag of butterscotch candies in the drawer beside the stove. And I don't think Charles will mind about your teeth. He is British, after all."

Lark turned on the bottom step. "Aren't you going to say hello and see how it went?"

Pam put the photos they'd separated into different boxes. "No. The second I do, I'll be cleaning and steaming Aaron's fish. I'm going to enjoy normal smells while I still can. You go on up. I'll be there in a while."

"Okay." Lark paused on the stairs, alone, and closed her eyes as gratitude washed over her. She hadn't spent that level of quality time with her mother in almost a decade. She placed a palm to her heart, smiled, and continued climbing.

Once on the main floor, she struggled not to go to the gas station for cigarettes and instead went to the kitchen. In the drawer her mother mentioned, she ferreted out a few packs of candies. She peeled open the wrapper of a butterscotch candy and popped it into her mouth, then tossed the wrapper in the garbage. It was a step-up from the grapefruit juice, but then again, *anything* was.

Aaron came around the corner with a big grin on his face. The silvery, cold smell of fish permeated the air. He was dirty and kicked his boots off. He carried a small cooler.

Bandit followed at his heels, meowing, purring, and meowing again, his tail as bushy as a squirrel's and curling like a question mark.

Her brother grinned from ear to ear.

"Hey," she greeted, suspicious of his overcheerful countenance.

He tried to keep a straight face but failed.

"What?" She grew suspicious there might be something on her face, or there was about to be from the twinkle in his eye.

Aaron set the cooler on the counter beside the sink and led her by the crook of the arm into the corner of the kitchen by the back door.

He glanced over his shoulder, lowering his voice as he spoke. "Okay, I'm going to get this out fast." He breathed. "Charles went upstairs to take a shower."

"Why?" she asked, recalling a showered Charles a few hours ago.

"He fell in the lake, checking out his reflection," he managed before he broke down. She joined in his jubilee before she could stop herself; his laugh was infectious.

Struggling to keep a straight face, she sucked in her cheekbones and controlled her facial muscles as much as she could. It was a losing battle. "Are you serious?"

"Yes. I swear I didn't do anything. Here," he said, taking out his cell phone.

"From the power cruiser?" she frowned, looking at the video Aaron showed her. The fall must have winded him, as the boat was at least four feet above the water.

"No, no, no. Dad's wooden rowboat. A new one Jim Patton made special a few years ago, varnished and everything."

"You took him out in a *rowboat*?"

"Shh," Aaron appealed to her, checking over her shoulder for signs of Charles. "Lark, I swear I wasn't being funny. I wanted to get to know him, so I took him to the old spot Dad and I used to go to." He held back a grin. "I had cast a line and sat there watching the lake. He noticed how crystal clear the water was, and he checked out the mountain in it. At least I thought he did. Then I thought he saw a fish, but instead, he picked his teeth, and he pitched in headfirst. Here, watch."

He played the video. It was beyond hilarious. Unable to contain herself, Lark let out a fit of subdued giggles as she watched Charles flip into the water. She covered her mouth in case the noise traveled out of the kitchen.

"I am *so* putting this on YouTube. It'll go viral in an hour."

"Don't you dare. Ha, you little shit. I can't believe

you *stood there* shooting a video instead of helping him."

"Play. Pause. Rewind. Play. Slo-mo. Pause." He teased. "Lark, it was hands down the funniest thing I've seen in a long time. He's, uh, not built for this sort of environment, is he?"

Lark sighed, clutching a stitch in her side as she used the candy in her mouth as a leveraging tool to control her laughter. "He's from London, Aaron. What do you think? I can't believe that. The water must have been freezing. Is he okay? Did he hurt himself?"

"He's *fine*." Aaron chuckled. "The fish were more shocked than he was. He wasn't too happy about it, though. I gave him an extra blanket I keep in the back of the truck. Kept going on about how much his pants are worth, how expensive they'd be to dry-clean. I offered to pay for it, but he blew me off. But it wasn't a wasted journey. I *did* manage to get us dinner." He opened the ice cooler and showed her three large, lifeless trout.

Aaron walked over to the sink to deal with the fish and considered her over his shoulder. "Hey Lark, can I ask you something?"

"Sure." She leaned against the counter.

"Well, after being with the guy for a day… I don't know. He doesn't seem like the kind of guy I picture you—are you happy with him?" he blurted.

Uncomfortable, Lark walked over to the fridge, opened it, and fiddled around with food she did not have one iota of interest in. "What kind of ham-handed question is that?" She turned and closed the door. "Of course I am. I wouldn't be with him if I wasn't. Why?"

He shrugged. "I don't know. We were out there for

like three hours, and the conversation never went past cars, money, and clout. He didn't act like I was even there. The guy's *into* himself. I mean, I guess you both have that in common. You both love him."

She shook her head, hurt, as he cleaned the fish. What sucked about the whole situation was he was absolutely right.

Aaron lowered his eyebrows with concern, as though he heard her. "I don't mean to upset you, but I won't apologize for having an opinion. I'm a no-holds-barred kind of guy, okay, and the guy's up his own ass. He's a textbook narcissist, Lark. You and he just don't make sense to me."

She frowned. "Aaron, you don't know Charles like I do, he's—he's—" She couldn't surmise in so many words what Charles was when she most needed to, because boy, did she have her doubts. Her brother turned around, his face filled with regret. She was pretty sure he knew he'd struck a major chord. He turned the faucet off.

"Mom should be in pretty soon to gut the fish. I better get cleaned up. Trout tonight," he said, patting her shoulder on his way out.

He and Pam were two opposite ends of her frustration spectrum. She craved some alone time in her UY office, a few pistachio nuts, and okay, a dream of Niall or two wouldn't hurt. An hour later, Charles still hadn't come down. Knowing him well enough to know he would prefer to lick his wounds alone, Lark settled in the library and curled up on the sofa with *Pride and Prejudice*, a book she hadn't read in many years.

The wind intensified outside her safe haven. She read on as the wind whooshed against the panes. The hiss of the stainless-steel steamer and the smell of warming fresh trout soaked in lemon juice and parsley flakes floated over to her from the kitchen. Contentment stole over her, and she relaxed. No matter how bad it got, there was always home-cooked food.

Engrossed in a chapter, she didn't notice Charles had come into the room. As she let out a yawn, he took the book from her hands and plopped dramatically on the other side of the couch. He lay on his stomach and rested his face in her lap. He'd changed into jeans and a dark-gray, long-sleeved top.

"Long day?" she mused.

"Rub my back," he pouted, his handsome face scowling as he turned it to the side.

"I heard what happened," she said. "You okay?"

Charles made a sound through his nose akin to a neigh. He turned over on his back and sulked up at her, his styled hair too crisp with gel to run her fingers through. She settled for rubbing his cheek.

"What's the point of fishing? It's some bored twat sitting around in a lake, getting wet," he moped.

A small smile played on her lips. "Fishing is kind of a spectator sport, like baseball. It's something you have to absorb and experience. Let the action come to you."

"Well, I'd ruddy well call falling in the lake absorbing it, wouldn't you?" He glowered at her.

"Oh, come on, Charles. You have to admit: it was classic."

"Your brother's a bit simpleminded, isn't he?" he blazed back.

Lark stopped stroking the side of his face. "He *happens* to have a 4.0 GPA and a full academic scholarship. He might be a wise ass, but he's smart as a whip."

Charles exhaled, put out. "Whatever. I had a bad day, and I'm stuck here in Hicksville until Monday with no... *Kiss me*," he ordered, readjusting the back of his muscular neck on her leg and tilting his head up. "We haven't been together in over a month now," he emphasized, putting his hand beneath her thigh and rubbing it with his thumb. "Give me something to go on here, Lark. Anything."

Despite her annoyance, she deemed falling in the lake worthy of a kiss, and as she leaned her head down to him, he cupped his hand around the back of her neck and drew her face closer. He kissed her, passionate and hungry, prodding her lips open with his eager tongue. It was too much at once after so long. He invaded her nice, quiet sanctuary.

After a moment of his bold, passionate kisses, despite her guilt at what had happened to him, what happened with Niall, she broke apart.

"Wait," she breathed.

"God, *what*?" he asked, irritated. "What is going *on* with you? You're turning into a damned country bumpkin or something out here, and you won't let me near you."

Lark touched the back of her neck. She couldn't pretend she didn't know or suspect. "Tell me the truth. What is going on with you and Gemma?"

He blew a harsh breath out and put a hand to his forehead. "Not this again."

"Yes, *this* again. I want a straight answer. Stop deferring it."

"I've *told* you," Charles growled.

"No, you haven't. You've avoided the question countless times. I want to know."

"You want to know what? Did I fuck her?"

Lark flinched at his cold tone of voice and moved his head off her lap. He sat up with a frown.

"Did you?"

He snarled at her. "Yes! Okay? Yes, I *shagged* Gemma. Many times. You're telling me you're surprised, after the way you neglect me?"

Lark shook her head, flabbergasted. "The way I n— H-how long has it been going on? Have there been others?"

The worst part wasn't the question. It was the silence after, which was answer enough. Trembling, she stood and walked toward the mirror above the fireplace, tears stinging her eyes. "I guess I have my answer," she said, twisting off her engagement ring. She extended her arm and took a step backward, holding it out to him, trying to keep it together. "Here. It's over."

He took the proffered ring as though he expected it and pocketed it. At least he had the grace to appear contrite. "I'm sorry, for what it's worth. I didn't want you to find out like this."

She snorted. "Oh, you're *good*. You know what? I think you didn't want me to find *out*, period." She paused. Shit. Could she have an STD? "Wait. Did you use protection?"

"Excuse me?"

"With those women. I deserve to know. I've *never* been with anyone but you, and for all I know, I could be infected with something if you've been sleeping around."

"No," he countered firmly. "I used a condom every

time I shagged someone. I insisted on it. The women were clean. You needn't worry."

"Well, bully for you," she snapped. "I'm having a hard time believing Gemma was clean."

"She *is*," he insisted. "She gets tested once every three to six months."

Lark shook her head, cackling at the irony. "Oh, I'll *bet* she does. She'd have to, considering she's slept with half of London. *And* you." She turned to the side, wishing the bitter tears would go away. He didn't deserve them. The last thing she was going to do was fall apart in front of him.

"Lark," he said softer, "you were too busy for me after you got promoted. You have to understand; I'm a man. I have needs."

"Unbelievable. And that makes it okay to *shag someone else* because you have needs? You—"

"I needed attention—for the love of... God, why don't you move in already, O'Hagan?"

She glanced in the mirror, and there stood Niall, unease written across his face, as though he was uncertain of what he'd walked in on.

Lark lowered her face so Niall couldn't see her tears in the mirror, and Charles remained seated with the exception of crossing his ankle over his knee, his face irate.

"What do you want, O'Hagan?" he seethed.

"Charles," Lark reproved, wiping her eyes as she tried to collect herself, half turning. "It's *Niall*."

Niall stood a few feet away from the couch, close to where he'd entered, and held a stack of papers, his eyes scanning her face. He gave Charles a warning look. "I have to check for a file I'm after in the office," he said in a tight voice. "I'll be there if I'm needed." His gaze fell upon her, but she turned to hide her face from him.

They waited while he crossed the room into the office. Charles huffed and stood. "There's no peace in this damned house. You *never* have time for me," he whispered harshly.

Her jaw dropped. "*I* never have time for *you*? You're the one who works late and goes on extended weekend conferences. Except now I know it was a lie, and what you've really been do—"

"You're damned right! I *deserve* to get some. You're too focused on being Little Miss Perfect with your perfect assistant. You don't care about fulfilling my needs. Gemma does, and she likes to please me. I can do whatever I want to her."

She shook with anger. "I see. Never mind the fact my dad died, and for the first time in our relationship, I need you. I never ask you for anything, Charles. *Anything.* But it's about your damned libido getting what it wants, whenever it wants, is that it?" Charles screwed his face up, angrier than she'd ever seen him, and it scared her.

"I'm going to take a long walk to stop me from saying something I shouldn't right now."

"You've said enough." She hated crying. "It's over between us."

"You're mistaken. We're not done," he snarled and stormed out of the house.

Sobbing, Lark sat on the couch and stared at a bookcase through blurred vision.

"*Aha.* Got it." Niall's voice came from the next room.

She picked up her discarded book and opened it as he approached, lowering her head and pretending to read.

"Sorry if I interrupted there, Shakespeare."

"You're fine." She turned a page her eyes didn't focus on, wishing her voice wasn't so nasal.

"But *you're* not."

She blinked, and he stood in front of her. He knelt before her and reached out to touch the side of her face, wiping her tears with his thumb.

"It's—it's nothing that concerns you," she tried to say, but her voice broke with constrained emotion.

He stroked her face, exhaled through his nose and took a seat next to her. He leaned forward and laced his fingers together over his knees.

"Maybe you're right. I should mind me own business. But if he was idiot enough to cheat on *you*, he doesn't deserve you."

"I broke off the engagement. We're done." She wept. "He's been sleeping around for who knows how long, and we've been together six fucking years. Some relationship that turned out to be, huh?"

"Don't beat yourself up about it, Shakespeare. Certain men have higher standards than others regarding relationships."

She'd had the last of what she could take, and she used him, angry and needing an outlet. "He was the first man, the *only* man, I ever slept with. What would you know about being in a relationship? Didn't you say it's been—?"

"Twelve years." Sadness flickered in his eyes.

Lark shut her eyes. She wanted to hide from this pain, to curl into a fetal position and not surface for weeks. "Niall, I'm sor—"

He took her hands in his and held them with both of his. "Don't. It's okay. Let's...let's sit here a moment."

She and Charles never sat in comfortable silence. They had at first, but over the years, it became more about being on time for things, going out with their respective friends, and giving each other distance, like being alone together for longer than five minutes was a chore.

Niall massaged her fingers, and she closed her eyes. The blood between her metacarpals heated and circulated, and relief traveled up her forearm, sending soothing endorphins through her. She sighed and leaned into him. When his fingertips feathered down her palm, and a surge of desire shot straight to her pussy, she tried to pull away, but he moved closer and took her hands in his again.

"No, relax. You deserve this."

Pleasant shivers erupted as she recalled a dream in which he'd said the same thing that his eyes now conveyed to her. *You deserve to be loved.* After a moment, warm, full lips pressed against hers in a kiss meant to comfort. Her eyes fluttered closed. The kiss ended way too soon.

"You *deserve* this," he repeated in a low voice, "If you belonged to me, I'd make it my mission to ensure you felt happy and loved, every single day, for the rest of your life."

She opened her eyes and glanced at his lips, wishing she could kiss them again. She licked her bottom lip. In one swift motion, he grabbed the back of her neck and pulled her toward him. She squeaked in surprise, but he drew her closer and planted his lips on hers in a solid kiss. There was nothing subtle or friendly about this kiss. If it had been a violent, angry liplock—as Charles was sometimes prone to do—she would have protested, but Niall's mouth was a sensual playground of delight. He nibbled at her lower lip, tugging it between his own as he tasted her. She couldn't help but respond to him as pleasant tingles warmed her pussy even more. He was the best kind of medicine, and she wanted more.

She slid her hands over his shirt, mapping the contours of his broad chest, and moved them to his forearms, where the delineations of his defined muscles pressed out. His strong hands roamed her back, comforting and arousing.

As she softened into his hold, he deepened the kiss, stroking his tongue against hers carefully, enticing it with gentle exertion as he tasted her. Lark's nipples tingled at the familiar taste she remembered from her dreams of oranges and chocolate. Her tears stopped. She was safe. This was Niall. He'd never hurt her. She wanted to moan, to express the effect he had on her, but she feared someone would hear. Or Charles would walk back in. She stayed as quiet as she could, touching her tongue to his, stroking it, letting him inveigle her into accepting this for the comfort it was.

And it went much farther than comfort.

She slid her arms around his neck and pulled him closer as he made her more and more unaware of anything and everything but him. *Hold me*, she wanted to say, but he already did. *Touch me*. As if he heard her unspoken demand, he kissed her deeper, cradling her face in his warm hands before gliding them over her neck and shoulders. From her back, Niall grabbed a fistful of her shirt and dragged her onto his lap.

Lark swung her leg over his lap, straddling him. *Make me forget.* Her breath came out erratic, and her heart pounded. He must be able to hear it. The hardness of his cock pressed into her through their clothes, and she gasped into his mouth. Niall groaned. He consumed her mouth with more ruthless kisses that left her breathless and yearning. His drugging kisses made it easier not to think about the ramifications of what they were doing, whether he intended to or not.

Overcome by the need to be closer, Lark lifted and lowered herself, rubbing her pussy against his cock as she kissed him. He growled into her mouth and slid his hands possessively down her back, into her jeans and inside her panties. He clutched her ass. He thrust against her, moving her toward him as he swayed torturously against her.

"We should stop," she whispered between kisses. He sucked her neck, and she gasped as wetness coursed through her pussy. This was way beyond out of control.

"I know." His dark curls touched her forehead. He slid his long fingers farther beneath her bottom, searching until they found her wet and responsive pussy. He buried his face deep in the crevice of her neck and groaned, clawing his fingers into her wetness, stroking it around her slit. "I know, but I can't, Lark. I love being close to you, and your pussy is so hot and wet for me. I can't tell you what that does to me."

Her body on fire, Lark looked frantically around to make sure they were alone and then lifted so he could move his hand around, to grant him better access.

She bit her lip as he moved his hand to her pussy

again and inserted two fingers into her nectar. Shaking, she rested her forehead on his shoulder and closed her eyes as he slowly pumped in and out of her, the friction delicious and tight. After so many dreams of this, nothing compared with the real thing. She couldn't think of anything but how amazing he made her feel.

She whispered his name as she milked her inner walls around him. He drew his fingers out, then thrust them forward, hard. She tensed her thighs on either side of him, grinding against him as her breath came in sharp gasps.

"I want you, Lark," he breathed into her hair. "I want to be with you."

He plunged his fingers in and out of her, fucking her, building a frenzied rhythm. All she could do was shiver, nod, hold on, and grip him tighter. He quickened his pace, jolting her body with each movement, impacting her front wall with each hit. His mouth claimed hers again, and she lost herself in the exploration of his tongue and his hand cupping and squeezing her breast as blood rushed into her sex in response to his ministrations.

Without warning, he flipped her over on the couch, climbed over her, and unbuttoned her jeans.

"We can't, not in here," she begged. He nodded, a dark tendril falling onto his face.

"Then I'm going to please you, make you come," he whispered, sliding his hand beneath her panties and commencing to do so. She shouldn't use him like this; he didn't deserve it. But his thumb pinpointed her clit, and her head fell back. He rubbed the tip of his fingernail over it, and she was in another world. He lifted her shirt with his other hand, pulled down a bra cup, and sucked the nipple into his mouth. He licked and sucked her, thrusting into her pussy, bringing her to the height of pleasure. Lark hooked her ankle over his foot, arched her back, and met his thrusts. Shaking, she exploded, warm wetness flowing out of her with her orgasm. She came so hard her vision blurred. He collapsed half on her, breathing deep and kissing her neck.

He took her hand and entwined their fingers, and they lay together in silence until their breathing returned to normal. She held on to him, not wanting to think, not wanting to move.

Pam's voice from a few rooms over hollered dinner was ready. They pulled apart and got clumsily to their feet. Niall helped her straighten her clothes. His eyes took her in.

"Lark, I'm sorry to complicate things, but I'm not sorry for this."

He leaned forward and kissed her, his heart in his eyes.

"Never for this. Don't regret it. I *never* will."

He kissed her once more, put a hand to her cheek lovingly, and bent to collect his file from the floor. Then he left the room.

She watched him leave, and a strong, pulsing hunger coursed through her.

She'd never have enough of him.

****

After she'd cleaned and joined everyone in the kitchen, Charles sat at the table. So. He'd returned to the house. She opted to give him the silent treatment over dinner. It worked. She had used it in the past when he'd come home drunk or had been acting like a jerk, but his indifference stung in a way which made her skin crawl. Why had she never noticed he was this callous? She picked at her food. As a younger woman, she'd been inexperienced, virginal, naïve, impressionable, and flattered that a man so good-looking would be interested in her. Had she truly stopped to question if they were right for one another? She'd been swept up in her new London career, too enchanted with the possibility of what lay before her to doubt his sincerity or if they were compatible. She'd pushed reasonable doubt to the back of her mind.

Niall was quiet and subdued and left halfway through, saying he had work to do. He seemed to sense she wanted space after what had happened, which she was thankful for. He scooted back his chair, and she met his eyes. He gave her a look charged with longing before he left the room. She wanted him in a painful, desperate way, and though he returned it, she knew he wouldn't push. After supper, Charles retired to the office to brood, which suited her just fine. She turned in early, too emotionally spent to be good company to anyone.

****

Lark awoke late on Friday morning and took her time getting ready. Charles's betrayal stung to the heart of her. She'd let her guard down in front of him after moving to London and had given him so much during a most vulnerable time. To think he had betrayed her this deeply was unfathomable.

She sighed. It was hard for her to work out what Niall was to her. She wasn't the type of girl to ever label someone "rebound guy," nor did she think he fit anywhere close to that category. After dreaming about him, then meeting him in the flesh and getting to know him, being with him—he meant more. Much more. And it frightened her.

She popped her head into Charles's room on the way downstairs to try to break the ice but found it empty and the curtains open.

"Hey," she greeted Aaron as she came downstairs.

He sat on a love seat in the visiting room, reading a textbook and making notes in the margins.

"Hi, sis." He continued scribbling.

"Getting ready to go back?"

"Yeah, I'm driving back Monday."

"Ouch. Nine to ten hours is a hard drive. Are you going to stop anywhere?"

"Nah. Just for food and meals. I prefer to drive straight through and get there. If I leave at first light, I'll get back on campus by six. But it's cool. I enjoy the scenic route."

Lark leaned against the wall. *I'll miss you*, she wanted to say. The house wouldn't be the same without his boisterous spirit. The soft tick of the grandfather clock against a nearby wall echoed softly. "Well, be careful on your way back."

Aaron smirked into his notes. "Yes, Mom."

"Wiseass. Where is Charles?"

"In the gym downstairs. He went about half an hour ago."

"Thanks," she said, heading for the basement. He'd left the door to the gym cracked open. She opened it and entered the large room, which had been modernized. She remembered it as having a lonely exercise bike and a TV her dad had used.

Two fans sat in opposite corners of the room and

were on full blast. The well windows were also ajar. Blue floor mats had replaced the carpet. A large, black-and-chrome exercise station occupied the middle of the room, and many different pieces of workout equipment aligned the mirrored walls. Charles was in The Zone as he lay on the black bench press. His discarded shirt lay on the floor beside him. Sweat covered his skin as the muscles bunched and contracted as he pumped iron. He strained as he resisted, pushing the bar he held up. A vein stood out in the middle of his forehead as he returned the disk-laden bar back to its cradle on the bench, then sucked in deep breaths and rested his hands on his chest.

"Hi," he grunted, breathing hard.

Lark moved into the room and over to his side. So, this was where he hid when he wasn't monopolizing her dad's office. She noticed an empty plastic water bottle and his cell phone in the cup holder of the stationary bike.

She curled her hand around the edge of the bench-press bar. "Aaron told me where you were. Have you been working out while you've been here?"

Still panting, he nodded and laid a hand on her hip, ogling her with unabashed lust. "A couple of times. I couldn't sleep at first. GMT's a world apart from PST." Charles's dark eyes darted to the open door. He swung upright and locked his arms around her waist. "Can we pretend the last three days didn't happen?"

Lark glared and pushed at his shoulders, but he tightened his hold. Her arms ached.

"Come on," he urged. "Clean slate, you and I. No one's here. We have the basement to ourselves, and I haven't had you in forever." In one swift movement, he drew her onto his lap and traced his hand down her front.

"Charles, no. *No*," she hissed, shoving his arm away. She stood. "I mean, what are you *smoking*? I found out yesterday you're screwing your secretary—and I'm guessing many others—and I'm supposed to be *okay* with it? How do you expect me to forget? Do you *know* me?"

He shrugged, assessing her with those same calculating eyes he reserved for tough meetings. "I know you better than you'd think, babe. It's *you* who's lost your sense of perception while you've been over here." He considered her, as though trying to figure something out. "Why not channel your anger at me into passion? It might make you feel better, and I bet it'll improve our sex life. Take it out on me. I don't mind."

She shook her head, incredulous. "Our se—are you *kidding* me? I know who'll feel better if I do, and it won't be *me*. Jeez, the whole point in coming here to find you was so we could at least have a conversation and make arrangements about my moving out of the flat. I'm sure we can at least be civil about this, Charles. Can't you—"

"Lark? Just, shut up. *Shut up.*" He rubbed his forehead as though he had a headache.

Stunned, her jaw dropped. Charles advanced and yanked her forward, seizing her mouth. She was too dumbfounded to object right away, and Charles pulled her onto the floor. He rolled on top of her and kissed her hard. She protested and fought, but he was heavy, and his hands trapped her wrists. Her weight was no match against his.

His assaulting kisses came at her too demanding

and fast, and he seemed to be in his own world, murmuring as he undid the top buttons of her blouse, "Come on, baby. Mmm, I'm hard, so hot for you…"

Lark bucked beneath him as hard as she could and, once she'd gotten him to take off his weight, rolled to the side and held up a hand to ward him off. "W-whoa. Stop it right now. What?"

"Huh?" he asked, coming out of his spell and breathing hard.

"What did you say?"

Charles sighed as he loomed above her with his hands caging the floor on either side of her face. His thick, sweaty hair fell forward. "I said I'm hot for you. What? You're ruining this, Lark. *This* is what I'm talking about when I say I have needs. I want to get some action here. Give a bloke a break."

Lark closed her mouth and frowned at him. This wasn't the guy she'd fallen in love with. He'd never really understood her. "Get off me. *Right now*."

He stayed there as if he might not. Then he rolled off to his side in a huff and watched her stand.

She took a deep breath and pointed a finger at him. "You are on thin, *thin* ice with me right now. I don't want you anywhere near me. Do you understand? It's *over*. I want you to figure out where you're going to stay while I get a new place. At Gemma's, your mate's, a damned hostel if need be, but I don't want you there when I get back. I'm moving out, and that's the bottom line."

Lark stormed out of the basement and hurried upstairs to the bathroom by the kitchen, where she could be alone.

She ripped open the door to her safe haven and

jumped. Niall jumped as well. He was in the middle of shaving, and his clean white work shirt and white T-shirt hung over the towel rack. Pretending not to look was out of the question. His defined chest had a black tattoo obscured by his left bicep, and it all but screamed at her to stare. In a second that stretched forever, she gulped drily, trying to get a grip, and fought the urge to lick her lips at his ripped abs. A striped, dark-green-and-white towel was draped over his shoulder, and a small silver electric razor buzzed in his hand less than an inch from his face as he turned from the mirror to her. He lifted his eyebrows at the close call and set the razor down, letting out a low whistle before he turned it off and unplugged it. *Great, I can't be alone even for a second.*

While Niall stowed away his things, she tried not to let her gaze linger on his bulging shoulder muscles shifting beneath delectable skin. His damp hair curled around his face. Had he come from the shower? A blush stained his cheeks.

Lark put her hand behind her neck and closed her eyes. "Sorry."

"Now, that's what I call a close shave." Niall wiped the left side of his face with the damp hand towel, considering her. "I was doing me neck literally a second ago. If you'd been any quicker or more alarming, I'd have a scar. Might be an interesting image, though, Irish and dangerous. Your, erm, blouse is open," he said, pointing to her open shirt. She glanced down. The upper half of her white lace bra and her breasts peeked over the top of the cups. His finger grazed one as he closed the edges of the blouse, but then he tensed like a dog sensing an intruder. "You're upset."

"N-no, I'm not."

His green eyes glittered, and a muscle in his jaw tightened. He stepped closer. "Yes, you are. I can feel it. Are you all right?"

"I'm okay." Lark buttoned up, avoiding his eyes, but he got in her face, worried, his warm skin inches from her own, and his apprehension settled like a thick fog around her. "I *am*."

His palm cupped her cheek, soft and warm. "Lark, did he hurt you?"

Now there was a loaded question. She leaned her cheek into his hand and shook her head. "We had an argument about the flat. I put my foot down and told him he needed to find another place to stay while I worked on moving out. I'm fine." His gaze searched hers, then dropped and did a scan of her body. She stroked his bicep, trying to reassure him. "I'm *fine*, Niall. You'd know if I wasn't."

She was grateful when he nodded. He cleared his throat and turned to put on his T-shirt and slide his arms through his white work shirt, though he left it unbuttoned. He collected his things on the counter.

"Why are you using this bathroom to shave, anyway?" she asked as she straightened her blouse and smoothed a hand over the back of her disheveled hair. Okay, it was rude to kick him out, but right now, her need was greater than his for a place to retreat.

"The power outlet is out downstairs," he said as he zipped his black mesh Dopp kit. It likely had more to do with Charles being there, but she nodded in support. "I tried to reset the breaker for the bathroom, but it didn't work. Must be a shortage in the system somewhere. I have my tool belt in the SUV. I'll see if I can fix it when I have a minute. I'll leave you in peace." He sidled past her.

Their bodies brushed against each other as she turned, trying to get past him, and he drew in a sharp breath as the tips of her nipples grazed his chest. They hardened into tight peaks. Oh my God, did he smell wonderful.

"Steady on there, woman."

Niall closed his eyes and rubbed his nose against hers while putting his hand on her hip. She wore no perfume, but she might as well have been lying in a fragrant rose bath from the way his eyes lit up with desire. She tilted her head up, and he stole a kiss from her lips.

They paused, pressed together, then turned to untangle themselves in the narrow doorway. She raised her head and met Niall's gaze. A soulful light danced in his emerald eyes.

They stood there breathing heavily, and she teetered on the brink of losing it. If he kissed her again, she'd climb all over him. She cleared her throat. "Uh, Niall, this isn't rocket science. You're there, I'm here. I want to get into the bathroom. Please."

"It's all yours, Shakespeare." He surrendered, breaking away from her with a glance at her breasts.

Lark swore off men forever and shut the door in his face.

Chapter Eleven
The Stone

Niall left for Portland soon after their encounter, and Charles had stepped outside to smoke and now watched the mounted flat screen in the living room. He'd passed her in the hallway earlier upstairs after his shower. He'd taken her hand and said, "I'm sorry about earlier," then descended the stairs without another word. He gave her space. She appreciated his knowing when to back off, but certain actions could never be erased. It scared her. Her life in England would never be the same.

She skipped lunch, too mentally distracted. Sitting by the fireplace, she checked out real-estate websites she'd bookmarked for London flats on her smartphone, but despite how much she made, they were all exorbitantly priced. She wanted to make a clean break with Charles, but it seemed foolish to throw away a career she'd worked hard for and achieved so much in, because of one failed relationship. Then there was the lingering guilt which gnawed away at her over what she and Niall were doing. There was no doubt what her body and heart wanted. It would be great to be able to go for it with him, but a sense of shame preyed upon her, paralyzing her with indecision. She hated herself for it, for being anything like her father. Until now, she'd had a clear vision about her life's direction.

She sighed. Maybe she'd go for a horseback ride. Something to take her mind off things, get her outside.

She went upstairs and changed into jeans and a shirt, then hurried downstairs. She paused at the living-room doorway.

"I'm going out for a horseback ride."

Charles nodded while watching *Survivor*.

She caught up with her brother, who moved a saddle from the fence post inside the stables to the flank of the Appaloosa in the pen next to him.

"Hey," he greeted her. "I'm going for one last ride before I have to drive back."

"Great. Just what I came out to do. Can I ride with you?"

"Sure." He seemed thrilled. "You want to take Penny again?"

Lark nodded, spotting the gray mare watching them with her head over her gate a few pens down.

Her brother slapped the top of the pen enthusiastically and reached over to plunk his black Stetson onto Lark's head. "'Bout time. I've wanted to do loads of stuff with you since you got here, but with the will and everything, it kind of didn't happen." He glanced at what she wore. "You may want to take this. It's cold up there," he said, unhooking a large, deerskin jacket with tassels from its peg on the wall. She'd seen him wear it a few times before coming in from the stables. She slipped it on. Tentlike, it kept her comfortable and warm.

Aaron grinned. "We have a Jane Wayne in the making."

Lark stuck her tongue out at him and helped him get the horses ready.

Their ride was unhurried and relaxed, unlike last time, but they went farther up the hillside than they had before. The wet smell of the light morning rain upon the pines seeped out their natural, fresh fragrance, and though it was chill and damp, the breeze was cool as their horses worked, each hoof crunching fallen, dead leaves as they clambered along the thin paths side by side.

Upon reaching the top, Lark and Aaron let the horses rest, getting off and tying their reins to a tree.

"Come on," he said. "I want to show you something."

He led her around a large boulder, and she gasped. A panoramic spread stood before her where the ridge dropped off. The wide-open sky was patched over in areas with clouds, but there was still enough sunlight. As a young girl, on a camping outing, she'd stare at the skies, where the colors from the great gems of the world came out together to dazzle when the sun rose and set, and at night, the hidden treasure diamonds revealed themselves, glistening in the dark.

Their father took her and her mother out to a field when she was nine with a pair of large, infrared binoculars and had told them to turn off their flashlights and gaze at the stars. Immersed in the darkness, seeing the night sky through the binoculars, had transported her to a magical moment, where the shadows surrounding them in the field took form, and the incredible, incandescent stars had souls, rendering her small, yet significant.

Below her and Aaron for as far as the eye could see were tall, majestic conifers so green they seemed blue. The tops of cabins and properties scattered around the countryside, and an interstate snaked its way around the hills in the distance.

"There." Her brother pointed. She followed his finger and hitched a breath. The ranch house spread out far below, rustic and inviting.

"Wow," was all she could say, and though she loved the English language, she could find no words adequate enough to describe what lay before her.

"Makes you feel small in the scheme of things, doesn't it?" Aaron asked. "Like our problems, everything that crops up day-to-day, don't mean anything compared to this."

Lark put a hand to her heart, surveying the ranch house with fond memories. Despite the more recent, unpleasant ones, it was still the place she learned in, matured in, was safe in. *Home.*

"Aaron?"

"Hmm?"

She almost didn't say it, but she had to. It had been in the back of her mind since she came home, but she had no idea how to say it. The solace of the mountain gave her the courage to. "Do—do you resent me? For leaving, when you were so young?"

He let out a whoosh, took off his hat, and rustled his light hair with his hand. "What? Nah. No, I never blamed you. I mean, at first, I assumed you were busy with college. You were always deep in it whenever Mom and I visited you at Berkeley. When I was like fourteen, and you got into grad school, I asked Mom one day why you never came around, and she took me up here and told me about Dad. She didn't bother sugarcoating it either. I don't blame you, Lark. I wasn't there and have no clue how it made you feel. Hell, if it had been me, I'd have punched him."

"Yeah, well, I'm not going to lie. I thought about it." Lark smirked. She nudged his shoulder with hers. "Thanks, Aaron. I love you guys. I never wanted to leave you, or Mom. I hope you understand that…" She looked out at the mountains.

"I know. You don't have to say anything. It's cool."

"Thanks," she whispered, patting his hand.

"You want to go back?" he asked after a while.

"Give me another minute." Aaron nodded and went to tend the horses, leaving her alone. She leaned against a boulder and gazed out.

It was for the best she made a clean break from Charles. Even if he'd never cheated, she would never be able to share any of this with him. He came from a different background and had no interest in ascending anything that did not begin with *corporate* and end with *ladder*. This would belong to her alone.

Lark lifted her head.

"I don't know if I'll ever see you again," she said down to the ranch, small as an ant beneath the ridge. *But you'll stay in my heart forever.*

Once they returned from the trail, Lark and Aaron walked their horses the last hundred meters to the stables to give them a well-deserved break.

Aaron slowed his pace. "Did you ever think…" Lark turned to him, her eyebrow raised. "Did you ever think Dad had a plan when he left you the house?"

In the sidewalks of her mind, green shoots of possibility emerged from the cracks in the ground. She could choose to stay, to keep it. She could uproot her life and start fresh, but London had become her stronghold after her family life went south. She didn't know if she wanted to give that up. Or if she should.

Aaron continued. "See, I've been thinking the last couple of days. Maybe it was like him saying he didn't want us to follow the paths we'd set for ourselves. It could be he wanted us to break out of our comfort zones and, I don't know, develop or something."

"I've no idea why he left us what he did. I know he loved to stir things up. This was one way to do it, without a doubt. But I...I don't belong here."

"You sure?" he asked. "Because you seem at home to me. *Appleyloothas*." He laughed as she gave him a playful punch as they approached the stables. The wind almost blew the black Stetson off her head, and she anchored it with her hand. She noticed someone watching them from the open stable doors.

"Niall," Aaron called. Lark stopped smiling and put a hand on Penny's neck to steady her. She watched as her brother greeted him.

Niall leaned against the stable doorway still in his shirt and tie, a black tool belt loose about his hips. He clutched a packet of hinges and a screwdriver in one hand.

"You're not breaking stuff again, are you?" Aaron teased as they neared him.

Niall grinned, and his eyes lingered on Lark. "Quite the opposite, lad. I'm waiting for Peter at the Estate Administration to call me back regarding the affidavit Pam and Lark signed a few days ago. He's an old friend. He may be able to speed things along and help it sail right through." He held up the packet of hinges. "Thought in the meantime I'd have a go at fixing the stall your mam's been going on about. Also came out to have a chat," he said to Aaron. "Where'd you go?"

"Crawman's Ridge."

Niall whistled low. "That's a great place to take 'er." Lark shifted beneath his gaze. "What did you think, Shakespeare? Must have been a long time since you've been there. It's charming, eh?"

Lark nodded. "It was nice." Niall's fingers wound around the open barn door, and his long forefinger slid along it in a casual way. He'd used it in a similar fashion on her yesterday. Blood rushed to her cheeks. She ducked her head, handed Penny's reins to her brother, and excused herself.

"Where're *you* goin'?" Aaron asked as she removed the black Stetson from her head and handed it back to him.

"For a walk." She turned toward the trail to the creek and path.

"But you just got back," Niall called. "It's going to get dark soon. Don't you want to rest, or at least get some water?"

"I'll be fine," she replied.

"Wait a sec," said Aaron. He fished inside the saddlebag on Penny's back and threw her a plastic bottle of water.

"Thank you," she told him. "I won't be long."

"Pam's got dinner cooking. Should be on at about six," Niall chimed in.

The knowing glare Niall gave her perturbed her because he understood exactly why she took off. She did care about what he thought of her, but she needed time to herself, even if it did make her look like a coward.

After walking for about five minutes, she discovered she'd left her iPhone in Penny's saddlebag. She'd meant to take it out, but Niall had distracted her. She turned back, wanting to listen to music and drown everything out. The trouble with walking without a partner or having music to listen to was that her brain often kicked into overdrive and she tended to dwell on things. Lark tried to clear her mind, but all she could focus on was Niall's hands. On the way back to the barn, she replayed in her mind their encounter on the couch—the sounds he'd made, how gratified he'd been when she came.

Her happiness affected Niall; it mattered to him. Though she warred with herself and compared her actions to her father's, it bothered her that during their engagement—not even married yet, mind you—Charles never considered her happiness something he had a duty toward. He only seemed to care about himself.

****

The barn door was shut, and no one appeared to be outside. Funny. She hadn't been gone long. She didn't see Penny in the corral, so she slid open the door. Niall. He stood beneath a dangling work lamp, which lifted the darkness from the back of the barn. Niall's shirt and tie were off and draped over a nearby saddle. He wore a snug white T-shirt as he worked, trying to fit the new hinge into the top half of the stall door. She prepared to announce her presence, but the sight of him took her breath away.

The sinewy muscles of his coltish back shifted fluidly beneath his damp T-shirt as he worked the screwdriver, power, and determination clear in the twist of his body. Out of sheer instinct, Lark reached out to trace her fingers over the crevice between his shoulder blades. Her mouth parted as she ghosted her fingertips down the length of his spine. She could smell him, earthy with a whiff of mint. Coupled with the sweet perfume of the pale golden hay, it brought to mind misty Irish mornings and ancient standing stones.

Daring to hope, she placed her palm beneath the hem of his shirt, the flesh on his lower back warm to her touch. It amazed her a man as strong as he could be so tender and loving. She brushed her fingertips along his torso, fascinated. He stood perfectly still, but turned his head to the side, aware of her now. Her insides were hot. She struggled but found it impossible not to touch him.

"Lark…if I turn around right now—" He drew in a staggered breath, and she could tell his eyes were closed. "—if I touch you, are you going to leave?"

Lark shook her head, her hand sliding up his side as she outlined the contours of his shoulder muscles with the other, then realized he couldn't see her. "I won't."

He turned around, pulled the T-shirt over his head, and cast it off. She came eye to eye with his pectoral muscles. She smoothed her hands over them, watching his flat nipples harden in the chilled barn air as they rose and fell with his breath. Lark slid her fingers to the tendons at his neck, splayed them along his collarbone, then glided them along the ridges of his shoulders. Gathering her courage, she met Niall's eyes. He watched her. She wished she could tell him how badly she ached for him, how much she wanted his touch and taste. From the hot-blooded fire in his eyes, though, she wasn't so sure he didn't already have it figured out.

213

The muscle in his jaw moved as he gripped her hips. Locking his eyes with hers, he walked her back to a secluded corner of the barn behind a haystack, where he pressed her against it, leaving no room between their bodies. It was reckless and dangerous, this dance of theirs, but she wanted him. He leaned in.

"Now," he said, his hot breath against her neck making her shiver, his lips a hairbreadth away from her skin. "I know you want to pretend yesterday didn't happen, but I can't. I won't. You're all I can think about."

Lark's breath caught. "I think about you too. More than I should—"

He swooped in and claimed her mouth, a swift, hard press of his lips. He opened her like a flower, and then he mapped a deliberate, unhurried journey with his lips and tongue. He moved farther into the cradle of her hips against the hay, and the blood pulsed in her pussy where his cock pressed into her through their clothes. He cupped her ass, kneading it as he rocked into her. He pulled her thigh around his hip, and she moaned. She moved to tiptoe, letting out a puff of air when the shape of his cock rubbed against her slit.

He moved to nibble her ear. "I have been thinking of you, nonstop, since we met." He licked along the shell of her ear. "You've taken over my head and heart, Lark. I think about being with you, and how you make me feel as a person, as a man. I think about fucking you, over and over." He moved against her with an impassioned sound, and she shivered and wrapped herself around him, her ankle weaving around the back of his.

His palm slapped the haystack right next to her

head. "I want to taste you," he said in her ear, trailing his mouth along the upper curve of her jawline. "Please let me. I can't get enough of you. You're so incredible."

A raw flush of exhilaration shot through her. He wanted her. He *wanted* her, and she needed that, needed *him*.

She clutched his raised forearm, her eyes screwed shut. She nodded, undulating her hips against him like an ocean wave against the sand, a whimper escaping her throat. He groaned in response and captured her mouth, his hands fisting into the hem of her shirt, clutching her ass, everywhere, as he pushed and pulled and kissed her. The low sound he made through his mouth traveled right into the pit of her stomach. He drew back, and then he knelt before her, his long fingers trailing over her breasts and her abdomen.

His fingers trembled as he undid the button on her jeans, and she swayed while he unzipped them and slid them down her legs. He wanted this as much as she did, and knowing so drove her to hurry. She toed off her shoes and held on to his shoulders for steadiness as he helped her step out of them. Desire lit his eyes, and the puff of warm breath he jetted against her pussy set off an arduous throbbing.

As if he could sense her need, Niall moved forward, stroking his hand over her slit through her panties, a featherlight touch. He placed a kiss there, humming against her folds.

"Niall," she whispered, inhaling and carding her hands through his hair.

"Be patient, love. I intend to enjoy this." Her panties had grown damp, the moisture seeping out between her wet lips as though crying out for him. She pressed her knees together to appease the friction, but he shook his head, prying her legs apart.

"No, darling, this is mine. All mine."

He hooked his thumbs into the waistband of her panties and yanked them down. She stepped out of them, and he brought them to his nose, inhaling her scent. He kept his gaze on her as he stowed them in his back trouser pocket. His nostrils flared as he brought her hips close again, his hands clamped around the backs of her thighs.

"Come here, Lark," his said, his voice rough and hungry.

The craving in his eyes floored her. No man had ever looked at her the way he did with such love and raw desire. "What—what are you thinking? Right now, I mean?"

He slid his hands on the backs of her thighs soothingly. "How very much I want to do this," he assured her, his eyes narrowing. "With *you*. Tell me I can. Tell me what you want."

Lark drank him in. Who was she kidding? She pushed the guilt and doubts to the back of her mind. "Fuck me with your mouth, Niall," she said, the sultry voice coming from her lips one she didn't recognize as her own. He gave her a dark, ravenous look, the first full drag of his tongue, soft and warm, swept into her slit and up. She cried out his name and clutched his hair for dear life, letting him take her away.

His lips explored every part of her, stopping only at the tiny button of skin at the top, flicking out his tongue in a rhythmic series of attacks. He sucked her clit with enthusiasm, and she whimpered, pushing against his eager tongue, swiveling into the rhythm of it like an exotic dancer. Her body coiled tight, and she ground her hips against him, her breath fast and heavy. Her skin flushed, itching with the need to be completely undone by this man. He stilled her movements, holding her hips in place with his strong hands as his tongue devoured her. The hay scratched her back, but she was too enraptured to care. He licked a path down her soaked slit, burying his tongue inside her, thrusting in and out. She bucked against him, tangling her fingers in his hair as a surge of pleasure coursed through her.

She rotated her hips against his hot, hungry tongue. "Yes. Your mouth feels so good on me, Niall."

He continued to lick and suck her clit, and two long fingers worked their way inside her. A feral, uninhibited grunt escaped her when he pulled them out and thrust them back in while he ate her out. Oh, he was *good* at this.

"That's right, Lark," he whispered as she cried out. "Let it go."

He stood, not slowing his fingers as they drove in and out of her. The tip of his finger pressed against her wet clit. She opened her mouth to let out a wail, and he kissed her, swallowing the sound. She wrapped her legs around him, and he moved her higher, supporting her ass with one strong hand as his other worked her into a frenzy. "Come for me," he said into her ear.

His fingers curved inside her, reaching the right spot, and when he pressed against it, she gushed over his hand. He brought his hand to his mouth and licked it clean right before her eyes, sucking on his fingers. He savored it, and she was done for.

"You taste incredible."

She was a mess of nerves, fighting to breathe,

fighting to stay up. "Niall, take me." He nodded and smoothed his hand down her back. She helped him yank off his trousers and boxers, rubbing his back as he stepped out of them. He pushed the weeping head of his hard cock against her, the warmth of his body pressing into hers.

"Your heart belongs to me, Lark."

She kissed him, knowing it did. As he entered her, she held her breath. This was about more than just the sex. He cared. He knew the leap she took by loving him after being betrayed. From the way his palms caressed her hips as he moved within her, with each grasp he made of her hip, to the way he enfolded her, told her he cherished what she gave him.

****

Lark blinked. She walked on the trail around the property, and dusk had fallen. She removed the earbuds and turned off the music on her iPhone, pocketing it as she turned toward the house. Oh my, what a dream. There was no shame in daydreaming about him, at least. Dreams were safe, and dreams remained private without the ability to change her life.

She detoured so she could arrive at the back of the house. She sipped the last of her water, and a cold breeze tickled the back of her neck. She looked up. Niall leaned over the patio banister in a contemplative mood. It seemed surreal to see him at his most human. The dreams made him out to be anything but.

She should go; she'd just fantasized about him, for heaven's sake. Like five minutes ago. The porch lights and lampposts glowed as the night sky turned a clear, dark blue, and she almost veered around. But they did need to talk sooner or later about what had happened.

She pulled the brown deerskin jacket closer around her shoulders, braved the steps, and looked anywhere but at him.

"Niall?"

He turned around, distracted. "Oh. Hello there, you. Didn't see you."

He scratched the bridge of his nose with his thumb. He gulped, his gaze on her throat, and she got the weirdest sense he'd been fantasizing about her too.

Keeping her hands in her pockets, Lark lifted her eyebrows, trying to be as casual as she could. "Did you get the gate fixed?" *By the way, I daydreamed you took me on a journey in the barn. It wasn't a dream, by the way. All me. Want to try a reenactment?*

"Yep." His eyes caught the light from a nearby patio light. "Works like a charm. So, I know why I'm out here. Mostly. I'm waiting for your mam's tasty roast beef to beckon me inside with its mouthwatering aroma." He glanced at the deerskin jacket she wore and fingered the suede collar, pulling it closer over her as the chill air settled in. "What's got *you* out here during twilight's tango, Miss Braithwaite? You've scaled a mountain on a horse and returned from a long walk. You sure you're up for another round tomorrow?"

Lark dipped her head. "Oh yes, I'll be fine. Penny did the work, anyway. I'm out, uh, stargazing."

"Ah…" Niall sighed and followed her gaze to the first evening stars. He leaned over the railing and recited: "*And yet, with neither love nor hate, those stars like some snow-white, Minerva's snow-white marble eyes, without the gift of sight.*"

"Frost?"

His face lit up. "And she nails it again. So, down to

business. Other than the magnificent three marble eyes, what else's got you out here?"

Much more than she could tell him. She settled for half the truth. "I wish I could tell Aaron and my mom about what's going on. With Charles, I mean. I don't understand why I can't. It feels like I'm a distant cousin or something. I wish everything could click," she admitted. "It's bizarre, not feeling relaxed enough to open up to them like I know I should be able to."

Niall sighed and leaned forward, clasping his hands together over the banister. "My guess is you're expecting it to be like something out of a Hallmark movie, eh? Truth is, if you go away for a lot of years, you never come back the same. People change. Aaron's different, but so are you. It'll never be the same again, as much as you'd like it to be. People go through adjustments, and there's nothing you can do about it but learn to adapt. Something I learned when my brother came over to visit from across the pond."

"What happened?"

Niall dipped his head and smiled. "We shared a strong bond, my brothers and I. My da passed away when I was five. He went to bed one night and didn't wake up the next mornin'. We found out he had undiagnosed heart disease. He was a grafter; he wouldn't ever go to the doctor unless his arm got broken or something. It's all right," he assured her when she winced. "We got through it. It didn't hit me as hard as the older ones. They remembered him better. Me mam put everything into raising us, making sure we turned into good men. It was barmy when Liam came over here, though, because I don't drink or smoke now, and we couldn't exactly go get drunk together unless he did it all. He'd changed too, more set in his ways, and he had his stubborn village mentality of how things should be. Got after me about 'why have I not remarried or settled with a woman yet,' you know. The point is, no matter how many things might have happened to you or them, they're your family. You have to get to know them for who they are, and trust if you tell them what's going on, they'll be there for you. Don't waste time being someone you're not to appease them."

Lark stayed silent. It was difficult with Aaron because he hadn't known about the affair when it came out into the open, though he did reveal to her their mother had told him later on.

"Any time you're away, things are different when you come back, whether you want them to be or not."

"Thank you for the advice. I wish it helped." He nudged her with his elbow and gave her a full, butter-melting smile.

"Me too. Lark, for what it's worth, I'm sorry to complicate things, but I'm not sorry for having met you. It's the best experience of my life."

He moved a strand of hair out of her face, and if she didn't keep him talking, she'd do something stupid, like attack him with her mouth. Inane chatter was good.

"Talk to me about yourself, Niall. I mean, we were…intimate, yet I feel like I don't know you as well as I should. What's the longest time you spent in Africa?" He moved in close again, rubbing her arms, and she wanted to rest her head on his shoulder, to have him hold her.

"About six months, three or so years ago. I left in late April and returned before Thanksgiving."

"You must have seen a lot there, done a lot." She leaned forward, wishing she could open him as she did a book and discover his hidden secrets. Niall's gaze flitted over hers as if he knew about her internal struggle. He drew a breath.

"It's…disheartening, being in the third-world parts of Africa where Dee and Anthony teach and knowing people elsewhere are enjoying their comforts, warm houses, and expensive meals. I saw a boy once, dying of malaria. He was so emaciated from not eating, his rib cage poked out of him. He was like a shrunken skeleton with a small amount of flesh stretched over him. His eyes were like huge, brown marbles, a fragmented, scrappy human looking out of enormous eye sockets. It hurt my heart, seeing him," he said in a strangled voice. "It can be a place of desperation, but also a place of tremendous hope. I suppose it's what keeps drawing me back. The way they don't let anything beat them, the children especially. They're *resilient*. We could all take a lesson or two from those kids."

Newfound respect for him washed over her. He was attractive, in spades. But beneath that, beneath the charisma, stood a good man with a purpose, at peace with things in his life.

"Coming back must have been pretty weird, hmm?" she asked. "I bet it wasn't easy to adapt back to regular life?"

He considered her. "Ah, yes and no. I've traveled, so I'm no stranger to finding my feet. Coming back made me grateful for what I have, but also made me aware that life isn't cut-and-dried."

"What was the best thing you were glad to have when you came back?"

Niall smiled. "Ice."

Lark wrinkled her nose. "Ice?"

"Aye. Where we were, the entire time it was hot and humid, and there was never any ice while we were in the remote villages. I like ice. But enough about me," he said. "You must be a good manager; you've a knack for turning the subject quicker'n a cop reloading a Glock. I understand about Aaron, but what about your mam?"

Lark sighed. "What about her?"

"Well, I know why you and Rick didn't speak to each other. But it seems like you two slipped apart. Pam didn't know your address after you moved. I tracked it down from your last flat in London. That's got to test you, not having any family to talk to."

His unspoken desire to ask more, to prod further into her life, hovered over them like a drone, but she also sensed his reluctance to, both because of his position and her uncertainty. She hesitated and then chanced it.

"We *did* slip apart over the years. I don't know. It was like we grew more and more distant when I moved to London after grad school. In a weird way, it was sort of how you and your friends grow older and realize you have less in common than you used to, and you drift apart. I couldn't be someone I'm not, and my mom knows it. She wanted me to be happy, and by leaving me alone, maybe she thought I'd either find happiness or want to come back. Can I tell you something?"

"Anything." The deepness of his voice reminded her of when it had dropped yesterday. "Client-attorney privilege," he assured her in a less sensual tone after a moment.

She took a breath. "Well, have you ever found yourself driving somewhere without any real memory of having driven there? That's sort of how I feel about where I'm going and what's happened between me and Charles and my family. I'm driving on a crazy highway with no direction. My life's floating in the air, and I'm terrified, and guilty, and *scared*. This is crazy. I have so much going on in my mind and heart right now, and I don't know how to process it." Niall took her hand and interlaced his fingers with hers over the railing.

"You can always talk to me."

He kissed the top of her hand, then tipped his head back to look at her. She wanted to crawl into the safe haven within his eyes. She swallowed hard.

"Always."

Lark slipped her hand out of his as frustrated tears filled her eyes. One escaped and spilled down her cheek. This was wrong. Guilt weighed upon her like an anvil. She turned away, but he pulled her back to face him.

"What is it? What's wrong?"

Lark wiped her face. "*Everything*, okay? I feel horrible. Look at what we've done. I'm no better than my dad." Her voice broke, and she couldn't stop the tears from falling.

Niall put his hands on her shoulders and steadied her, calm and intent. "Lark, listen to me. You are *not* horrible, okay? We have a connection between us, something special, and I think you feel it too. You shouldn't feel guilty about it. I'm drawn to you, and for being celibate as long as I have, it's a *big deal* I feel comfortable enough to talk to you, let alone touch you. It means something, and it's significant. I haven't known you longer than a week, but I can tell what you're feeling. I know when you're sad but pretending to be annoyed, and I know when you're worried but pretending to be fine. I can feel it inside if you're upset. I feel it right now. I don't know how, but I do. Now, being engaged to someone who's been unfaithful to you and then developing feelings for someone else, doesn't equate to being married and having a well-established family, and then cheating and throwing away everything you have."

Lark blinked, sobering at his words. He cupped her face in his hands, his eyes glistening with emotion.

"You're on the cusp of creating your life as you want it. I know, because I feel it in you. I've been there, and exploring your options doesn't make you a bad person. It makes you human. Let's say you up and married someone."

"Like you?" She smirked.

"I'd be lying if I said I was opposed to the idea." He grinned. "So yeah, for instance, me. We fall in love, have a kick-ass wedding, create a couple of cute, moderately well-behaved kids, and settle down somewhere nice. So essentially, you follow your dad's path, yeah? But there's a world of difference between what Rick did and what you're doing now, okay? Don't think less of yourself or beat yourself up about it. You're not with Charles anymore. If he was a good, stand-up guy with a generous heart who put you first in everything and loved you without limits, yeah, it'd be wrong. But he's not, he hasn't, and you deserve so much better."

Lark shrugged, frustrated. "See, that's exactly it. I—I don't feel like I *know* you, but you understand me better than *anyone* in there. How is it I can have a whole conversation with you and not feel like it's one-sided, or wonder if you understand what it is I'm trying to say? You seem to know what I mean. It's strange."

"It's because we're connected." His thumb brushed along her lower lip, and his eyes softened. "I know you feel it too. You're an honest woman. I love how you articulate what you want to say in a straightforward fashion. I like you being comfortable with me. You *should* be. You do know why we're comfortable with each other, don't you, Lark?"

She shivered as he took her right hand, turned it over, and traced his index finger down her wrist to her palm. He laced his fingers with hers while he watched her. Her hand tingled. He drank her in with intense eyes.

"I have a confession to make," he said in a low voice. "I saw you in my dreams after we met. I don't sleep very well, but when I do…" His face went red, but he stepped in even closer, mere inches from her lips. "Let's just say you're in them. A lot."

"What?" She licked her lips against the fall air. Her heart pounded so loud he must have heard it. He stared at her lips like he wanted to devour them. "In these dreams of yours… Were we, uh—?"

"Yes," he growled, the thirst in his eyes way too transparent to be misconstrued.

"I see. Can you tell me any more about them?" She'd give anything to know if his were anything like hers, or if they were even one and the same. Was that possible?

"I might tell you one day," he said, moving closer to her lips. "But I'd prefer to show you." He pulled her to him and kissed her. Lark melted into his embrace, dizzy at the heady sense his kisses gave her.

"Dinner," Pam called from the cracked kitchen window.

They broke apart, and she withdrew from Niall. His gaze burned into her backside as she slipped away, turning to walk toward the house.

"Coming, Mom," she called back, surprised how out of breath she sounded. She kept her face blank but savored the thrill fluttering in her stomach. *He dreams of me too!*

When Lark got to the back door, she turned while holding the screen open. Niall leaned against the patio railing, watching her.

Later, during dinner, she was overtalkative and couldn't look him in the eye. It was like he could see right through her. And despite her education and managerial training, she had no tactics to hide how much she cared about him. He'd wrenched open her heart like a tin can and had its contents on a silver platter right in front of him. So much for playing it cool.

****

The Saturday morning air cooled her cheeks, breathing new life into her as they ran. Niall waited for her outside as she left the house, not a word spoken about the previous night beyond his bright-eyed and eager, "Well, let's go," before they'd taken off. Once again, he let her set the pace.

Lark clutched a stitch in her side from the physical activity of the last twenty-four hours, but she didn't say a word. Niall could probably leave her in the dust if he so chose, for he was cheerful as could be beside her, humming a tune beneath his breath as though they'd gone for a country stroll.

"Hang on, Niall," she panted, stopping near the last stretch and bending to put her hands on her knees. "I'm dying here. Let me catch a breath."

"You've got it. Wind's at your back," he said with zest. Sunlight obstructed his face from her view.

"What?" she puffed, shielding her eyes.

"'The wind's at your back.' It's something me mam used to say as kind of an encouragement if me or my brothers ever did something spectacular. Which was pretty rare in those days. We were incorrigible." He laughed. "It goes in line with an old Irish blessing, 'May the road rise to meet you; may the wind be always at your back—' *Oof.*" Niall shifted his left foot around in pain.

"You all right?" Lark frowned.

He crouched and unlaced his sneaker. "Got something in me foot. What the—" He sat on the ground and shook out his shoe. A flattish gray stone, the size of a quarter, fell out. "So that's the devil that's been driving me mad the last few minutes." He chuckled, turning the stone over to inspect it.

"Chuck it to the side," Lark said, ready to go.

Niall set it on the ground as he put his sneaker back on. He picked it up and stood. "No, this one's special."

"A special rock?" Lark laughed as if he were out of his mind.

He glanced at her as he inspected it between his thumb and forefinger. "Aye. Stop for a moment." He walked over and showed her the stone. "You see the lopsided half-moon there, like a smile, and the two wonky holes above it that look like eyes? This here is a genuine smiley-face rock. He's a cute little fella."

Lark couldn't help smiling as she checked it out. It did bear a resemblance to a smiley face, with an attitude.

Niall's dark green eyes were gentle and amused. "Keep it."

Lark blushed. She took her hand off his and resumed walking. "Nah, it's all right. I'm good."

"No, come on, take it. He's cute," he persuaded, dancing the rock in front of her face as he walked beside her.

"It's not cute. It's a rock."

Niall moved the rock in time to his words as though it were speaking to her in a high-pitched falsetto Irish accent. "Oh, look how cute ah am, Lark. Take me home, oh please—go on, take me home. I've got no one. I'm alone on the road. Go on, lass, give us a chance." He made several kissing noises and moved the rock to Lark's face as if the rock was going to kiss her.

"No." She laughed, batting his hand away. "Come on, Niall. What would I want with a stupid old stone anyway?"

Niall's hand touched hers. They stopped, and she turned around. He studied her with a knowing expression as he placed the rock in her palm and closed his other hand over it. "It's not a stupid stone. Why, this here could be the smartest rock in the world. The Stephen Hawking of rocks."

Lark scoffed.

"He'll write a book someday and call it *Diamond in the Rock in a Nutshell*. Go on and take it," he said, his eyes twinkling. "It'll bring you luck, no matter what happens."

She faltered under his gaze but kept the stone clutched in her palm. She nodded, and they resumed walking.

"All right, then. Thank you. But I don't believe in luck. You make your own luck," she muttered, turning the stone in her hand. She'd learned the hard way during her rising career.

"That's what you believe?" he asked from the side.

She nodded.

"Oh…I hope you don't mind this being a personal question and all, but what do you think about faith, then?"

"Faith in God?"

"In *anything*."

She didn't know how to answer him when she was still so unsure of everything. Feigning indifference, she rambled, "I don't believe in God or anything. I think we're here for a time, and what you get is what you get. One shot to make your mark. No one does it for you. You push yourself or don't push yourself as far as you want, and whatever happens, happens." He appeared to consider her answer. "Why? What about you?"

Niall lifted his eyebrows as they walked. "I'm surprised. You've struck me as being spiritual at times. Me? I'm a big believer we're here for a divine purpose. We're here to be tested, and what we do in this life will reflect where we go in the next. I don't think this is our only shot, but I do think it matters what we do with it."

Lark considered he was at least half right. The rift in their budding camaraderie irked her, knowing they held separate beliefs. "You honestly believe that?"

Niall stopped walking. "Of course I do. Without faith, we're like a…a group of people, sitting in cold,

230

dark houses, unaware of electricity. Until we acknowledge the switch, we can't turn the light on and see what darkness was."

A tremor passed through her, and his words impacted her more than she cared to admit. She laughed.

"Where on earth do you come up with these things?"

"Common sense." The sparkle in Niall's eyes went from passionate to playful. "You should try some once in a while; you'll be amazed what happens."

"Hey," Lark jostled his arm and ran away at full speed ahead.

"That's it, woman," she heard him say, and she gunned it toward the house, squealing with glee and trying not to trip as he chased her. He had almost reached her when she spotted Charles sitting by the patio deck table, glowering at them. She wiped the ear-splitting grin off her face as Niall halted right behind her.

"Charles." She said, out of breath. She straightened and walked toward him, keeping her body language subtle. Charles scowled at Niall.

Lark and Niall met each other's gaze, and he took his cue. "Well, I should, uh, go get ready. Good run, Lark." He touched her back as he walked past her.

"Yeah, you too." She grinned.

She swiveled into the empty space beside Charles, caught her breath, and offered him a small smile. Maybe he would work with her on the flat situation. He nursed a cup of coffee, and the newspaper lay on the table, crisp, tri-folded, and still unread. Had he been waiting around for her?

"Am I allowed to talk to you now?" he asked acidly.

Lark considered him and nodded. "All right."

"The curse has been lifted. Well, don't you two seem *chummy*?" He took a sip of his coffee.

"Niall likes to run, and so do I. It's nice to have someone to run with. Keeps you motivated." Lark slid the paper toward her and unfolded it.

He drummed his fingers on the table. "Let's say I went somewhere for a week or two. Have you looked at flats? You do realize anywhere in London is bound to be high-end leasing at best, right? And I'm sure Maisie can't take you in with Graham and their football team of kids."

She shook her head, pissed at how businesslike he acted about the whole thing. "I would never put her in such a position, and frankly, it's not your concern what I do from here on out. I'm planning on looking online tonight for places."

He tilted his head and gave her a shrewd look. "What about work? How do you see this working between us?"

At least he was talking to her about it. Lark leaned forward, scratching her eyebrow. "Well, you're two floors up, and I'm sure we can be professional and polite to each other. We have separate friends. I don't see why we couldn't be civil. We're both professionals. We make a clean break. Move on."

"I don't *want* a clean break." He brooded.

It was way too early for an argument, and she couldn't focus on anything in the paper due to nerves about this whole situation. Figuring she wouldn't get any real leeway from him, she stood and stretched. "We can set aside time to talk about this later. I'm going to go drink water and hop in the shower."

"You should," Charles said, taking the paper from where she'd laid it. He opened it and buried himself in an article. "You smell of sweat."

Casting a dirty look at his back, Lark walked into the house.

The minute she got to her bedroom she turned on the shower to get the bathroom warmed, then went to get ready. She'd spearheaded negotiations before. There was no reason why they couldn't break apart on decent terms. She had no desire to get back together with him or seek counseling, despite how uncertain her future seemed. Cheating was the worst possible betrayal in any type of relationship. In any companion she sought, she needed trust. She needed security. After removing the elastic from her hair and releasing her ponytail, Lark spied the smiley stone she'd set on the nightstand. She picked it up and smiled back at it, then deposited it in the pocket of the coat she'd brought over from London.

It's funny, lackadaisical face gave her hope.

Chapter Twelve
Comings and Goings

A warm, sweet smell drew Lark to the kitchen later on that morning. "What are you making?"

Pam turned around at the stove. She'd applied more makeup today, and her skin had more color. She tapped the end of a small bottle of essential oil into a double boiler, then mixed it in. The energizing smell of peppermint filled the kitchen.

"Hi, hon. I'm making lip balm. Open the fridge. I put two small pots in there to cool earlier."

Intrigued, Lark found two small, metal lip-balm pots with glass tops in the fridge door, one marked on top with the letter *L*, the other with a *P*, in black permanent marker. Taking out the pot with an *L*, Lark unscrewed the lid. The citrusy scent of lemon oil wafted up to her. Using the edge of her pinky finger, she spread a thin layer across her lower lip and rubbed it in. A tingling sensation buzzed on her lips, along with a sweet taste.

"This is nice. What's in it?"

Pam donned pot-holder gloves and poured the balm from the double boiler into another small metal pot on the counter. "Everything," she said, focused on screwing a lid onto the pot of salve. "Sweet almond oil, beeswax, other stuff. It doesn't take a great deal of time to make, plus it's toxin free and great for your lips."

"Can I take one back with me?" Lark asked, in love with the stuff.

Pam set the pot on a cutting board to cool. "Yes, you can keep that one. It looks like it's firmed up, so no need to put it back in the fridge. I've also got a bag of homeopathic goodies for you to take along. Lark, I'd like you to consider getting into it," she continued in a niggling tone. "I got the information your dad's grandma gave me before she passed away, who got it from her mom, who got it from hers. It'd be a shame not to continue a Braithwaite tradition."

Lark shrugged, holding the little jar. "I haven't got the time, Mom. I wake up, go to work, churn out innovative ideas, deal with a bombardment of problems, then crawl home, sleep, and go do things in between if I'm lucky. I love my job, but time is a luxury."

"Doesn't Charles support you?" Pam asked. "He should. You shouldn't have to work so hard."

Lark picked up the new pot her mother had filled and put it in the fridge. She wasn't ready to tell her mother what had happened yet. "Some people *like* to work hard, Mom. Me included."

"And are you, um, going to have kids, do you think?"

Lark caught the too-light tone of her mother's voice and knew Pam wanted to say more but was worried she would drive her away. Sighing, she leaned against the counter and folded her arms to hide her naked left hand. "I'm not sure, Mom. We haven't talked about it."

"But you *do* want them?" The question floated in the kitchen like a fragile soap bubble.

"Of course I want kids. I love 'em. I watch Maisie's kids once in a while. It's not like I don't want to settle down. Maybe in a few years. I don't know. It has to be the right time." *And with the right guy.*

"I understand. And you should also be married before you think about having them," Pam added. "You'll need a support system when you have kids. They're a lot of work."

"Yes, that too." Lark smiled, trying to appease her.

Charles walked in from the living room. "What are we talking about, ladies?"

"When you're going to make an honest woman out of my daughter and set a date," Pam said, standing there with her hands on her hips.

"That old chestnut, eh?" Unfazed, he pulled a chair out from the table. He stretched his long legs out and crossed them at the ankle as he leaned back. He rattled the table with his knuckles in high spirits, commandeering and back in action. "Aaron said he'll give me a lift to the airport Monday on his way back to the university," he told Lark.

"How nice of him," she replied. "They're sending someone to take back the rental car tomorrow morning, so it's better to go with him and not waste the gas." His eyes scanned her, as if he were trying to work out if she acted politely because of her mother, or if she'd forgiven him.

"Yes, it's good of him. Pam, would you excuse us, please? I need to speak with Lark." He jerked his head toward the arched kitchen door as if saying, *There's the exit.*

Lark pinched the bridge of her nose. "Charles, this is my mom's kitchen, you can't kick her ou—"

"No, Lark, it's fine." Pam filled the last jar of lip balm and left it to cool on the cutting board, then took off her apron. "I need to go see if the laundry's done anyway," she said as she left the room.

Lark shook her head at Charles. "You were *beyond* rude. This is my mom's house. You can't order people around like they work for you or something."

"Sit down," he said in a mellow tone.

She stood, resentful and perturbed by the serious glint in his eye. He wore his hardball face, and it meant trouble.

"I'll get right to it." He took out her engagement ring from his pocket, held it to the light, and set it in the middle of the kitchen table. "Here. Put it back on."

"No."

Charles chewed his lower lip. "I know you're not thrilled with me, to say the least, but we're not done. We have things to work through, and it would be foolish to throw away six years of a relationship due to a slip of weakness."

"A *slip*? Oh my God. I love how you're downplaying it here. It was *your* weakness, Charles, not mine," she said coolly.

"Be that as it may, I don't want you spending time alone with O'Hagan anymore. Period. Do you hear me?"

Lark scrunched her forehead. She didn't like the tone of his voice. "Okay. First of all, you don't *own* me. The engagement is off, in no uncertain terms, so I'll do *whatever* the hell I want with whoever I want. It's not your place to interfere with my decisions. You've never cared what I do before—"

"Well, I do *now*."

His serene control disturbed her, because she knew a stealthy Doberman pinscher lurked beneath his calm demeanor. She took a seat. Maybe being on his physical level would get him to dial it down a notch.

"I see the way he looks at you, and I don't want you around him."

She clasped her fingers together in front of her on the table and met him head on. "What I do from here on out is none of your business, Charles."

"Yes, it is. You said it's over, but you're not thinking clearly, and in all likelihood, you'll change your mind after you get back."

"Never going to happen." She tried to keep her voice from rising. The worst move would be to escalate things. "My mind is already made up. As I told you, I want you gone when I get back to London."

"No. I want *your* word you'll stay away from O'Hagan. No running together, no talking to him other than things pertaining to the probate and settlement. *Nothing*. Promise me."

Lark leaned forward. "I'll do *no* such thing." He narrowed his eyes, but she was more than ready for him. "Come on, Charles," she challenged. "Stop bullshitting. You're going to go right back to corporate and bang that slut of a secretary the minute you land. And you know what? Go ahead. I don't care anymore because it's over."

He pouted and shifted the ring around the table as he glared at her. "I don't want it to be over, Lark. I want a second chance."

You don't deserve one. She took a deep breath. Over the years, she'd learned Charles was the proverbial, spoiled private-school kid, and he had to be dealt with in a certain way. "It's not going to happen, and you need to understand that. I'm sorry. You seemed fine when I called you out on Gemma, Charles. I assumed you'd be happy to be at liberty to do whatever you'd like with her. Why are you so hung up on Niall, anyway?"

Charles sat upright, angry. "I don't like the way he's always around you, all right? He's doing his job, but he's crossed the line. You told me when we first dated that you like assertive men. Well, this is me being assertive and guarding my interests. Stay away from him."

"I'm no longer your *interest*," she managed calmly, though she wanted to throw something at him.

His face grew serious. "Lark, stay away from him."

"No. I'll do what I want. You lost all rights to me when you cheated. I just wish I'd known sooner."

"Give me another chance."

She stared. "Find somewhere else to stay, so I can get sorted and move my things out."

Charles stood, and leaned over to her. "Listen to me. Whatever this is, whatever this…*phase* you're going through, has something to do with your father passing. I'll let it slide while we're here and chalk it up to emotions. What happens here stays here, but it ends as soon as you get on that plane and come home. I need you back, in top form, primed, in becoming clothes, sleek and together. We'll deal with my indiscretions when you get back, and we'll make it work. You want to go to Paris or Rome? I'll book us a trip and make it up to you. We'll fix it. End of discussion." He stood, straightened the hem of his shirt, and turned to walk out.

"*Hey*."

He turned around, and she stood, closed her fingers over the ring, and threw it at him. He staggered but caught it. Charles pursed his lips. He clutched the ring in his fist and stormed out.

Lark sat, bucked in her chair, and threw her head back. She stared at the ceiling and breathed out in frustration. A chill breeze hit her neck. She glanced out the corner of her eye. Crap, the back door wasn't shut. She stood to close it, but then changed her mind and left the house. The steady wind prickled her skin, and she spotted dark-gray storm clouds in the distance.

She rubbed her arms as she walked across the patio. How dare he? Charles had never been this controlling before… Had he? She was smart. If he'd been a domineering sadist, she would never have gotten together with him in the first place. But he'd changed over the last six years. Her eyes were opened to the fact that he'd transformed. Power did that to some people.

To her far right, Niall approached from the path to the stables. He was dressed down in dark jeans, a gray shirt, and a worn black leather jacket. She watched him turn around the side of the house, then stop when he noticed her.

"Oh, hey."

"Hey."

He rattled the keys in his jacket pocket and glanced to the woods. "I was about to go for a ride and clear me head. You want to come? Get away from here for a bit?"

Lark glanced back at the house. She nodded and walked around to the front with him. Whether he sensed the change in her or not, she didn't care. She needed an escape.

Niall opened the door for her to his silver Ford Explorer parked farther down the paved drive. She got in and buckled her seat belt, then watched him walk around the front and open the driver's side. Two duffel bags and a carry-on were piled on the backseat, but the front was clean, save for a folded, silver Leatherman tool on the floor and a few empty pistachio nut shells in the coin console near the gear shift.

"You—you like pistachios?" she asked as he keyed the ignition. A song by Flogging Molly poured out of the speakers.

"Aye." He leaned over her to open the glove compartment. "They help me concentrate. Better'n chain-smoking, which is what I did back in the day." He winked. "I keep extras in the glove box." The large bag in the compartment had been torn at the top edges and resealed with the built-in Ziplock.

"What?"

Lark blinked. What would he say if he knew about her jar back in her London office? She helped herself to a few nuts. "Nothing."

Neither of them said much as he drove. He turned up the music. Perhaps he understood her need to escape and wanted to give her legroom. Or maybe he was in a quiet, contemplative mood.

Tall, golden tares in the wheat fields and harvested pastures passed by in areas where the forests broke off before they rejoined. She blocked Charles from her mind. She relaxed against the comfortable seat and tried to phase out. The ears at the tops of the tares swayed toward the left as if pointing at something she couldn't see. Their uniformity and the way they moved with the breeze calmed her. There was no pressure to have to say anything with Niall, and it was nice.

After a while, the Explorer slowed. She turned to Niall. "Why are we stopping?"

He switched off the music and drummed the steering wheel with his fingers. "Whenever I need to think about stuff, the last thing I want is a bunch of people around me. Sooooo…"

Lark braced against the dashboard and let out a grunt as he drove uncouthly off the side of the road, straight into an unfenced, overgrown wheat field.

"We're gonna give you someplace to think."

The view from her window grew obscured by golden tares as tall as the SUV, oscillating over the windows like underwater kelp. She rocked around as he drove over bumps and patches in the ground.

"Uh, Niall? Do you have any idea where you're going?" She held on to the grab-handle above her window for dear life as the SUV rattled, and he drove farther into the field, with glee.

"Not at all, lass, but I'd say this is good enough." He chuckled and slowed the Explorer to a stop. He put it in Park, killed the engine, and turned to her. The jungle of wheat canopied the windows like a soft sky. It was so quiet and still, the cadence of their breathing carried in the cab.

"Wow," she said in a hushed voice.

He nodded. He seemed to consider something and then eyed her. "Wait. You're not claustrophobic, are you? I'm sorry, I didn't think to ask."

"No." She closed her eyes and relaxed against the headrest. The silence of the car and being secluded with him compelled her to talk to him, and to her amazement, she began to talk and opened up to him with stunning ease about *everything*—her mother, her brother, Gemma, her reluctance to discuss her problems with Maisie, what happened with Charles. Niall remained quiet and attentive, listening with a careful demeanor as she vented. He nodded when she spoke about her pain over Charles's infidelity and her uncertainty. "Charles told me to stay away from you," she said after a while.

He shook his head, guffawing. "Well, how convenient, for *him*. What do *you* want?"

She bit her lip. *I want you.* "I-I'm not sure. I know I don't want to give him a second chance, though. What he did burned me. I could never do that to someone."

"He's a class *A* twat, Lark, the same kind of git who used to pick playground fights and belittle me and my brothers for wearing hand-me-downs and being poor. Be glad you found the courage to stand up for yourself and break it off. I don't understand why someone of your caliber was with a guy like him."

She rubbed the side of her forehead. "He was different when we first got together. He changed, but I was too blind to see it. Charles tends to become a big baby if he doesn't get his way."

Niall narrowed his eyes. "He shouldn't be telling you what to do, though. What pisses me off is he doesn't care who you are inside. You could be anyone. He doesn't even *know* you. You're a convenience for him because with you he would have gotten to have the beautiful, successful trophy wife, plus a little on the side. C'mon, don't look like that; it was clear after talking to him for a few minutes." He extended his arm over the back of her headrest and leaned in, his familiar face a mix of anger and passion. "Now, let me be clear about this, Shakespeare, because this may be my only chance to tell you this before you go back to London. I don't know what these dreams mean, but I know it terrifies me how much I *care* about you. I'm not saying this out of nowhere, and I think you feel that. This may surprise you, but you and I, we've more in common than you'd think. Besides the dreams, I mean. For my own reasons, I've a hard time letting people in."

He reached for her hand and placed her palm on his chest. The steady rhythm of his heart thumped beneath his T-shirt.

"You know, where it counts? I haven't been intimate with a woman since my wife died, but since I met you, everything's connected. It's insane, but you have me at full throttle with a mere glance."

Lark gasped. "Are you saying you haven't had sex in twelve years? At *all*?"

He nodded.

Lark scoffed. "Oh, come on. You're pulling my leg. Look at you. I mean, *please*." He was a walking sex god. Of course, that might be her being biased from her dreams, but still. There was no way.

He sighed, and a dark shadow passed across his striking features. He wasn't joking. "I did *try* to," he ruminated. "After I got myself sorted out—and it took years—I took women out and tried to get into a relationship many times. But for the longest time, I felt guilty for the way I'd been with Melanie and responsible for what happened. I'd no desire to move on. I didn't feel worthy."

"Why didn't you feel worthy?" He wouldn't look at her, and an alarm bell went off in her head. Could his reluctance have something to do with his health? "Oh. I don't mean to pry, but do you have an STD or something? Is that why you haven't had sex?"

He lifted his head, and his eyebrows rose in surprise. "What? No, not at all. I'm clean as white linen. I never slept with anyone but Melanie."

"Same here." It seemed only right to lessen his burden in divulging his personal life by sharing some of her own. "With Charles, I mean. He was my first." She shifted her fingers nervously in his hand. "Of course, God knows how many women he's slept with. He swore he wore a condom every time, but…" She looked away. That particular wound was still too fresh.

"Doesn't make it any easier to bear, eh?"

She nodded, and he massaged her fingers. His skin was warm, and she moved closer.

"Are you taking any birth control?"

When she met his eyes, a thrill shot through her at the intensity in them. Why was he asking? Her heart raced. "Yes. I, uh, have an implant in my arm. It's long-lasting. I have to change it out every three years."

"Good to know." His voice dropped a notch, and he stroked her face with his free hand.

She cleared her throat. "Niall, what you said, about feeling like you don't deserve to move on? It's all in your head. You're an incredible person. Of *course,* you deserve to." She ached for him. She'd had a taste of his passion; to punish himself for so long was unthinkable. "Do you mind if I ask what happened to Melanie?"

He exhaled and rubbed his thumb over her hand, then held it to his chest like he needed it there. "I'd rather not talk about her now. But someday." A gleam of pain laced his eyes, and something told her not to push.

"It's okay. I understand."

"Thank you."

He smoothed his hand along the length of her arm, caressed it. His eyes darkened as he leaned in, and his chest rose and fell quicker. She wanted what he wanted, just as badly, but she needed to be responsible, conscientious. "Niall, no. We should stop doing th—"

He ate her words with his kiss, drugging her with his hot mouth as he moved over her, cradling her face in his hands. He kissed her with an intense hunger like he'd never have enough, and the voice of doubt, of needling guilt, floated farther away the more he kissed her. This was *not* Charles kissing her. This kiss contained passion, emotion, and strange magic. No boy—or man—had ever kissed her like this. And definitely not Charles. In fact, she never had this spark with Charles.

Her seat jerked backward, and before she could tell who'd moved it, Niall was over her, pressing the hard line of his body into hers as the seat reclined. His lips adored her throat, and he trailed a line with his tongue, making her shiver, making her want him. She nuzzled his hair.

"Love, I won't push you. But I have to touch you. I can't be this close to you and *not* touch you."

Niall lifted his head, searching her eyes for consent. Lark touched his cheek and nodded. He paused, then removed his jacket and peeled off his shirt. She drew in a breath at the sight of his warm, muscular body, the intricate black tattoo above his heart. It looked primal: a sun with a star in the middle. She traced it with her fingers, curious about its origin.

Niall's eyes were ablaze as he watched her. He roughly balled his jacket and shirt and tossed them over the seat. He placed his hand over hers, his eyes dancing with tremulous intent. With his other hand, he undid the button and zipper on his tight jeans, and she eyed his hardened cock, straining to get out.

A sigh of relief left him once his cock was freed from its confines, and it jutted proudly out, tenting against the cotton of his boxers. She wanted to touch him. She spanned her fingers and raked them over his broad, well-defined chest; first grazing his flat nipple, then gliding them over his ripped abs, and lingering on the sharp V of his hip flexors, which all but begged to be stroked. He caught her wrist and shook his head.

"No. Don't," he said, his breath coming in quick gasps. "I swear I'll lose control and take you right now. I want—I *need*—this to be about you."

Lark frowned and withdrew her hand, then met his gaze. His eyes were alight with the blatant sexual appetite he kept carefully banked. A hot pulse pounded in her pussy. This wasn't a rejection; it was delegation, and right now, she was the designator. Oh, they understood each other.

He bent and pushed her shirt up and off, his knifelike gaze never leaving hers. The intensity of his eyes told her he was about to take her on a journey. He flung the shirt over her head. She leaned forward to unclasp her bra, then shivered as her breasts sprang free. Her dusky-pink nipples puckered as if they wanted to kiss his lips.

Niall groaned and moved forward, cupping her breasts and seizing a nipple in his warm mouth, laving the underside with his tongue while he caressed and massaged the other with his warm fingers. She breathed heavily and held on to his shoulder. She carded her free hand through his thick, dark curls as he licked and sucked, teasing her with his teeth. She undulated beneath his touch. She had no idea how he could incite her so, but she wanted to lose herself in him. It scared her how much she wanted him.

She'd never known such a feeling before, had never experienced anything like this.

Niall unbuttoned her jeans. Lark kicked off her shoes, then lifted her hips as he slid the jeans down her thighs, taking them off. There was not an inch of skin he didn't touch, or a shallow breath they didn't share. His gaze roamed her body. She shifted beneath its intensity, her self-consciousness rearing its ugly head. She sighed. Niall was such a beautiful man. What would he think of her? She didn't have to wonder long. His breath warmed her neck as he trailed his nose along her cheek, and his lips tugged upward against her skin.

"You're exquisite, Lark. It's all I can do not to take you right now."

She drew him closer, unable to tell him what his words meant to her. She licked his neck; its salty tang left a spicy imprint on her tongue she hoped would last forever. His words gushed lighter fluid onto the fire inside her. She pulled him close and kissed him ardently.

His hands caressed the dip of her waist, went around to the curve of her back, and then over her ass. She hooked her ankle over his, desperate to feel him against her. Despite her prodding, he took his sweet time. Though it must have been torturous for him to go so slow, she loved that about him, how he mapped her out like a mystical mountain, worshipping her with his lips, venerating her with his hands and teeth and tongue. Niall slid a large hand beneath her panties. She gasped and closed her eyes, pleading with him to hurry while she rotated her hips toward his touch. His teeth scraped her throat while his hand made a slow descent past the light hair on her mound.

Lark bared her throat to him while she rubbed his back, his bum, anything she could touch. His hand dipped into her pussy, and she opened for him, gasping as he moved his thumb over her clit and then into the dewy wetness inside.

"Niall," she murmured. He thrust two fingers into her, and she jerked. So exquisite. She tightened her thighs around his hand.

"Do you like this?"

He moved slowly in and out of her. God, their dream sex did not in any way compare to the real thing.

She inhaled. "I *love* it." Desperate to touch him, she coasted her hand over his chest, further, until she wrapped her finger around the unmistakable bulge through his cotton boxers. He sped up his thrusts, going in deeper, and she fell back against the seat from her half-seated position, too distracted by the sensation as her hips thrust in time with him. She slid her fingers beneath the waistband of his boxers and touched the seeping tip of his hard cock. He bucked against her. His fingers pounded inside her, unremitting. "Niall," she whimpered. "Oh yes!"

He pressed his lips to hers, tender despite the burning friction between them. He pulled back, and she looked at him. "Lark, I have to taste you. Please."

Lark searched his eyes. There would be no turning

back, but damn it, she wanted it, wanted *him*. She nodded, her insides dancing. *Yes. Hell, yes.*

He drew back, the side of his mouth lifted as he yanked down her panties. He took her legs in his hands and draped them over his shoulders. She pressed her feet against the warmth of the console behind him and scooted as far as she could go to give him room to work.

"I'm going to open you up, Lark Braithwaite," he said, his voice low with desire.

True to his word, he spread her out like a sacrificial lamb. He stared unabashedly at her body, taking his time. She flushed with arousal and embarrassment as he made love to her with his eyes alone.

"Every single inch of you is perfect," he murmured, trailing his hand along her inner thigh.

Lark squirmed a bit. It had been a long time since anyone went down on her. Sex was a way to de-stress after a hectic week, to unwind or regroup. Until now, she'd never used it for her own personal pleasure, not in this manner. Charles never had any interest in that sort of thing. She watched Niall moved his face closer to her dewy nether lips, then lick her pussy from bottom to top with the flat of his tongue. She jumped. Hot blood rushed through her core as her heart sped up. She moaned and closed her eyes as he used his supple tongue on her sensitive clit, swirling around it like an ice-cream cone.

"Look at me."

She opened her eyes and sucked in her breath. He stretched her pussy lips to better expose her, lifting the hood of her clit and working her aching nub with the tip of his finger. He alternated between his teasing tongue and little licks along her entrance. She lifted her ass toward him. It was too much and yet not enough. She bucked against him, rationale disappearing from her desire-clogged mind.

She slapped a hand over her mouth to keep from shouting as he moved to suckle her exposed clit in slow drags, his soft tongue darting out every few seconds to stimulate it. Her thighs shook. He stilled them with his elbows. He reached up and pulled her hand away from her mouth.

"Don't you *dare* be quiet, Lark," he growled. He blew a breath of warm air against her clit, and sweet vibrations shimmered through her oversensitive body. "Let me hear you."

She cried out, a raw and impassioned roar.

He growled his approval and did it again before licking her. His arousal pressed against her hand, and she squeezed him. He moved his hips against her hold.

"It's just you and I, love. You and I."

He feasted on her, and she let him. Niall shoved two wonderful fingers into her sopping wet pussy, filled her to the brim, and pumped them in and out, driving her absolutely mad with lust. Those animalistic noises—were they coming from *her*? She should be embarrassed, but she was too far gone to care. Her body was on fire, and she wanted to attack him in the best way possible. She let go and gave in to the pleasure he wielded like a sword, gyrating her hips and writhing into his face to get closer, closer to him.

Something told her she'd seek him out again and again. She would never have enough of this man. He thrust deep into her, hitting a particular spot on her back wall. Her body quaked and sent delicious shockwaves up her spine. She squeezed and stroked his hard cock, while he held her captive to his touch. There was no escape. He curled his fingers inside her, and an orgasm ripped through her. Niall watched her with rapt attention.

Like an overfilled dam brought to the breaking point, her nectar burst forth, and he lapped it up, his face buried deep inside her, his hands stroking the undersides of her thighs.

Her whole body trembled. Tendrils of need unfurled inside. She wanted him. She wanted him to take her, fill her, fuck her—anything. She just needed this itch scratched. As if sensing a change in her, Niall resurfaced, breathing hard, his lips and chin glistening with her essence. He moved over her with blazing eyes and dived into her mouth, his tongue roughly claiming hers. She tasted herself, sweet and heady, and she sucked his tongue, hoping he'd take the hint. He removed her hand from his cock and laid it on her stomach, where he trapped it with his.

He groaned into her mouth and shifted his hips closer to her. He shoved his boxers down and pumped himself against her. She released his tongue, and he pulled his face back. All he had to do was say the word, and she'd surrender. She hungered for him.

He put his forehead against hers and dipped the glistening head of his cock through her slit, gathering her wetness and rubbing deliciously against her, bumping her clit with each stroke. She shivered at the contact, at the breaking point.

"I want to come on your pussy, Lark."

Not what she had in mind, but he was honoring his promise and respecting her, trying to assuage her reactions and what she wanted. She nodded, opening her legs wider for him. Was he into watching her pussy as he got himself off, as Charles was? But Niall surprised her. He ignored what lay between her legs, and locked gazes with her. She breathed deep, transfixed in the bond of his vast, green eyes. He increased his pace, his muscles tightening as he focused on her face, furiously pounding his cock into his hand and grunting openly. It was the sexiest thing she'd ever seen, made more prevalent by knowing he did it with her in mind. She broke their stare and watched him work his long cock. He was bigger than what she'd grown used to. She licked her lips. What would he taste like? His cut-off moan brought her attention back to his face, and she licked her top lip. Niall leaned forward and braced one hand against the headrest above her.

"I'm about to come."

"I *want* you to," she urged, her breath hot against his neck.

He kissed her on the lips and shifted a bit, then guided the tip of his cock around her clit and pussy as he ejaculated. A smidgen of semen splattered onto the edge of her hand, but she didn't care. She raised her hips. He called out her name as his seed spurted over her pussy.

"Oh *fuck*. Oh *yes*. Lark."

He threw his head back, the tendons in his neck straining as he released on her. This was all for her—his raw passion, the evidence of his desire made manifest. Lark blinked the tears from her eyes. He was beautiful.

"I like seeing you like this," she admitted.

He relaxed his shoulders as the last of his climax

washed over him. He smiled at her, then moved his hand over her mound, smearing his essence over her entrance. Without warning, he shoved two fingers inside, and she arched her back. "*Mmm.*"

He put his mouth next to her ear, his voice husky. "I want my seed inside you for the rest of the day. I want you to remember this, Shakespeare."

She put her arms around his shoulders and clamped her thighs around his hand, not about to forget this anytime soon. Their lips met in a slow, gentle kiss, and Lark laid her head back and tried to breathe. Niall panted, collapsed on top of her, and laid his cheek against her breast. Spent liquid heat dripped from his cock onto her, pressing against her thigh. She stroked his back with the flats of her palms while his fingers stayed buried inside her. She kissed his sweaty forehead and watched the wheat sway outside the car windows. The waving wheat sounded like the ocean, the faint, sweet smell of it like perfume. Sated, she hooked her right leg over him and pushed back the hair from his eyes.

"Niall, how old are you?"

He chuckled, propped himself on his elbow, and carefully withdrew his hand. He took his weight off her. "Thirty-three." He lifted her hand and interlaced their fingers, gazing into her eyes.

"How old were you when you got married?"

He cleared his throat, his gaze darting away.

She raised her head. "I'm sorry. Is it painful to talk about it?"

He caressed her outer thigh. "No," he said. "Not with you. I suppose I'm not used to talking to anyone about my earlier life. Your mam and Aaron don't know.

We were young, married right out of our sixth year at eighteen."

"Eighteen? God, that's so young."

He eyed her hair. "Yeah. People in love do crazy things, and kids are no exception."

Sensing his discomfort, she asked him about his tattoo. He showed it to her, pointing at the sun surrounding the star. "I got this while visiting Dee and Anthony a few years ago. It means transformation."

Lark smiled. "Seems pretty fitting with all you've been through."

"Aye," he smiled back, his thumb rubbing her fingers. "Lark, tell me I have a chance here," he murmured. "Please tell me this isn't fleeting. I need to know you feel the same for me as I do for you."

Oh, Niall, I do, she wanted to say, but daggers of shame shot through her as they lay there bathed in each other's pleasure. She was no better than Charles, no better than her father—but Niall had a way of making her forget herself and the world. They'd given and gotten exactly what they needed from each other, and the way he touched both her body and spirit rivaled anything she'd experienced. "I'd like to. I *want* to…"

He sighed against her and caressed her thigh. "No worries, Shakespeare. I told you—I won't make you say or do anything you're not ready for."

Lark pulled him into a hug and clutched him tight to her, torn inside. Their interlude would be over soon, but she wanted it to last forever.

"Lark?"

"Mmm?"

He lifted. "What do you think the dreams mean?"

She shifted beneath him. "I'm not sure what they

mean. I had one the other night of being out on a lake somewhere. The moon seemed bigger than usual, and there were large, exotic plants and bamboo plants. The ground was rough."

He kissed her breast and hummed. "That sounds like Rwanda. They integrated bamboo in their forestry over three years ago, but there wasn't vegetation around Deidre and Anthony's village. I've seen it, though. Interesting."

"You had a horse too."

He looked amused. "A horse?"

She nodded, looking expectantly at him, but he shook his head.

"I can't help you there, love. There's one place I know where they have horses—Mount Kigali. They do trail rides and holiday stays, but it's for wealthy vacationers, not locals."

"Oh." She didn't mean to sound disappointed, but a desperate part of her longed to find a connection through the dreams.

"Though," Niall sounded thoughtful. "In psychology, horses *do* have a sexual connotation in dreams."

"You're making that up."

"I'm not. It might have something to do with your sexual energy." He squeezed her breast lightly, and she giggled. "Or passionate desires." He nipped teasingly at her neck.

"Ha-ha. Stop it."

"Insatiable sexual appetite," he growled. "What kind of horse was it? A mustang? A black stallion?"

"Uh, no, an old, spotted gray mare."

They laughed.

"Figures." He sighed dramatically.

She stroked his back and smiled at the sunroof. "What about the lake I told you about? Have you ever been to it? Do they have similar lakes in Africa?"

"Well, yes. Dee and Anthony's village is near the Great Lakes. Before there was an Ebola outbreak a year back, I did bathe in a lake once with men from the village, when shower water wasn't available. What happened in the dream?"

Despite being skin to skin with him, she blushed. "I'm sure you can figure it out."

He tickled her side, and she squirmed beneath him, giggling. "Niall, stop it."

"No, tell me." His smile was infectious, and she put her hand to his face lovingly.

"I'd like to tell you, but talk is cheap." She closed her lips over his, and he moved over her, his hand sliding up her leg. He thumbed her clit again, and she tightened her legs around him, arching into his touch.

Niall's phone went off with a text message, and he groaned, pulling back. He kissed the top of her head and reached for the phone, checking it. "I'm sorry, but if it's regarding the house, I can't miss it. It's your brother, asking where I am." He sighed, burying his face into the crook of her neck. "We have to get you back."

Using napkins Niall found in the glovebox, Lark cleaned as completely as possible under the circumstances. She felt decadent, knowing Niall's seed remained inside. They dressed in silence before driving out of the wheat field and back onto the road. They'd moved comfortably around each other, but the issue at hand lingered like an unwelcome visitor between them.

She was forlorn when the SUV pulled into the path past the ranch gates, gravel crunching beneath the tires. Back at the house, he put the Explorer in Park. She closed her hand over the door handle, ready to exit.

"Hey, hang back."

"I'll never forget that, no matter what happens," she said, leaning her head back against the seat. Being with him gave her peace and clarity. She'd wanted to consummate the magic between them, but their time in the wheat field was a close second. "Thanks for taking me away. And for, uh, everything else." *Way to undersell it, Lark.*

"My pleasure. I'm glad you're staying longer. I enjoy being around you."

She wanted two things at once: to grab him and kiss the life out of him, and to get out like she should do. Getting involved with, literally, the man of her dreams was insanity, and a niggling pang of guilt filled her at it being so soon after Charles. It bordered on cheating, and cheating was a no-go. She'd gotten lost in a real fantasy back there, but there would be consequences. What was she doing? She needed to knock herself upside the head.

She glanced down. "I've enjoyed it too, Niall. I should go back inside, though. My mom will wonder where I am." She made to open the door again, but he caught her hand in his.

"Lark," he whispered. "Please. Think about what I said. Think about *us*." His fingertips left her hand and traveled to the side of her neck, a gentle lover's touch. She shut her eyes. "I believe we're having these dreams for a reason. The ancient Greeks believed significant types of dreams to be visions of the future, of things which were meant to happen. Think about it."

"I will." She opened her eyes, and he kissed her softly, leaning forward as he inclined his head toward her. Gathering her inner strength and cursing the way things were, she pulled away and opened the door. "Sorry. I have to go. Thank you," she added, turning to climb out, but not before seeing the love in his eyes as she shut the door.

She toed off her shoes as she entered the house. Charles, Pam, and Aaron sat on the wide sectional in the living room, watching a movie on cable.

"Hey, how's it—"

"Shh," Pam urged.

Relaxed, Charles glanced at her over his shoulder and grinned. Okay, so he played the let's-pretend-what-happened-didn't-happen card.

"The new commercial's coming on," he said cheerfully.

Did he have any clue she'd been gone for the last hour? It was the same thing as coming home to an empty flat and finding out he had a "late night meeting." When things were going Charles's way, he seemed oblivious to her.

Not a huge fan of the advertising for UY, she bore with it, biting the inside of her cheek. Aaron and Pam applauded at the end.

"Wow. Is that something you thought up, Charles?" Pam asked.

Charles nodded. "The commercial here's different than the English version, but yes, it's my copy line. Lark, what'd you think? I don't think you've seen it."

"I haven't. It's good," she said. She was grateful they'd at least taken a more tactful and less-sexy approach to the commercial. She checked the time. "How long have you guys been in here?"

"Not long," Pam replied. "There's a good movie coming on."

"Corporate called to make sure I was coming back on Tuesday," Charles said. "I got off the phone about five minutes ago." He checked Lark out, and she patted down her hair, which sported its own landmark since the wheat field. He narrowed his eyes. "Where've you been?"

"I needed to get out, so I went for a walk," she lied, noticing Aaron gave her a funny glance.

Charles grunted, oblivious. She sat several feet away from him, but he put his arm over the couch behind her as if straining to reach her, which irritated her. Her insides were warm, coated with Niall's cream. She crossed her legs to spread the comfort, wanting to hold on to the happy, content spell between the forever.

Niall came in a while later, said a quick hello, and holed up in the office. He deposited several books and his briefcase on the desk, shrugged off his leather jacket, and acknowledged her with a forthright nod before closing the door.

In the hallway later, she came back from using the bathroom, and Aaron stopped her, his expression serious.

"Hey, I saw you leave with Niall earlier."

Lark froze, guilt knocking her over like a tidal wave. Her eyes stung. Her brother took her hand and stepped closer.

"And I won't tell anyone," he whispered. "But if you guys do ever get together, the dude is like a *brother* to me, so you have no idea how happy it would make me."

He drew her into a hug, then returned to the living room. Lark shook her head, feeling like the wrong actor in someone else's movie.

****

Sunday morning dawned, and Pam asked Lark to help her make cinnamon rolls. They spent quality time visiting. Later, they watched a few movies and reminisced about her father and funny childhood moments. Aaron was in a cheerful mood and even got Charles to take a few selfies with him. Charles was on his best behavior and gave her a wide berth, which saved her from doing something stupid, like telling him about Niall.

The paperwork was on hold, as it was Sunday and most places were closed, but Niall kept working in the office, stopping once to come out for dinner. In the afternoon, she passed him on her way to the bathroom, and he took her hand in passing. She caught his eye and stroked his palm. A delicious tingle passed between them. His eyes shone with need, and he stepped close and pushed her against the hallway wall. He was warm and hard, and she both hated and loved how he turned her into a raging creature of desire in a damn millisecond. She was supposed to be on her way to wash her hands, not standing there playing the staring game with Niall set-my-pants-on-fire-with-a-glance O'Hagan.

"Niall, no," she whispered as he pressed his lips against hers. "We can't. Not here." He rocked against her, his arousal stiff against her stomach. She moaned.

"At least I'm still inside you," he said into her ear.

It took every ounce of effort to push against his

chest and walk away, unbalanced, to the bathroom.

Charles was subdued, but he watched her. She couldn't decide what she wanted more—to have him leave her alone or to have it out with him. Tired and overwhelmed, she spent most of Sunday evening searching online, bookmarking London maisonettes and flats. They were all the size of a broom closet and way overpriced, but she was determined to move out, even if it meant finding a flat mate. Bandit joined her on the bed, circled, and plopped down. Frustrated at the piddly findings, she closed the laptop and got ready for bed. She fell asleep the moment her head hit the pillow.

Her dream, though, was distorted. Something to do with getting a little, curly-haired girl to school on time and making plans to travel, then changed to a boardroom meeting, where Mr. Osaka pulled out of the merger. She slept restlessly.

****

Lark awoke early on Monday, groggy. She took her time in the shower. It was light outside, but the house was quiet. No one stirred.

Her craving to smoke was still there off and on, but less than before, and it seemed like she might actually quit for good this time. She went downstairs and got things underway in the kitchen. She prepared a fruit salad for her mother.

She laid out the cutting board, knives, and Tupperware then attacked the pineapple first. After she cut up the fruit, Niall's voice approached from the hall. She looked at the microwave. The digital clock said it was close to eight a.m.

He entered the kitchen in the same black suit and tie he'd worn the day of her father's funeral, the well-cut jacket slung over his arm. He talked on his cell phone, listened and nodded.

"No, it's not. Hold on, Jake. Let me write it down."

He lifted an eyebrow at Lark. She pointed to the magnetic Post-it notepad-and-pen set on the fridge and resumed the fruit salad.

Thanks, Niall mouthed as he grabbed the set and scribbled something down. "Uh-huh. Just a sec, it's burning up my pen. Okay. Yeah, I'll call them and get back to you. Cheers." He ended the call, split the yellow Post-it note from the pack, and replaced the pack on the fridge. "Well, good news," he said, sitting on the stool opposite Lark at the island counter.

"What is it?"

"We may be able to put this through as soon as today. We'll still have to sign the final papers tomorrow or Wednesday, but it should be wrapped up by then."

Relief swept over her. "Niall, that's excellent. I was worried I'd have to get another flight again."

"Well, see, the delay is part of my grand master plan: to continue devising ways to keep you here all to myself." He kissed her hand, and sucked honeydew melon juice from her fingers. The heat of his tongue swirling about her digit shot straight into her. Her eyes glazed over. The man was like a drug.

"What, so you can have your way with me and be done?"

He narrowed his eyes. "Oh no, I'm not a love-'em-and-leave-'em type lad. And you're no ordinary lass. You're extraordinary."

The sensual tone and energy in his eyes roused her and sliced through the fun of the moment. She withdrew her hand and returned to dicing melon cubes, working harder than necessary. Charles's words about staying away from him flashed like railroad lights in her mind. Crap. There was that to deal with too.

"You're mistaken. I'm plain. And I used to be fat, so you must be delusional."

Niall leaned his chin onto his palm and studied her as he draped himself against the counter. "You know, Lark, what comes out your lips at times sounds colder'n an icicle. But your eyes are warm. Like a doe's."

Lark continued working, flushed. "Well then, trust what's coming from my lips and not what you think you see in my eyes," she said, making her voice cool, hoping he would take the hint as she moved the cut-up melon from the cutting board to the open plastic bowl beside it with a spatula.

"Will do. You do have beautiful lips, by the way. I've been obsessed with them since I met you."

He stared at them and took the opportunity to lean farther over the counter and kiss her, his full lips tugging her bottom lip before releasing it. Her body responded, tingling and ready for him.

"I love your eyes too," he murmured. "They're shiny and reflective, like a lake. You remind me of Ireland."

She pulled back, both exasperated and turned on as he stole another kiss. "Mmm. You're nauseating. But so damn tasty."

"You love it," he purred.

He was totally right, but she said nothing as she closed the lid to the bowl. She slung the dishcloth over her shoulder and put both hands on the edge of the countertop, then blinked and leaned toward him with what she hoped was an annoyed expression.

"Niall…you undoubtedly have the gift of the gab. While I would love to get you to follow me around all day and say these things and continue to set my panties on fire, I'm confused right now. I need you to back off. Okay?"

He gave her a lawyerly look which told her he didn't buy it. "Why?"

Lark sucked in a breath and lowered her voice. "You *know* why."

"So—what? You're not engaged anymore, and Charles can continue to shag his secretary, but you have to stay away from me? How does that work? Because he's still with her, in case you haven't figured it out. I heard him on the phone with her yesterday morning when I went into the office, and I'm here to tell you it *wasn't* work related. At all."

"Spectacular," Lark fumed, folding her arms and glaring at him. "Thank you for the update. I give up. You're infuriating," she growled, turning to place the bowl in the fridge. Heavy footsteps sounded on the stairway above them. Charles.

The current in the air shifted, and Niall appeared beside her, brushing his arm against hers.

"I'm sorry to be the bearer of bad news, Shakespeare, but don't pretend you don't like me close. I can feel you do," he whispered in her ear.

Lark turned as his lips grazed her earlobe, and a rush of blood pooled in the pit of her stomach as she remembered the powerful spasm that had rocked her body when he'd taken her with his mouth in the wheat field. Niall twisted in midstep and caught her eye as they passed. She turned her head away, flustered. He smiled, turned, and his footsteps retreated. She heard him bid Charles a reticent good morning in the hallway.

Charles approached her dressed in khaki trousers and a dark sweater, which made him seem taller than usual. He gave her a pointed glare.

"He was passing through," she said, ducking her head.

He held her engagement ring in front of her eyes. She sighed and shook her head. "No, Charles. It's over."

"It's *not* over."

"I'm not marrying you," she said, putting space between them. "And we need to talk about the flat. Let's be decent about this, okay? I want to have some time to find a new place. I need you to go somewhere when I get back so I can get sort—"

He huffed and put the ring in his pocket. "Lark, you're stressed out with being back here, you're not think—"

"Oh, and your sleeping around with Gemma and whoever else has *nothing* to do with it? You're delusional, Charles."

He stood still, watching her. "You'll come back. You'll come to your senses, and this will get resolved. I know you. You wouldn't throw everything away. Are you certain you don't want to hop on the flight with me? It's still not too late. We can see if there've been any cancellations."

Lark sealed the remaining cantaloupe in plastic wrap. "No. I told you," she said, grumpy and fed up. "My mind is made up. I'll come back when I said I would to pack my things and find another flat, but this has got to get taken care of. I need you to uphold your end once I get this paperwork out of the way. I don't want to be signing things back and forth for the next year. Don't forget what I said. You need to go."

Charles leaned against the counter, watching her. "C'mon, Lark. Don't give it all up. Tikka Masala in London, the West End. Us." He took her hand and rubbed his fingers over hers. Niall did the same thing yesterday, but it had nowhere near the same effect. "I'll miss you."

She shook her head, conflicted at the sentimental tone in his voice and torn between guilt and righteous gratification about her feelings for Niall. Charles had made his bed, and he needed to lie in it.

Lark took a deep breath and turned away to wash the cutting board. "You better go make sure you have your things."

****

Charles and Aaron set off that morning, at half past eleven so they could get to the airport before one. Pam said her good-byes inside. She gave Charles a hug and wished him well, and Lark led him outside.

Niall talked with Aaron as Charles and Lark approached. He said something to Aaron, who shook his head, and they hugged. Niall barely nodded to Charles in passing, then stopped at his SUV to lean against it and watch them from a distance.

Lark watched Niall in speculation. Had Niall and Charles spoken at all about her, given the cold send-off they were giving each other? For the most part, Niall ignored him. It seemed unlikely.

She hugged Aaron before he got in the driver's side of the truck, but he dismissed her hug and instead pulled her into a full-on bear hug.

"I wish we could have more time," she said.

"Me too." His blue eyes shone. "We only had a week, and now we're both going back again. Look, I'll need to download your damn brain and get advice from you on the business, so don't expect this to be the end of it."

"I don't. I'm here whenever you need *anything*. I'll fly over for your graduation. You also better come visit me in London too."

Aaron was on the brink of tears. He nodded and got in the truck.

"Hey." She stopped him before he shut the door.

"Yeah?"

Lark wrestled with her emotions. "Thanks for taking me up to Crawman's Ridge. I love you, and you'll always be my brother."

That seemed to do it for Aaron. He hopped back out of the truck and hugged her hard. "Love you too, sis," he whispered. "Take care of yourself, okay?" He passed a fleeting glance at Charles, who loaded his suitcase into the bed of the truck several feet away. "And keep in mind what I said about Niall." He gave her a thumbs-up before getting back in the truck and shutting the door. She shook her head fondly.

Lark put her hands in her pockets and meandered over to Charles. He seemed upbeat as he loaded the last suitcase, then pushed the tailgate shut.

"Had enough mingling with us commoners, hmm? I know you're one who's happy to be heading on back," she smiled, trying to part on good terms.

"Well, I won't lie."

She smirked. *That'd be a first.*

Charles touched her arms and looked in her eyes. He seemed to be in good humor despite it all, his movie-star face winning as usual in the gloom of the overcast, hazy day.

"Now, I'll be at Heathrow to pick you up on Friday night from the airport. I'll smooth out this whole mess with Osaka-Nayaweni and close the deal. In the meantime, get things here settled and"—he eyed her jeans—"come back how you were. I want my sexy fireball back."

She pinched the bridge of her nose. "No. Don't pick me up. I'll get a taxi. I told you, it's ov—"

"We'll see," he challenged.

She frowned at him. "Charles—"

When he leaned in to kiss her, she turned her face, and his kiss landed on her cheek. His breath stank. She checked his eyes for any redness around his dark pupils but didn't see any.

"Stay away from O'Hagan."

She couldn't tell if he were drunk, or delusional, or both. Either way, it meant trouble. Charles got in the truck, and Aaron pulled away, leaving Lark standing there in the dust.

Niall joined her, and they walked in silence to the porch. She sighed and sat on the porch swing. "Niall, yesterday, when…when you and I went to the wheat field, you asked me if there was a chance…"

His eyes darkened, and he sat next to her. He touched her neck with his fingertips. She held her breath. He touched his forehead to hers and closed his eyes.

"Aye. I've thought about it. The dreams we both have, how I can feel what you feel—it has to mean something, don't you think?"

She nodded. He made her feel impossibly good,

but what would a future with him hold? Could she give up her job and move back to the States? He kissed her forehead, put his arm around her, and put the swing into motion.

"Lark, if you give me a chance, I'll give you the world," he whispered into her hair. "I've fallen in lo—"

She moved to sit up, about to cut him off.

"Don't," he pleaded, drawing her back, his lips mere inches from hers now. "Don't do that." He stared at her and glanced at her mouth. "I know you want this as much as I do." Niall took her hands in his and touched his lips softly to hers.

As she closed her eyes and gave in to the kiss, the front door opened. She moved away from him and turned toward the front door, running her hand through her hair.

"So, it shouldn't be sold," she rattled on as her mother stepped out with a jar of canned peaches.

"The estate again, eh?" Pam asked.

Niall cleared his throat.

"Yes," said Lark. "It'll be over soon," she added in Niall's direction. "And then I'll be back in London." She fished into the back of her jeans for the one cigarette and lighter she'd squirreled away a few days ago, in case she needed it, and tried to light it. Her hands shook, more from nerves, though, than lack of nicotine.

Pam handed the jar of peaches to Niall. "Open this for me, please. My carpal tunnel is acting up. I've made peach cobbler. Lark, please don't. You've been doing so well. I can get you a scoop of ice cream instead?"

Lark threw the unlit cigarette over the balcony. "*Fine*." She left the swing in a huff and stormed into the house, fed up with everyone pitching their two cents.

"And you don't need to be rude," her mother called after her. Lark ignored her and went upstairs.

Chapter Thirteen
The Orchard

Niall left not too long after their encounter on the porch to go teach a lit class in Portland and check in with his office. Pam seemed to sense the friction between them, and to avoid playing a game of twenty questions with her mother, Lark escaped to the office to catch up on hundreds of work e-mails, answer queries, and change her out-of-office assistant to reflect the extended days she'd be out. Maisie had texted her and left messages, but she didn't want to talk to her yet. She'd tell her everything, but it was still so tentative. Going the safer route, she sent a nice e-mail, thanking Maisie for taking care of things.

With Niall gone and the house vacant for the first time, Lark sat next to her mother at dinner. The lack of testosterone was nice for a change. Pam had a gift for continuous chatter, regardless of the subject, and Lark listened to updates on the lives of people she'd forgotten even existed. They discussed recent movies and how things were in England compared with America. They chatted long past the tasty peach cobbler with a dollop of cream on top. For whatever habitual ramparts ever existed in the Braithwaite house, there was nothing proper dessert and girl talk could not fix.

"How long will Niall be staying here?" Lark asked, playing with the last morsel of dessert on the edge of her fork.

"Until he's done," Pam replied. "He's stayed over before plenty of times. It might seem strange to you, but it's normal for us. He and Rick hung out. They took weekend fishing trips with Aaron to the lake too."

Lark changed the subject to the rosemary and sage herbs growing in terracotta pots on the kitchen windowsill, which got Pam rambling about the vast uses the spice plants had for healing and skin treatment. Lark developed a keen interest in all things herbal and pushed Niall as far back on the mental burner as possible.

****

She bolted awake when the alarm clock rang Tuesday morning. Her heart beat so fast, she swore she was on the verge of a panic attack. Even her hands shook. She needed to get up and move. Lark licked her parched lips, and her throat scratched as if someone had stuffed a jar of cotton balls in it overnight.

She drank the remaining water in her glass on the nightstand, then went to the bathroom, refilled it, and drank the whole thing in several long gulps. She dressed in her sweats and went downstairs, where she stretched in the foyer.

She went outside, and the wind assaulted her. Light rain pitter-pattered on her shoulders, but she didn't let it deter her and ran hard. The extra adrenaline of nerves gave her a much-needed kick, and she stretched out her legs the more she ran, using her arms and breathing to help, glad of the solitude.

She passed the mile mark for the fourth time, her hands above her head as she ran. It helped. The nervous tension left her. Cool sweat slid down the sides of her face and throat.

She walked from the path toward the back patio. It stopped drizzling, and the sun peeked through the clouds. A water bottle awaited her on the lowest patio step with a white envelope perched against it. They had been set under the step above so as not to get rained on.

Lark walked to the stairs and looked around. No sign of Niall. She had been out for almost an hour, and he'd come and gone.

She picked up the water and the card, then turned and sat on the step. She unscrewed the cap and guzzled half the bottle like a spring breaker chugging a keg. When her thirst was satisfied, she set it aside and slid her finger under the envelope flap. She extracted a small folded white slip of paper.

In neat masculine handwriting he'd scrawled:

I was a twat.

Lark lowered the paper, a hint of a smile on her lips. He hadn't been, not by a long shot, but the fact he waved the white flag first made her feel bad. Sighing, she folded the note and put it back in the envelope. Her bum and calves were sore. She spent a good deal of time stretching out on the deck and finished drinking the water.

Passing through the hallway on her way upstairs, she bumped into Niall much sooner than she expected. It threw her off guard.

"Hi," she nipped out before she could help herself. It came out more like a cold snarl. She cringed. Not how she wanted to sound.

"Hello, Lark." He tipped his head with a theatrically menacing voice. She made a fruitless effort to not smile, and he chuckled when she gave up and grinned. "I'm glad I caught you, for more reasons than one. I need you to sign some papers." He handed her the clipboard in his hands. Each paper had a red-and-yellow SIGN HERE tab, the way she liked it.

"Pen?" she asked, her eyes skimming over the Confidentiality Agreement.

"Here you go."

"Thanks." She tried to take the pen he offered, but it stayed clutched in his large palm.

"Oh sorry, caught me too early, there. Still morning. Try again." He offered it to her with a wink.

Lark pulled the pen from his fist, but he tugged it playfully back.

She bit her lower lip. "Look, can I have the pen, or what?"

"Hey, Shakespeare, I'm not stopping you. You must not be trying hard enough," he replied with a straight face. He handed the pen to her with a smile, then watched as she signed the documents.

He leaned over her, inhaled her scent, and sighed in satisfaction. "Ah, I love the smell of sweat after a good run. Well, you'll be left in peace today." He scratched his eyebrow. "I'm heading downtown to get things done. I'll be there most o' the day. I've got my mobile. Number's on the kitchen counter if you want to text me."

Lark smirked, her head hidden in the paperwork, and finished signing.

****

The rain stopped, and the weather warmed when she came back downstairs. Her mother sat out on the front porch swing, her feet nestled in the cushions beneath her as she sipped a cup of coffee.

"When your dad built this place, he claimed it had a soul," Pam said after taking a sip.

Lark walked along the porch and rubbed her arms. She placed her hands on the railing and leaned forward, taking in the straight row of trees and looking past the winding road and into the horizon. "There used to be magic," she said. "I loved growing up here, playing in the woods, watching you plant flowers and fruit trees. Ha, I spent half my teenage years studying under the apple trees, reading to my heart's content. It was a place where I felt accepted, not judged because of my weight."

"The trees still have harvest apples on them, if you want to go over there," Pam suggested.

"That doesn't sound like a bad idea. Thanks, Mom. I think I will." Lark hurried into the house to get a few things, then walked out to the modest apple orchard. Past the hill from the stables and a few hundred feet away, a wooden, fenced-off patch of fruit trees had been paired off in three distinct rows. Sunlight fell over the apple, plum, and apricot trees. The autumnal grass browned around them.

Lark tied a red sweater about the waistband of her jeans beneath her white shirt. She held a plastic water bottle and carried a copy of *All Quiet on the Western Front*, which she'd pilfered from her father's library. She stopped in front of a gala apple tree. A few mature apples remained strong on the higher branches, and several littered the ground.

Her cell phone rang from her back pocket. She took it out and flipped it open; another Dow text update. She found Niall's number she'd saved in her contacts earlier and sent:

Thinking of you. —L.

Smiling, she turned the phone off and pocketed it, set the book and water bottle near the mouth of the tree, and climbed the tree to reach for two apples near the upper branches.

****

A while later, she stood and wiped the leaves off. She hiked up the hill with a fulfilled heart, toward the stables. Travis, the old ranch hand, was back after being off for a few days while Aaron manned the barn. He said hello before he returned to work. The horses grazed in their outside corral.

Lark leaned on the fence post and watched the Appaloosas mill about. Penny, with her dark-gray diamond forehead and spotted body, trotted around the enclosure. The horse stopped on the other side of the corral and stood still, watching her.

"Hey, Penny."

The old mare whinnied and bobbled her head, then clopped straight over for a fuss. Lark petted her nose and scratched the top of her mane, telling her what a good horse she was. Penny seemed to agree, moving her long neck forward for more attention.

On the spur of the moment, Lark decided to take the horse out. Travis set her up. The ride was nowhere near as long or adventurous as the rides she'd gone on with Aaron, but it was nice to go out to the pasture.

Later, after she'd returned from her ride and had taken time to brush Penny, she sat to eat a light supper with her mother and checked her messages. Niall had responded to her text:

That is the best thing I've read all day. ALWAYS have you in my thoughts. And dreams. See you soon,

Shakespeare.

Every time Niall came near her, her insides screamed at her to go for it. Yet something held her back. The biggest issue was her break up with Charles. She'd never use Niall to heal from the hurt Charles caused her, but the guilt gnawed at her. Like Niall was a rebound relationship—and she didn't want him to be a rebound anything. Deep down, inside her heart, she grasped that Niall was what her mother would call a keeper. And like he'd said—he wasn't the type of guy to have a passing fling. Images flashed through her mind of the wheat field, their talk about their dreams meaning something, his lips adoring her body.

She sipped the tall glass of grapefruit juice on the desk before her, grateful for the oral destruction it brought. It tasted vile, but it worked. She didn't crave a cig.

Charles sent a text earlier in the day, saying he had arrived home and would call her later. Lark checked her watch. It would be around three in the morning back in England. Sitting at her father's desk, she stared at her e-ticket online. If she changed it, she'd have more time with Niall. She curved her forefinger around her mouth. Charles would go ballistic if she did. He'd fought her every step of the way on cutting him off, and she'd tried to coast around it so as not to damage their working relationship.

He didn't call until one a.m. Wednesday morning, her time, and she'd fallen asleep. She reached over for the phone, scraped it off the nightstand, and held it to an ear covered with tousled hair.

"Hello," she croaked.

"Lark?"

"Charles. Hey," she slid up in bed.

"Did you get my message?"

"Yeah, I got it. But my cell phone was off, and I didn't read it. Figured you'd be asleep."

"I was. It's almost nine here. What've you been up to?"

"Quite a bit." She yawned, not awake enough to register that they'd broken up. "I had a good day yesterday. I went for a long walk in the orchard and read a book under an old tree where I used to—"

"Sounds great." He sounded preoccupied. "I went into work yesterday. I'm about to head off again."

"Oh," she frowned. "Do you want me to let you go?"

"No, but I wanted you to know I'll be there. At work."

"Okay." Lark took the phone away from her ear and gave it a strange look. *So?* She put it back to her ear.

"Are you packed for Friday?"

She clicked on the nightstand lamp. She had to tell him. "No. I made the decision to cancel my flight last night."

"You *what*?"

She winced at the sharpness in his voice. "It's not any of your business, Charles, but I want to stay a while longer and spend time with my mom. I have the holiday time, and if I go back after such a short time with her, it doesn't feel right."

"Lark, no. You need to come back now— Is O'Hagan there?"

She shook her head, floored. "What? No. I haven't seen him since yesterday morning."

279

"It sounded like someone."

At the foot of her bed, Bandit lifted his head and front paws, stretching out as he gave her a cute, sleepy meow. "That was me, rearranging the covers."

"He's there, isn't he? I can hear him."

"Charles," she groused. "It's the damned cat on my feet and the bed covers. I'm not going to have this conversation with you acting like this. What I do from now on is none of your business. I don't know if you're having male PMS or what, but you can eat chocolate or something and call me back when you're ready to act like a grown-up. And find another place to stay. Good-bye." She shut the phone down, turned off the lamp, buried her face in the pillow, and pulled the covers over her head. "I hate men," she mumbled as she drifted off.

****

In the early afternoon, Lark leaned against the back porch railing, looking at the ranch. She'd managed to get more sleep after Charles's early-morning phone call, for which she was grateful. Her sleep schedule was still erratic from traveling and jet lag. She sighed, soaking in the essence of the place. These quiet moments were so hard to come by in fast-paced and noisy London. She savored the peace. The sun bathed the back garden in soft-hued golden light, and a pleasing, gentle breeze kissed her shoulders. The leaves blew and shot overhead like wondrous, tan-colored missiles. Fall was here, and winter wasn't far behind. Her eyes followed a few of them to the ground, where they collected together and rolled, herdlike with the wind, toward the woods. She'd helped plant daffodil bulbs in her mother's garden and found it wonderful there was still time in the day to take a break to enjoy the scenery of the woods and mountains in the distance.

Time had suspended itself as if it knew what was up with her chaotic life, to let her breathe in the fresh air and be at peace, away from men and the constant work they required. Pinecones adorned the evergreens, kissed by the low-slung autumn sun, and the fresh smell of the perennial pines filled her nostrils.

She was lighthearted and calmer than she'd been in years, but she couldn't explain why. The old, white sundress her mother once wore flapped delicately about her calves.

"That becomes you."

She turned, and Niall stood there, gazing at her. Sans jacket and tie, the two top buttons on his white shirt undone, and his sleeves rolled to the elbows, showing his strong forearms. Combined with the dark trousers, white shirt, and dark shoes, his thick, dark hair accented his handsome Irish face.

Lark smiled as she drummed her fingers on the railing.

"Thank you. I couldn't have worn it ten years ago." She gazed into the distance. "Charles never liked these types of dresses on me; he said they look too homely."

Niall set his cell phone on the patio table and walked over. "Well, Charles is a tool. It looks beautiful, and you look beautiful *in* it."

He gazed into her eyes, then at her wide-brimmed straw sun hat. The honest determination in his open expression touched her more than she wanted to admit. It was the same type of look she could picture him giving her in fifty years.

He lowered his chin and fixed his eyes on her. "Let's make a rule today. No walls. It's too pleasant an afternoon to argue. Spoils the magic."

She removed the hat and unwound the elastic at the end of her long braid, loosening the plaited strands with her fingers until her hair fell about her shoulders in wavy curls. He watched her every move, and it seemed strangely more erotic than taking her clothes off.

He leaned down and kissed her. "You're breathtaking, Lark." A breeze wafted past her, lifting hair off her shoulder. She had the funniest feeling it might be her father. She couldn't tell Niall in simple terms what his words meant to her, because nothing between them was simple. He brought her soul to life and reignited her passion, made her feel alive and feminine, supple and strong, all at once.

She edged the rim of the hat and watched Niall walk to the table and pick up his cell phone. The heat of the setting sun warmed her back. Niall pressed a button and then set the cell back down. He came back and took the hat from her hands and placed it on the wooden deck railing. He took her into his arms as an upbeat electric guitar played a love song by Ed Sheeran. Niall's eyes twinkled, and he moved in close, invading her personal space. He pressed his cheek against hers, taking her right hand in his left. A natural, familiar calm washed over her. The tempo played light enough not to be overwhelming, and a gentle calm settled upon her, quelling her hesitancy.

Thank God she didn't have to look into his eyes, or he would see her smiling. Her eyes fell to half-mast as she put her left arm around his shoulder. She had danced with Charles many times, sure, but in the company of others, at company functions, never as intimate as this. Niall's fingers stroked the small of her back, and he brought her in closer. His soft breath on the back of her neck made her nipples tighten, as did his touch.

This indecision wasn't fair to him. Giving him hope when she wasn't sure meant leading him on, even if she did want to stay and be with him. She should go. "Niall—"

"Lark?" He whispered her name in her ear, sending frissons through her. "The rule. Shut up, and dance with me."

She did.

He spun her once the music beat increased, and she laughed, letting go of her inhibitions.

This feels good. He smiled back, holding her to him and keeping his hand on her back while he led her.

"Mmm, you smell like autumn flowers." His lips skimmed the edge of her ear. "Nice."

He smelled nice too, masculine and woodsy. Their bodies swayed to the rhythm. He was a good dancer, at ease as he moved in time with her.

As the song neared its end, she closed her eyes. The crown of his fingertips skated along the nape of her neck, a quick, feathery touch. They stopped dancing, and Niall drew her closer. She trembled. *Stay.*

Her heartbeat thundered in her ears, her breath labored as his fingers traveled around her neck, then traced the contours of her collarbone. His scent—earth and grass and goodness—filled her senses until there was nothing but him. The music picked up.

His nose nuzzled her behind the ear, and his lips pressed against the base of her neck. Déjà vu settled in, and Lark opened her eyes with the strangest sense of watching herself in his arms from a distance, having been here before, possibly in her dreams.

He pulled her closer, and the heat of him warmed her like a good fire. She understood it then; he took whatever she would give him.

"Niall, I can't. This isn't fair to you," she whispered, wanting to go, wanting to stay. His hands spread on the small of her back, coasting slowly up her spine as he adorned her neck with his kisses. Hot lust bloomed where he touched her and spread throughout her body. Screw their emotional connection, she physically needed him.

"Yes, you can. You want to as much as I do. I can feel it," he murmured. The breath from his parted lips warmed her flesh. She looked into his eyes, as dark green as wild Spanish moss after rain.

What am I doing?

Lark broke free. She didn't trust herself to stay. He tried to touch her arm.

"Lar—"

"No, stop it." She raised her voice, blinking. "Why does everyone always assume they know what I want?" Her voice broke. They separated, and his wounded look made her ache.

"Lark? Please, wait a minute."

"Leave me alone," she called over her shoulder. She stalked into the kitchen through the back door.

Her mother sat at the kitchen table, peeling an orange and perusing a glossy magazine. "Lark? You all right, honey?" she asked, broken out of her reverie.

Lark held up a hand as she walked past Pam on her way to her bedroom. "Not now."

Once upstairs, she closed her door and locked it behind her, then leaned against it, panting. She closed her eyes and breathed deep, trying to still her galloping heart.

Heavy footsteps sounded on the stairs a few minutes later, and she dreaded what he might do, what *she* might do if she let him in. All it would take would be the unlocking of the door, and she'd surrender.

Silence met her from the other side. Was Niall right there, with his palm and face pressed against it?

She placed her hand against the door and shut her eyes. She touched her forehead to it, waiting until the sound of his footsteps retreated. Later, she gathered the courage to open the door. Her mother's straw hat hung on the doorknob.

Lark sat on her bed and watched the dimming light descend over the horizon. "I have no idea what to do," she said, her voice sounding loud in the room. "I'm choking on choices here, and it feels like I'm living someone else's life. But you understand, don't you? You always have. In the short time I've been here, you've been the only one who hasn't shoved the past down my throat or tried to goad me on." Bandit lifted his furry feline head from the foot of her bed, yawned, and laid his head on the other side of his elongated front paws.

"Ah, you fat, lazy cat. Do you know about my problems?" Lark chided him as she scratched him behind the ear. Niall's Explorer still remained in the driveway the last time she'd checked. She didn't want to face him, not yet. *Chicken.* But she needed to preserve her sanity.

She drew a hot bath and poured in a few drops of lavender oil her mother had left in a small, dark brown bottle in the medicine cabinet.

Sinking into the warm, enveloping haven worked miracles on her shoulders, neck, and sore back. She slid a leg through her wet hands and ran her fingers along her ankle to the back of her thigh as she stretched. She appreciated the soothing warmth and gentleness of the water for helping to make her feel better but hated it for washing traces of Niall off her skin. His scent. His taste.

She let out a sigh and tried to clear her mind but found that she could not. Niall was there, moving his hands over her, tantalizing and invoking the sensitive places of her skin. His lips caressed a delicate, erogenous spot behind her ear and traveled lower. Lark leaned her head back against the tub and closed her eyes. She soaked for a long time.

****

Half an hour later and wrapped in a towel, she peeked around her bedroom curtain. Below on the ground, Niall opened his SUV door. He paused before getting in and raised his face to her window. She moved away, knowing he'd seen her. Things were moving so fast, and so much had happened. If he came near her right now, she didn't have it in her to push him away anymore. Being with him excited her, and she longed to go to him and have uninterrupted time together.

The skies clouded over, and the first claps of thunder rumbled as she made her way downstairs after getting dressed.

"Warm as summer to cold and dreary…weather can't seem to make up its mind today," Pam said, sitting on the visiting-room sofa with her feet raised and crossed as she read a fat paperback. The table lamps to either side of her were turned on. "A lot like someone else I know," she added, with a special look at her daughter.

Lark descended the stairs. "Mom, please don't. I'm not in the mood."

Pam shrugged and went back to her book. "Fine. But if you want to talk about a certain someone and a certain something, I'm here," she said, turning a page. "There's chili con carne in the slow cooker if you want some. Bread's in the fridge. I got more grapefruit juice earlier. Should be behind the bread."

Lark glanced at the clock hung above the visiting-room window. It was late, nearing ten. The rain outside trickled on the ground, the sound carrying inside, soothing and metrical. She headed to the kitchen. "Thanks."

The warm chili had a nice, spicy kick to it. She had a small glass of milk, then rinsed out her plate and glass in the sink. Psyching herself up, she wrinkled her nose and poured the grapefruit juice into her glass, then headed to the living room. Pam had moved from the visiting room and sat on the couch in the library, a cheerful fire crackling away in the stone hearth as she read a fat romance novel.

"Wow, you're deep in it." Lark smiled, nodding at Pam's book as she sat cross-legged on the couch next to her, putting off the inevitable grapefruit juice for as long as possible.

The wind whipped against the windows, startling them both.

Pam glanced at Lark, then at the open curtains, where streams of rain slashed against the panes.

"It's going to town out there," she said. "The weatherman said it's supposed to rain for the next few days and then turn to snow. But oh, how they lie. We'll need sunblock by tomorrow, mark my words."

"Yep." Lark bit the bullet and sipped her juice. She wished with all her might to the Powers That Be that it tasted as good as the chili con carne. The Powers ignored her, and her taste buds suffered.

Her mother marked her place in the book and set it aside, supporting her elbow on the top of the couch as she leaned toward her.

"Okay, kiddo. Let's chat. The house is devoid of men, and I am *dying* of curiosity here. Are you going to tell me what in the Sam Hill is going on with Niall? The poor man is *mesmerized*. First, you storm through the kitchen earlier and stay upstairs. He follows you and comes back looking disappointed. I ask him where he's going at six at night since he's waiting for the bank to call us to go downtown and sign the trust over tomorrow. He mumbles about needing to clear his head and drives off. Lark," she demanded, "What is going *on* with you two?"

"Nothing," Lark said. "We were arguing about the estate."

"Hon, there's nothing left to argue about. It's done and dusted. All we have to do is sign and date along the dotted lines. You're in love with him, aren't you?"

Lark lifted her nose. "Of course, I'm not. That's ridiculous."

"Being engaged to Charles doesn't mean you can't care for someone else. You're human, Lark."

Recalling Niall telling her the same thing before everything went down, Lark set her glass on the coffee table and leaned her head back on the couch. She slid her hands together over her forehead and into her hair.

She sighed, looking at the ceiling. "Mom, I'm not in love with Niall, okay? This is all some kind of, I don't know, phase—"

"No, it's not. Niall's special. He would treat you right, and he's down-to-earth."

Lark pursed her lips. "What are you saying, then?" Her mother's eyes shone brightly. She wouldn't hold anything back, and Lark wasn't sure if she preferred her to or not.

"Well, if we're being open here, I think he represents what you want in a man. He's kind, thoughtful, not superficial. What you want your ideal companion to be. And the fact he's interested in you has got you so scared, you're defensive."

Lark sat up straight. "Spare me the dime-store psychology, okay, Mom? I mean, I'm sorry to slash open old wounds, but you're a fine one to talk about the 'ideal husband.' You must have cowered to Dad like, what, a thousand times?"

"Lark, be careful here," Pam warned. "I don't want this to end badly, to have you go away again. I couldn't stand it." Her eyes glimmered with the hint of tears. "I love you so much. But all the same, I won't let you talk to me that way. You're getting defensive because you *know* I'm right, and you have a habit of throwing other people's problems in their faces when you feel threatened. You're in love with Niall, honey, and it's got you scared to death. I can see it as plain as day. And what's got you even more scared is he loves you too."

Lark pressed her lips together, willing herself not to cry.

"Now, I don't know how Charles factors into this, or what's going on here, but you have a decision to make, and soon. What are you going to do?"

Lark took a deep breath. "Mom, there's nothing *to* do. I'll pack my bags, get on my plane, and be off in a few days, back to my nice, cushy job. I'm not about to make an impulsive decision which could risk everything I've worked for, based on a strange guy I've known for what, two weeks?"

"It can take less than five minutes to fall in love. It happened with me and your father."

"Get real, Mom. It's the twenty-first century. Since I was a kid, you've adopted this insane notion the guy is supposed to be the breadwinner and the girl the homemaker; they meet and *smack.* They fall in love, get married, pop out two-point-five kids, and drive a minivan. Unfortunate news flash here, that's not how the world works for me, or how I see things. Situations are different, people are different.

"You don't kiss your husband's ass, cook him dinner every night, let him get the last word in, and think it's okay. You *especially* don't let him cheat on you, then go back to acting like everything's fine," Lark seethed, on the edge of her seat, and it dawned on her with a growing horror she spoke about her own situation, not her mother's.

Pam scanned her eyes. "All right, then…Lark, I don't blame you for still having hang-ups about what happened, but you shouldn't use them to change the subject because you're uncomfortable. It speaks volumes about your insecurity."

Lark couldn't handle it anymore, and she buried her face in her hands, sobbing and shaking. Her mother's arms wound around her, and she cried into them for a good long while.

"I love you, Lark," her mother whispered into her hair. "You're my flesh and blood. I'll be here for you always, no matter what. No matter what."

Lark wiped her tears, sat up, and shook her head. "Mom, I love you, but I don't understand you," she said. "Dad pretended to be this great, committed, family-oriented man, with so many values and morals, and then he cheated on you. You, who he pretended to love. He built his business on his good, wholesome reputation, but it was a lie."

"He wasn't pretending, Lark," Pam said. "He did love me."

"He played you like a puppet, Mom, and us right along with you," Lark fumed. She stood and grabbed her glass from the floor, ready to leave. "I don't want to argue with you either. But it pisses me off to no avail to have watched you cower your whole life to someone who's not worth it. He owed you *so* much more than he ever gave you."

Pam looked up at her with a hurt expression, tears sliding down her cheeks.

"I'm going to bed before I say anything else I'll regret. I've got a lot I'm dealing with right now. I-I'm sorry." Lark turned and left her mother in front of the fire, angry and put off by the nineteen-sixties brainwashing mentality Pam seemed to embrace. Okay, so she'd been bitchier than she should have been. After all, Pam was only trying to help. Lark closed her bedroom door and got ready for bed. She should apologize or at least have a makeup ice cream fest at some point. After all, her mother had been right, about everything.

The wind rushed against the windows as she lay

there, listening as it created a rhythmic, thwacking sound as a branch tapped the window pane. Outside, the storm raged on. After a time, she was able to close her eyes. Sleep was a long time in coming.

Chapter Fourteen
Rain

The wedding was bright and colorful. Silver, red, and white decorations swooped from lampposts and covered tables set up behind the ranch house. Charles dazzled in a black-and-white tuxedo, holding her hand as they laughed and cut their three-tiered wedding cake in front of their guests. Her sleeveless white dress fit around her bust and torso, flowing from the waist down. Her hair was curled and loose. Picture flashes went off as Charles fed her a slice of cake, and everyone cheered and clapped.

Charles was extra-attentive and kept feeding her cake after she told him to stop. His expression grew demanding, and he said under his breath, "Eat the cake," in a malicious, unforgiving tone. "Just fucking *eat the cake*."

Frightened, she shook her head and broke free of him, holding the skirts of her wedding dress. She pushed past the crowd of onlookers and banked toward the stables. She glanced back. The decorations remained, but everyone had disappeared. The chairs were all vacant, the presents and food on the table untouched.

Lark turned her face back and collided with Niall. Relaxed and handsome, he put his hands on the outer edges of her arms and looked at her. He wore a white shirt, open at the throat, and it seemed out of place, of the past and not of this world.

"Whoa, there," he chided her with a kind smile. "Almost ran me over, Shakespeare. Where you goin' with the devil on your tail?"

"I'm trying to get away from him," she breathed, afraid to look back in case Charles was there.

Niall looked past her to the wedding pavilion. He nodded and took her hand in his. "Come with me."

He led her past the stables to the small fruit orchard and kept looking at her. A red-and-white-plaid picnic blanket lay under her favorite apple tree, and he took her to it. She sat in her wedding dress, and he stretched out beside her.

Lark did not know how it happened, but she lay down, looking up at the trees, her hand above her head. Niall supported himself on his elbow next to her, his eyes riveted on hers.

"You are magnificent," he said, and he leaned over and kissed her, his full, sensual lips warm and soft. The deeper the kiss went, the more she became lost in it. His fingers caressed her long, full hair fanned out on the blanket.

"You're an angel. My angel," he murmured, his hands rubbing her inner thighs as he inched her dress up, the pads of his thumbs nearing her pussy, making her quake with anticipation.

****

A loud noise woke her, and Lark opened her eyes. She rubbed the back of her neck as the thunder outside growled and rumbled. She reached over for the glass of water on the nightstand. She grimaced at the sour taste. It was the grapefruit juice from earlier. She checked the bedside clock. Near midnight.

The juice tasted like crap. She brushed her teeth to get rid of the taste. Still thirsty, Lark changed into black sweat bottoms and a white T-shirt and put her slippers on. She held on to the empty glass, intent on getting more. The bedroom door opened with a slight creak, and she stepped out into the dark hallway as the cat slunk past her. A soft glow from the stairs lit the path enough for her to make her way down, the microwhisper of the Berber carpet beneath her slippers soft and comforting.

She took her time going downstairs, half-asleep and not wanting to trip. It was quiet below, except for a small, random sputter that did not sound like rain. The soft glow she'd seen upstairs belonged to a fire in the living room to her right and a small table lamp someone left on. The room appeared empty. A few low flames fought their way for survival in the stone fireplace, on the verge of dying out.

She went into the kitchen and over to the fridge, where she depressed the valve for cold filtered water. She scratched her leg with the opposite foot while also rotating her neck and getting the kinks out. She took a few deep gulps of the cold, refreshing liquid, then padded with glass in hand back toward the stairs.

As she placed a hand on the railing and a foot on the bottom stair to go back up, a strong roar of thunder reverberated throughout the house.

Clutching the glass and shaking, Lark turned and instead made her way to the living room and around the couch, where she stood in front of the dying fire. She placed the glass of water on the mantelpiece next to a framed photo of her dad, then warmed her hands to avoid having to look at his picture. She tried to get her head around the dream, but she still fought that in-between state between consciousness and being asleep and didn't want to think about the argument she'd had with her mother.

Watching the flames in the fireplace, she backed up and sat on the sofa. She squeaked when she sat on a pair of legs. Strong arms slid about her waist.

"Hey, I've had this dream," a familiar Irish brogue whispered in her ear. Lark yelped and turned in shock. Niall's face was mere inches from her own, amused and taking her in. The firelight reflected in his eyes as he smirked.

"We've got to stop meeting like this," he said, deadpan. "Would you like me to tell you a story, ma'am? You see, I happen to have a knack for storytelling, goes way back in me ilk for generations. If you're having trouble sleepin', I'll be more than happy to—"

Lark disengaged from his arms and lap and stood. He chuckled. She folded her arms, pursed her lips, and went to a nearby window, watching the rain and storm outside so he would not see her blushing.

"Burning the midnight oil, are we?" she asked, wishing her voice wasn't so tense. There was enough light thrown from the small lamp and fireplace to vaguely see him in the windowpane. She didn't need his reflection, though, to remember what he'd been wearing. Niall was relaxed in a cotton dark-blue pajama top that opened to a white T-shirt beneath, with matching bottoms. His thick, dark hair was tousled.

He made a noise, and she turned to see him. Niall stretched out his long legs, crossed his ankles, and went back to his book, which he held one-handed. His thumb and little finger were extended on either side of the outer edge, and it struck her as a sexy way to hold a book, attractive in its own right. With his other hand, he massaged a purring Bandit behind the ears. So, the cat had been two-timing her with a hot Irish guy. It figured. The cat curled on the cushion next to Niall like a furry pretzel. Niall's long fingers stroked the feline cheekbone, and Lark pressed her lips together.

"Ah, like I said, I have trouble sleeping," Niall said, seemingly engrossed in what he read.

How could he shun everything that had happened into oblivion and act so relaxed? He seemed to have a knack for overcoming embarrassing moments, letting them pass him by without a care.

"I'm going back to my condo tomorrow since business is pretty much wrapped up here. We should have everything settled."

The book he held was a thin, dark-brown hardback. The dim light made it hard to make out the title in bold gold lettering along its spine. She turned back to the window and listened to the rain, not daring to speak to him, but not wanting to go upstairs yet either, her dream still too fresh and lucid.

He closed the book with a muted *clap*. It made a soft *thump* as he placed it on the table. He paused, then recited: "*Day after day, day after day, we stuck, nor breath nor motion; As idle as a painted ship upon a painted ocean.*"

Lark did not skip a beat. "Coleridge," she murmured without turning around.

"Mmm," he approved. The sofa creaked as he shifted position. "Well, young Miss Braithwaite, what's got you up on an auspicious evening such as this? The thunder keeping you awake? Hasn't stopped blowing all night. Was loud enough t' wake a hibernating bear earlier. The walls shook."

"No, it's not that," she said testily, looking outside. "I...had an argument with my mother," she said, shaking her head. "She comes from a generation of women who think no matter what a man does, he's always right. And I'm a hardheaded, cold battle-ax. Ergo, we clashed."

"No, you're not," he assured her, chuckling. "You're clear-thinking. Pam's also stronger than you give her credit for." He stretched out. "If she fought past the conflict in her heart to forgive Rick his philandering, I expect she had her reasons. Don't punish her because she put it behind her."

Lark watched the rain outside hit the pavement, then shoot upward, ricocheting like mini water pellets.

"It's so easy for you to defend her, isn't it, Niall? You're a man. If a man cheats, it's supposed to be okay, isn't it?"

"You know I didn't say that," he countered.

"Well, what the hell? Why do you defend her?" Lark asked his reflection in the glass. He stood from the sofa. Bandit lifted his furry head and meowed, annoyed by the movement, then lay over his front paws and fell back asleep.

"Because someone's got to. Hey, look at what I do for a living. I'm an attorney, an advocate. Everyone needs an advocate. Don't hang your mother out to dry because she happens to be your father's. She gave him a second chance. Haven't you ever been given one?"

Lark put her palm against the windowpane. Cold,

fat rain droplets slid down on the other side as the storm beat a musical *pitter-patter* rhythm on the pavement, pool, and roof shingles. "I think I'm being given one now," she whispered, loud enough for him to hear.

Niall came up behind her and put a warm hand on her shoulder. "I'm no one to dole out advice, but the one thing I do know," he said with deep conviction, "is we make decisions daily which determine our future. We're in our own world, aye, but we also live *in* a world. We make choices. It's important to make the right ones."

"Don't you ever get tired of sounding like a fortune cookie?" she bit out.

Niall laughed. His hand squeezed her shoulder, but it irritated her. She whirled around.

"No, I want to know," She raised her voice. "Seriously, what makes you such an *expert* on forgiving someone who's wronged you? What's ever happened in your life that was so damned trying you had to forgive someone for the hurt they'd caused you?" A chasm of pain surfaced on his face as he withdrew his hand, taking Lark aback. She must have struck a nerve because his face filled with intense sorrow.

He drew a deep breath and considered her. "All right. If you want to know, I'll tell you. Please have a seat, and lower your voice." He turned to click off the side lamp. He sat on the carpet a few feet away from the fire and propped a knee up, resting his right arm around it as he leaned forward to place another log upon the low, orange flames that licked the dying logs. She walked over and sat on the carpet cross-legged, next to him. His features became illuminated and dark at the same time, the lines in his face etched from the shadows and firelight, giving away his age.

"Lark…I'm going to tell you something I haven't told anyone but your dad. I'll ask you to keep it between the two of us."

"All right." She leaned forward, interested.

Niall's voice dropped, his tone steady. "A long time ago, I was married…" He lifted his head, gazing into the fire. His eyebrows lifted. "We were twenty-one. Melanie was six months pregnant, expecting our first child. We lived in Ireland at the time. I grew up in east Dublin and lived in Achill Sound for a while. We had a small maisonette there and were doing all right. I'd graduated from uni and worked as an apprentice solicitor in a law firm close to where we lived. I'd use the train every day to save on petrol, and Melanie used the car. She worked as a nurse in the maternity ward at our local hospital. She was beautiful, Lark. Her smile would melt the sorest heart. She was full of spirit and clever as they come. She had a fond love of the bluebells in our garden each May."

"How did you two meet?" Lark leaned back against the bottom of the couch and drew her arms around her knees.

He smiled. "We grew up on the same street. She couldn't stand me, though. She called me arrogant and rowdy—which I was, by the way. We didn't fall in love until secondary school. She had a knack for putting me in my place, as you do. That's perhaps all you two have in common. She found the good in me, and it made me see the good in myself."

Lark watched his face as he spoke. The firelight danced in his sharp, dark green eyes. He stared into the flames, which crackled and shifted as though recounting his story for him.

"One night, a few weeks before Christmas," he went on, his voice faltering, "my firm had a party we went to. It was late, and Melanie didn't want us to stay. She kept on me, wantin' to leave before it got too dangerous on the roads with the pub-dwellers and riffraff about. I drank back then, but I didn't drink because I knew I'd be driving. I kept saying, 'in a moment, love,' and 'we'll leave soon, I know you're tired.' But my colleagues were full of good cheer, talking my ear off and pissed with spirits. It came close to midnight, and we left because Melanie had had enough.

"I was horrible to have made her stay there with smoke in the air, the smell of the drink around us... To this day, I regret it with every breath I take." His voice broke. "Not a day goes by that I don't think about it. It's why I don't drink or smoke, to honor her in some small way as much as I can. I regret a lot, Lark. I didn't know at the time how to properly care for a woman, and I acted young and selfish, a foolish git who should have known better. Anyway," he continued, sighing as he moved forward and nudged the fire with the poker. "The roads seemed clear enough. My work's Christmas party took place at a fairground they'd converted for use into a large, heated tent. They threw nice, catered parties and live entertainment," he added with a slight smile.

"We had about a half-hour drive back to our home, and as we drove back, Melanie let me have it for having kept her there. The one thing you both have in common is you don't hold anything back. By all rights, I deserved it," Niall mused. "I was concerned with myself back then, scalin' that old bottom rung with the promise of a bright, shiny hole at the top of the climb, working sixty hours a week, and never at home. She tried to plan for the baby and do everything herself, always tired and frustrated. She was under the weather that night, but I made her go anyway." His voice was thick with bitterness. "I made her go. I wasn't as loving as I ought to have been, nor concerned with her well-being." He shot a lopsided smile at Lark. "Never underestimate the wrath of an Irishwoman. Anyway, like the git I was, I argued back and had the bottle to call her unsupportive of my new position in the firm. We argued when I turned into a roundabout, and then it happened." He turned away, but not before his face contorted into a mask of pain. His shoulders hunched, and his voice broke. She ached for him.

"What happened?" Her tender tone gave away her deep adoration for him, but he stared into the fire, preoccupied and locked in the past.

"A beat-up, blue Ford Escort came careening into the roundabout from the wrong direction at top speed. I remember the heavy-metal song blaring from the speakers. It's etched in my brain like a bad taste in me mouth. I'll never forget it. It collided head-on with our Mini, and I couldn't stop in time or steer around it. It smashed the front end of our car, and the impact caused us to roll over and crash into the median. I woke up, and they'd put me on a stretcher. I'd broken ribs, a broken leg, and I later learned I had a concussion."

Lark leaned forward and placed a hand on his back. He turned his head when she touched him but did not turn around. Instead, he lowered his chin.

"It's funny," he choked, sounding nasal. "When I

came to, I turned my head to the side, and there was this young lad.

"This ginger-haired, punk-rock lad with nose rings and a leather jacket. He sat on the open, back end of the ambulance van with a shock blanket over his shoulders, shakin' like a leaf on a tree. He saw me, then burst into tears, holding his bloody face in his hands in a way I'll never forget. I woke, and I asked for Melanie. The medic said, plain as rain, 'Mr. O'Hagan, your wife and her baby were killed in the crash tonight.' Offered his apologies."

"Oh, Niall," Lark choked out, tears spilling down her cheeks. She moved next to him and took his hand in hers.

His eyes shone, brimming with moisture. His voice steadied, his urban Irish accent thick. "The medic *did* sound like he was sorry, but I will never forget that shivering boy. My world was torn apart in a heartbeat. Me life ended; it's true. She was my heart's song, Lark. I loved her. I should have been a better husband to her and a better father to our unborn son. But in a twisted turn, the kid's agony hurt like it was my own. It haunted me."

"You're so generous. I would have hated him," Lark spat out.

"*Hate* him? No, Lark." He turned to her and covered her hand with his. "Love, I *pitied* him. Every hope and dream I had for the future extinguished with the death of Melanie and the baby, but I could go on and keep them in my heart as long as I lived, and somehow do good in the world to make up for the wrong I'd done and had been done to me. It was clear to me from then on. But the *boy*." Niall shook his head.

"His name is Sean Malley, and he was a kid. Seventeen, Lark. He'd been drinking and had so many drugs in his system he could tranquilize a fucking elephant. He didn't know what he did. I didn't have to wonder. His body language alone told me how sorry he was. I had the power to lock him up for the rest of his life, but it wouldn't have equaled the punishment he has inside him he's got to live with."

"You forgave him so soon?" asked Lark, astonished.

"I *had* to," Niall said. "Hate is a cancer which will eat at your core, devour you whole if you let it until you're consumed by it. I know Melanie forgives him, and she would have wanted me to do the same. I did.

"For the first while, I turned to God to muddle through, and it helped. But then I grew depressed, missing her. I drank to ease the pain, and before long, I spent more time at the pub than the firm, my work fell behind, and I got sacked. Father May from the parish took me under his wing, having me help out in the soup kitchen and work in the gardens when all I wanted to do was die."

Lark flinched. "Are you telling me you never took that kid to court?"

Niall shrugged. "What would have been the point?"

"I—I can't believe you didn't press charges, Niall! You had every right. You *should* have done."

Niall furrowed his brow. "That's what they kept saying. Colleagues at work, my family, her family. 'Hang him out to dry, Niall.' 'Don't let the shoddy wanker get away with it.' But I did what I had to do, and soon after it happened, I was a wreck, anyway. I mean, imagine. The guilt and pain of killing a woman and her unborn child, eating away at you for the rest of your life. Knowing you'd caused unimaginable grief and anguish to someone's life because of one stupid decision you made. He was a confused kid."

Lark put a hand to her heart. There was no way in hell she'd ever be as magnanimous as he had been.

"When I got better, I visited him in prison a few times. He shivered from head to foot whenever I came into contact with him. He couldn't be in my presence without becoming a scared little boy. His sorrow ate at him. He apologized from the depths of his soul to me with tears in his eyes, and I chose to forgive him. I was in a sore state, meself. I helped out Father May, but my heart wasn't into it. It served as more of a resting ground, so I didn't have to think. I didn't press charges. He did, however, serve nine years for several counts of drug charges and driving under the influence, and despite my not pressing charges, Melanie's family did. He wrote me at the parish while I lived there. I had a small room without so much as a picture to remind me of Melanie. But in an odd way, it kind of helped. When Sean got out, I sent him a letter, telling him I forgave him and that he should get on with his life. I haven't had any contact with him since then."

Lark shook her head. She would never be able to turn the other cheek in the same situation. Shame filled her. She'd be too hurt to do anything but hate Sean Malley. She marveled at Niall's strength and spirit. Her weakness lay in holding grudges and not being able to forgive and forget.

"A church would burn down if I walked into it," she admitted. "And you lived in one. I can't hold a candle to you for forgiveness."

He inclined his head with a knowing look in his eye. "I doubt that. You're more compassionate. All people are. We're so caught up in the daily grind, our true natures get slammed aside in the fallout."

She waved it off. "What happened between the time you were living in the parish and now?"

Niall sighed. "Well, I'd been living there for over five years, keeping to myself and getting visits from family from time to time. One day, I got a visit from someone unexpected. Your father's attorney, and my old partner, Craig Fernelius. Good lad, he was. He was an American, from Portland, who worked with me at my old firm in Ireland. He got wind of what happened, and he flew over and convinced me it was time to move on. We got on like brothers, and he railed into me and told me my talents and hard studying to become a lawyer were being laid to rest by staying where I was, and the efforts I put into my earlier career were being rendered fruitless. I wanted to move on, but I didn't know *how* to. A life of isolation wasn't in the cards for me, as much as being around kind people might bring me peace. Craig convinced me to go to Oregon on a visa from his law practice to try to rebuild me life.

"It took persuading. I mean, I was happy there. The work was quiet, and I enjoyed listening to people go on about themselves, never asking about me. Those who knew what happened were good enough to never bring it up. I left the parish and moved to Portland to live with Craig and his family for a while. When I was established, I bought my condo downtown. I worked as an associate for three years before he made me a partner, and he passed away soon after. He wanted to make me a partner before he went. When he died, I took over your father's account, and I've been good friends with Rick ever since. He's the only person other than Craig, and now you, who knows of my past. I think your mam has an inkling, but she's never let on as much," he concluded, letting out a small sigh of relief.

"That kid… I can't believe you," Lark said, wiping her eyes with her fingers and casting a hurt look to the side.

Niall placed a finger beneath her chin and turned her toward him. "Hey," he chided.

She had no idea how he did it from merely widening his eyes, but his gaze kindled her insides as though she'd stepped into a warm, welcoming, firelit cabin from the freezing arctic cold of the tundra.

His sharp eyes gleamed in the firelight as they searched hers, and she knew he could tell she struggled to forgive.

"Everyone deserves a second chance, Lark," he said, keeping his eyes on her while jerking his head in the direction of the framed black-and-white photograph she'd touched earlier on the mantel above them.

She turned her head and looked at the professional studio photo from the eighties of her father perched on the edge of a mahogany desk, his arms folded as he smiled and frowned at the same time into the camera. He wore a nice, dark-blue business suit and silk tie. How foxlike he had been—cunning and sharp. Funny, the details you remember once someone is out of your life.

"Don't hate him because of one mistake he made, eh? Forgive him." Niall stroked her cheek with the back of his hand. "After all, that's what we're here to do."

Lark closed her eyes and took a deep breath. "You're right, of course. You're right," she murmured. Her mind flooded with memories of her father's indiscretions, of her mother's words, of poor Melanie O'Hagan and the child Niall would never hold in his arms, of Sean Malley, maybe back in prison, still living with his guilt.

Niall's thumbs brushed away a few tears on her cheeks, and he held her face in his hands. She opened her eyes, not wanting to look anywhere else. She placed her hand over his, brushing the underside of her thumb over his fingers. "You're an amazing person, Niall."

He leaned his head to the side and raised his eyebrows. "I wouldn't say so, but I do have me moments."

Lark nodded and smirked, and the expression in his eyes said it all. She remained still, her heart aching for him with both respect and desire, for the power of forgiveness he possessed, for the unique person he was inside *and* out.

She leaned into him, her lips pressing against his. He stayed still at first, as though anticipating she'd leave, but then he responded, and the kiss took on a life of its own. With a slight breath, she cast off her inhibitions and let go.

He slid his arms around her, pulling her close. He nipped at her bottom lip, deepening the kiss. Lark opened her mouth, moaning as she allowed Niall's tongue access, not hesitating to twine with his. A low growl of approval sounded against her lips. The kiss grew from passionate to all-consuming. He moved to devour her neck, and his hands explored her, his fingers caressing her nipple through her shirt, and when he squeezed it, a moist, throbbing response between her legs demanded attention. She rubbed her legs together to try to appease the friction and let her head fall back as his lips explored her, allowing herself to feel.

"I want to see you," he pleaded in a deep tone, sliding his hands beneath the hem of her shirt. "All of you."

Words from my dreams. She nodded, holding her hands up as he slid her shirt off. His eyes held hers as he pushed her down to the soft rug, and she helped him remove her sweatpants and panties.

Lark gulped, vulnerable at being laid out so bare in front of him. She'd been bare in his truck in the wheat field, yes, but this seemed...more exposed. And although she'd lost a significant amount of weight, some insecurities never went away. She attempted to cover her breasts, flustered, but he tenderly took her wrists in his hands and placed them above her head, opening her to his intense gaze.

"No. Let me see you, Lark."

His eyes drank her in from head to toe, lingering in one place before travelling to the next, and the ache between her thighs pulsed.

"You are so amazing. So beautiful," he murmured. "May I touch you?"

"Yes," she whispered.

His hand slid to her breast. "Here?"

She nodded, gasping when he took her breast in his mouth, laving the areola and dusky-pink nipple with his warm tongue until they grew taut. He repeated the same with her other one, and she squirmed to quell the burning between her legs. He trailed his hand to her waist, spanning his fingers out over her flat abdomen, asking with his eyes.

"Yes," she whispered again, and he kissed her stomach, nearing her exquisite torment. He waited for consent, and she smiled shyly, opening her legs for him and nodding.

Niall cupped her mound, massaging it. She wasn't bushy down there anymore—she'd just shaved—and he seemed pleased by it from the way he stroked the thin thatch of dark hair. Looking into her eyes, he slid his hand into her teeming wetness, spreading it over her swollen slit. Lark moaned as he found her clit. He rubbed it with his thumb in a quick, chafing rhythm. She tossed her head from side to side.

"I love the look on your face when I'm doing this to you," he murmured. He slid his middle finger farther in and pushed it inside her, feeling around her inner walls, while his thumb continued its assault on her swollen nub of pleasure. Lark trembled, staring at him, wishing she could keep him.

He groaned and kissed her, his tongue enticing hers with a languid slowness. She arched for more. He withdrew his finger and then slowly inserted two. She moaned as they filled her, at his complete disposal. He continued to assault her clit, his fingers taking her to a feverish pace. She writhed beneath him, her hips rolling against his hand unashamedly. He consumed her, and she'd never been this turned on in her life. Her skin came alive beneath his touch. She was lost to it.

Her thighs trembled, and her pussy tightened with anticipation when his sopping fingers pushed farther inside her, curling up. She seized up as the orgasm came over her, wailing with the rain. He held her with tenderness and kissed her, slow and absolute, smoothing down her damp hair.

"Lark, I want to be with you, *inside* you."

He searched her eyes, and she nodded, her heart leaping for joy. She touched his cheek. "Yes. I want you inside me."

He smiled and kissed her, lifting to yank his shirt off with one hand and toss it away. He stood to push off his pajama bottoms.

Distracted by his hard cock, which sprang free and jutted out as if coming to attention for her, she sat up. She moved forward on all fours, admiring his nakedness. He was a virile, well-built man. The firelight illuminated the delineations of his muscles and the light smattering of chest hair. He froze, watching her move toward him, until she sat before him on her knees, having made up her mind to do it the second he stripped.

She slid her hands along his muscular legs, noting the few, sun-kissed freckles on an otherwise perfect body. "I have to confess. It's been so difficult to look at you and not believe you're still in my dreams." She spread her fingers along his leg and kissed his knee. "I've struggled, feeling guilty, but I want you so bad, Niall. I can't help myself anymore." She stroked the perfect globes of his ass and kissed his hip bone. She ran her tongue along the warm skin toward his cock. He drew in a deep breath, fingering her hair as she enclosed her hand around him. The tip of his cock glistened with pre-cum, and she rubbed the bead of moisture with her thumb, spreading it over the head and along the shaft.

"I crave you." She lifted to lick the salty tip, her mind reeling with how long she'd wanted to do this.

Niall wound his right hand in her hair, his face a battle of raging lust and concern.

"Lark, you know you don't have to, right? Oh, sweet God…"

She took him into her mouth and learned in the next few minutes what it finally took to shut Niall O'Hagan up. Smiling, she moved her tongue from side to side, licking him like an ice-cream cone. She loved both the power it gave her and the inimitable taste of him. She gave him a long, drawn-out suck, and he inhaled harshly, carding his fingers through her hair, saying something gruffly in Irish Gaelic.

"Shakespeare, if you keep that up, mmm, I'm going to go sooner than I'd like. You have no idea how much I want you…have dreamed about you."

He trembled with unfulfilled desire against her, but before she could bring him to the height of his pleasure, he stepped back and withdrew from her mouth, picked her up, and laid her back on the rug before the fire.

He kissed her and positioned himself over her. "I can't wait anymore. I have to have you. This is everything," he whispered.

She nodded. It was. The tip of his hard, swollen cock nudged her wet flesh, and as she opened for him, he laced his fingers with hers, bringing them to either side of her head.

"Lark, I love you."

He kept his gaze on hers as he entered her. Lark entwined her fingers with his, held by the love in his eyes. She groaned as he stretched and filled her.

He continued to push forward, sinking into her wetness, until it felt like the final, long-lost piece of a puzzle returning to complete it. He sheathed himself to the hilt, deeper inside her than anyone had been. She lay there, filled and stunned by the sensation of being stretched in the most delicious of ways. Her dreams were hot and enjoyable, but this was unexpected and more wonderful than she could hope for.

"*Is tú mo ghrá*," he whispered. Lark had no clue what he said, but she returned his tender kiss and put her arms around him. Nothing would ever be the same again. She'd fallen in love with him.

He kissed her forehead, shifting to slide out of her, before thrusting back in, deep. Lark tossed her head back with pleasure and lifted her hips to meet him in eager anticipation. He was made for her, unquestionably. The word *magic* formed, and it floated around her like a cheerful little cloud. Her breasts brushed against his chest hair as they built a feverish rhythm. Pleasant hot bursts flowed between them with each roll of the hips, each sharp thrust of his cock into her eager pussy. He kissed her, pushing and pulling and digging into her, drowning in her, and she clutched him like a lifejacket.

To give credit where credit was due, it'd been forever for him since he'd been with a woman, but he lasted a lot longer than most men would. She clutched his shoulders and tried to match his frenzied, tortuous cadence, but the more he fucked her, the more she lost control and clenched her buttocks, the harder he drove into her. She cried out as he brought her to the edge. He stopped as she seized up, and fell into her neck. She put a hand into his hair, frowning. His body stilled, tense against her.

She regained her breath. "Niall, are you okay?"

"I want to take your perfect pussy from behind," he

rumbled into her ear with constrained emotion. She gasped, and he pulled out and flipped her over. The hard contours of his abdomen rippled along the smoothness of her back as he moved. He prodded her entrance and pushed his hard, demanding cock into her dripping-wet channel, a guttural grunt escaping through his clenched teeth as he slid home. Lark sucked in her breath and hissed, full with him as he brought her to her hands and knees. Oh, she loved this position. She hadn't been in it for a long time, and he felt amazing inside her.

He pulled out and plunged back in, unremittingly, his whole body tight against her as his muscles moved over her with the single intent of consuming her. It was pleasure and pain, and she loved it.

"You're so wet, love. I'm going to make you come. You deserve to. You deserve it all."

He reached between them and stroked her clit as he snapped his hips into her. Lark reared her hips back, meeting him thrust for thrust. His body moved powerfully over her, and she tightened with the tension. He sped up his ministrations on her clit, chafing it with his fingernail. It hit the right chord with her body, and she was done in.

"Y-*yes*," she roared. "Please, Niall. Please!" He encouraged her with each impact of his cock, panting cut-off, garbled words as he gripped her so rough she would have bruises in the morning. But right now, she could care less, because he was fucking her, fucking her so hard.

The fire shifted, and the sweet smell of the wood invaded her nostrils. He slammed his cock into her, and it was like time stood still, suspending them in slow motion. His sweat mingled with hers, the taste of saliva and sex upon her tongue a provocative perfume. Every twist and pull and delicious thrust.

She tried to grasp his buttocks but failed. She dug her fingers into the side of his thigh instead, squeezing it as she would his ass. He sped up, and she reared back to meet him, hard. The impact of it hit her cervix, and she cried out as he tensed behind her.

"You're amazing, Lark. So incredible." His hand clenched at her hip, and a hot spurt of his seed shot inside her, warming her delectably. "Oh yes. *Fuck.*" He rubbed her lower back as the rest of his semen exploded inside her. "Yes, sweetheart. Oh God, Lark, you feel so good. I love being inside you. Love *you.*"

He reached over and pinched her clit, and she cried out as she came again. She threw her head against his shoulder as a searing wave of pleasure rolled over her. He sucked her neck, growling. This man was like a narcotic.

He fisted her hair and turned her head to the side, his mouth claiming hers in a rough, passionate kiss. His tongue dominated hers at first, and then he slowed and took time to languidly taste her. She loved the way he kissed. They trembled together, soaked in each other's nectar, and she slid to the rug on her stomach, the softness stimulating her nipples as she brushed against it. His arms buckled, and he collapsed on top of her, burying his face into the crook of her neck, inhaling.

"That's it. I'm keeping you, and there's nothing you can do about it."

She smiled at the rawness in his voice, his heartbeat thundering against her back, matching her own.

With the weight of him against her back, she learned his soft and hard places with the edge of her hand, traced the curve of his bum, the back of his neck, the thick curls on his head. He stroked her hip to the sides of her breasts and throat, slid his hand down her forearm, and entwined their fingers together. Life could be pretty messed up, but this made up for it. He remained inside her, limp now, but she was reluctant to move, too content. He pressed his lips against her shoulder and pulled out, rolling to the side.

"Are you cold?" He stroked her back as she smiled at him.

"A little."

Niall handed her a box of tissues from the nearby end table. He reached over and extracted a throw blanket from the edge of the sofa, covering them after they'd cleaned up. The orange embers of the fire crackled in the hearth. She rested her head on his chest, cuddling as he brought her in close and put an arm around her. She laid her palm over his steady heart. He traced the soft curve of her breast over the blanket, and she sighed.

The euphoria of lying in his arms, sated, was sheer bliss, a mindless escape where she only experienced the sweet glow of their love. She'd enjoyed going down on him. It gave her a tremendous sense of power, the kind she could get drunk off if she was so inclined. There was a certain inherent royalty in knowing a man so impressive and strong came apart in the most primal of ways from her touch.

She nestled into the warmth of his arms. He kissed her hair tenderly, stroking her arm, and they both fell asleep to the gentle, sweet rhythm of the rain.

Chapter Fifteen
Choices

Hands roused her a few hours later, roaming her curves, lips coaxing the side of her neck. In truth, Lark had already been stirring, but she let him carry on until she opened her eyes.

"Hey." He smiled.

"Hey," she whispered.

He nodded to the fire, which had gone out. It was still morning, judging by the darkness outside the curtains. "What's the time?" she asked, sitting up.

"Half past three. I figured you may want to go somewhere more comfortable."

Lark rolled her stiff neck, touching his forearm. "And private. My room?"

"Sure," he whispered, gathering their clothes and helping her stand. They dressed against the morning chill and walked into the kitchen. Lark turned the stove light on and poured them both glasses of water. Niall searched the fridge and took a small plate of chicken legs out, then followed her upstairs.

Pam's room was on the opposite side of the house, and she took something to help her sleep, but as a precaution, Lark locked her bedroom door behind them once they were inside and propped the top of her vanity chair against the handle so they wouldn't be disturbed. Niall set his glass and food on the nightstand and turned on her bedside lamp, surveying the room as he ate a bite of chicken.

"You're the first guy I've made love to in this house." She draped her arms around his torso.

"I'm honored," he assured her, taking her chin in his hand and bringing her mouth up for a quick kiss. "In fact, we should christen your room."

She wasn't about to say no. She blushed, touching his cheek. "Okay, but let's clean first. C'mon." She took his hand and led him into the bathroom.

Lark looked in the mirror. Her pupils were dilated with arousal and a puffy from lack of sleep. Niall sported a morning stubble. Several splotchy red marks garnished her neck and his from their exertions, and their hair was disheveled. Kissing the top of her hair, Niall wound his arms around her from behind and rested his chin on top of her head, cradling her to him. Their reflections swayed. She closed her eyes and placed her hands over his on her stomach.

"I don't want this night to end."

Niall clutched her tighter to him and spoke softly in her ear. "It's not over yet. I've got plans for you, love, and they involve lots of time in your bed."

When they'd both cleaned up, she hugged him, kissing beneath his jaw. "You're so much more than I ever imagined. You make me feel special."

He pulled back, his eyes drinking her in. "You *are* special." His hands caressed her face, neck, and shoulders, and then slid to her waist as he kissed her. "I love talking to you, and you feel so good whenever I touch you. All I want to do is be near you, Lark."

She hugged him. What would happen now? She'd bared herself to him, and it was more than simple physical intimacy. It was emotional nakedness of the soul.

Despite the uncertainty of what would come, she believed without question she was in safe hands with Niall. Being with him soothed her. As though to reassure her, he turned her to the side and lifted her, his arm beneath her knees as she clung to his neck. To be able to be picked up was gratification in and of itself, but more so was the solid strength of his arms as he carried her to the bed. He lay her on the coverlet and stretched out over her, kissing her again.

She glanced at the nightstand. "Turn off the light."

He shook his head. "No. I want to see you." The mattress dipped beneath their weight, and he pressed into her, piquant and heavy, the hard line of his body molding to hers. His tongue slid into the cavern of her mouth, exploring and tasting her. The savory flavor of chicken lingered on his tongue, and she dived in for more, eliciting a low rumble from him.

"If you keep that up, Shakespeare, you'll get your comeuppance."

He grabbed her ass and rolled them over, and she squealed in delight. He moved her legs apart, so she straddled him on top. Lark sat up. His erection pressed between their layers of clothes, and her eyes fluttered at the sensation. He grinned, rubbing the tops of her thighs, her hips, pushing up beneath the hem of her shirt. She helped him take it off and tossed it over her shoulder. His hands came to rest at her breasts, and he traced her nipples over her bra with his thumbs.

"Your breasts are so lovely, Lark." She shivered, leaning forward as he pressed his thumbs in and lightly kneaded them. "I love the way they fit in my hands. I swear I'll never have enough of you."

She bit her lip, and he sat upright, attacking her neck with his mouth, his teeth plucking her skin, sending tiny shivers down her throat.

"I dreamed of this." Her voice sounded husky.

"Oh, yeah? You dreamed I was in your room?"

He slid the strap of her bra off one shoulder, freeing her breast to latch on to it with his lips. He licked it lovingly, and she moaned, grinding her hips against him. He yanked her other bra strap, not so gentle this time, taking her nipple into his mouth. He sucked harder, tugging it with tender insistence, and then laved the underside with his tongue.

Lark unclasped her bra, letting it fall to the floor. "Mmm. Yes."

"Interesting."

Preoccupied, he slid his hand along her upper thigh, spreading and sliding his fingers along her leg. Each time he got higher, his thumb abraded her pussy, taunting it as he used more and more pressure in his touch with each visit. She raised herself on her knees, gazing at him as he hooked his thumbs into the waistband of her sweats and panties, helping push them off and toss them to the floor. She leaned forward to kiss his chest, his stomach, and down his navel. His breathing grew harsh, and he lifted up, grinding his covered cock against her.

She helped him take off his pajama bottoms, and kick them off the bed. He wore no underwear. His cock sprang free, hard and ready, and he stroked himself, a roguish gleam in his eyes as he looked at her.

"Touch yourself, Lark. Please. For me. Spread your gorgeous pussy and let me see you."

She wasn't an exhibitionist by any stretch. If anything, she still had severe body issues she'd carry forever. But something about the weight of his stare, the way he asked, prompted her to put a hand to her pussy. She used her middle finger to coax her clit. She moved toward him, rubbing her wet pussy against his sac, her mouth open at the roughness against her. She gathered her moisture and spread it over him.

He inhaled unsteadily and joined her hand as he stroked her wetness, spreading it around his cock and breathing through his teeth as he worked himself with one hand, touching her with the other, his fingers smearing her clit even as she teased it.

"Oh, yes. Touch your clit. I want you so much, Lark. I *look* and you just—have no idea what you do to me. Please keep doing that. God, you're so beautiful and brilliant, and you don't even know." He groaned and circled her entrance with two fingers. He slid them forward, filling her pussy. She lifted her hips and moaned. "I think of you every minute." She moved her hips to the flow of his hand, her eyes closed and her head thrown back. "Every second."

"I think of you too, Niall."

"I'm serious. I never thought I'd find someone again," he breathed, fucking her with his hand. She rolled her hips against him. "I love who you are, and when you're spread out for me like this, so beautiful, all I want to do is fill you up with my hard cock, ram it into you until your hot, wet pussy shatters around me. I like knowing it's me you come apart for. I like making love to you." He curled his fingers inside her, and she cried out, palming her breasts and arching her back.

She was so turned on, it made her almost angry.

"Yes, love." He slammed his fingers into her back wall, and she let out a primal grunt. "You're so stunning. I like watching you burn like this."

Lark clenched her inner walls around his fingers in response. She moved his hands, and unable to wait any longer, she slid forward, positioning his wet tip at her entrance, and she sank down on him, impaling herself to the brim. The depth of him inside consumed her. It bordered on pain but was on the best side of pleasure. They both breathed in, and he fell back with his eyes shut, caressing her hips, threading his fingers through hers. He raised his ass, lifting her, and she swayed.

"You feel so good inside me," she gasped, savoring the sensation. She raised up and slid back down, a spirited cry escaping her lips. He bucked beneath her, hands gripping her thighs harder each time. It amazed her he filled her so completely, to the point where she didn't know where either of them ended or began.

She held a hand over his as he cupped and kneaded her tender breasts, offering words of encouragement, words of love the faster her pace became. Her thighs were on fire, but the cataclysm of ecstasy and heady power drove her on, flowing into her like an ocean current as she rode his hard, wet cock. He enticed her clit with his thumb when she tensed up. He took control and sat forward, clutching her to him. He thrust up with a demented fervency, his cock pushing farther into her, his fingers abandoning her breast to grab her ass. His thighs smacked into hers with each impact, and she bounced with rapture as he thrust harder. She couldn't speak. His other hand traveled from her clit to cup her breast. She put her hand over his, rubbing the hard ridges of his knuckles, which shouldn't have seemed sexy but were the sexiest knuckles ever. "*Ahh…*"

"Yes. Come on, Lark! Fall apart. You're so fucking beautiful."

Delicious spasms shot through her pussy. A wicked pressure built inside her, contracting the muscles of her pelvis. He drove her with the honest intensity of his love and moved his hand to torture her clit with his thumb again. Instead of calling out when she came, Lark exhaled into his ear, a gentle whisper, like she was telling him her deepest secret. He groaned as her wetness gushed forth, bathing them both in the essence of their love. She wrapped her body around him, her inner walls clenching around his cock, milking it. He came, whispering her name like a prayer.

They sat tangled in each other, trembling. He cupped her cheeks and kissed her tenderly, pushing the damp hair away from her face. He put his forehead to hers as she fought to catch her breath.

"Thank you," he whispered. "Thank you for tonight, for opening your heart to me. I'll always cherish it. Always."

****

For surviving on about two to three hours of sleep, Lark felt pretty damn good, all things considered, without even having had any coffee yet to give her a boost. She'd donned the sundress Niall liked. He was upstairs getting ready in her bathroom as she wandered through the house, clearheaded and pleased.

The cogs in her brain had kicked in, but she was still too gratified from the night before to consider engaging any kind of guilt. Niall had given her the greatest sex of her life in the space of mere hours, and she didn't know what to do with that, or how to hold on to something as raw and beautiful as his love.

She entered the kitchen. A few large pots and pans commanded attention, sticking out of the sink as they were from the previous night. Her mother stayed on a roll when it came to having everything tidy, but the last several weeks must have overloaded her.

In a gracious mood, she donned the yellow rubber gloves draped over the edge of the sink. With the dishwasher full of clean dishes that still needed putting away, she squirted lemon-scented dishwashing liquid into the stainless-steel basin and filled it with warm water from the faucet.

She dampened a blue-and-green sponge and scoured a deep pan, smiling and humming beneath her breath. Niall was a cuddler. Waking up lying on his chest, in the warmth of his arms, had been like taking a soothing, hot bath after a long day.

The back door opened, and Pam came in. She paused to unlace and remove her dirty sneakers. "It's getting cold out there." She grabbed a tissue from the box on the kitchen counter and blew her nose. "I'll have to use the treadmill soon. You may want to change into something warmer if you're going out. Oh, you're doing the dishes? Thanks, hon, it saves me time."

Lark glanced over her shoulder. "It's the least I can do."

If her mother noticed a difference in her, she hid it tactfully. She gave Lark a small hug from behind. "I'm glad you've decided to stay longer." Pam put her hands on the back of Lark's shoulders, and she leaned into the backward hug. "I didn't like leaving things the way we did last night."

"Neither did I. I love you, Mom. I'm sorry I've

been so hardheaded."

"We both have. Why don't we pitch the white flags and call it square?"

"Sounds good to me."

"You take after me in so many ways." Pam touched Lark's hair. "Thanks for cleaning up. I'm going to go take a shower. I'll see you in a little while."

"Okay."

Pam's footsteps retreated on the stairs and then, a few minutes later, large, strong hands slid around the curves of her waist. She'd smelled his earthy aftershave when he entered the kitchen. Since the first time she met him, she sensed when he was in a room with her.

Niall set his cell phone on the counter and drew close behind her as she placed the pan she'd scrubbed into the drying rack. He traced his fingers down her left arm, humming against her hair. She closed her eyes, enjoying being held close.

"I want to take you out."

She smiled. "They have hit men for that, you know."

He laughed low and rubbed the tip of his nose against the back of her loose hair. "I do my own dirty work. Hit men are overrated." He rested his chin on the top of her head. "Cute, though. Where's your mam?"

"In the shower. Do you want breakfast?"

"A kiss'll do," he said, trying to turn her to face to him.

She giggled, resisting. She had dragon breath. "You don't want to kiss me right now. Trust me. I haven't brushed my teeth yet." She dodged him when he tried again, turning her head. Niall reached over her and shut off the faucet. He turned her around and put his hand on the side of her neck.

"No, don't. Morning breath is hot."

She snorted. "Yeah, right."

"It *is*. I'll show you how much."

He smirked and unbuttoned the front of her dress. He hit the fourth button, and it slid from her shoulders onto the floor with a gentle whisper. Lark took off the dishwashing gloves and tried to pick up the dress, but he grasped her hips, turned around with her, and walked her backward to the kitchen table.

"What are you, like, a button ninja? Niall, my mom's upstairs taking a shower."

He wasn't listening. His twinkling eyes focused on her lace bra and panties. He loosened his tie and yanked it off over his head, then swiftly unbuttoned his shirt and let it fall to the floor.

"Well, we best be quick about it, then," he murmured.

He moved forward without preamble to cup her pussy as he kissed her, his tongue attacking her mouth, waking it with the shock of spearmint flavor. His fingers moved against the thin fabric of her panties, massaging her clit, and she flushed with embarrassment. Her panties were already damp. She couldn't believe he wanted to do this here with her mother upstairs. Her ears burned as he thumbed her clit and stepped in to assault her neck with his lips, and she wrapped her arms around him, despite herself, laughing nervously.

"You're insatiable. You know that, right? Don't you at least want to get breakfast? Mmm?" He took her earlobe in his mouth, pressing against her. Lark held on to his arms for leverage, dizzy with pleasure.

"Sod breakfast," he mumbled into her neck, undoing his trousers and yanking them down along with his boxers. They pooled above his shoes. "*You're* my breakfast." His cock jutted out, ready for action. He lifted her onto the table with whip-smooth speed, then parted her legs with eager fervor. He moved the barrier of her panties to the side and drove into her in one solid, quick stroke, his eyes on hers.

A rough breath escaped her, and she closed her eyes, putting her arms around his shoulders as he moved inside her, thrusting his tongue into her willing mouth in the same sensuous manner that he took her. His pace slowed and then grew determined, and Lark braced her hands against the wobbling table as he built a delicious, burning friction between them, his sac smacking the flesh of her ass as he sank deep into her tender, craving flesh.

"I love being a part of you. Watch, Lark. Look at what I'm doing to you. Look."

Lark leaned back, watching as his long, wet shaft pulled out of her soaked pussy lips, coated with her juices, and then plunged back in, jostling the table and disappearing to the hilt inside her as his crisp black hairs blended with hers. She gulped, shaking from the impact and powerful sight of it.

"Watch," he breathed again.

She did and gasped when he pulled out and stroked them both where they were joined with his fingers, before thrusting back into her. He slowed down, taking her hand and entwining their fingers and kissing her palm, sucking on the tip of her finger as his hips rotated into hers, slow and intoxicating.

"This is us, right now," he whispered, his eyes on

hers. "You're mine." He sped up, letting go of their fingers, grabbing her hips and pummeling her hard. "Mine!"

"*Yes*." She *was* his, heart and body and soul. She threw her head back, unable to articulate anything but gasps of air and grunts as he fucked her into the table.

"You're everything I've ever wanted," he breathed, kissing her with a slow drag of lips.

He drove in deep, clutching the back of her thigh, and Lark cried out against his mouth as she came. She soared into the sky like a bird, her body free of inhibition and full of life. He didn't slow, though. He continued to take her, his hips freezing when his seed spurted into her. She clenched her thighs around him and milked him with her throbbing pussy, wanting every last drop inside her.

The tendons in his neck stretched when he threw his head back as he poured into her, his broad shoulders and chest glistening with sweat. Aware of him all the way to her womb, Lark lay back as he slid out, dazed and spent as he stood there, breathing harshly, like a man who'd just conquered a mountain.

He helped her sit up and slide off the table, kissing her hand.

"Sorry to attack, but I told you, you're like a drug. I can't stop touching you." He wiped his glistening forehead with his forearm.

She smiled, something she hadn't been able to stop doing since last night. "I'm not complaining. At all. But we *should* get dressed."

He nodded, gathering their clothes. They dressed in cheerful silence, and Lark cleared her throat as she straightened her dress. "Now, Mr. O'Hagan, if you'd be so kind as to grab the Clorox wipes under the sink and clean the table, I'll get you something to eat." He did as told, slapping her ass in passing as she put a few on-the-go pastries in the toaster. She loved how he *got* her; they moved in tandem.

"Clean as a whistle," he murmured a few minutes later, putting his arms around her from behind as she finished making them both plates. "Last night was amazing. *You* were amazing."

Lark leaned back in his arms, pleased. "Thank you. *I do have me moments*," she teased, with a surprisingly decent imitation of Niall's Irish brogue.

He kissed the top of her head while he rubbed her arms. "I have to go, unfortunately, but I'll be back later on tonight, around six or so. I'd like to take you out on a proper date if that's all right."

She nodded. "I'd like that."

His cell phone went off and danced along the kitchen counter. Niall parted her hair and kissed her once on the back of her neck, then checked his phone. "Work. I've got to take this. Thanks for, erm, breakfast. I'll eat on the way there," he said as he scooped the cooled toaster pastries off his plate. "See you tonight. We can talk about everything then."

"Sounds good," she said as he backed off, answering his phone with his free hand, his eyes trained on hers.

****

Her mother wasn't an idiot. Of course she knew something was going on. She sprayed air freshener in the kitchen when she came down, then carried on her usual morning routine and didn't saying anything about the matter. Niall had left the final drawn-up probate paperwork on the counter, ready for signatures, but Lark moved it out of the way during lunch and avoided discussing it.

She reveled in the peaceful, happy state he'd left her in. It lasted for a few hours. But being without Niall after last night was torture. His scent and seed, the feel of him on her, *in* her, still lingered after her shower and as she went about her day. She kept her phone off and set it on her nightstand to avoid the elephant in the room. In the late afternoon, wanting to text him, Lark turned her cell phone back on. Her stomach sank as several icons popped up for missed calls and texts from Charles, the most recent being two hours ago. The subject line said: *Read this NOW*.

She had taken no action to get another plane ticket, but they expected her back to work next Thursday. She sighed. Soon she would have to either rebook her ticket or forfeit its cost. Everything had happened so fast. She held off checking Charles's messages until tomorrow. It was avoiding the unavoidable, yes, but she didn't want to disturb the magic between her and Niall.

It clouded and rained all day, and she stayed in the living room, napping on and off, curled on the couch with a soft, cream-colored fleece blanket. When she wasn't dozing, she perused the book Niall had read last night, which turned out to be her favorite play by Ibsen, *A Doll's House*.

Pam seemed extrasensitive to whatever she suspected was happening, and she let Lark have breathing room, which she appreciated. Her mom had always been emotionally intelligent. Pam popped her head into the living room around four.

"Hey, hon. I thought I'd let you know. I'm going to

go out to dinner tonight with my friend Sue. She's been concerned about me, and I want the word spread that I haven't become a complete recluse, and am okay. Sue's a damn gossip, and I trust her to blab about it. I'll be home pretty late, so you and Niall have the house to yourselves." Before Lark managed to deny anything, Pam smiled and left her in peace.

Her mother hadn't been gone long when Niall came to pick her up after six. It rained cats and dogs outside. Lark met him at the front door, ready to go in a warm jacket she'd borrowed from her mother. They were both dressed in casual jeans and tops.

Before he uttered a word, she put her arms around his shoulders and kissed him. He supported her back and drew her to him. Satisfying chills shot up her spine.

"Now, that's what I call a nice welcome home." He splayed his hands over her back and drew her close. "Hi."

"Hi, yourself."

His eyes were bright gems, and warmth spread through her body as he put his hand to her cheek. She wanted to bottle the warmth and keep it forever. A rumble of thunder sounded, and the *pitter-patter* of the rain changed to a torrential downpour, hard and bulletlike drops that sounded more like hail as they pounded on the porch awning. They both turned and looked out on the balcony, where it rained hard.

"Crazy," she murmured. "Do you want to wait before we go, and kill fifteen minutes or so?"

Niall nodded. "Sure. The Explorer almost got stuck in the mud on the dirt stretch out from the highway." His phone went off, and he pulled it from his jacket as Lark closed the door. He answered it, mouthing *Jake from the office* to her as he took it, walking through the hallway as he spoke.

Lark took off her jacket and followed him into the library. He'd stopped by the bookshelves, his back turned when she entered.

"Well, thank you for all you've done," he said into the phone. "I'm glad we were able to get this taken care of. Aye, I'll be there to drop the papers off tomorrow after they sign them. Uh-huh."

He looked over his shoulder, and Lark gave him a flirty little wave as she poured a glass of white wine at the minibar. She licked her lips slowly, teasing him, and he prowled toward her with the phone still to his ear and a look which spelled trouble.

"Listen, Jake, something's come up which needs tending to, but I'll be in touch and let you know how the signing goes. Yeah."

She took a slow sip of wine as Jake's garbled voice from the other end echoed a bit. Niall ended the call and threw the phone on the couch, hauling her to him with a mischievous glint in his eyes as he set the stemmed glass down and walked her over to the bookshelves.

"Well now, aren't you the naughty one," he murmured. "That deserves a reprimand, wouldn't you say?"

A thrill of excitement surged through her. A second later, he'd pinned her against the bookshelf, and they kissed each other full-on. He seemed to enjoy the lingering sweetness of the wine on her tongue from the way he engulfed it with his own.

She slid off his leather jacket, moving it down his shirt, and her mouth watered at the outline of hard muscle beneath. Even after meeting him and knowing him for over a week, she couldn't believe he was hers. She slid her arms around Niall's torso, rubbing her hands up his warm back. He groaned and kicked between her feet, pinioning his thigh between her legs. The pressure at her apex set off a steady throb, and she hooked her right leg over his hip, rubbing against him as he engaged her tongue in a wicked duel. He grabbed her ass, clutching and kneading it as she ground against him.

If this gave any kind of glimpse into their future, she was all for it.

His cell phone went off again, but they were both too involved to move away, kissing each other with a fiery passion. If the way he devoured her served as any indication, last night had been a mere taste. He curved his hand around the side of her slim waist, tracing his fingers over her blouse. The cell phone went off again, and Lark broke her lips free, delirious.

"Are you going to get that?" She breathed as his fingers explored her left breast, a tingling, tantalizing caress. His touch surrendered and commandeered at once, and she loved being able to give control to him but still be empowered.

He held and kissed her palm, attending to each finger with full, hungry lips. "I'm busy," he muttered.

She sucked in her breath as she held the back of his neck and closed her eyes. Tingly endorphins raced through her.

"I haven't stopped thinking about you."

She touched his jaw, where the stubble lent a hint of danger to his striking features. "Neither have I. Last night was—"

Niall shut his eyes and nodded. "It *was*. It's safe to

333

say you've got me where you want me, Shakespeare. I've no words for what being with you does to me."

He unbuttoned her jeans and kissed her earlobe, then tugged on it, whispering poetry to her of her gracefulness, muttering in his melodic Irish of the crook of her arm, the camber of her neck, her softness and strength, the loveliness of her spirit.

He made her come alive in a way she never had before, and she wanted him again. "Niall," she pleaded as he teased her, nibbling her earlobe and kissing her neck in turns.

"What have you done to me," he murmured, falling to his knees. "It's like I'm spellbound. I swear, I'll do anything you ask. Anything you want."

He tugged at her waist; her jeans pooled at her ankles, and his hands slowly slid her panties to her thighs. He kissed her mound with devotion and slid his fingers between her wet folds. She sighed, opening her thighs to him like a flower to the sun. He licked her clit, caressing every inch of flesh his hands came into contact with.

Lark leaned her head back at the pressure of his mouth, drunk on sensation. "Make love to me."

"Yes. A thousand times over."

He lightly suckled her clit. She wound her fingers into his curls as his fingers slid into her pussy, soaking in and spreading her wetness all over her hypersensitive, glistening folds. He took his time, caressing her backside as he sought out her most responsive places. His tongue stroked her like velvet, coaxing her toward him, his long, slow sweeps evocative and lovely.

"Niall, that feels so nice. So good," she breathed.

He hummed against her, and then he stood, his mouth claiming hers. His tongue slid against hers, unhurried and searching, and she tasted herself on him. She worked his belt, unbuckling it and undoing his button and zipper. She needed to feel him again. She slid her hands beneath the hem of his T-shirt, putting her arms around his solid torso to draw him closer as he touched her. His hand travelled down, and he reentered her with two fingers, whispering in Irish Gaelic between impassioned kisses.

"I'm going to take you," he murmured, pumping his fingers in and out of her pussy as he thumbed her clit. "And I'm going to do it right here. Put your legs around me, Lark." He tugged his jeans and boxers down with his free hand. She lifted her other leg, he withdrew his fingers from her, lifting her ass to meet him at his full height. The tip of his steel-hard cock pressed through the wet folds of her sensitive flesh, and he drove forward, pushing her into the bookshelf as he filled her. She tilted her head back and shut her eyes.

"No. Look at me," he breathed, driving forward until he came flush against her.

She did, and he was less than an inch from her face, his eyes like green flames. He flushed red from their exertion, and his fingers gripped her bottom. He pinned her there and didn't move. "Tell me we weren't made for each other." He pulled out to the tip and slammed back into her hard, jostling the books behind her. Lark cried out and clutched his shoulders.

"Niall!"

"Tell me you don't think this is meant to be, right now," he demanded, repeating his actions. Lark kissed him, wanted to suck his tongue, but he moved his head back. "Say it." He reared back and slammed into her again. It was too much, and yet never enough.

"We're destined," he urged.

She sucked in her breath, held there by his weight and filled to the brim with his long cock.

"I...*yes*." He sped up his actions, cushioning the brunt of the shelves by shielding her with the backs of his hands.

"Say it," he rasped, fucking her hard into the bookshelf.

Lark gasped as his frantic thrusting grew erratic. She pushed her heels against his thighs. "We—ah…"

He slowed, punishing her with long, slow thrusts that threatened to make her come apart. He put his lips against her ear. "Tell me we belong together like you *know* we do," he whispered, working his hips in and out of her. "Those dreams weren't for nothing. Tell me, Lark."

"We do," she whispered as he circled his hips and slowly took her. "We belong together."

He kissed her longingly and moved her away from the bookshelf, carrying her to the couch. The love in his eyes, the rapture on his face, overwhelmed her. How, in the space of a couple of weeks, had this man come to love her so much? To adore her as he did? It was like receiving a magnificent Christmas present and not knowing how to thank someone. She touched his lips as he lay her down on the couch and crawled over her.

The rain pounded on the roof, the tinkling music of it echoing throughout the house. Niall caressed her hair, his eyes gentle.

"Lark, I want to bury myself in you and never resurface."

"Come into me." She opened her legs to him with unreserved trust. He reentered her in one swift move, sinking his cock deep into the cradle of her hips. She wrapped her legs around him, wanting to cry at the tenderness and vulnerability in his eyes. He'd lost so much, and, it seemed, loved so deeply. He moved within her, slow and thorough, and she raised her hips to meet his.

"I love you. Oh God, I love you."

Lark shivered at the rough emotion in his voice. Saying it had cost him something, and she wound her arms around his neck, bringing him close, bucking her hips in response to show him she was grateful for such a precious gift, even if her lips weren't ready to reciprocate yet.

Thorough and deliberate, he pulled back only to surge into her again, nourishing her hungry heart with the food of love. Blood rushed to her core, and she needed what he could give her. "Niall." She lifted her hips. "More. Faster. Please."

"Soon, Lark. Soon."

He put a hand to her hip and then quickened his pace, growling and screwing her into the couch. She couldn't speak beyond cut-off, unintelligible words and throaty cries as he pounded her. She hooked her legs at the ankles over his back, moving in time to the *plink plink* of the rain on the roof as he relentlessly took her. The couch moved with each thrust.

"I'm not letting you go, Lark," he said against her ear, and his fingers moved between their bodies, finding her clit. She surrendered to his touch, arching into his body and throwing her head back against the throw pillow, baring her neck.

His lips adored her bare throat, and he sucked the skin there as they both came, his seed exquisitely warming her insides.

Niall collapsed against her, and she caressed the muscles of his back. She carded her fingers through his hair as he breathed against her neck and kept a heavy hand on her hip. The beat of his heart thumped above her rib cage, his face against her breast. He propped his elbow up and leaned his head on his hand as he drank her in.

"You need a poem. An ode."

Her breathing back to normal, she smiled. "There once was a girl named Lark, who had so much grapefruit, she let out a fart."

He chuckled. "Doesn't quite work, does it? Let's try something else. Your hair is like burnished copper, so soft I could fall into it at night."

Lark turned her head to the side as her face burned. He smiled gently when she looked back at him, but the intensity in his eyes meant business, and she stirred again. How the hell was that even possible? Did he drug her?

"Your eyes remind me of delicious chocolate—smooth, heavenly, delectable." He drew his finger down her face. "Melting."

"Oh please." She giggled.

He rocked his hips into her, a warning, and a pleasant hot spurt warmed her insides. "Mmm."

He kissed her cheek, his lips lingering. "Your cheeks are beautiful, lofty pillars that bloom like fragrant, dusky roses."

She grinned. "This is good stuff, Niall. Don't stop."

He interlaced his fingers with hers and traced her palm lightly with his thumb. "I don't intend to anytime soon. Your hands are soft conduits by which I can read and navigate your deepest emotions, hidden like a sunken, buried treasure."

Her breath came quicker. He glided his hand over her left breast, his thumb caressing her soft nipple, then past the curve of her waist to her leg, where he reached between where they were joined to stroke her inner thigh as his eyes devoured hers. Tingles shot through her pussy.

"Your legs are sylphlike guardians of your most coveted sanctuary, tightening and writhing against mine in a tempestuous dance for passage when we mate."

She opened her mouth, her breath coming out labored as her breasts rose and fell beneath him, her tightening nipples grazing his own. He hardened inside her, his cock stirring against her walls.

"Your mouth is a stocked vessel of compassion and kindness, yet capable of wielding words sharper than any sword." He paused, and chuckled. "And that's all I've got for now."

"Thank you. That was wonderful," she admitted, smiling like a lunatic. "I don't think anyone's given me an ode before."

"*Anything* with you is wonderful," he purred, kissing her. She pulled him in and embraced him. His cock relaxed within her. She sighed contentedly. They needed a break.

"Why don't we go out soon, though, hmm?" He kissed the tip of her nose. "It can't spit like this forever. Let's wait for it to lighten up, and then we'll go. I could easily stay like this, but I want a proper date with you. I want to treat you like you deserve."

Lark smiled, serene. "You just *did*, Niall. Let's get cleaned up, and we can head out."

He withdrew slowly, his semen rolling deliciously down her pussy. He watched it a moment, smiling, and lifted himself. He kissed her again and grabbed a box of tissues. He helped her clean up as she lay there. He touched her tenderly as he wiped her with the tissue, and she loved how he seemed to know when to be soft, and when to be rough. After they cleaned up, they got dressed, touching each other with little strokes and random nuzzling. She had no idea sex could be so intimate, so exceptional. She'd never known the emotional aspect to it, and it made for an entirely different experience, especially because it was Niall. Lark finished her glass of wine, then followed Niall as he opened the front door to check on the rain. He took her hand as he leaned his forearm on the doorjamb. "All right, come on, you old storm. Get a move on so Lark 'n I can hit the road."

"Let me go use the bathroom. Maybe it will let up, and then we can go." She slipped her hand out of his and handed him the house keys so she wouldn't forget them in the bathroom. She kissed him. "I'll be right back." He nodded, smiling warmly at her.

After using the toilet, she looked in the mirror. Her reflection sported a huge, goofy grin, her skin flushed from their exertions. She studied her eyes. They'd never caught the light so much before. "I have no idea what I'm doing," she said out loud, "but I don't ever want it to stop." Tears of joy sprang to her eyes, and she blinked them away, smiling at herself. Shrugging and taking a deep breath, she opened the door and walked—

twitterpated—down the hall toward the front door.

Niall was nowhere in sight, and the door was closed. She walked into the library. He might have gone back inside as it still rained outside. Huh. Vacant. She checked the kitchen and the stairs; still dark. A loud crash reverberated throughout the house, and she jumped, shaking. It came from the front. She turned and walked toward the visiting room and the front door. Another crash sounded as she turned into the room. She found the front window smashed in, Niall in a chokehold, and Charles standing above him.

"Charles," she gasped. She rushed forward. "Get off him! What are you *doing*?" Charles lifted his head, distracted, and Niall took the opportunity to punch him in the face. Charles retreated, and Niall got up, moving away from the bashed-in window to the porch. Lark ran over, careful not to step on the glass, and stuck her head out the window. The porch light was on via the automatic timer. "Stop it," she screamed, watching in horror as Charles swung an uppercut with his large, muscular fist, and sunk it into Niall's stomach. It knocked the wind out of him, and he doubled over as his face went a frightening purplish-blue.

"Niall," she shouted. She ripped the front door open.

Niall regained his feet, gulping, and pointed at her. "Close the door. Stay in there—" He went silent as Charles's shoes kicked him hard in the ribs. He curled into a defensive ball on the porch floor.

"That's right. Stay…*there*," Charles bellowed, and with each word he kicked Niall, who cried out in pain from the strong blows, shielding his head with his hands. "Watch me kick the shite out of him. You can have ringside seats, you lying bitch!"

Niall howled on the fourth blow, and Lark couldn't watch anymore. Roaring, she hurried onto the porch and grabbed Charles from behind by the waist, tugging him as hard as possible away from Niall. "Charles, stop it," she begged. "You'll kill him."

Charles stopped, turning incredulously to her. He had a black eye, and his lip bled. His eyes were wide and excited, and darkness possessed his smile. "Oh, this is *good*. What—now you're standing up for your *lover*?" He sneered with a strangled sort of voice. "Tell me, did you wait until I'd gone, or did you bang each other while I was still around?"

Standing in front of the curled-up figure of Niall on the floor, Lark tried to get Charles away from him and did her best to appeal to him. "Let's talk about this, okay? We don't have to hurt anyone. Let's try to deal with this without—"

In one swift movement, from the corner of her eye, Niall lifted both his feet high in the air while Charles was distracted, and he kicked hard on the front of Charles's shins.

Charles screamed in pain and almost fell headfirst down the stairs, but he caught himself on his hands on the top of the porch, wincing in agony.

Lark wasted no time in crouching down, helping Niall to stand.

His attention focused with a concentrated frown on Charles, who lay prone on the porch floor as he held a hand to his ribs. Lark brushed the tears from her cheeks and held the crook of his arm as he regained his footing.

"Niall, are you okay?" He pushed her down onto the porch swing with a surprising amount of force. She fell against the pillows, grateful they were there to cushion her.

"Stay there no matter what happens. I don't want you hurt." He pointed at her in a contained way, then staggered to Charles.

While the latter struggled to get up, Niall scoffed at him with disgust, as one might consider a pile of animal droppings on the road. Wincing with pain, he sat on Charles and put his full weight on him, straddling his back and pinning him to the porch floor while rain pounded their heads.

Charles remained still and then rolled over, catching Niall off guard. He got to his knees and punched Niall hard in the face.

Lark shouted Niall's name again, wanting to jump on Charles and wring his neck. She made a move to get up, but then reality dawned as she watched them struggle. They were two full-grown, angry men fighting with each other, and she was significantly smaller, with no experience in fighting, despite how riled up she was. She searched around for something to use as a weapon if she needed to.

Charles turned his head toward her, and Niall surprised them both by bringing his fist up, landing a blow in Charles's undamaged eye. Charles howled, standing and covering his eye with his hand, staggering backward.

"Lark, stay there," Niall told her firmly. Bright headlights beamed through the porch railing, the rain pouring in front of a taxi cab.

Charles swung his fist out as Niall struggled to stand, and his blow found its mark as Niall tried to steady himself. He moved in time to miss it, leaning to the side, still favoring the right side of his ribs. He grabbed Charles's other hand, and in the blink of an eye, he pressed Charles's knuckles down toward his wrist and pushed it into him. Charles cried out, crumbling to his knees as Niall grunted and winced. He brought Charles's arm behind his back and moved around him.

"Charles," he said with restraint. His face contorted with pain. He winced but didn't let go. "It's over. You are going to leave now, and you're not coming back here." He held Charles down, and Lark watched, amazed at his steady tone of voice despite the pain he must be in.

"I'm going to tear you apart, you son of a bitch," Charles yelled through gritted teeth. Blood trickled down the side of his mouth as Niall held him there.

Lark had never seen Charles so angry, so violent. Ice-cold prickles of fear and guilt seeped through her. Was this her fault? Could she have done anything differently in handling the breakup with Charles to prevent this? She couldn't, but it had only been twenty minutes ago she'd been on fire from Niall's touch, and now here he was, fighting for her.

"That's not going to happen."

Niall sounded as calm as he could, and Lark marveled at his restraint. His head bowed as he held Charles there despite his struggles, but Niall's face twisted as he fought to control his pain. Charles continued to wriggle to get free, but Niall pressed against Charles's pressure points in his hand, causing Charles to howl.

"Let me go. Right now, you bastard."

Niall was quiet, though a muscle in his jaw ticked.

"I won't until I know you've calmed down." Charles struggled, and then exhaled when he couldn't move.

"Should I call the police?" Lark asked, standing. They both seemed injured.

"No," Charles sneered at her. "The last thing UY needs is my face on the news. Let me go, O'Hagan. I'm calm. I'm calm."

Niall searched her eyes, then focused on the man in his charge. She crossed her arms and rubbed her dry throat.

"It's not your company's reputation I'm concerned with, mate," Niall grunted. "And I hate to point out the obvious, but you're the one on the ground here, not me. I want your word you won't harm her. You'll leave here, and never come back."

"I would never hurt Lark, and she knows it," Charles snarled. He tried to look at Lark from his kneeling position, but Niall had him locked up tight. "Lark, tell this bastard to let me go."

She glanced away, not wanting to.

"Hey, what's going on up there?" shouted the cab driver, poking his head out the window. "Mister, do you want me to call the cops?" he directed at Charles.

"Niall," she urged. "For heaven's sake, please."

Niall raised an eyebrow at her, and she nodded, knowing Charles would not do anything else to put his work reputation at risk. Niall let Charles's arm go and moved in front of Lark, safeguarding her like a German shepherd.

Charles stood to his full height, rubbing his arm and wrist. He sneered vindictively at them both from a few feet away.

"The hell with this, and the hell with *you*," he said

to Lark. "And you." He pointed at Niall. "This isn't over." Charles burned his hate-filled glare into her, and she took a step behind Niall, closer to his back. Niall stood his ground, taking her hand from behind, his eyes fixed on Charles, who limped as he made his way to the cab.

"Airport," he barked before he slammed the door.

As the cab drove off, Lark stepped closer behind Niall and put her hands on his shoulders, laying her cheek against his back and closing her eyes. He placed a hand over hers, and he let out a low breath, his body sagged with fatigue.

"Niall, are you all right?" He turned around to face her. His right temple sported a large red mark which would leave a bruise.

"Aye. Can't say I've had worse, but I'll survive. You?"

Lark nodded. "Let's go inside." She stopped to collect his wallet and her mother's keys from where they'd fallen on the porch, pretending not to notice the droplets of blood by the window. Whether Charles's or Niall's, she didn't know.

They went in and locked the door. Rain dripped into the living room from the broken window. She focused first on rendering first aid and spent a good deal of time in the kitchen cleaning him and tending to his bruises. She'd helped him slowly peel off his damp shirt, and nasty, black-and-blue marks bloomed where Charles had kicked him. She cringed.

"Oh, Niall. Your ribs might be broken. He's so horrible. I'm sorry," she whispered, her voice breaking as she pressed an ice pack to his forehead. The meager things she did were not helping, as much as she wanted to heal him. She had no knowledge of first aid beyond the basics. Her mother, on the other hand, a seasoned homeopathic expert, would know exactly what to do.

"You need to go to the emergency room."

"I'll wait a few hours to see if I get any better. I can breathe fine. These rib bruises might be superficial."

Lark preferred he go to the ER rather than wait. The fight scared her and shook her to the core. She changed the subject.

"I didn't know you knew self-defense." After cleaning and disinfecting the cut on his arm where he'd encountered the glass, she applied a dollop of aloe vera gel. Thank God her mom had a whole pot full of the stuff.

"I don't. It's pressure points. Before I left for college, my brother Frank was goin' through the Police Academy, and he used me as his practice dummy when he came home on the weekends. He beat me up so he could pass his classes, and in exchange, I learned stuff. Guess it's stuck with me. I'll have to tell him."

"Well, it showed."

Niall took her hand with concern. She stopped treating him and met his gaze. "Lark, why don't we go patch up the window and then light a fire and sit for a bit, hmm? I'll pay to have it replaced tomorrow."

She complied, searching the garage for plastic sheeting and duct tape. She did most of it herself, as he had a hard time moving, but there seemed to be enough to seal the windowpane and keep the cold air and rain out. How she planned to explain to Pam what had happened, she didn't know.

Done, she changed into tracksuit bottoms and a T-shirt. She searched Aaron's room and brought back a pair of her brother's old sweats for Niall. She returned to the kitchen to get him and then supported him as they walked into the living room.

"Here," she said, kneeling before him. "I've got a towel. Let's get you out of these wet clothes and dry you off." Careful of his ribs, she helped Niall step into the sweatpants, but he resisted peeling off his shirt. He winced.

"Leave it for now."

"Okay." She wrapped the towel around his shoulders to help sop up his T-shirt and helped him sit on the sofa, then threw a lit match onto the logs in the hearth. Leave it to her mom to have the fire ready to go. The cream-colored fleece throw she'd used earlier still lay across the top of the couch. Niall gingerly pulled it down, mindful of his ribs, and spread it out. Lark handed him two Excedrin and a glass of water she'd poured in the bathroom. "Here. Take these." He swallowed the pills, then turned sideways. She frowned and folded her arms. "Niall, you shouldn't be sitting here. We need to take you to get checked out."

He sighed and held out his hand. "Come sit with me. Let's stay here a little longer and cool down, okay? I'll see if the pain subsides. If it doesn't, there's an InstaCare close to my office, about an hour from here. If I do have to go, I want to wait till the roads clear, or I can go first thing in the morning. I'll be fine."

"Well, that's stupid. Let me drive you, and we can go right now," she insisted, reaching for the keys to his SUV he'd left on the end table next to the couch.

"Lark," he chided, putting his hand on hers and taking the keys back. "It's late, and these may be surface bruises."

"But they may *not*. Niall, you need to get checked out."

He sighed. "Listen up, milady, I'm breathin' fine right now, so long as I don't move around too much, and nothing feels too out of place. This isn't the first fight I've ever had, after all. I had about a hundred of 'em growing up with my brothers, though they never kicked me when I was down. That plonker's a nasty piece o' work. Fights dirty. Also, I don't want you to sit there in a crowded emergency room, worrying about me. You're upset enough as it is."

"I'm not upset, I'm *angry*. I can't believe him," Lark said. Tears stung her eyes. She paced, furious. Charles appalled her, kicking Niall like he was a rugby ball.

"Aye, but who won?" he offered, a hint of laughter in his emerald eyes.

She gave him an exasperated look.

"Please, don't worry."

Lark knelt and put her hand on top of his thigh, stroking it as she gazed at him, concerned.

"Mmm… Feels nice," he said as he slid his hand around the back of her neck. "'Tis a shame I'm in no shape to take you, now that I've got you right where I want you. Let's sit here a while and try to unwind, eh? Maybe watch a movie on Netflix? I wouldn't be opposed to *Rocky*."

Lark tried, but her nerves hopped in every which direction, and she struggled to keep her hands from fidgeting. Spotting her cell phone on the lamp table, she grabbed it and turned it on.

His breathing steadied beside her, and she went to

her in-box, wishing she had checked her messages sooner. The most recent text message from Charles read: *In the taxi on way to ranch. Y haven't u answered v/m or texts? I'll see u when I get there. 7ish.* She deleted his other messages without reading them. He was gone now; that's what mattered. Her phone rang as she finished deleting Charles's messages, and she scrolled back to answer the call.

Niall shifted. "If it's Charles, send him my love."

"No," she guffawed, reading the Caller ID. "It's my mom." Lark answered her phone and said hello. Ladies' laughter and country music played in the background.

"Hi, hon, it's me. I wanted to give you a head's up that I'm staying out later with the girls than I planned. They've been so darling. We're going to go play a board game at Sue's, so I should be back pretty late."

"Okay."

"How are things there? Sounds quiet."

Lark drew a breath, debating whether or not to tell her. "We're on the couch."

"Ohh," said Pam, and Lark cringed as she mistook her meaning. "I'll stay out later tonight, then. You two have fun."

"Oh no, Mom, I didn't mean— You don't need to—"

"I insist," Pam said. "Talk to you later."

The line clicked, and Lark turned to Niall in disbelief. "What an entirely one-sided conversation. I'm sure she thinks we're going at it like rabbits."

Niall chuckled, holding a hand against his side with a wince. "Argh, if only it were true. I'd take some TLC over aches 'n pains right now." He took the cell phone from her hand and set it aside, massaging her palm. "You didn't tell her about the window?"

"Nope."

"I guess she'll find out when she comes home."

"Most likely. Niall?"

"Hmm?"

Lark blinked at their joined hands. "What—what's going to happen to us now? I mean, I'm going to be going back to work soon. Charles and I are over, but with you in Oregon and me in England, how is this supposed to work, exactly?"

His thumb stroked her fingers, and he pushed hair away from her eyes. "We're going to *make* it work. I'd never ask you to give up anything for me, Lark. I realize how fast this happened, but I want to be with you. I'll move for you if it comes to it."

She shook her head. "No, I couldn't ask you to—"

"To what? Reinvent my life with an incredible woman somewhere fresh? I'd do it, you know, if you want me in your life."

Lark bit her lip. "I have no idea what to say. This is so—"

"Crazy?" He kissed her. "Insane?"

Lark nodded, smiling as he tugged on her lower lip with his own.

"Amazing?" He kissed her again but then pulled back, wincing.

She frowned again. "Okay, no. Niall, you *need* to go to the hospital and get checked out. What if it's something internal or a broken rib?"

"I'm still breathin', aren't I?" he wheezed. "Let's hold off."

Unsatisfied, Lark sank back against the couch

cushion and held his hand, staring into the fire. "No. If you're not better in the next hour, we're going. I still can't believe how he was. Charles, I mean."

"Well, would you rather have found out *after* you married him?"

She shuddered and shook her head. They would have had such a messed-up marriage, him shagging anyone he wanted and treating her like a consolation prize. She'd dodged a major bullet, and she was glad to be done with it.

Niall stroked her palm. "You don't think he's coming back, do you?"

"No." She sighed. "Trust me. He's at the airport right now, demanding business class, hopping on the next flight home."

Niall lifted his eyebrows. "Well, maybe he'll broaden his mind at the airport with a few hundred drinks and grow a new personality. Good bleedin' riddance."

"You got *that* right." Lark rested her head against Niall's shoulder. "I love being with you." Somewhere between the crackling of the fire and his fingers entwined with her own, she drifted off.

Chapter Sixteen
Ultimatum

When Lark woke, she lay face down on the couch, draped by a blanket. The fire had gone out, though the lamp was still on, and the coldness seeped into her bones like someone had decreased the temperature by twenty degrees. Damn, was it chilly.

She slipped off the couch, stood, and wrapped the blanket around her shoulders for warmth. She blinked, and the ornate analog clock on the mantelpiece came into view. After midnight.

"Niall?"

She checked the temperature on her way out of the living room, looking for him. Still set at sixty-nine. A strong breeze blew into the house. She went to check if the duct tape on the broken window had come off but instead found the front door stood ajar, letting in the wind. It had stopped raining, but the wind still howled.

"Niall?" Still no answer.

Lark drew the blanket closer about her shoulders, gathered her gumption, and approached the door. Maybe he'd gone out to get something from the Explorer; he'd more or less lived out of it the last few days. She turned on the porch light and opened the door, peering out at the driveway. Neither the Explorer nor Pam's car was there.

A terrible feeling sifted through her. She closed the

353

Roxanne D. Howard

door and turned the deadbolt, hoping this was another lucid dream. Her cell phone went off in the living room, making her jump. Nope, not a dream. She walked into the living room where she'd left it, fumbling as she picked it up, spotted Niall's number on the Caller ID, and answered.

"Niall?"

"Oh good, you're up." She relaxed at the sound of his voice. "I've been trying to reach you for the last half hour."

Relief and fear gripped her at once. "Where on earth are you? I woke up scared out of my mind."

"Are you okay? I'm sorry to have frightened you. I'm in the waiting room at InstaCare."

Lark rubbed her closed eyelids. "Niall, why didn't you wake me? I could have driven you. You're in no condition to drive."

He hesitated before answering. "Lark, you were upset. I wanted to let you rest. I don't know how long the wait'll be. It's busy tonight. Let me get checked out, and I'll call you as soon as I'm done, okay? I'll drive back when I'm finished."

Lark sighed. "Okay. Hey, you left the front door open, by the way."

"I did? Are you sure?"

"Yeah, it was wide-open."

"No, I'm sure I shut it. I didn't know where you put the keys after we came back in. Sorry 'bout that."

"It's okay. I bet the wind blew it open."

"Hmm. Listen, Shakespeare, do me a favor and turn on the lights in the house and check the rooms. I want to stay with you on the line while you check. Has Pam come home yet?"

354

"No, she's still out," said Lark, flipping on the light to her father's office. "Not that I can blame her. She's been cooped up in here for at least two weeks. Hmm, everything *seems* clear. Maybe the wind did blow the door open. It's been pretty strong lately, and with the broken window, air pressure might have pushed it open." She sighed. "I've had about all the spooky horror-movie crap I can take for one night. I'm going to go make a cup of hot chocolate and read after this." Someone called Niall's name in the background on his end.

"Damn it, I'm going to have to hang up. They're calling me. Can you text me, though, so I know you're okay?"

Lark flipped on the light to the staircase, checking up and around it. "Of course."

"I might be back earlier, with any luck. Enjoy your hot chocolate, love."

"Will do. See you later." Lark ended the call and leaned her head back against the wall. Knowing Charles would, in all likelihood, trash her stuff when he got back to London after tonight's events, she tried to get it out of her mind. At least her options were open. Her mother did say she could have the house if she wanted. What would it be like to live here as an adult? It would mean moving and uprooting the life she'd had until now, but maybe a clean slate, possibly with Niall, was just what she needed.

The trickling, leftover rainwater dripped off the roof past the windows, stilling the house to a quiet, peaceful calm that seemed off-kilter. She glanced through the sheeted-up visiting-room window.

She rounded the hallway. Light spilled out from the

kitchen. She froze. Wait, hadn't she and Niall had left it on earlier when going into the living room? She sighed. "Get a grip."

She entered the kitchen and jumped.

Charles stood by the sink, drying his spiky hair with a dark-blue towel. He turned and threw it at her. She caught it before it hit the floor.

"I let myself in." The bitter smell of alcohol lingered, but he seemed sober. And angry.

"Get out of my house," she said, clutching her cell phone and scared to death, but there was no way in hell she'd let him know. "I'm calling the police."

Charles turned away and retrieved a clear, crystal drinking glass from a nearby cupboard. He pressed the valve on the fridge and filled the glass with water. The lack of his usual domineering stature told her all she needed to know about him being unhinged.

"*Your* house? That's good. I suppose you're planning to live here, then. This is what I get after going back to save our investments, hmm?" he asked, his tone acerbic. He took a sip of water.

Lark stood her ground. She acted brave, but fear crashed like a tsunami. This was a Charles she didn't know. And she was alone with him. She glanced at her phone and dialed 911. She scanned around for a weapon. The knife block sat on the counter behind him.

Still facing the fridge while drinking his water, Charles spoke. "You fucked him, didn't you?"

Lark waited until he'd turned around and met him eye to eye. What a bastard. "Yes, I did. What was the phrase you used with Gemma? *Many* times. And you know what? It was *making love*. He gave me everything you never did, and I loved every second."

His face turned red, contorted with anger. Lark moved her finger to hit Send when Charles threw his glass across the room. It shattered on the wall right next to her face. She threw her hands up to shield herself, and her cell phone fell to the floor. Despite the false bravado she'd mustered, reality dawned on her. He came back here after what he'd done.

He could *hurt* her.

It wasn't the loud shatter of glass and the jagged shards everywhere that alarmed her. The fuming mask on Charles's perfect face, incensed and ominous, made her realize she'd never really known him. He moved toward her, glass crunching beneath his shoes. What would he do? She couldn't move, like a paralysis dream, despite how much she wanted to. Primal fear rooted her to the spot. His face darkened, and he lifted his hand.

"You bitch."

Before she could duck or move, Charles punched her hard to the side of her left eye.

She cried out as searing, white-hot pain blinded her. Red spots danced around in front of her while her mind spun and she tried to get a hold on reality. Dizzy and crying, Lark attempted to get away, holding the stinging side of her face as tears flowed down her cheeks. But Charles backed her against the counter. Fuck. He'd had the same countenance on his face when he kicked Niall.

She glanced at the hallway on the fat off-chance Niall had magically appeared since she'd spoken to him on the phone. Charles trapped her, putting both hands on either side of the counter as he leaned in close. He'd done the same many times in the past, except those times had been flirtatious, never menacing.

"Lark, look at me. There. Now, you believe me when I say I'm sorry, don't you?"

She nodded, controlling the whimper that wanted to surface in her throat. She wouldn't give him the satisfaction.

Charles glanced in the same direction she had. "What—is someone here? O'Hagan's SUV was gone when I got here." He turned back and studied her eyes, his handsome, elevated cheekbones tight. He considered her small frame and backed up. "Clean it up." He headed to where a broom and dustpan leaned against the side of the fridge and closed his hand around the handles.

"Clean it up yourself," she spat, batting his hands away.

He sighed and briskly swept the tiny shards of crystal, first around her, then farther away where stray ones had shattered on the floor. She watched him as angry tears slid down her cheeks. He'd never done something like this before. She had seen him freak out when deals didn't go right, or someone in the company had flubbed up, but this was the first time she'd seen him physically violent. But how much time had they really spent together alone?

Charles emptied the last of the debris into the garbage and put the broom back. "I'm sorry."

He sounded sincere, but Lark wanted to wipe the floor with him. She folded her arms, hugging herself. The area above her eye throbbed. The tender spot begged for an ice pack, but she would not play the victim.

"Can we talk now?"

"Go to hell, Charles."

Charles sighed and stepped toward her, and she hated his light, pleasant tone. "Now, come on. Let's talk and work this out. We all do irrational things in the heat of the moment. It was an isolated incident."

She blinked. He was deranged. He truly believed he was in the right, so handsome and crazy in his black polo shirt and trousers.

"Lark, what is going on with you? What in the hell happened while I left? You've become soft as a one-minute egg. Where is the woman who, a few months ago, took charge in the conference rooms and turned the eye of all the blokes? You're buying whatever rubbish he's shoveling at you? You've got to be kidding me. You're an educated woman. He says a couple of poems in his damned Irish brogue," he enunciated, "and he has you eating out of his hand in the space of two short weeks. What the hell has gotten into you that you'd piss away your life and go off with *him*?"

"I might ask you the same question." He narrowed his eyes at her tone, incensed. Perhaps trying a different tactic to keep him from hitting her again might work. "You never dance with me!"

"What?" Charles fired back, bemused. "We've danced loads of times. What the *hell* are you on about?"

"In public, sure," she said, wiping her cheeks as her eye burned. "But when did you ever put your arms around me when we were alone and—"

"Whenever we've been together. I can't count the times, Lark—"

"No," she yelled and stamped her foot. "Name one time, if ever, you put your arms around me when we were alone, no one else in the room, and told me you loved me or danced with me barefoot on the carpet? Never. Not once, Charles. In six years of being together."

He laughed at her. "Is that all you want? We can do it right now. Come on, darling." To her horror, he crouched down to move her feet, but she kicked at him and pushed his broad shoulders away.

"You're a crazy asshole."

Charles sat back on his haunches, still kneeling. "Well, then help me to understand here because I'm lost. What is so damned amazing about O'Hagan you'd throw away what we had?" He shrugged. "I thought we were fine. Sure, I shagged Gemma and other birds, but we weren't married at the time. You should let it go so we can move on."

"We were *together*!"

He raised an eyebrow at her as if to say, *Oh, please.* "Where's the Lark I used to know? Where's the self-confident, take-charge woman? It's like you've gone away and been replaced by Miss Wishy-Washy."

Lark turned away from him and looked out the kitchen window onto the patio deck, to the same spot she had danced with Niall. She drew a breath to calm down. Niall might be getting his ribs x-rayed right now with no idea Charles had returned. They did have a special connection. Did he feel her distress? "She never left, Charles. She came out from under her shell."

Charles stood behind her. "Lark, let's dissect the practical facts here, shall we? Take a step out of la-la land and *think*. We're closing upon a multimillion-pound merger with a prominent corporation, and you have a personal emergency that needs attending to. I hop on a plane to give you a shoulder to cry on, and instead of wrapping up your life business like you should have done, you—"

Lark turned around, and a rhythm of blood throbbed beneath her temples. She shut her eyes. She didn't need a headache right now. She held up a hand, tired and fed up. She opened her eyes. "Charles, wait a minute. Please. I hear what you're saying to me, yes. But give me a break. I'm a human being." Charles stood still as he listened, and it gave her the courage to continue.

She tucked a strand of hair behind her ear. Thunder rolled outside. It had begun to rain again. "I can't keep living like a damn machine, saying the right words, acting the right way, being picture-perfect every day of my life. I need a break. I have a heart, and it beats as much as anyone's. I'm not made of stone. I need to be free to think and feel."

Charles cocked his to the side and gave her a calculating glare. "What in the bloody hell are you on about? You're a perpetual free spirit, Lark. You've had nothing *but* freedom with me. It seems like with him you should be so lucky."

"*Have* I been free?" she asked in earnest. "Have I? Dressing as you wanted me to so you could impress your *mates* and other directors of sister corporations at parties, telling me not to laugh too much if someone made a joke, feeling tight and bitter, a-and *cold*—" Lark twisted her face in disgust, recoiling from the pain his fist had inflicted as well as her ambivalence in staying in a relationship with an egomaniac when, as Niall had said, she deserved better. It wasn't emotionally honest, and in a lot of ways, she'd been living the life of a different person.

Charles took a step toward her, and she clutched the edge of the counter behind her, staring him down. If he tried to hurt her again, she'd fight back.

He held up his hands, appeasing her. "Whoa, now. I'm not going to hit you. If you felt cold, it's not my fault, Lark. Don't put that on my doorstep. I don't commandeer what you feel, and I don't know why you think I should."

She didn't shy away from the weight of his dark eyes. "Fair enough. But you don't treat me like he does. I've known you six years now, Charles. But in the short time I've come to know Niall, I've learned what happiness, respect, and personal freedom mean. Charles, Niall makes me feel warm and cared for. He's thrilled if he makes me *smile*. It matters to him if I'm happy. I see it. I can relax and be myself, and not worry about what I look like or how I act with him. It's not down to what other people think of us, but what we think about each other. He completes me."

What scared her next was not so much what Charles said, but the sharp, quiet way in which he said it.

"Are you listening to yourself? You want me to play along with this while you sugarcoat it. You want me to stand here and pretend this is a blasted fairy tale and be the better man and step aside with the amount involved? You're doing a huge disservice here. Not to me, but to yourself."

She narrowed her eyes. The bastard wanted the money. "Wait a minute. That's what this is about? The money?"

He hesitated. "What are you— No. You're twisting my words."

"You said the *amount involved*, and I know you're not referring to the number of years we were together. Are you trying to secure a payoff here?"

He appraised her scathingly. "Of course not. It's clear O'Hagan doesn't have any plans for you. It's obvious. How many times do you think he's done this, Lark? Come on, think about it. You're an intelligent woman; you know how these things go. I'll bet he seduces every aggrieved widow's daughter he comes into contact with, shags them, then dumps them the second he gets some action. You might as well get a tattoo that says *O'Hagan's fiddle* and be done with it. He's playing you. Think of Ivan from marketing a few years ago. How many of his assistants did he go through before they fired him?"

"You're a fine one to talk," she pressed. "I don't ever recall you having to kick someone in the stomach like a gang member, throw a glass across the room, or *hit me* to prove a point! And Niall is nothing like that, Charles. You don't know his past, and you don't know *him*."

He scoffed at her. "Oh, and you do? In the meager space of a few weeks as opposed to six years with me?"

"Do I know you, Charles? *Do* I?" Charles glared at her and then toned it down a notch. On one level he might regret hitting her, but it didn't excuse him by a long shot. "Because Niall seems pretty damn good from where I'm standing. He would never lay a hand on me, and I know it deep down."

"I said I was sorry. You have to let it go. It was a one-off. I may have my faults, Lark, but at least you know without a question where I stand. I make it clear. What makes you so sure he cares and isn't stringing you along for a purpose?"

She stood her ground, familiar with his intimidation techniques. "Niall wants me for *me* and doesn't want me any other way. You need to accept it." The odd, hurt expression on his face sent a cold dagger of fear through her.

"He 'wants you for you,'" he scoffed.

"Yes."

"Did he say that?"

"Yes, he did."

Charles folded his arms. "Hmm. It's obvious you believed it. And let me guess…"

Lark glanced at the floor, then looked straight into his eyes. She didn't say it, but she might as well have. She never *was* good at masking her expressions. Still, it wouldn't do to goad him on, as volatile as he was.

Charles stood there for several moments, brooding. "So, what we have…" He pursed his lips with a glower.

"You threw it away when you cheated on me. You made your decision."

Tears formed in his eyes, something she'd never seen happen. Guilt flowed through her and then evaporated when she noted his pursed lips and clenched fist. Letting him go was the right thing to do.

"So, what, this is it? Without another word?"

Lark shut her eyes. "I'm sorry. But that's how it's got to be."

Charles nodded. "Fine." His tone became vindictive. "Fine," he snarled.

Lark opened her eyes, and her heart sped up. He was about to play hardball. This was the tone from hard-edged meetings back in London, right before he lay out his cards in the cold, calculating way a CEO is capable of.

"Charles," she cautioned.

He reached into his back pocket and withdrew an envelope. His lips whitened with rage as he spoke, articulating each word in his clear English accent. He held the envelope up.

"This is your ticket for the eleven o'clock in the morning to Heathrow. You'll be on it. A car will come pick you up to take you to the airport at half past eight. I suggest you pack tonight."

"Excuse me?" Lark asked in a shrill voice, ready to fight tooth and nail if she had to. "Charles, what did I just say? I am going to stay here for the time being and be with Niall. I'll be back at work next—"

"You can't."

Lark blinked. "What are you talking about? Yes, I can, and I *will*."

Charles took a deep breath. "I didn't want it to have come to this, Lark. But you leave me with no choice. I know things." He glared. "I hacked into your father's computer. What I found would *shock* you. I know things about your father and his dealings with the company, how he acquired everything, that would ruin your family's name and all he's built." He reached into the inner pocket of his coat spread across the dining-room table and took out a blue jump drive the size of a small vial. "It's all here. I sent the electronic files to my office a week ago, and I have more copies of these. Feel free to take a look. This jump drive contains your father's bookkeeping, computerized journal entries, and pictures of meetings with certain elected officials. It will bring everything your family has crashing down, and don't think I won't do it."

Lark crossed her arms. "Say this is true, Charles. You still can't do anything. He's dead now, so what's done is done. And everyone knows about his affair with Susan Grant if that's what you're referring to."

"I'm not referring to his affair, which I found out about ages ago before you'd told me. See, I dug up information on you, sweetheart. I had you investigated. What, you didn't think I would do something like that?" he patronized her. "And incidentally, it might interest you to know he had many more affairs—a long line of secretaries for a span of about twenty years. Susan Grant was just the tip of the iceberg. Your mum might not like what's here."

He continued as if encouraged by the blatant dismay on her face. "Your father gambled and embezzled the majority of the company's stock. He gambled it with known criminals who are behind bars and would no doubt testify if it meant shorter sentences. I have photographs of him with them, written and signed testimonies from the people he dealt with on the side, and witnesses they can call in a heartbeat. If I bring this out in the open, your family won't just lose all this *and* the legacy he built." He spread his arms to indicate the property. "You and Pam and Aaron will be in severe debt for the rest of your lives."

He came dangerously close. "We're talking about millions, Lark. I bet I could get a jail sentence for your mum if I pressed for one without too much effort." Lark glanced at him in disbelief. "Oh," he said, feigning remorse. "Didn't you know? Your mother was in on it too. She knew what was going on, minus the affairs, and she was privy to the extent of the illegality. She is as much to blame for not having done anything about it."

"And in your twisted mind, what," Lark seethed, "am I supposed to do to make you stop extorting my family?"

"Marry me."

She gave him a withering look. "Please. If I'm not happy with you now, what in the world makes you think I'm going to be happy with you after this? I hate you now."

"Hate me all you want. But you'll marry me. You'll come back to London with me, and we'll get married. You'll get your share of the inheritance when it sells, and we'll use the money. Everything will go back to normal, and you'll do your part as my wife and colleague."

Despite his earlier evasion about it not being related to her money, Lark had to laugh. "You're such a liar, and you're insane! I'm not surprised what it boils down to *is* the inheritance, but this BS you're slinging about *I'll do my part as your wife*?" He was delusional if he assumed she'd lie down and take it. "Let's get one thing straight. I will never sleep with you, *ever* again, for as long as I live. You couldn't drug me enough to do it! I regret having ever done so in the first place. Hell, you were a different man back then."

He chuckled. "You're going to look back on this and laugh," he mused. "Lark, listen. I still want you. You belong to me. But do you think I find this country-hick phase attractive? You're a sexy, powerful woman, and you were fated for me. I need that woman, not this whole cotton-dress-wearing, big-haired, Tammy-Wynette's-love-child person you've become. I'll give you points for your figure, love, but your mind has

367

taken a hiatus."

Lark wanted to slap him, to punch him the way he'd punched her, but she feared what he might do. She balled her fists tight. "If you think I'm going to—"

"You'll act your part in public. You're too well-respected and revered at UY for me to let you go. I need you, and there's a lot I can do with your timeshares when you get your payout. Otherwise, I wouldn't bother with *any* of this. I investigated it, and eight percent of Oregon tax, plus four percent sales tax and inheritance tax, would make your share somewhere around one million five hundred when everything's gone through. It might take up to a year as you'll be overseas, but we can wait. As soon as we're married, you can sign the forms, and we'll be in business. It'll belong to both of us."

A choking sound escaped her throat. So that's why he wanted to get married so badly. "You bastard. You total, *unimaginable* bastard."

He shrugged, unbothered. "This is strictly business, babe. Think of it as a chess move. I have the forms ready, and my attorney will handle it. I mean, consider what we've accomplished, merging with Osaka-Nayaweni because of how much Mr. Osaka took to you first off. You're too valuable an asset to walk away from, Lark, and you're a damned good business partner. I've invested six years of my life and time in you," he said through his teeth, "and I expect to be paid on *all* my investments. We'll get married, and you'll come around and want me again. I'm a patient man, and if I must, I'll find someone who can…take care of my needs in the meantime."

"You're sick," she yelled. "Who *are* you?"

He grimaced. "I may be sick, but like it or hate it, you're stuck with me. Deal with it, or make your *family* deal with it. I'll go through with it. You should know better than anyone else that I don't bluff."

He *didn't*, and the possible repercussions her family would face terrified her. Her mother was a soft, sensitive soul. No way would she last a day in prison. "Hold on, here. If you're going to dangle this over my head, I want the information you have on my dad, and I mean e*verything*. I also want my own place to live, and your guarantee you won't use what you know." She wouldn't put it past him to be vindictive if things didn't go his way.

He pursed his lips. "And how do you propose I do so?"

"I don't know, but you figure it out, or I'm not doing *anything* but staying right here, even if it means giving up my job and you extorting us."

Charles nodded. "All right. When you get back to London, I'll turn over everything I have on your dad to you."

"Not good enough. I want a written statement too," she pressed. "Word it however you want to, but it has to say you won't use what you have as long as I uphold my end of the bargain, and you'll leave my family alone for good." If he was going to do this to her, she wanted leverage. Screw wanting it—she *needed* it.

"No," he frowned. "It could land me in legal trouble."

"Yeah? So could blackmail."

He stared her down, his eyes moving about as he weighed his options. "Very well. We'll draft up an agreement when we get back, just between us.

Everything I have on your father is on that jump drive. Have a look if you don't believe me. After we return to London, if you do your part, I'll give you the additional documents and hard copies."

"No. I want them the second we get in, or I don't go *at all*."

"Done." He flattened the travel pouch containing the airline ticket against her chest and smashed his lips against her cheek. "Get packing."

Lark turned to the side, sickened and violated, wanting to scrub the places he'd touched her with a harsh loofah.

"You best say your good-byes to your lover before you go," he said close to her ear. "Because he's not welcome at our house anytime, day or night. You don't breathe a word of this to him. Let him know it's over for *good* unless you want me to go after him too, which I'll be more than happy to do. I expect you to be in the car at half past eight." He left her standing there. "Don't forget your passport," He barked over his shoulder.

"I hate you!" she yelled at his back, infuriated. She threw the envelope containing the ticket at his retreating back and let out a primal scream. Papers scattered over the floor.

Once the front door closed loudly, she hurried over and locked the deadbolt, shaking. She then went back into the kitchen, put her hand on the back of a kitchen table chair, and slid it out. She sank into it with a heavy heart. The tears she'd been holding back trickled out, and she laid her forehead on her arms, cringing as she hit the sore spot above her eye.

Lark got back up and retrieved an ice pack from the freezer, pressing it tenderly to her forehead. She bent to retrieve the ticket from the floor when her cell phone rang. She answered the call on the fourth ring. It was Niall.

"Hello?" It came out a whisper.

"Hey, you. I planned to leave you a voice mail, but I'm glad you're still up. I finished with the doctor." He sounded cheerful.

"What did he say?" she asked nasally.

"He— Are you all right? You're upset."

Lark shut her eyes, wincing at the developing bruise on her face. It would be a shiner. "I'm fine," she lied. "I've been worried about you, and I haven't had much sleep over the last couple of days. What did the doctor say?"

"Well, first of all, I'm going to live, so you can stop worrying. I do have a couple fractured ribs, but they're superficial. They gave me pain medicine and a cooling adhesive pad to put on my chest for it. Beyond that, a few cuts 'n scrapes. I'll be okay."

"Good," she breathed, grateful. She pressed the ice pack to her eye.

"Love, I want to come back out there, but it's raining a lot, and it's ridiculously late. I'm dying to lie down and hold you, but would you mind if I go back to my condo and come round in the morning?"

"No, no, I *want* you to go home and rest," she said in a high voice, trying to steady herself.

"Lark, I know I asked this, but what's wrong? You sound off."

"I'm fine," she replied. "I'm tired, and it's been draining."

"I know it has. I'm sorry about that. But we made it, didn't we?"

Roxanne D. Howard

"We did," she agreed, glancing with a sinking heart at the plane ticket in her hand. He would hate her. Hell, *she*'d hate herself.

"I'll see you in the morning, Shakespeare. We'll work out where we go from here. Get lots of rest."

"You too," she said. "Good night." Lark disconnected and set the phone on the table.

Charles would be on his way to his hotel, or wherever it was, he was staying. She scowled at the ticket. She hated him. Lark opened the freezer and put the ice pack in to refreeze it.

A few minutes later, the front door opened. Lark rearranged her hair to hang in her face, covering the reddish area that would soon darken.

"Hon, what the hell happened to the window?" her mom asked, shocked.

"Charles," she replied in a flat voice.

Pam gasped and hurried over to her. "What? Did he— Oh Lark, did he hurt you?"

Lark turned to the side to hide her developing bruise. "No. He came back, and he and Niall got into a fight. I'm sorry about the window, Mom. Niall said he'll pay to have it replaced."

Pam put down her purse. "What on earth is Charles doing here?" She looked around. "Is he still here?"

Lark shook her head. "No. He left. He was upset I'd cancelled my flight, so he flew back because he wanted to make sure things were okay between us."

Not buying it, her mother gave her The Look. "Lark, what's going on?" Pam took her by the arm into the living room, sitting her on the couch. "Why did he come back? I thought you and Niall—"

"What *about* me and Niall?" Lark feigned, acting

372

unbothered.

"I know when sparks fly around this house. You're in a real mess."

Lark buried her face in her hands, not wanting to think. "I know. I know, Mom." She clasped her fingers together and brought them to her mouth, blinking back tears.

Pam rubbed her mouth. "What are you going to do? Do you have any idea?"

Lark shook her head, still pressing her lips against her clasped fingers. She'd get on the plane in the morning; she had no choice.

"Well, you'd better come up with something soon."

"I know."

Pam stood. "Let me know what you decide, okay?"

"I will."

Pam paused in the doorway, fiddling with her keys. "And Lark, with the house... We can still go back if you want to keep it in your name. It's not too late. You may *want* a place of your own in the future; who knows? And for what it's worth, I've known Niall for years, and I know that you can travel to Timbuktu and not find anyone half as wonderful. And he pretends to like my cinnamon cookies, although I know they're awful. Don't stay with someone violent. Please. I love you."

She left Lark sitting there, miserable.

Chapter Seventeen
London

Lark found everything on the jump drive that Charles said was on there. With a sinking stomach, she packed, unable to sleep. In the morning, she slipped downstairs as quietly as possible, leaving a note for her mother and one for Niall on a small table near the front door.

She padded into the kitchen, pausing by the final probate papers on the table. A pen lay in wait for her, but she turned without signing anything and walked out. It was a simple, unproblematic moment that did not hit her as hard as it would later.

She'd struggled to write Niall a letter, discarding many long-winded versions. In the end, she kept it simple, short, and full of lies.

Dear Niall,

Charles came back late last night, apologizing for what he did to both of us. He is sorry and wants to work things out. After talking with him, I realized I do love him, and I want to be with him. I know this will hurt you, and that he hurt you. I'm so sorry.

Thank you for our time together. Good-bye.

Lark

Thumbing the handle on her carry-on, she left the house amid a mountain of regret before she changed her mind.

The taxi ride to the Portland International Airport took an hour, and she mentally battled with herself the whole way.

She made her way through check-in and sat in the waiting area at her gate. Charles discovered her there. He sat beside her, crossed his ankle over his leg, and busied himself with his BlackBerry.

"I've set our wedding for the day after tomorrow at Hammersmith Town Hall at half past two," he mentioned in an offhanded sort of way. "I e-mailed you the list of what documents to bring with you. They normally do ceremonies by appointment only several weeks in advance, but Gareth Townsend from Finance knows the superintendent registrar. He owed me a big favor, so I had him pull a few strings. The ceremony itself will be simple and short, about thirty minutes long, including the signing with the registrar, and then we're going out to dinner with my mum and dad."

Lark nodded, nauseated with the pollution of his cruelty.

Once they boarded and the flight was on its way, she moved to a vacant window seat in coach to avoid having to sit next to him. "Niall, I'm so sorry," she whispered, looking out the window as the commercial jet sped down the runway and lifted off the ground.

****

The flight into London touched down at half past eight Sunday morning. They got into the flat, and Lark retreated straight to their home office, opened up the futon, and slept. Sunday pretty much disappeared, and she slept deeply, with no dreams. Lark had contacted Maisie on their flight back, telling her she needed to talk. When Maisie knocked on their front door early

Monday morning, Lark opened the door and tried to smile. She was on edge and dressed down, with a black baseball cap pulled low over her swollen temple to hide the bruise. Thank God she didn't have to say anything or explain. Maisie's intelligent, wide black eyes read her well enough to know something serious had happened. Lark eyed the car keys in Maisie's hand and put her hands in the front pockets of her jacket.

"Hey," she whispered.

Maisie nodded, scouting past her for any sign of Charles, who was still asleep. "Come on, mate."

During the ride to the coffee shop, Lark gazed out the window. Maisie seemed to sense something going on, and as usual, she didn't say anything until Lark felt ready to talk.

They sat at a table in the far back after ordering their coffee. Lark shakily poured sweetener into her cup and wiped her tear-streaked face with the back of her other hand.

"Lark? Are you all right, darling?" Maisie asked, placing a hand on hers. "Do you want to go have a cig?"

"I quit smoking."

"Lark, that's brilli—"

Lark pressed her lips together. The tears continued to fall, and her mind spun. She was in pieces, and it would take a world-class surgeon and a hell of a lot of sorting out to ever put her back together again.

Maisie leaned forward, concerned. "Darling, *what* is going on?"

Lark gave her a half-pitched story. She couldn't tell her the truth, despite how much she wanted to. Maisie worked in the same corporation and had once been

Charles's personal assistant. In the end, she told her more or less the same story she'd fed Pam in her letter; she and Niall had had a brief relationship while in Oregon after she'd discovered Charles's affair, but Charles came back for her to work things out. They'd talked it out and were now going to get married that afternoon at Hammersmith Town Hall.

"Whoa. Back up." Maisie raised a hand, blinking owlishly. "Let me try to get my head round this. First, you go back to America and meet, literally, the man of your *dreams*. Then Charles comes back, and you're giving everything up and getting married today, although he cheated on you. Why?"

"Be—because I love him." Maisie's face said she didn't believe her. "What?"

Maisie hesitated, but then she leaned closer and lowered her voice. "Okay, what I'm about to say doesn't leave this table, *capiche*? You asked me in my original interview why I switched. I told you I wanted a change. I did, but it wasn't the main reason why I moved."

"Why *did* you?"

Maisie sighed and glanced down, twisting her fingers. "Lark—all I can tell you is you have the power to decide your fate. No one has the right to govern what you do or don't do with it. Graham and I've been married for over thirteen years now. He's still the love of my life. But if we ever had a day in our relationship where I'd been bullied into it, I would be effing miserable, okay? Marriage is enough of a constant roller coaster as it is, and you have to make sure the person in the seat beside you are as willing to throw up their hands when you're speeding downhill and to hold on with you when you're going around sharp curves.

"If you go through with this wedding, I'll be there to support you no matter what." Maisie took her hand. "But if you love this man Niall, you need to love him and not give Charles the power to make you stay with him out of a sense of duty, or whatever it is. Charles is a powerhouse, Lark. I've worked with the bloke for a while and have seen him in action. He has no conscience if it means getting his way. If I'm fessing up here, no holds barred—I never liked him. You deserve someone a hell of a lot better. Please be careful."

Lark covered her face with her hands. She wished the decision hadn't already been made for her.

****

When she returned home a couple of hours later and entered their flat, Charles spoke to her as he checked his hair out in the hallway mirror on his way out, smoothing it down.

"As we're getting married this afternoon and it's still relatively early—" He glanced at the hall clock, which said nine a.m. "—you can take a few hours for yourself. But be home by one. And remember: We're going out to eat with my parents after the ceremony, so wear something nice. If you behave, I'll give you the contract agreement and hard copies afterward."

She seethed, waiting until he left the flat before using the bathroom to shower and get ready. She didn't want to interact with him at all. She hurried and got dressed.

As she gathered her coat and purse to leave, Charles sulked out at her from a nearby photograph, posing in front of an Italian garden with red roses adorning a trellis behind him. Resisting the urge to throw Charles's handsome, pouting face across the room, Lark instead placed the picture face down on the table harder than necessary so she wouldn't have to see him. She slid her keys off the end table by the front door with a metallic swoosh, shouldered her small handbag, and walked out the door.

The morning air hit her cheeks, fresh and cold but warmer than earlier when she'd been out with Maisie. She adjusted her cream-colored scarf inside her brown leather overcoat and secured the top button. Her hair hung loosely in her face, covering the tender bruise Charles had left. She descended with a cluster of people down the steep concrete steps, moving through the turnstiles to the London Underground. After purchasing her day ticket, she made her way through the throng on the escalators, which seemed to stretch for miles.

She didn't pay attention to which tube station she got off at; she walked on and tried not to think, lest she explode.

Her cell phone rang as she stood waiting for another underground train to take her to the London Bridge tube station. An unfamiliar number from the States appeared on the LCD screen on her phone, and she frowned with trepidation, pausing before she hit the button. "Hello?"

"Lark?"

"Mom." She exhaled in relief.

"Hi. How you doing?"

"I'm all right." Lark glanced at the dark tunnel as she waited for the train to approach. The overhead display stated the train would be there in four minutes.

"You're a horrible liar, sweetheart."

Lark choked up. "Well, I have to try. What time is

it there?" Her mother yawned loudly as she stretched.

"About one-thirty in the morning. I'm relaxing with Bandit out on the porch. I couldn't sleep. Been thinking about you. I've got my winter coat on. They said it was supposed to snow tonight, but it hasn't yet. It's cold, though."

Lark smiled, despite the solemnity of her circumstance. Pam Braithwaite would spend her dying day on her front porch. "It sounds it. I can hear the wind. You don't need to worry about me. But I'm glad you called, Mom. I…want to talk to you."

"Niall came by."

Lark folded her arms while holding the cell phone. Her stomach tumbled down the Grand Canyon.

"He did?"

"Yes, dear."

Lark closed her eyes tight, as the metallic whine increased from the approaching train on the steel tracks. "Mom, I have to go. The train's here."

"Okay," Pam said. "Can I call you later?" Lark glanced again at the dirty concrete floor, lost.

"Lark?"

"Yeah. All right, then. Talk to you later."

"Bye, honey."

Lark closed her cell phone, wiped the tears from her cheeks, and got on.

She got off a few stops later and walked along the pier by the Thames River, hands in her pockets, observing performance artists standing statuesque, mocking her emotional state as she passed by with their eerie, dramatic mask faces cast downward in despair. She guessed they did it in an attempt to make her laugh. She wasn't laughing.

An old, gray-haired vendor with a careworn face smiled as she walked by. He sold warm, honey-roasted peanuts with a thick, crusted coating. He wore a dark-blue coat and a flat cap. The sweet, warm aroma floated over to her from several feet away. Her stomach grumbled. She meant to pass the stand, but it smelled heavenly, and she hadn't eaten since last night.

"Can I get you something, love?"

"Yes, I'd like a bag, please."

The old man smiled at her and scraped the roasted nuts around on the oven with a metal spatula. "It'll be two quid. Getchya the warmest ones yet, right off the cooker. Too fresh out to be without 'em, eh?" He scooped up several crisp-covered warm nuts into a small white paper bag.

Lark glanced at the Thames and Big Ben and the Houses of Parliament, which aligned in the distance. Her nose was cold.

She put her hand into her coat pocket to get the change and touched something hard and cool and flat amid her coins. Pulling it out, she gasped in disbelief at the smiley-face stone.

"How in the world did you get in there?" It must have been in her coat since the day Niall gave it to her. She'd stuffed the coat in her luggage before leaving Oregon.

"Pardon?" the old man said. She showed him the stone, and a smile lit his old face.

He leaned over his stand to admire it and laughed. "Well, I'll be... A li'ul smiley face. Not every day you see one 'o them, eh? Ha, that's nice. It'll bring you good luck." He cleared his throat, and Lark glanced up from the stone in her hand.

"What?"

"The shrapnel, darlin'," he said kindly.

"Oh yes, excuse me." She handed him two one-pound coins from her pocket.

"Ta," he said and pocketed the money away.

She ate the peanuts and entered the British Museum at twenty to twelve. She was cutting it close, but every minute away from Charles was a small victory. She checked her cell phone, which showed her mother as being the one caller of the day. Charles wouldn't call; he had no reason to. He'd won.

Encased in a prison-cell-sized display case lay the remains of a five-thousand-year-old man a cheeky British archaeologist had christened "Ginger" due to the tufts of red hair on his head. Lark contemplated the scrappy, shabby remains of the preserved man curled into a fetal position. Is that how she would feel for the rest of her life as Charles's wife? What in the hell was she doing?

Her cell phone vibrated in her hand. Her mother again.

Opening it, she continued walking through the gallery. "Hi, Mom."

"Hi, honey. Where are you?"

"The British Museum. Why?"

"It sounds noisy."

"I can go to a quieter area so we can talk if you want," Lark offered. A distinctive beep sounded on her mother's end.

"Hang on, sweetheart. Someone's calling on the other line. Let me get rid of them."

"Okay, go on." Lark turned up the white, curving stairs in the large main hall. She kept the phone to her ear and smiled back at an elderly couple she passed on their way out of the gallery she entered. She watched them go, obviously happy, weighing what it would have been like to grow old with Niall. She pictured him with her as she walked through the gallery, allowing the daydream to ease her pain.

"Lark? You still there?" asked Pam.

"Yep."

"Darned telemarketers. Forty extra dollars a month and the solicitation block still doesn't work. What a joke. So, how are you? Can you talk?"

Lark sat on a bench. "I'm surviving. Yes, I'd like to talk to you."

"I want to talk to you too. Where are you, by the way? The sound is a lot better."

"I'm in the Mesopotamian Gallery. There's like no one here. I guess the Code of Hammurabi isn't as sexy as it used to be."

"Well, stay there while we talk, okay? The line kept cutting out before, and I don't want to lose you."

"All right."

"Good. We should have about ten to fifteen minutes before my calling card dies. I'll get a new one soon. Let's cut to the chase, Lark Suzanne. You're one miserable cookie."

Lark smiled at the use of her middle name and baking euphemism. "Well, I guess us Braithwaite women have never been known for our subtlety, have we?"

"Lark, what in the world is going *on* with you? One moment you and Niall are head over heels for each other, and then you're hopping on a flight to London with Charles. What happened?"

"It's complicated." Lark made sure her hair covered her bruise as a few people walked by.

"Try me." Her mother sounded annoyed. "You'd be surprised at what I've been through myself."

Lark closed her eyes. "Mom, listen. I want to tell you, but I *can't*."

"Do you love Niall?" Pam asked. "Lark?"

"I can't be with him."

"Explain."

"I told you I *can't*. It's complicated."

"Are you pregnant? Is that why you're back with Charles?"

Lark stood. "What? No. Mom, I—coming back here was the right thing to do."

"Right for who? Lark, I love you, but it seems like the only one getting anything out of this but heartache and misery is Charles. Do you love him that much?"

She loved him about as much as she loved the idea of crawling along on her hands and knees across a busy highway full of broken glass, but she took a breath and lied.

"Yes."

"No, you don't," Pam said, and Lark's heart shriveled. "I'm your mom, kiddo. I know when something's going on. Would you like to know, Lark, what Niall did when he found out you'd gone with Charles?"

Lark closed her eyes and pinched the bridge of her nose. "No, please don't tell me." *I couldn't stand it.* She pictured Niall in her mind's eye, leaving the house in a rage, hating her for the rest of her life.

Pam stayed silent. To take away the guilt and pain, Lark imagined Niall there with her, placing a hand on her back as she strolled farther into the gallery. It helped to slice through the veil of remorse, which fell over her like a heavy drape.

"All right, then. I won't for the time being. Tell me, how's it going with Charles? I know you didn't want to tell me you broke it off, but I figured it out for myself. What is it like being back over there after all that's happened?"

Lark paused in front of a display case along the wall, which housed artifacts dating back to the first record of man upon the earth. Bits and pieces of flint tools and clay vases recovered from ruins were set in neat rows. "We're sleeping in separate rooms," she admitted. "I haven't spoken to him since we got back."

"Oh, honey—"

"I know." The distinctive beep sounded again.

"Darn it. Sorry, someone's on the other line again. Hang on."

"Okay." Lark stopped in front of a display case, contemplating a model of a slave ship with miniature, brown-skinned figurines swathed in white clothing. Fascinating how people throughout history seemed fixated on leaving a vestige of their culture or existence so future generations got a glimpse of what they were like, even the brutality and sufferance of classes. It seemed everyone wanted to make their mark and prove they existed, whether the causes and plights of their peoples had been for ill or good.

"Lark? I'm back."

"Hey."

"Listen, hon, I don't know what's happening, but it's not worth staying with Charles for anything if you're unhappy. Do you hear me?"

Lark stared at the slave ship. "Yes, I do. Unfortunately, what's done is done, Mom."

"Nothing is ever *done*," retorted Pam. "And by the way, I'm going to tell you what Niall did, whether you want to hear it or not."

Lark winced. "Mom, please don't. I'm in enough pain as it is." Catching a reflection in the display-case glass, she imagined Niall behind her, not some stranger. She stretched her fingertips out to trace the outline of his face on the glass to the left of her own.

"He got on a plane and went after you."

Chapter Eighteen
Mesopotamia

Lark's heart plummeted. This was no fantasy.

She whirled around.

Standing with a determined look on his face, in the flesh—dressed in jeans, a dark shirt, and his black leather jacket—was Niall. A dark, fist-size bruise covered his upper right eye and temple, and she understood his pain, her identical one covered by concealer and curtained over by her long hair.

"Lark? Lark, what's going on?"

Lark did not break her gaze. "He's here," she said into the phone as he stared at her. The blood in her head rushed to her toes.

"Oh good; he found you."

"I assume it was him on the other line?"

"It was. My work here is done," Pam said with a flourish in her voice. "I'm going shopping. If you're as smart as I know you are, honey, you'll do the right thing." Her mother hung up.

Lark pushed her phone into her pocket, never taking her gaze from Niall's. Her heart pounded.

"*Believe me,*" he recited, taking a step toward her. "*If all those endearing young charms, which I gaze on so fondly today, were to change by tomorrow and fleet in my arms, like fairy-gifts fading away, thou wouldst still be adored, as this moment thou art. Let thy*

387

loveliness fade as it will, and, around the dear ruin, each wish of my heart would entwine itself verdantly still."

Lark caught her breath. "You got me. I don't know it. Shakespeare?"

He shrugged. "Two out of three. Thomas Moore. It kept playing in my mind on the flight over." He looked weathered, and his cheeks were flushed from traveling. He set his black backpack on the floor.

"Niall, you look so tired."

Niall put his hands on his hips, hanging his head. "Shakespeare, I'm bleedin' *exhausted*, if I'm honest."

And indeed, he looked it. The outline of an adhesive cooling pad lumped beneath his T-shirt, where Charles had kicked him.

She blinked. "How did you find me or get here so quick?"

"My flight landed two hours ago. Your mam said you were on the Underground the last time she spoke with you, so I've been riding it around the city, looking for you. I was less than a block away at Tottenham Court Road ten minutes ago, when she told me you were here." He stepped forward, his posture tense. Trepidation came off him in waves. "Lark, tell me you didn't sleep with him," he intoned, his face dark.

Lark shook her head, trying to keep her voice steady, but it broke. "I didn't. I wouldn't."

He relaxed and ran a hand through his mop of curls. He drew in a heavy breath. "Oh, thank God." He covered his eyes with his hand. "Thank God."

"Niall, it was beyond romantic of you to do what you did, but you shouldn't have come here. I—I meant what I said in the note I left you."

He straightened up, chuckling, and shook his head. "What a load of absolute rubbish," he said, enunciating each word. "I knew something wasn't right. I knew it in me gut when I talked to you on the phone. More so when I saw you hadn't signed the paperwork at the house. That told me more than that phony, crummy note you left ever could about where your heart lies."

Striding forward, he put his hand around her lower back and hauled her to him. He took a moment and looked deep into her eyes, daring her to break away. Lark opened her mouth to speak when he anchored her cheek with his other hand and dived into her. His kiss consumed her, his lips taking hers, his tongue laying claim. She tried to fight it. This was the wrong way to go about everything, with a dark cloud looming over her head. But she responded to him in an instant, melting into his arms and clutching his open jacket, drawing him nearer. He kissed her like a man possessed, drowning her senses in a pool of desire. He slowed down and pulled his face back, searching her eyes and nodding.

"Yeah, I thought as much. You're still my girl. Come on."

He turned with her hand in his, but she remained rooted to the spot, knowing Charles would extort her and her family if he found out Niall was there. He huffed and let go of her hand, beyond irritated. He set his backpack down again and folded his arms over his chest, glaring at her.

"Love, you and I need to have it out, but I have got to do two things before we can." He ticked off his fingers. "One, I'd like to check into the hotel my assistant booked and take a much-needed piss and damned pain medication whilst I'm at it, and then I'd like to sit, have a meal with you, and discuss what's going on. I can tell you've got a lot happening upstairs, and I can feel you're torn inside. But no matter how confused you are, do me this favor and come with me, okay? You owe me that, at least."

She did owe him. She nodded and let him take her hand. He hailed a parked black taxi outside the museum gates. He opened the door for her, getting in after her. "Kensington, please," he said to the driver, a middle-aged burly man with a receding hairline. "The Marriott hotel."

The taxi pulled away from the curb, and Niall took her hand in his again. He stayed quiet as he turned his head in the opposite direction, but his fingers and thumb massaged her own, comforting her. Too numb to cry and too shocked to move, Lark stared at their joined hands, overcome by the fact he'd followed her all the way here. They passed by London architecture, lots of traffic, and red double-decker buses as they moved through the traffic.

The driver dropped them off in front of the Marriott, and she went inside with Niall. "Is that all you brought with you?" He'd shouldered the backpack.

"Yes." He held the door open for her to the lobby. "I had to pack fast."

Guilt-ridden, she walked with him to the ornate check-in desk, and he showed the tidy male desk clerk the reservation on his phone.

"Ah," the young man said, searching his computer. "Mr. and Mrs. O'Hagan. Here we are."

Lark eyeballed Mr. O'Hagan and swore he stifled a smirk.

"I've got you in the Executive suite, one king bed, nonsmoking. It has a view of Big Ben. Excellent. I'll need to see your passport and credit card, please, sir, to solidify the reservation."

After Niall had the keycards in hand, they went to the elevators. He pushed the floor number to the suite. Lark slipped her hand out of his as the elevator moved, and that got his attention.

"Kind of presumptuous, don't you think?"

He blinked a little too innocently. "What?"

"Mr. and *Mrs.* O'Hagan?"

Niall's eyes glittered at her. "What can I say? I'm an optimistic lad. Let's get settled and order room service, and then we'll talk, okay? You promised."

She hadn't, but she did feel like she owed him something after what they'd been through together. "All right," she said, guarded. "But I can't stay." She'd give him the closure and respect he deserved, and then go back to the flat, alone.

He took her hand again and pressed her against the wall of the elevator. Thank God they were alone. He gave her a gentle kiss, and despite knowing she shouldn't, Lark tilted her head for more, sliding her hands through the folds of his leather jacket and holding him around the waist. He cupped her face with his hands, then pressed his forehead to hers as they reached their floor.

"Come on." He kissed her again and led her to their room.

The room was beyond lavish, and she took in the sleek yet warm design. It opened to a suite lounge with a dining table, couch, mounted flat screen, and a bottle of wine chilling in an ice bucket on the coffee table. It

391

was spacious in London terms, and indeed, out the balcony window, Big Ben looked close enough to touch. Niall locked the hotel door behind them, set his backpack on the couch, and took her coat to hang up. That done, he headed to the toilet.

He paused, turning to her. "Don't leave." It was a simple, light request, but the air permeated with a fragile heaviness.

Lark put a hand to her heart. "I won't."

"Good. Why don't you open the wine and have some, then have a gander at the room-service menu? Let's order food from the Atrium. I'm starving."

He closed the bathroom door, and Lark moved into the bedroom area, staring hard at the king-size bed. The duvet and pillows were white, and it appeared beyond comfortable. She was in way over her head. Her stomach growled. She hadn't eaten since buying the roasted peanuts, and she'd barely touched anything yesterday. Definitely not enough food. She spotted the room-service folder on the nightstand and sat on the bed, flipping through it.

Niall came out a few minutes later and sat carefully next to her on the bed. He put a hand to his ribs and let out a whoosh of air as he got comfortable. "Oh, *yes*. Yes, this is heaven," he murmured, snuggling his back into the bed. He lightly grazed the top of her thigh with his knuckles. "Have you picked something you want?"

Lark tensed at his touch and then stood. She had to stop this and leave. It wasn't fair to him. "I don't care what we get. I'll eat anything. Go ahead and order for me. I need to use the restroom."

"Okay," he said, sitting up and taking the folder.

Once alone in the clean, sparkling-white bathroom,

Lark sat on the toilet and put her head in her hands. She had no idea what to do, and it terrified her, knowing she would have to break Niall's heart. She stood and cleaned up in the sink. Her reflection appeared fresh and clean, but inside, she might as well have had a bucket of manure dumped over her head. This man was good and did not deserve the pain she would inflict on him. It stung like a thousand swords to know she couldn't make it right.

Her cell phone vibrated on the counter, and she checked a message from Charles.

It's getting late and close to the ceremony. Why aren't you back yet? Where are you?

She turned her cell phone off and set it back down, her eyes stinging. "Oh, God."

"Hey, Shakespeare?" Niall's voice came through the closed door.

"Yes?" she called, blinking up at the ceiling to stop crying.

"I ordered steak, salad, and vegetables. I got yours well-done. Is that okay?"

She smiled at herself. Trust Niall to cotton on to how she liked it. "Yes, that's fine. It's how I normally take it, anyway."

"Good." He sounded relieved. "It'll be here in about fifteen minutes."

"Okay," she said, opening the door. He stood right there, like a sentry guarding her door.

He'd taken off his jacket, his wide shoulders less tense than before. "Come here, you," he said, taking her hand and pulling her into him. She laid her cheek against his chest, reveling in the warmth of him as he rested his chin on top of her head, then pressed a kiss there.

"I can't believe you came after me, Niall."

His hand skimmed her lower back. "Of course I did," he said as if it were a no-brainer. "I would've been here sooner, but I had to go home to grab me passport, and I couldn't get a flight out until six hours after you. I had a bleedin' conniption fit when the connecting flight out of JFK got delayed. I can't believe you're surprised." He put an arm around her shoulders and walked her to the couch in the sitting area, his emerald eyes blazing. "Sit. Please. Let me pour you a drink."

Lark sat on the couch and watched his long fingers work the corkscrew on the wine bottle. He glanced at her and poured a glass of the white wine, holding it out to her. She took it, noticing the ice water in his glass. She brought the glass to her lips, her hands trembling from hunger and nerves, but he stopped her, taking the glass back. "Hold on. First things first." He took her left hand and slid off the engagement ring Charles had insisted she put back on.

"Niall, no."

He removed it.

"Wouldn't it be great if this, I don't know, flew away?" He put a finger to his lips and strode to the balcony door, opening it. He put one foot out and threw the ring hard, casting it far over the walkway and into the Thames River.

Lark let out a huff of air as he closed the door and came back, pleased with himself. Charles would kill her. The ring had cost a fortune. "Niall! How could you— How am I going to expl—"

"Shh." He placated her, lifting a finger as if to say,

one moment. He moved the backpack next to him and opened the front zipper, taking out something that suspiciously resembled an old ring box.

"Now, hold *on*," she said sternly. "You're missing the whole point of my coming back here. If you think you can—"

To her horror, he got down on one knee, opened the tattered box, and a beautiful gold Claddagh ring surrounded by tiny diamonds shone up at her.

"It was my mother's," he said softly. "The Claddagh represents loyalty, friendship, and love, with the heart, hands, and crown. After Melanie died, me mam gave it to me, telling me that though my life was in shambles and I believed I'd never find happiness again, someday a good woman with a brave heart would come into my life, and I'd find love with her and magic, and that I should give her this. I didn't believe it at the time, but I *have*, and I *do*. I love you, Lark. With my whole heart and my whole soul and body. I want to spend the rest of my life with you."

It terrified her, for so many reasons, yet she stayed still as he slid the ring onto her finger without preamble or waiting for her to respond. Surprisingly, it fit. Despite the pain she'd caused and *would* cause this man, she regarded her hand with a spark of hope, closing her eyes and daring any of this to be real.

He cupped her cheek, his eyes filled with love. "I swear I'll always be faithful to you and what we have together. I will never stray or want anyone but you. I'll be your friend too, in every way. You can count on me and come to me for anything, and I promise to listen and pay attention to how you're feeling and be honest with you. I will love you unreservedly for the rest of my life. I'll make sure you smile every day, and that you'll always have a reason to."

She wiped a tear from the corner of her eye, and gently pushed his hand away from her cheek. "Niall, you're wonderful. You need to understand... I *want* to be with you, but—"

"No." He took her chin, turning her face to him. "Look at me." She opened her eyes. "I'm done takin' no for an answer from you, Lark Braithwaite. I'm not the type of man who goes where he's not wanted, but you want me too. I know it because I *feel* you. You can't hide what you feel from me, the way your body responds to mine." The intensity in his eyes burned into hers. "We were meant for each other, and *you know it*."

Lark covered her eyes with her hand. She didn't want to cause *anyone* pain, least of all him. "I *do* want you, Niall. I do love you. More than anything. But I—I can't do this. I'm so sorry."

He lowered her hand from her eyes, and when she removed the engagement ring, he covered her hand with his, his eyes shrewd and assessing.

"Okay," he muttered, standing and helping her to stand as well. "Okay. Let's have it out, then. Keep it on, though. The ring is yours now. Here," he said, placing the wineglass back into her hands. "Let's sit at the table and talk about whatever the hell that wanker has on you. The food'll be here soon."

"Niall, he doesn't have anyth—"

"Rubbish," he countered knowingly. "I can see it in your eyes and feel it in my heart, Shakespeare, sure as me ribs are killing me." He pulled out a seat for her at the small dining table, and as soon as he pushed her forward, a knock came at the door.

Niall opened it, and he wheeled in the cart of food, then shut and locked the door behind him. He made his way back to the table, removed the warming covers from the plates, and handed Lark a rolled linen napkin with utensils inside. She took it, grateful for the food and temporary reprieve as he placed her plate in front of her and she cut up her steak.

"I can't imagine what all this is costing you," she muttered, then took a bite. It was cooked to perfection, succulent and tangy and thick all at once.

"It's nothing compared to the cost of not being with you." He took a bite of his own steak, and she watched as the fork tines slid slowly between his teeth. Niall put his fork down, took a sip of water, and she met his gaze over the brim of his wineglass.

"How are you feeling? Are you in pain right now?"

He shrugged. "No. In the end, it was all very minor. They're better, and the painkillers are workin' their magic. I'm fit as a fiddle for playin'. And"—he lowered his voice—"other things."

Her pussy stirred as if on cue at the look he gave her, and never in her life had she wanted to wish all her problems away so she could be with him. He cleared his throat and set down the glass.

"All right, level with me. Let's be honest with each other. What the fuck is going on here?"

She took a sip of her wine, trying to calm her nerves. "I'm not at liberty to explain it to you, Niall. I'm sorry. I never wanted to hurt you; you have to know that. I can't stand that I did. But it's something that's beyond my control."

He narrowed his eyes, suspicious and shrewd. He'd seen her forehead. He leaned forward and moved her hair from her face, and his countenance darkened as he discovered the purple welt. She turned her face away, humiliated, wincing at the fresh pain his touch caused.

"He did that to you? *Bugger*. Listen to me." He put his hand on hers in the middle of the table, his eyes bright with anger. "He's never going to touch you, ever again. I swear it."

She set her fork down, miserable. "Charles and I are supposed to get married in less than two hours."

Niall flinched. "The *hell* you are! We'll elope and get married right now if we have to." He skidded his chair back as he stood. He angrily laced his fingers together behind his head and turned away. She followed him.

"Niall, I'm sorry. I know you're upset. You have every right to be. But what's done is done, and you can't—"

"You're not getting the bigger picture here," he said with a harsh laugh, turning around to face her. He unlaced his hands. "Let's get one thing straight."

She gasped when he strode up purposefully and pinned her against the wall with his body, lifting her arms above her head and holding them securely at the wrists with one hand. He leaned in predatorily, his eyes so close she could drown in them.

"I'm not going *anywhere*, Shakespeare," he said against her mouth. "You're *mine*, and I'm invested in what we have together. Whatever this is, whatever *game* he's playing, we're going to figure it out."

"What if it can't *be* figured out?" she whispered, afraid of what she'd do if he kissed her. Through the cracked balcony door, the Westminster Chimes went off and played atop Big Ben, and she glanced toward it.

Niall let go of her hands and grasped her waist, and she looked into his eyes. His thumbs stroked her hip bones and soft flesh with tender pressure. His eyes searched her face, for what she was uncertain, but she arched, rubbing her aching pussy against him. She raised her thigh and crossed it over his, drawing him in. He made a distinctly male, pleased sound in the back of his throat and thrust his hard cock against her while nuzzling his face into the crook of her neck.

"You can say all the lies you want," he murmured, then licked her neck, "but your body doesn't lie to me. It never has. I *know* what you want."

Tired of fighting it, Lark lifted her face to kiss him. She fumbled to open the button on his jeans. If her life was going to be stripped from her, she was going to have one last fucking hurrah, and damn the consequences. His warm skin brought to mind soft clothes fresh from the dryer, soothing hot towels on the back of her neck on long-distance flights, afternoon sunlight teasing her desire-warmed skin the day they'd danced on the deck. She unzipped him, stopping when his large palm covered her cheek.

He pulled back from their kiss, searching her eyes. "Can you honestly tell me you don't want this? Because every time I look at you, I— This is hard for me to say, but you're *it* for me, Lark. Your heart, your compassion, and courage."

He stroked her neck, and she wanted to cry at the raw love in his eyes.

"Your impossible beauty. I want a life with you so bad I can *taste* it. I want to see your belly filled with our child, to travel, have adventures, and grow old together. But if you were honest before, and you don't want what we have…if you feel absolutely nothing at all for me, tell me. Otherwise, I won't stop. I *will* fight for you."

She blinked, stunned. This was her out. He was actually giving her an out, despite his well-deserved anger. The simple solution would be to peel away from him, quietly gather her things, and leave while she could, to save her family. She ought to. But his eyes compelled her, and it wasn't the weight of him molded to her or the way her body responded instinctively to his. It was the unspoken proclivity to do the right thing and the fact that she loved him.

Shutting her eyes, shutting out the world, she whispered, "I want you so much it hurts," and moved her face to his, pressing her mouth fully against his parted lips. A rush of adrenaline shot through her.

He trembled in response and passionately kissed her back. He slid his fingers down the indent of her back and clutched her ass. He kneaded the flesh there, moved his cock sensuously against her, and sniffed her hair, breathing in her scent. She quavered with sweet anticipation when he teased his lips against the side of her neck. A fresh sensation flooded her body, setting every nerve ending ablaze when he tasted her with a long, sweet lick along the underside of her jaw, savoring the tip of her earlobe and nibbling on it.

"Don't fight this anymore," he murmured. "Be with me. Your mouth can only say no so many times when your body's telling me the exact opposite. Surrender to what we are together."

"Yes." She shook.

His hands were on her blouse, and the fabric split with a loud rip when he tore it open, buttons falling and scattering in all directions. She'd be hard-pressed to wear it again after this, and that would present a problem in leaving the hotel anytime soon. Cool air teased her breasts, hardening her nipples into stiff, aching peaks begging for his touch. He yanked the torn folds of her shirt around her elbows and jerked down a cup of her bra, then took her breast in his warm, wet mouth. She moaned and slid her hands through his hair and all about his shoulders as he used tongue and teeth, licking around her nipple as he sucked her, then lavished the same attention on her other breast.

"I," he urged, the green flames of his eyes bearing into hers, "am going to take you to the bed, worship every glorious damned inch of you, and then I'm going to ravish you."

Her breath caught at his fierce, enamored expression. She had no idea what to do about Charles and his hold over her family, but Niall was right. This was a love worth fighting for.

Wincing slightly, he bent and swept his arm beneath her knees, lifting her up.

Lark frowned as he carried her to the bed. "Niall, don't. Put me down. You'll injure yourself."

"I'm fine, Shakespeare. A little ache is all. I wouldn't do it if I couldn't."

Lark hooked her arm around his neck, stroked his cheek with her other hand, and met his eyes. She touched his lips, and he enclosed his mouth around it, sucking and scraping it with his teeth. Her insides liquefied, and a stream of hot desire gushed straight into her core.

When her back hit the bed, and he crawled over her, the warmth of his body pressing down on hers, she moved against him in instinctive recognition, not giving credence to her actions until after she'd enveloped him as though he were home. His forehead pressed against hers. With a rueful smile, he grabbed her wrists from around his shoulders and pressed them to either side of her face, trapping her beneath him most decadently.

He trailed his lips along the new expanse of skin, along her shoulder, and down her collarbone, moving lower until he lingered tantalizingly close, his hot breath against her exposed nipple. He closed his mouth over it, nibbling the taut peak gently. Pain and pleasure rolled into one. Her pussy tensed, and she raised her hips to his, trying to appease the friction as he soothed her nipple with his soft tongue, trying to obtain relief. But it wasn't enough.

"Not yet," he chided, letting go of her wrists to kiss down her rib cage. She kept her hands by her face, straining as the faint slap of leather swished through a buckle, a zipper came undone, and the rustle of cloth dropped to the floor. He slid her trousers and panties off, marking a map upon the flat of her stomach with his tongue and teeth as he went along, tantalizing and gnawing every curve and line.

She curled her hands into fists in his hair as he neared her throbbing core, but he took his time, exploring her inch by inch as if trying to memorize her and catalog each and every detail. His fingers reached her dewy folds, opening her to him, and he slid down her body, his supple tongue caressing her clit, enticing it with little licks and swirls. She shuddered when he let out a groan against her, the vibrations from his voice traveling through her body.

"Do you like that, Shakespeare? Do you like my mouth on you?"

"Yes," she whispered.

His fingers took over her elated bud, rubbing it back and forth to either side and pinching it as he brought his mouth close, hot breath on her as he gathered her moisture with his hand.

"And what would you like me to do, hmm?" He pressed his fingers against her pussy, and she moved her hips up eagerly. He pulled his hand away at the last minute, teasing her. "No, darling. You have to say it. I flew ten thousand miles to be with you. I want to hear it."

Her nerves were on fire, and she tightened her grip on his hair. He seriously wanted her to beg? Fine. "Inside. Put them inside me. Please, I need you to touch my pussy." The sheer craving in her voice disarmed any qualms she might have had about this being the right thing to do. Her body was certain of what it wanted, even if her heart remained trapped. As the pressure of his fingers dived into her sopping wet pussy, she arched her back. The caged beast in her heart broke free from her lips. "I love you, Niall. Oh, I love you!"

"I love *you*, Lark."

He fucked her with his fingers and moved to capture her mouth. The succulent tang of the steak lingered upon his tongue, and she couldn't get enough of it. She moved her hands to his shoulders, noting the cooling pack around his ribs scraping against her stomach. Was he okay to do this after his fight with Charles a few days ago? His free hand cupped the side of her face as he thrust against her.

He peeled the cooling pack off and cast it aside, then moved deliciously against her, his hard cock jutting into her hip and dripping pre-cum as he kicked his boxers down his legs and off. She opened her legs to him, but he shook his head, taking hold of her calves and pushing her legs toward her so that her knees were bent to her chest and she was entirely exposed to him.

He moved to his knees on the bed, caressing her slit as he stared at it. "I thought about what I wanted to do to you on the way here," he said darkly, grabbing the globes of her ass and giving them a firm squeeze. "How I wanted to make you pay for leaving me without saying good-bye."

He rubbed his dripping cock slowly along the cleft of her raised ass, teasing her puckered hole and nudging it. She gasped. His large hand smoothed over her butt cheek, his fingers stroking her entrance. "That's right. I intend to have you in every way, Shakespeare, but right now, I'm going to bury myself in your beautiful pussy and fuck you hard."

Lark shivered. How could he make her feel so vulnerable and sexy at the same time?

She bit her lip, excited and scared. She never cared for dirty talk, but coming from him, it thrilled her. He smiled wickedly as if hearing her thoughts and gave her ass a light slap, and then another, harder. She jolted, her breasts tingling as her nipples hardened, and she breathed quicker. She knew why he acted rough and welcomed it. Niall let out a noise that might have been a grunt in the back of his throat as he stared at her breasts. The wet tip of his hard cock lined up at her entrance, his hands roughly parting her legs as he moved forward between them.

"Everything I am"—he breathed against her mouth, fitting his cock against her wet pussy—"all that I have is *yours*."

He surged forward, his cock plunging into her in one powerful stroke, and there it was, utter fullness and the sweet, electric charge between them. Lark moaned.

"I'm yours, Lark. And you're mine."

"Yes. Oh, *yes*."

He set an unwavering rhythm, and she caught it, meeting him thrust for thrust as they climbed together. "That's it, love," he approved with a roll of the hips, the head of his cock ramming into her back wall just right. She arched her back and threw her head back, groaning at the sensation.

"Oh, fuck."

"Yes, sweetheart. Exactly."

She pressed the heels of her feet into his ass as he pumped into her, holding on to his back as he clutched her even tighter, changing the angle to thrust deeper, stretching her. The pleasurable pain raised her like an eagle soaring for the first time.

When she couldn't bear the sweet torture anymore and tensed, he attacked her clit with his fingers as he continued to fuck her, sending her over the edge. A low, animal sound ripped from her chest and rent the air with an impassioned cry.

Niall let out a harsh breath against her ear, thrusting his hot cock into her once more with a soft moan before pulling out. He reangled his hips, his fingers grasping behind her thigh and lifting it, and he sank deeper into her than he'd been before. She yelled, surrendering to the raw ecstasy. He spanked her clit, hissing in a breath between his teeth.

"Oh, woman! I love you."

He pulled back and then pushed forward firmly, kissing her. He breathed her name with tender reverence as his seed spilled into her for what seemed a blissful eternity.

With a soft sob, Lark wound her arms around him. After finding her breath, she spoke into his hair. "Niall, I dreamed of you for half a year before we met." She prayed she could tell him before she lost her nerve. "I used to think you were a figment of my imagination until I met you."

Niall lifted, bracing on his hands over her. He scanned her face, the length of her neck, her breasts, her abdomen, their joined bodies, then traveled slowly back to her face. She caught her breath at his enamored expression.

"Well, I'm not. I'm real, as are you, love. I think someone was trying to tell us something. What do you think?"

"I think you're right." She nuzzled into him as he buried his face in her neck, reveling in the way he sought her out. Whether in dreams or awake, he'd sought her out every time. He breathed hard, and a conviction spread through her that this had all been meant to happen. The dreams had led them to this moment, no matter where they'd come from. She placed a sleepy kiss over his sweaty, warm brow.

A tickle of lips feathered her ear, his voice husky. "No more running from me, Lark. Promise me."

"I promise."

She'd almost drifted off to sleep, holding him in her arms, when he rolled to the side, rubbed his neck, and slowly stood. He held a hand to his rib cage.

"Are you okay? Where are you going?"

He strode naked to the couch, unzipping and rifling through his backpack. "I'm getting something you need to hear." He took out an iPad. He came back to the bed and sat next to her, turning it on. "I want to finish telling you what I meant to say back at the museum. On the plane, I couldn't sleep. I checked my messages and e-mail, and there was a modular voice message on my e-mail. Hang on," he said, searching through his applications. "Here it is. Listen." She took the iPad from him and heard a high-pitched beep.

"*You have three new messages*," an automatic female voice stated. Another high-pitched beep ensued. Niall rubbed her back as she turned to face him.

To her surprise, Maisie's voice spoke, her English accent crisp and tense. "*Hi Niall, this is Maisie Robertson. Lark's mother gave me this number. I'm her best mate and secretary, and I've made the decision to get something out in the open I've kept quiet about for far too long. I'm copying this message to James Vermouthe, and he can consider it my basic resignation as I'm graduating with my degree in Dentistry next month. Let me get straight to the point in case I'm not making any sense. Six years ago, I spent a year working as Charles Chase's personal assistant.*" Lark listened hard while Niall watched her.

"*During that time, I saw him firsthandedly using company money for personal vacations and then lie on the expense reimbursement forms. Charles embezzled petty cash and would take two-hour lunch breaks, betting on horse races and using company funds to gamble. He would use his corporate purchasing card to buy expensive jewelry and clothes for the women he went behind Lark's back with, and the only time he worked was when other managers were around.*

"*I had small children at home and feared going*

407

over his head to bring it up with you, Mr. Vermouthe. I approached Charles about it before we both went home one night, and he backed me against a wall, holding his hand to my throat." Maisie cried now, and Lark remembered how terrifying he'd been when he'd approached her in the kitchen.

"*I couldn't breathe. Charles said if I told this to anyone, he would hurt me and my family, and he'd make sure I never became a dentist. My husband wasn't working at the time, and I was our sole source of income and going to school. The next day, I went to HR at the same time Lark got promoted to manager. They told me she needed an assistant, so I applied for the job. Charles hounded me and sent me threatening e-mails and letters for the last five years, reminding me to keep my mouth shut. At one point, he sent me a Hamleys Toy Shop gift card for my children, for my silence, which I sent back, of course.*

"*Mr. O'Hagan, Mr. Vermouthe, I've lived in fear for my life and for the life of my family for the last five years. I don't know what's going to happen, but I know I'm doing the right thing. I don't know what's going on with him and Lark, but he has something on her too. Charles never knew this, but I kept a file on everything he did: copies of faxes, receipts, e-mails between him and his girlfriends about their gifts, his national lotto and horse-betting tickets, all of it. I've kept it locked in a safe-deposit box, and I've sent them via courier overnight to your attention, Mr. Vermouthe. I've also made a copy that I'm sending to Mr. O'Hagan for whatever legal purposes he deems necessary. So, that's my testimony, I guess. Niall, on a personal note, I believe Lark was coerced into coming back here. She loves you, even if she's too stubborn to admit it. Ignore whatever she told you about Charles. It's bollocks. He's blackmailing her as he did me. Well, I've said all I needed to say. Please don't let this sit, Mr. Vermouthe. I'm willing to testify in court. My solicitor's contact information is in the packet I've sent you, and he'll be in touch. Thank you.*"

The message ended.

Lark stared at Niall, tears coursing down her cheeks. That son of a bitch. Six years together, and the entire time, he… She and Niall remained quiet, the gap between them like an immovable chasm.

"What has he got on you?" he asked, putting a hand to her cheek. "What is it? Tell me, damn it, because I know you don't love him. You love me. If just now didn't prove it, I don't know what will."

"I *do*," she whispered. "I do."

The concern on his face broke her heart. He set the iPad aside and stretched out next to her on the bed, taking her in his arms as she buried her face in his neck.

"I want you to be my wife," he said into her ear.

Lark smiled against his skin, and she kissed it. He needed to see something. She drew apart from him and, wrapping the sheet around herself, got up and made her way over to her coat.

"Where are you going?" he asked, faint alarm etched in his voice.

She placated him with a hand and fished through her coat pockets, drawing out the small, smiley-faced stone and the jump drive Charles had threatened her with. She hadn't been able to let it out of her sight since looking at its contents back in Oregon. At first, she kept it close out of fear that someone else would find it, but it served as a constant reminder of the chain about her neck. Niall met her halfway back to the table, and she held both items out. He smiled with nostalgia at the stone and then took the jump drive from her, holding it up questioningly.

Lark took a deep breath and secured the sheet beneath her armpits. "Charles has proof of my dad's involvement with illegal gambling and embezzlement of his company stocks. He said my dad had ties with organized crime."

Niall laughed. "What a load of shite. And you believed him?"

"Well, yeah, I did. I mean, it's all there on the thumb drive. I checked everything. And he said my mom knew about it too, and she could be held accountable."

Niall seemed to weigh this, then sighed. He took her hand and led her back to the bed. "Lark. Did I ever tell you what I did before I became an estate attorney?" They sat.

"Do you mean about how you lived at the parish?"

"No, before that. I studied criminal law at university. *That* was why Craig wanted me at the firm, and why they brought me on as an attorney on your father's case."

"What are you saying here? All this is true, and you were hired to, what, come in and scrub his bad history?" She frowned. He wasn't making any sense.

"No, not his. His *partner's*. Dustin Clemence helped your dad build Braithwaite Boxing Company, but he's also the one who nearly destroyed it."

Lark blinked. "Wait, what?"

"Clemence gambled away an exorbitant amount.

He went on weekend trips to Vegas and bet on horse races with company funds he had access to. While he lived it up in Vegas, he made friends with lowlife criminals, and he almost got your dad involved."

"Almost?"

"Yeah. They hired me to close Clemence down, so to speak. Rick paid a cash settlement to get him out of trouble with shady characters, and then he cut Clemence off entirely. Your dad didn't do a damn thing but be a good Samaritan."

Trembling, Lark put a hand to his arm. "Are—are you sure?"

He stroked her hair, his eyes firm. "As his attorney, I'm positive."

"But…Charles said my mom realized what was going on, and she'd be held accountable too. And that my dad had a lot of other affairs." She really didn't want to know if he'd slept with more women, but it slipped out.

He took her hand, squeezing it gently. "I can't help you on the affairs part. It may or may not be true Rick had other indiscretions. I don't know. He confided to me he did a lot of things he regretted and said he and Pam went through tough times. But as for her knowing about him helping Clemence, Charles speculated and made it up to scare you, I expect. I advised your dad to keep records in case any ties to Clemence or a lawsuit came up. That's where Charles got the notion of it being your dad. If Pam *did* know about Clemence, it's all done and dusted, so there's nothing they can hang over your family's head. Charles wanted to control you," he stressed. "And you let him."

Lark's eyes stung with tears. "What have I done?"

Niall kissed her.

"Well, as far as I know, today you've gone to the British Museum and started a shag fest with your fiancé." He held his ribs as he leaned forward to press his lips against her neck.

"Started?" she smiled. He was ambitious, considering his fractured ribs.

"Give me time, Shakespeare." He smirked. "And aspirin. Lots of aspirin. But I intend to keep you prisoner in this room for at least the next twenty-four hours. We're not leaving this bed." He leaned toward her but clutched his side, wincing.

Lark moved forward instead, helping him change positions, so his back rested against the headboard. She touched his jaw and kissed him softly, careful not to put too much pressure on his chest. "I love you," she breathed. "Thank you for coming after me."

"I always will," he murmured, touching his forehead to hers. She cuddled close, covered them with the duvet, and buried her nose in his neck.

"Niall, what's going to happen to us now?" she asked after a while. "I mean, I never signed the probate papers. I was supposed to, but the house is still in my name. All my belongings are still in the flat I share with Charles, I'm meant to go back to work soon, and—"

The vibrations of his chuckle tickled beneath her. He smoothed his hand on her back. "The only thing I'm concerned with right now, Shakespeare, is you saying 'I do' in the near future and me taking you home to meet my family in Ireland. The rest will work itself out. No matter where we end up, it's you and I, love. You and I."

About the Author

Roxanne D. Howard writes sizzling erotic romance. She is a U.S. Army veteran, and a Columbia College alumni. She loves to read books in every genre, and she is an avid Star Wars fan, musical theater nut, and marine biology geek. Roxanne resides in the western U.S., and when she's not writing, she enjoys spending quality time with her husband, children, and furry companions. Roxanne loves to hear from her readers, and encourages you to contact her via her website and social media.

~*~

Visit Roxanne at
www.RoxanneDHoward.com

~*~

To chat with Roxanne D. Howard and other Wild Rose Press authors of erotic romance, join us at
www.groups.yahoo.com/group/thewilderroses.

Also Available
from The Wild Rose Press, Inc.
and major retailers.

Melt in Your Mouth
Mocha Magic Book One
By Skye Kohl

After her parents are forced to sell their bakery due to the economy, Elizabeth Carpelli wants security, and that means a dependable man with a college education and a stable job. No matter that her degree in marketing is being wasted in a coffee shop. She wants it all. But then, with the help of her boss, and the most deliciously sensual chocolate, she discovers lust beyond her wildest dreams in a no-commitment arrangement with an uber fit carpenter—a blue collar worker.

Having his heart ripped in two by a cheating fiancée, Hank Lehman wanders into Mocha Magic to drown his sorrows in a steamy black brew. When the sweet and sassy barista gives him an offer he can't refuse, chocolate body paint and a canvas of silky flesh with no strings attached, it may just help him forget his past and turn his future toward a more tasty adventure.

Also Available
from The Wild Rose Press, Inc.
and major retailers.

Catching the Cajun
By Ursula Whistler

Paranormal blogger Felicia Li wants to show she's more than an Internet flash in the pan. Her Paranormal Pest website is taking off as she debunks ghosts and monsters across the country. Her next gig involves busting a New Orleans tour group for a fake Loup Garou haunting the swamps. But the formidable tour owner kicks her off the boat, and she's not above cozying up to the sexy Cajun to catch the fake monster.

Jacques Mercier, owner of Cajun Boy Tours, isn't about to let petite Felicia bring down his family business. He's overcome oil spills and hurricanes, but something about the feisty Internet phenom tells him she's going to be trouble for his business—and his heart.

Thank you for purchasing this
publication of The Wild Rose Press, Inc.

For questions or more
information contact us at
info@thewildrosepress.com.

The Wild Rose Press, Inc.
www.thewilderroses.com

To visit with authors of
The Wild Rose Press, Inc.
join our yahoo loop at
http://groups.yahoo.com/group/thewildrosepress/